All Together Now

Also by Gill Hornby

The Hive

All Together Now

A Novel

GILL HORNBY

LITTLE, BROWN AND COMPANY

New York   Boston   London

For my mother

Copyright © 2015 by Gill Hornby

Little, Brown and Company
Hachette Book Group
1290 Avenue of the Americas, New York, NY 10104
littlebrown.com

First United States Edition: July 2015

Originally published in Great Britain by Little, Brown and Company, an imprint of Hachette Book Group, June 2015.

Little, Brown and Company is a division of Hachette Book Group, Inc. The Little, Brown name and logo are trademarks of Hachette Book Group, Inc.

The publisher is not responsible for websites (or their content) that are not owned by the publisher.

The Hachette Speakers Bureau provides a wide range of authors for speaking events. To find out more, go to hachettespeakersbureau.com or call (866) 376-6591.

For further copyright information see pages 327–28.

ISBN 978-0-316-23474-0
LCCN 2015931478

10 9 8 7 6 5 4 3 2 1

RRD-C

Printed in the United States of America

And each town looks the same to me, the movies and
the factories.
And ev'ry stranger's face I see reminds me that I
long to be
Homeward bound.

Simon and Garfunkel

Her eye caught the clock: half past five. She felt the stirrings of a familiar low-level panic and put her foot down. It wasn't that she was late—she was never late; prided herself on it—it was just that there weren't enough hours in the day. And the governors' meeting dragged over just those few extra vital minutes. Still, if she really belted, she should be there just about on time. Well, she had to be and that was that. The electric piano and all the sheet music were right there on the back seat. They could hardly start without her.

The rain pounded onto the windscreen. It had been pounding on and off all day, now she thought about it, but she had been dodging around, running into one thing and out of another, and it hadn't really mattered. Until now. Her panic moved up another notch. Now, it really mattered. Oh please. It couldn't rain on them tonight. Not tonight of all nights. They had to be out in that High Street and they had to sing. Tonight was crucial. The future of their choir depended on it.

What were they actually going to sing, though? It had been such a busy week, she hadn't quite got round to working that bit out. Should they kick off with something from the musicals? Not the Sound of Music *medley, for God's sake. She was desperately, subtly, trying to bury that one but it wasn't easy. They did not exactly embrace change, her lot. She smiled, shaking her head. What about* Les Mis? *Had she even packed the* Les Mis? *She turned and looked behind her, reached an arm to the pile on the back seat – just at the moment that a lorry pulled out and flung around her a curtain of spray. And when she turned back, it was to find the whole world was now invisible. Then she was spinning ... spinning ... spinning ... quite out of control ...*

All Together Now

1

At ten to six, Tracey was, as usual, steering her way through the tunnelling that would take her up to the surface of the earth. Even on a good evening it took a while to get out of the car park. She always used those few minutes to select the soundtrack for the journey home – an eye on the bumper in front, a hand rifling through the CDs on the passenger seat. According to Billy, this was the last car to drive across the First World with such a pre-historic sound system. He was always on at her about it, like she was an Amish, or Fred Flintstone. He didn't seem to notice that they would need to win the lottery just to upgrade to central locking. And anyway if he wanted Tracey's opinion – yes, *if* – the CD player was the best thing about this car. It gave a physical dimension, an extra sensation, to her music that advanced elec-tronics denied her. Here in the excellent Flintmobile she could still touch it, spread it out, sift through the albums of the gods of rock like a jeweller her diamonds ... And tonight, it looked like she would have even more time to play with than usual. She settled in to the long slow queue for the barrier and set about making her choice.

'Here.' The parking attendant knocked on her window. 'Something's up.' She wound it down. 'It's terrible out there tonight. Keep away from Bridgeford if you can help it.'

'Ugh,' Tracey tried to say, but nothing came out. 'Wish I could.' She cleared her throat. 'But thanks ...'

She slumped back against the car seat and clutched at her hair. She'd already put up with a bog-standard, run-of-the-mill, utterly dehumanisingly normal day at ONS Systems – emails, contracts, emails about contracts – sitting alone, sit-offishly, in the corner. She coughed again – her vocal cords were in serious danger of atrophy. There had been a 'Bless you' to a sneezing junior and a twenty-second sing-song for a birthday – it being the office and there being the law of averages, it was bound to be somebody's birthday – but apart from that, nothing. She needed – she really, properly needed – to hear the sound of her own voice. Something shouty, that was what she wanted tonight – straightforward and shouty. She found just the disc, flicked it out of its cover and into the machine and waited. The driver of the car ahead stopped to take on a couple more passengers; windows opened, hands stuck out, fingers waved. Someone called, another laughed; Tracey growled. At last, it was her turn. She passed through the barrier, back into the world and pressed Play. 'Meat Loaf,' she announced, 'you may escort me home.'

... paradise by the dashboard light

Tracey emerged and scanned the dark sky. It throbbed with the rhythmic blue of the emergency lights but was giving no sign of what sort of day she had missed. Tracey, as usual, had no clue. They didn't really go in for weather at ONS: it didn't bother them, so they didn't bother with it. The enormous metal-box structure had its own climate, permanently set to 'very pleasant'; a little patch of northern California, just handy for the M4. Still, the roads were sodden, it was the middle of England in the depths of winter: it could only have been grim.

She took to the slip-road, thumping on the steering wheel, singing – bellowing – along until she came out to the roundabout and a sudden stop. Craning her neck to look ahead, Tracey saw straight up and into the van in the next lane. Three young blokes, all lined up on the front seat, still in their overalls, were laughing away at her. So she shouted a bit louder. Not what they expected from a woman in her forties dressed in her sensible office clothes? Didn't they like it from someone old enough to be their mum? Just because she didn't look like a rocker, didn't mean she wasn't a rocker. She stuck out her tongue, showing them her stud, pressed it to the window and pulled her Ozzy Osbourne face. She might even have mooned them, but then they inched forward and her sport was over.

'Oh, come *on*.'

Nearly twenty years she had been doing this commute, and it generally pulled some sort of trick on her at least once a week. It had caused her no end of trouble in the past – especially when Billy was little – and yet she had never been tempted to look for some sort of job on her own doorstep. Living in Bridgeford was dismal enough; she couldn't possibly work there, too. It might not be exactly exciting coming out here every day but it did at least throw in another dimension to her existence, increase her imprint upon the earth, just a bit. Tracey tried to imagine her days and years without it and felt a shiver – her whole life would seem such a little thing. She leaned forward, switched off Meat Loaf and fiddled with the tuner.

Officially, Tracey never listened to *Dave at Drivetime* – soft pop and local radio being, obviously, landmarks in the Valley of Musical Death. Unofficially, though, she had to tune in quite often for the traffic updates, so she always made sure to keep her guard up. For the more vulnerable listeners, the traffic update could just be a dangerous beginning, like a gateway drug. Tracey worried about them, innocently tuning in to hear about a pile-up on the A-whatever and suddenly find themselves filling their brains with all that other stuff: humming along to Maroon 5, smiling dopily to a bit of Michael Bublé . . . She shook her head in sorrow. Of course, that could never happen to her, but still, even as she waited her own brain was being filled with 'News from Your Neighbourhood'. 'Ugh, please, spare us,' she muttered, drumming her fingers on the gearstick.

'... the demonstration tomorrow night at the proposed site of the new superstore planned on the London Road ...'

That reminded her: she needed to stock up the fridge yet again. The sooner they built a superstore the better, and London Road would be very convenient. She would be able to swoop in on the way home without battling into town, so let them get on with it. Honestly, of all the things to protest about. Third World hunger all sorted then, was it? World peace in the bag? People round here could do with some real problems.

An air ambulance clattered into the sky and one by one the cars ahead of her started to move.

'... recruitment drive. Yes, the Community Choir has announced that they are going BACK to the County Championships this year after a few quiet seasons. And this time they are in it to win it for your town. But they really need some new voices. So come on, you lot. We know you're out there. All you belters of Bridgeford ...'

Tracey hooted as, at last, she shifted up into second gear. 'Belters of Bridgeford!' There was an image. She must remember to tell Billy when she got home. They would have a right laugh at that one.

She crawled on to the motorway – past the wreckage piled on the hard shoulder, the flashing lights, the police in high-vis jackets and the traffic cones – and pulled out into the middle lane.

♩

'Where can she have got to?' asked Annie. 'Let me try her again ...'

'What are we going to do?' worried an alto.

'We'll just have to start without her,' shrugged Lewis, stamping his feet to keep warm.

'Without her?' echoed a soprano. '*Sing?* Without *Constance*?'

The Choir had arranged to meet outside the supermarket at six o'clock, but it was now quarter-past, the turn-out was still low and even their leader wasn't there yet. She was always a little bit late, but not quite this late. Annie fiddled in her bag for her phone as she scanned the dark High Street and the damp Market Square. All the other shops were shut: most just for the evening, of course, although a few had closed for good in the weeks since Christmas. The rain had just stopped, so the usual kids were back in their customary position on the war memorial, waiting out the years, swigging out of tins, until they could get served in the pub. Otherwise, there was almost nobody around. She dialled Connie's number again, listened to the tone, frowned and shook her head: it really was quite out of character. Still, Lewis was right: they were here now and they would have to carry on regardless. Annie tried to put on the sort of inspirational, mood-changing, charismatic leader's voice that Constance always used. 'Shall we start?'

It had seemed like such a good idea after choir practice, but then everything seemed like a good idea after choir practice: they always came out on a high. Even with their sadly depleted membership they still sounded so amazing to themselves that at the end of every number they burst into wild, spontaneous applause. There might not be many of them at the Tuesday-night session in the Coronation Hall, but it always felt electric, ground-breaking, a whole new dawn for music – like the opening night of *Cats*.

So when Constance announced her recruitment drive, it had seemed the easiest thing in the world. All they had to do was get out there and put on a cracking performance to the hundreds of potential new young members and there they would be, back to the highest levels of competition standard, like they were in the glory days. To be fair, even in that atmosphere of buoyant self-confidence, nobody had actually suggested a proper concert. They knew, from the past few attempts, that the whole bookings-and-tickets-and-bums-on-seats thing was not exactly the right vehicle for the Community Choir at the present moment and they had accepted that. Well, most of them had. There was still a little residual bitterness in some sections after that rather grim business with 'The Magic of *Les Mis*'. But they did agree that if Bridgeford wouldn't come in for the music, then the music should go out to

Bridgeford, and so here they were. They shuffled into a semicircle. Annie clung to its outer edge.

A bit of everything, that was what they had decided on for tonight's showcase. They were, as Connie was fond of saying, an eclectic bunch and Lewis, one of their more outspoken members, did like his folk music. He stepped forward and raised his hands. Annie – she had perfect pitch; town tuning-fork was one of her many voluntary roles – hummed the note and they began.

Earl-y one mo-or-ning, just as the sun was ri-i-sing

They sang up and out into the empty night. A few members had argued in favour of a lunchtime event, but they were all the sort of people who were out of town all week working, and had no real understanding of how nearly everybody these days was out of town all week working. It was in a perfect position, Bridgeford, handy for everything – and that was its problem. There was an excellent train service and a choice selection of arterial roads and only the residents left behind who didn't get on one or other of them, like Annie, could really understand quite how they sucked the life-blood out of the place every single day.

So they came up with this idea, to catch the commuters on their way home, and the last-minute shoppers popping in to what was still, just, the only supermarket. And everyone did agree that Bridgeford was at its best in the evening. A bit of darkness did the town centre a favour. You couldn't immediately see that most of the shops sold only posh knick-knacks or second-hand clothes, that the bakery was now a tattoo parlour, that the gutters were full of scratch-cards. Of course, it didn't do quite as good a job as snow. Bridgeford in the snow was Annie's absolute favourite – when you couldn't tell which century it was or even if it was the real world; you could pretend you lived in a period drama. Shame it only happened once a year. But still, the dark nearly did the trick. Standing out here, they could almost, at a pinch, through a squint, kid themselves it was the 1950s.

. . . a po-or maiden so?

It was always a little dispiriting to finish a song to no applause whatsoever. But onwards and upwards and they decided to do musicals next. There was a little hiatus, as they all had to change positions, even Katie in her wheelchair. Lewis came forward, fiddled about with the brakes and tucked the rug around his daughter's knees. Once that was sorted, it was time for Maria's big moment. The rest stood back in deference as she pointed her mouth towards the streetlamp, took careful aim and belted:

Sum-mertiiiiiiiiiiime

And the liv-ing is ...

Maria's soulful performance had brought tears to the eyes of past audiences. Tonight, though, all that could be heard was that ugly, barking laughter peculiar to the adolescent boy – half man, half sea-lion – slicing through the beauty of the song.

Over on the war memorial they were, rather deliberately, seeing the funny side. The boys were pretend-fishing, the girls were lying back for a sunbath. Annie's spirits sank a little further. It might not be the perfect set for a Wednesday night in January, but it was still the best set they could come up with for a Wednesday night in January. That was what happened when you did something for everyone – not everything was perfect. Anyway, what was the alternative? No singing at all? Was that what these people really wanted?

There was a deep rumble as the 6.18 pulled out of the station and the first consignment of commuters started to rush through. Most of them kept their heads down and their eyes averted; several crossed the road; a few took leaflets, but then dumped them in the bin down the street, by the cashpoint. Annie watched Jazzy, in her waitress uniform, standing at the door of the Copper Kettle, leaning on a broom, looking deeply unimpressed. She just caught the retreating back of a chap in a suit – now who *was* that? – carrying one large potato and pressing past in a hurry. Like everyone else around, he was not in the mood for music tonight. They were all just desperate to get home.

One of the many beautiful things about a choir of long standing is that the members can develop a telepathy, a corporate sixth sense – as Annie, who had been one of the Choir for over thirty years, understood only too well. She knew what it felt like, to be able to sense what your colleagues are thinking while they are singing. And she knew that, right then, what they were thinking was: this is a right waste of time.

♩

Tracey signalled and turned left on to the High Street, towards the shop. They were bound to be low on bread and milk, they always were – Billy had, apparently, to consume one or other at all times simply to stay alive. It was but one of the many similarities between having a young adult son and keeping a baby bird. Billy was, basically, a baby bird just on an epic scale. She parked across the road from the supermarket and reached down for her bag. The 6.18 was just leaving, and there was a rush of commuters walking through, so she did not immediately notice that there was a small crowd over there. In fact, she was dangerously close to getting out of the car and walking straight into them. She might have had to listen or talk to someone or accept a leaflet or something. Thank God she spotted them just in time. She sank back into her car seat, locked the car for good measure: safe. Trapped, but safe.

She couldn't quite work out what was going on at first. Bridgeford was famously – or not at all famously – the town where nothing happened, and yet clearly something was happening right in front of her this very evening. Her mind ran through the most obvious options – hunger riot; extremist political rally; wild midwinter Home Counties Mardi Gras – until the truth finally hit her. They were the actual belters of Bridgeford. And, what's more, they were actually belting. What were the chances? This was her lucky night.

A home-made sign was propped precariously in the corner of a young woman's wheelchair: THE BRIDGEFORD COMMUNITY CHOIR, it said. Hardly, thought Tracey. She would concede they were in Bridgeford, but 'choir' was pushing it. And as for 'community', well ... who did they think they were kidding? This was not exactly a representative sample: it was mostly women, for a start, and they all looked pretty ancient; well, certainly middle-aged. Tracey peered more closely. The few that she recognised straight off, she knew to be certifiably bonkers. There was that swimming teacher who put Billy off water for good, and the weirdo who ran Cubs, and the woman who poured tea at Outpatients – and that was just the front row.

The only person who wasn't about 120 was the girl in the wheel-chair. She must be the same age, or thereabouts, as the kids taking the piss over on the war memorial, but that was where the similarities ended. While she was singing out with uninhibited enthusiasm, the others were heckling at the tops of their voices. And while she could only dance along with her arms and rock in her seat, their long, nimble bodies were thrashing around in ex-uberant mockery. Tracey shook her head. Life: even for an irony fan like her good self, sometimes it went way too far.

The number came to an end and, in the absence of any immedi-ate audience response, the Choir clapped themselves. For a happy moment it looked like they might have finished; sadly, they had even more to share. Tracey wound down the window to have a listen –

Sing, sing a song
Make it simple . . .

– and wound it up again quickly. Criminal, that was. It should be on 'News from Your Neighbourhood'. Forget the superstore; here was the real story. She should call in, do an on-the-spot: *This is Tracey Leckford, with an eye-witness report, live from the High Street, where right now The Carpenters are being MURDERED on the pavement outside Budgens . . .*

♩

It was time for their showstopper. They often discussed how it might be better to open with 'The Rhythm of Life', but the choreography was pretty ambitious and some of the older members – Lynn, Pat and the like – needed to warm up to it first, especially this winter with the rush of joint replacements. Only the other day, Dr Khan had said to Annie there was more titanium than calcium in the altos these days. They did have to be careful, but it was worth it. The audience – when they had one – always loved the actions, all the swimming and the crawling and the flying. It was an absolute scream.

Yes, the rhythm of life is a powerful beat.

However, it was always a bit nerve-racking for the sopranos, because at least two of them had to stand next to Katie's dad, and while Lewis was indisputably one of the finest human beings on the planet, he was not one of the finest dancers.

They click-click-clicked, did a shimmy and a shake . . .

The 6.42 came and went and another delivery of people started to pour down the station steps. This was lucky timing: they were just hitting the 'swim to Daddy' verse. Two basses broke through the ranks and did the crawl across the front. Katie, positioned right in the middle, was doing the breast-stroke. They knew their joy to be infectious when they did this one; they had been told exactly that a million times. And what was this? A smartly dressed chap was heading straight for them. This could be the breakthrough. Annie felt a prickle of optimism. He might be a whole new tenor . . .

Rhythm in your bedroom, rhythm in the street

He took some change out of his pocket and looked around Katie for a collection box. Then he stepped forward, gave her an encouraging nod, smiled at the rest of them and placed the money on the blanket in her lap.

Tracey swung off the busy road straight into her garage, turned off the ignition and sat for a second. That girl in the wheelchair, the raw pain in her poor dad's face – she couldn't get any of it out of her mind. Why did she always feel things so much more when she saw them reflected through a parent? It was the same watching all those talent shows on the telly: when acts got through, they were always pleased, but their families were ecstatic; when they got thrown out, well . . . the visceral agony of those mums had Tracey all choked up every time. The girl herself made a joke of it when that bloke threw his change at her – she tugged at her forelock, thanked him for noticing her, promised not to spend it on booze – but the dad . . . He looked like a man having his heart torn out. She wouldn't be telling Billy about the belters now; they wouldn't be having a right laugh; the joke had gone clean out of it.

Music was thumping through the building as she got out of the car. Keys between her teeth, carrier bags hanging from both hands, she kicked the door to and closed the garage by flicking the switch down with her nose. With this much shopping, she always had to take a sideways approach up the internal stairs to the living room. Space was at something of a premium in their housing develop-ment, but even with just the two of them, it was certainly cosy.

Billy was deep in the sofa, holding a half-gallon of milk in his lap, his feet perched up in front of him on a kitchen chair. The music was pretty loud up there. Tracey crossed in front of the TV, forcing him to pivot in his seat.

'Hey, Mum.' He didn't take his eyes off the game. 'How was work?'

'Yeah. Brilliant, ta.' She stopped to take in what was going on. Billy was controlling a heavily armed figure walking down a burnt-out street in some post-apocalyptic horrorscape and playing against one of his little cyber-mates from the other side of the world – Japan by the looks of it.

'Sorry, love.' She stepped over a pizza box on her way through to the kitchen, dumped the shopping on the table and went back in to pick it up. 'Haven't heard this before,' she shouted, putting the crusts in the box and closing the lid. The song – a string of exple-tives with a bass undertone – was pounding somewhere in her solar plexus. 'Who's it by?'

It was a matter of pride to Tracey that not only did she listen to the same music as Billy, they listened to it together. Music was for sharing. They didn't have many house rules, but one of them was No headphones – the iPod stayed in its dock. Billy never disappeared into his own audio bubble as all the other kids did, and Tracey never screamed, 'Turn that bloody racket down', as her parents had done. She was not that sort of mother. She wanted, needed, to know what her son was listening to. She liked to embrace his choices.

'WHO'S IT BY?' she shouted again, more loudly.

'THE BLOODSHITTERS,' he roared over his shoulder, and swigged some milk. 'NEW BAND. NOT BAD.'

'COOL.' She put the rubbish in the bin and started to unload the shopping. 'WHAT DO YOU FANCY FOR SUPPER?' she bellowed, her head in the fridge.

'NOTHING.' Billy rose, turned the volume down a notch and hitched his trousers a little closer to his buttocks. 'Got a job. Start tonight.'

Tracey span out into the room, astonished. 'A job?'

'Yeah,' he sniffed. 'Look, Mum – I can't live off Dad's money for ever, you know.'

'Yes, of course.' Finally. Thank Christ. 'What? Where? When? How? That's so great, Bills!'

'All right. Calm it. It's no big deal. Me, Curly and Squat are taking over the bar down at the Square.' He grabbed his jacket off the table and in two strides was through the door. 'I'll be late.'

'Hey. Good lu—'

But he was already down the stairs, through the garage and out in the street.

Tracey picked up the milk, screwed on the lid, turned off the TV and silenced the music. To be totally honest, she wasn't really in the mood for The Bloodshitters right now. Billy's career path so far had been paved with disappointment and Tracey knew, from long experience of his various job opportunities, that this one was unlikely to last beyond the week. Still, she must hope for the best. 'My son, the barman . . .' It had a certain ring to it. And even if it didn't turn out to be his thing, she did at least have the place to herself for the evening.

She looked around her. The L-shaped kitchen/lounge was nowhere near big enough for both of them now there was so much more of Billy than there used to be. She picked up one cereal bowl from the floor, stepped over a games console and reached down for a second. Of course, it would be much easier to live in if it were actually tidy. When you looked at these places – ground-floor garage beneath first-floor living area, with two beds and a bath on the second – they were a masterclass in space management: such a small footprint on the earth, yet just enough room for living crammed up above. No doubt they had neighbours who were even rattling around, but as they had never spoken to any, they couldn't possibly know. She balanced a third bowl on top of the others and picked her way back to the kitchen.

There was more cereal detritus in there. She poured herself a glass of wine, took a hearty swig and started to potter around the work surfaces.

La, la, la, la-la

Le la la le la-la

She picked up two knives caked in butter with crumbs stuck on, removed the spoon poking out of the peanut butter and put them in the dishwasher.

La, la, la, la-la, le

An unfamiliar sense of contentment began to creep over her while she wiped down the counter. Of course, her relationship with Billy was about the best between mother and son since . . . since . . . Her memory scanned through the respectable amount of history and literature that she had taught herself, but came up with no positive example. Surely there must be one famous one where they didn't end up either shagging or killing each other? Anyway – she squirted neat washing-up liquid on to the filthy frying-pan – the thought of an evening at home without him was not an entirely unpleasant one. Her wine glass was unaccountably empty; she poured herself some more.

Tum tum ti tum tum

Tracey became aware that, rather than the raspy, throaty one that she used when she was singing along with Billy, she was using her chest voice for once, and she could feel the calming, anti-depressant effect of it on her stressed-out body. But it wasn't until she was back in the living room, tucked up with her glass and the bottle on the sofa, that she realised exactly what it was she was singing. Christ almighty. Those bloody belters had wormed into her ear, through to her brain, down to her lungs. They had regressed her. She was regressing. For the first time in nearly thirty years, she was spending the night in alone pretending to be Karen bloody Carpenter. How sad was that?

Tragic, she thought, as she bounded out of her seat. The one great thing about being Tracey Leckford was that she was so much cooler in her thirties and forties than she ever had been in her youth. She opened the cupboard under the iPod and rootled around in the back. Billy had no idea about her past, and she was determined it would stay that way. Aha, there they were. Their unit – such a depressing little word, 'family'; she never used it – was founded on rock and metal, hard and heavy; strong, firm, reliable. And that was how they both liked it.

She pulled out the ghetto blaster with the box of her old cassettes and blew off the dust. The sense of recognition and familiarity was almost overpowering – like being reunited with an amputated limb. The music of her youth had been so hard-won, looking back on it. All that saving up and borrowing and hanging out in record shops; all that transferring and organising and arranging her day around airplays on the radio. Tracey would never say it out loud – she had an Old Fart Warning signal hard-wired into her brain now to stop her saying anything like that out loud – but she wasn't sure, in this click-click-download world, if songs had quite the same value that they used to. So much care had gone into the making of the tapes in this box, so often were they played, that Tracey still knew immediately what was on them, just by looking. The ones labelled TOP OF THE POPS, for example, probably did not bear revisiting. She had made those herself with the mic pressed up to the screen and the quality wasn't marvellous: one ABBA performance, which might have been rather precious, was ruined at the point where her mum asked her dad for a cup of tea. But it was the mix tapes she was after tonight, and one in particular. She took it out. GIRLS' NITE IN, it said, in pink felt pen. Wow, so she was that lame? She looked around, nipped over to the kitchen window and snapped shut the Venetian blinds, opened the garage door to check the coast was clear ... No one need ever know. Dimming the lights just in case, she put the tape on, stood stock-still in the middle of the carpet, gave a smile and a nod in the direction of Richard on guitar – or, in this particular instance, the bookcase – and began:

I'll say goodbye to love ...

All Tracey had ever wanted, for her interminable teenage years, was to be Karen Carpenter: to sing to, to be heard by, to sway beneath the gaze of the whole world out there. In her more realistic moments she was prepared to settle for being a mere slice of Bananarama, such was the measure of her determination and – at times – desperation. But, no. Even her most humble aspirations were to be denied her. Fate, it turned out, had other plans. She waited, as she sang, for that familiar stab of grief, disappointment, humiliation; to be shocked once more by the way her story had ended; to be derailed by one of her interminable enquiries of 'What if ...?' But, much to her surprise, nothing happened. She was just having too good a time: lying on the sofa being Sheena Easton, making cheese on toast doing her best Bonnie Tyler. She was actually up, barefoot, on the dining table singing 'Theme from *Mahogany*' into yet another wine bottle – *Do you know where you're going to?* – when the doorbell rang.

It had been many years since anyone had rung their doorbell, and it took Tracey a few moments to identify the sound. She heard it again. Her first response was to ignore it, until she realised that for once Billy was actually out. She climbed down from the table and tottered over to the cassette player. Supposing something had happened to him? She turned off the music and looked over the window sill. Was it a policeman down there, come to play out her very worst fears?

Tracey couldn't even remember the last time she had used the front door. They had a mailbox fixed to the outside wall. She, Billy and Billy's mates always came through the garage, and nobody else ever turned up, ever. As a consequence, the stairs down to it had become, over time, jam-packed with all the stuff they didn't quite have room for and had never quite got round to chucking out. She stood at the top and peered down, over old bicycles, a rowing machine, a mini-fridge that didn't smell too healthy, a guitar, a lava lamp, a rucksack, a lot of Warhammer, bin bags full of indeterminate cast-offs, a keyboard, a train set and finally, at the bottom, a pram. There was definitely a man down there, she could tell by the silhouette on the frosted glass. He rang again. Better get this over with. She picked her way through, like a warden in the Blitz. Eventually, she found and opened the door. It was him. The dad. Of that girl. The one in the wheelchair. Admittedly, she felt quite pissed now she was standing up and having to communicate with someone, but still, she was sure. It was him.

'Evening. Sorry to bother you,' he said, although he didn't sound it. 'Only I couldn't help overhearing—'

'Overhearing?'

'Yes. Sorry' – he put his hand to his chest – 'I'm Lewis. We're neighbours and—'

'Hi. Tracey. You listen to us?' She was starting to get, in Billy parlance, weirded out. This bloke was like one of those Stasi officers who spent their lives bugging East German homes. Tracey had never seen him before and suddenly there he was, twice in a night. Was she under surveillance?

'Well, no. Of course not. We don't have a glass to the wall, or anything. We live across there,' he jerked his thumb over his shoulder, 'on the corner. We can't help but hear your music and—'

'All our music?' Oops. She pressed her forehead to edge of the door. The Bloodshitters. He'd come to complain about The Bloodshitters ...

'No. Really.' He held out his hand. 'You don't understand. This isn't a complaint. I'm just here because, well, you were playing different songs tonight. And you were singing. I've never heard you sing before.'

OK. This was quite weird ...

'And you sounded brilliant.'

... but, you know, not *that* weird.

'Thanks.' They stood there looking at one another. Tracey felt rather at sea. She had never knowingly met a neighbour before and certainly never gone in for any of that neighbourly chit-chat stuff. 'Very kind.' But, much to her own surprise, she found that she did want to be friendly, just this once. After all, she'd watched this one with his daughter; she'd witnessed how much he cared; she'd seen him make a total arse of himself dad-dancing outside Budgens. Even Tracey Leckford couldn't shut a door in a face after all that. She smiled, while racking her brains for something to say. 'Anyway.' What was it people talked about? Compost bins ... Rubbish collection ... Gutter-clearing ... Surely this was a bloke who could bang on for hours about gutter-clearing ... As it turned out, he was a bloke with his own agenda.

'Actually, I have come to ask you a favour.'

'Um. Yeah. Of course.' Neighbours? Favours? Now she was seriously out of her depth.

'We would like you,' he pressed a leaflet at her, 'to join our choir.' She looked down at the leaflet, made a snorty noise, looked back up at his face, all ready for a good old laugh ... and was struck, instantly, by the absence of a sense of joke where really, under normal circumstances, she would expect some sense of joke to be. 'We have a competition to win.'

She straightened her face. 'Yes,' she said through a cough. 'I heard it on the local news.' Amazingly, for once she actually had.

Lewis was not as amazed as he should have been. 'Yup.' He thrust his hands into his trouser pockets, rocked on his heels, paused for a bit of teeth-sucking. 'It is a pre-tty big deal.' Tracey couldn't reply to that; if she did, she would only get the giggles. 'And you are exactly what Bridgeford needs.'

'Yes ... but ... you see ...'

He pulled back his shoulders, raised his voice a bit. 'Can all the voices of this town at last unite?'

'Um ... well ... haven't got a clue ... I doubt it ... Christ ... sound bloody awful ... but I'm afraid ... '

'Are we better together or are we better apart?'

Apart, on the whole, obviously, thought Tracey – though she could see it wasn't the moment to bring it up. Instead, she kept quiet and watched the spectacle unfold on her own doorstep. He was well away now, this Lewis – rather fancied himself as quite the inspirational public speaker, if she was not mistaken.

'Can we go to the County Championships and bring back our pride?'

Tracey studied him as he blathered on with his fists clenched and his eyes shining. A funny thing, the power of the human voice, she thought: not just for the effect it had on others, but for the effect it could have on ourselves. Tracey was entirely unmoved by Lewis' rhetoric, but clearly he was under the impression he was transformed.

'Can we *win* the County Championships?'

She was looking at a shortish, fattish white bloke in supermarket jeans, but somewhere inside that shortish, fattish white exterior was a self-image of someone else entirely.

'Yes we can!'

She cringed and let slip an involuntary moan of pain, but Lewis didn't notice.

'And we need you, Tracey. We really need you.'

'Oh ... um ... Lewis ... I would love to help, obviously, but ... but ... '

'We are your local singers ... '

'Oh ... OK ... I did get that bit ... but ... '

' ... and we need YOU.'

'Oh.'

'Oh what, Tracey?' He was getting rather demanding now. 'Oh what exactly?'

Oh hell.

2

Bennett rolled over in bed, stretched down to the floor and slammed off the alarm with a force that sent his phone skimming across the bare boards. In one movement he swung his legs round, stood and strode across to the clothes rail, straight into a waiting shirt. There wasn't much to be cheerful about at the moment – this morning felt no more glad or confident than any others of the past miserable month – but he did smile to himself when he felt that clothes rail; it was a new addition to the getting-up process, and one with which Bennett was quietly pleased. The simple act of purchase had seemed like a positive, proactive step in the right direction. For a start, it filled up that gaping hole between the window and the corner of the bedroom. Even better, it had taken him hours to put the thing together: when eventually he had finished it, the whole evening was behind him and it was time to go to bed. But most satisfying of all was this: compared to a wardrobe it cost almost nothing, and yet it did everything that a wardrobe did. Why, Bennett was now desperate to know, did anyone ever buy a wardrobe in the first place? All that wood, all that money, all for nothing. Perhaps he was one of the first people to work this out: a clothes-rail early adopter. Very satisfying indeed, that would be, if it turned out to be the case.

In the old days, his policy was to be fully dressed in under two minutes without making a noise or putting the light on. He'd had to leave for the train so early, and he didn't want to disturb Sue or the kids. Curiously, in this new life, his routine was, for the most part, unchanged. There was no point in heating this whole house for just him, so he still had to get dressed quickly; it was too cold to do otherwise. And he was back to doing it in the dark, because Sue had come round over the weekend and, somewhat to his surprise and contrary to all previous agreement, removed not only the bedside table but also the light that had for so long sat, rather helpfully, thereon. Bennett had a sort of hunch that perhaps that last confiscation might have had something to do with the new clothes rail in some obscure way. Certainly the sight of it, while she was on her routine inspection of the property – there was a definite *Carry On Matron* air about his wife these days – did seem to cause a further dip in her already low mood. Quite why that would be the case, though, he couldn't even begin to explain. Was it envy, perhaps? Was she a bit put out to be in possession of their wardrobe, when all that was required was a simple clothes rail?

He shook his head and tightened the knot of his tie. He did get these little snatches sometimes, of possible motives or plausible explanations, but they were few and far between – hazy glimpses rather than a proper sighting that you could log or record. If he was completely honest with himself – and there was nobody else to be honest with, literally nobody – he was beginning to think that this inability to understand his wife might not be a particularly new development. Sometimes, as he lay alone in the dark – the very profound dark, since the lighting in the house overall had been significantly reduced – and tried to look back over the majority of his twenty-five-year marriage, his overriding emotion wasn't grief or relief or anything in between, it was just bafflement – as if he was watching a foreign film without subtitles. He could make out what everyone was doing, because he could see them doing it, but any explanation as to quite what on earth could possibly have motivated them to do it in the first place lay somewhere beyond his understanding.

He hooked a finger in the loop of his jacket, slung it over one shoulder and took the stairs, two at a time, down to the kitchen. The toaster had disappeared, without a word, a couple of weeks back, so he slid two slices of bread under the grill, draped his jacket over the door handle and pulled himself backwards up on to the work surface to wait. This was another of his furniture revelations, in direct antithesis to that re the wardrobe: a kitchen table and chairs had several uses, wider than just the eating of one's meals. Sadly, once again, there was nobody in the immediate vicinity with whom he could discuss it.

Sue had definitely been more demonstrative in their early years; he could see that quite clearly. When they were courting colleagues, and then living together ... And a few years into that, when she had said – rather sweetly, he had thought at the time – 'OK, don't worry. I can take a hint. We're never going to get married. Obviously. Excuse me while I just bloody bugger off,' and they had of course got married forthwith. It had seemed, at the time, rather rude not to. He smiled. Looking back on it, that was one of their key romantic moments.

It had continued like that for a while and, as Bennett remembered, he found it very helpful. Yes, things could be a little uncomfortable. There was that evening when, in his commuter's boredom, he had read the daily recipe in the evening paper and gone through the back door waving it in a cheerful way: it looked so simple, he had said, and so delicious. Why didn't they spare themselves anything too complicated and have that for a change? He genuinely had had no idea that there was any possible cause for offence. But when she picked up first one saucepan then the other, scraped the contents of both into the bin, flew out the door and drove off up the road very fast in first gear – shouting back at him to cook his own bloody dinner and shove it up his arse – then he understood that she had taken offence anyway. He didn't completely understand it, even when she explained her position at length, but he certainly never did it again. The system might have had a certain inherent violence, but it worked.

All that had been replaced in subsequent years, although Bennett couldn't quite put his finger on when or how. She had given up the swearing once the children started to talk, he knew that much. It was a shame, from his point of view: swearing seemed to work with him somehow, like writing in bold or illuminating in neon; his brain lit up in response to it – though quite right for the children, absolutely; quite right for the children. But then, something else crept in in its place, some sort of subtlety – at least, he could only suppose it was subtlety – and that didn't work at all. Bennett's brain did not, he was pretty sure, respond to subtlety: he had a dim sense that it remained firmly dark while the subtlety went right over it. Recently, when he was negotiating his settlement with the firm, she started to say things like 'Yes, so *courageous* of you, to leave in this particular economic climate,' and 'Of course *I'm* thrilled but it might be tough for *you*, being home for a long stretch. We're terribly boring, you know. For such a *clever* chap. Used to such an *interesting* life.' And frankly Bennett found it all most disconcerting. He was pretty sure she didn't really think he was clever, he knew she thought his job the dullest thing on earth, and he couldn't believe that she didn't think he was a bumbling fool to get himself squeezed out of a company he'd worked with for decades – it was certainly his own view. So why, these days, did she always say the complete opposite of what one was expecting to hear? Baffling. 'Stuff it up your arse' may be neither pleasant nor elegant, but it did at least have a certain clarity.

He was drumming his heels against the cupboard door as he pondered. Then he heard himself and stopped short. That thumping, on the wood: that meant children. It was the noise of his children. He could see them clearly, sitting up there, swinging their legs from the knees, swigging juice straight from the carton, moaning about homework, laughing about their day. Then his own voice came through to him too, lecturing them about paintwork, pointing out the rubber marks on the door, and he chewed his lips. So he didn't understand himself either. He jumped back to the floor and ran his hand over the cupboards. There wasn't any real damage, and anyway, who would care if there was? Not Bennett, he was almost positive. And yet he definitely told them all off about it, he could hear himself doing it. What did he do that for? How did that happen?

He seemed to understand himself as little as he understood Sue. He could hear himself shouting at Casper about a B in Maths but he couldn't imagine that he was really bothered about a B in Maths. And why was he even living here in this house? He could see himself sitting in the solicitor's office, signing the separation agreement, helping his family move out to that funny little house the other side of Bridgeford, but he couldn't say why all that had happened. It certainly wasn't because he wanted it to. None of it. On no account did he ever want to live here for a day without them, and he desperately didn't want them to leave. At the end, when he begged her not to do this right then, pleaded that redundancy and separation all at once was more than he could bear, all he got was her shaking head and 'No, no, no. It's your house' – when of course it wasn't just his house – and 'You want your fresh start. We all understand that,' when he had never wanted a fresh start in his life. The fresh start had always been anathema to him. Sue knew that better than anybody. Every life change – however minor, however obvious – had caused him some sort of deep psychic pain. He wasn't entirely sure that he had ever quite recovered from the shock of leaving prep school. Yet he had apparently signed a piece of paper drawn up by his lawyer, and they had gone.

It looked bad, even Bennett could see it looked bad. He could tell, from the way his neighbours responded to him, that living here alone was something of a public-relations disaster. Outsiders could take one look and feel justified in leaping to the conclusion that he was somehow the bad guy in this whole miserable situation. Sitting here in the family home, amid the spoils of war, he did not look, to the untutored eye, like the injured party. Yet he certainly felt like the injured party. And what was more – he shifted uncomfortably on his buttocks – he was injured; deeply, horribly injured.

The toast was burning. He flicked it out from under the grill and on to a plate – black on one side; white on the other was, on average, at his reckoning, a golden brown. It should taste just right. He added butter and marmalade, propped himself against the counter, tucked in to his breakfast and drew up the timetable for his day.

3

Typical Bridgeford. Of all the glorious moments in British history to commemorate, it had to pick the 1953 coronation – all
austerity and post-war struggle; pebbledash and dodgy taste; the
only regal pageant in centuries they'd had to knock off on the
cheap. The stolid, mixed-material, mongrel-architectural Coronation Hall sat back from the corner of Church Street in an
apron of its own car park and stared out at the town like a plain
and disapproving old aunt. It eschewed comfort – its windows
were high, its floors dull and dusty, its walls a distempered
cream – and offered only the basic barrier to the elements. A bit of
weather, in its opinion, never hurt anybody; if it could talk, it
would tell you to put on a vest. In the summer it was too hot in
there, the rest of the year it was too cold, and on this particular
winter's evening – one of those that before Christmas might have
been romantic but now, in January, was simply *de trop* – it was
almost freezing.

The heavy door groaned open, and a gloved hand poked in
and felt down the wall for the switch. As the strip lights clicked
on, Annie came in and stood for a while, watching the cloud of

her warm breath catch in their beam. She was a nice-looking woman, Annie: slight build, fair hair worn in that no-nonsense bob of the frightfully busy. She dressed well – always keeping it politely age-appropriate and, on the whole, looked pretty good for her fifty-nine years. She would probably look even better if she spent less time on others and a bit more on herself, but if she did that – well, then she wouldn't be Annie. Her face was broad, its smile semi-permanent, it made reference to neither mood nor ego and as a result never quite got the attention it deserved. If people were to notice her at all, it was for her eyes. They were a bright hazel and flickered about her in an urgent sort of way, like there was too much human warmth building up in there and if she didn't find another human to warm up asap she might just self-combust – those sort of eyes. In a better world, perhaps, judged by a different set of criteria, Annie Miller would be thought a beauty. In this one, no one thought about her for long enough to form a view.

Annie was first to this evening's choir practice, as she was first to every Tuesday evening's choir practice. She kicked the door shut with her low-heeled boot, tucked her wicker basket in the crook of her arm and slipped off her gloves as she trotted across the hall to the little kitchen.

La-la-la-la, lo lo lo

They always began their sessions with an exercise like this – drifting down the tonic scale and then up again, C to C, changing the syllable when changing the note – each singer joining in as soon as they walked in the door. It was one of Lewis' many, many team-building ideas.

Tea-tea-tea-tea, toe toe toe

Tonight, though, Annie's voice was a little wobbly. For once, she was singing a mournful minor scale, and she sang it as if unsure whether anybody should be singing at all.

Fa-fa-fa-fa, foe foe foe

Putting her basket on the counter, she reached up to the cupboard and took down the chipped and stained cups and saucers. It had long been her job to organise the refreshments for the break, because there was no one else left in Bridgeford with a working knowledge of that kitchen. She would be running the Evergreens' Lunch Club for the rest of her days simply because she alone knew how to get the urn to boiling point. Word was that yoga on a Wednesday were having to bring their own flasks. If anything untoward were to happen to Annie, there might never be a communal cup of anything in that town again.

Ma-ma-ma-ma—

The door banged.

—moe moe moe

At last, more voices were joining in with hers. The altos had arrived. She darted back into the hall, wringing a tea-towel in both hands. 'Oh,' she cried, running towards them, 'girls!' Of course, they were nothing of the sort; it's just how females – be they six, thirty-six or a hundred and six – always address one another. It's like shouting, 'More or less direct contemporaries!', only not such a mouthful. 'Girls, thank God you're first. It's all so awful. You do know, don't you? You have heard the terrible news?'

There were all sorts of reasons why the regulars belonged to the Bridgeford Community Choir and, interestingly – some might say regrettably – singing was not always among them. Take Judith, for example, who as soon as she arrived went straight across the hall to use her solid bulk and strength to collect and carry all the chair stacks. In her late thirties, she was a junior in the altos – in fact, when set against the rest of them, she was more like kindergarten – and music was not, as far as anyone could gather, her first love. Still, she never missed a Tuesday with the Choir, like she never missed any of the other local classes and groups that she went to every evening and most weekends – from Indian Head Massage to Construction. There was a general assumption that she was less a polymath, more a saddo on the hunt for a mate. Of course, that was rather sexist and not really fair, but then that was the current batch of Bridgeford sopranos for you: rather sexist and not really fair.

'Shame she can't find an evening for Weight Watchers.' Pat and Lynn were just tipping into their seventies now – way too old for their voices to reach the high notes – but they stuck with the soprano section anyway, for emotional rather than vocal reasons: it was their spiritual home. They watched Judith move all the furniture and then sat down with a sigh, Pat getting out her knitting and Lynn her new catalogue. They never seemed pleased to be there – where Judith was always trying to engender team spirit, they were all for killing it stone-dead – but they still had good reasons to turn up every week. For a start, they came out of habit – they had been coming, after all, for thirty years. In addition, they came to spend time with each other. But above all they came to obstruct any form of choral progress. They came to protect the role of classical music and religious song. They came, most importantly, to stick out their aching feet in front of the march of modernism and watch it go arse over tip.

'Evening, Lewis,' called Pat, eyes on her knitting needles, thumbs pushing up the wool. 'Got something nice for us there, have you?'

Lewis wheeled Katie towards the refreshments area. Every Tuesday afternoon, she baked something for the group. The results were a little hit and miss, but she didn't have anything else to do on a Tuesday afternoon so she carried on regardless.

'God, we need something to cheer us up,' called Lewis, parking Katie at the table and watching her unload. 'Nice bit of short-bread—'

'Dad. Cupcakes . . . ' Katie corrected.

'Doh, my eyes . . . Nice lot of cupcakes. Just the ticket.'

Lewis, almost uniquely, couldn't sing or dance or even click his fingers. And any song that made no reference to either the history of the English peasantry or the international labour movement seemed to render him temporarily deaf. It didn't even count as music as far as he was concerned. While he could – almost – hold the tune of 'The Red Flag', give him a line from a Disney song and he was all over the shop. But then, he was a keen member of the Bridgeford Players and he couldn't act; he was a member of the

Chamber of Commerce and he didn't have a business. He was Bridgeford Man, was Lewis – he just had to be part of everything – and he was also Katie's dad. And when you're nineteen and a half and in a wheelchair and all your mates have gone off to uni and you've missed a couple of years of schooling, there's not a great range of things you can do with yourself on a week-night. Katie loved choir and that, to Lewis, was more important than anything.

Some enchanted evening

That was Maria, crashing through the door, still in her green carer's uniform, her preternaturally short arms outstretched towards the room.

You may meet Lew Stanford

Now Maria did come for the singing. That squat, square body was perfectly designed to produce the sort of rich, round sound that could fill the upper circle in a noisy matinée. Had she not spent her formative years in an Eastern European war zone, she might even have ended up a stage professional. Of course, she was never the leading lady type, but musical theatre had, over the years, provided enough nurses, nannies and maids to keep a performer like her going into a ripe old age.

You may meet Lew Stanford

Somehow – as if Fate had got the memo but hadn't quite read it properly – Maria found herself cast in the role of real-life carer instead of the fictional version. She brought to it the various skills and weaknesses, charms and irritations of every nurse, nanny and maid in the history of musical comedy, and sang her way through happily enough.

Across a crowded room

Although her name was not in lights, she was most definitely one of the most well-known characters on the Bridgeford stage. And that, after all, was a fame of sorts.

'Pass me my revolver, would you, Lynn love?' Pat cut in loudly – on top of modernists and secularists, Pat had it in for soloists too – but the hall was filling up now and nobody took much notice. A scattering of basses were noisily settling themselves into the seats on the left; the altos were all arranged in the front seats in the middle; the sopranos were huddled in a group, giggling. Annie looked about her, aghast. Either the rest of the Choir didn't know how to behave, or they really didn't know what had happened. She found Lewis and whispered behind her hand. 'You know, I don't think they can have heard.'

He stood up and hitched his waistband over the protrusion of his tummy. 'We need an announcement,' he said, with grim pleasure.

'Yes. Will you?'

'Annie, I think this is one for the both of us.'

They walked in an important sort of way to the front of the hall. Annie coughed and Lewis began: 'I'm afraid I have some terrible news. Last week, the night in fact that we were singing outside Budgens—'

'No need to apologise. But I'm never doing that again,' muttered a soprano.

'—our beloved Constance was in a terrible accident on the motorway.' He paused. The Choir was stunned. Then, 'No,' they started to say; 'Not Connie . . . ', 'Of all of us, not her . . . ' Constance they knew to be the best of them. Constance was what held them together. Constance was why they came.

Annie opened her mouth, thinking it might be her turn to speak.

Lewis continued. 'I've been in touch with her family a few times, and I spoke to them just this evening. Everyone is very hopeful that she will make a full recovery.'

Annie looked out at the hall, serious, concerned, mute – the female half of the nightly news anchor at one of those moments of national emergency that require the particular gravitas that, it is generally believed, only a man can bring.

'And the message is: she is still determined that we are not only still going to the Championships, we are going to WIN! She just needs to get a bit of strength up, and then she will decide what songs we will be performing and let us know.' Annie nodded some more. Lewis continued: 'Of course, I know you will all join me in wishing her the speediest recovery.'

'Hear, hear.'

'Poor love.'

'But until she is back with us, there is now at the very heart of the Bridgeford Community Choir A POWER VACUUM.' He thumped the fist of one hand in the palm of the other. Fifteen years as an Independent on the council had not dulled his enthusiasm for public speaking. Annie gave up, ducked and tiptoed to her place in the altos.

'Well, fancy that,' said Lynn.

'Don't tell us' – Pat was unravelling her knitting. It was going to be a Homer Simpson for a grandchild, but it could just as easily be a bed-jacket if Connie could take the yellow – 'you're the man to fill it.'

'No!' Lewis began to stride around the hall. 'On the contrary.' He jabbed a finger. 'There is no one in this room who is worthy of Connie's throne. She is an impossible act to follow. There is not even a likely regent who can carry us through this crisis.' Annie wriggled in her seat, looking a bit put out. 'Without her, we are all equals. Until she returns, we will behave as such: equal power, equal choices, equal respect. No longer shall we sit in rows and face the front. From now on, we face each other in a circle.'

'Ooh. The circle of trust,' said Judith. 'I like it.' She jumped up and started to rearrange the chairs.

'We will have no programme, but just sing according to our own moods. We will learn no more harmonies, just sing the same notes. We shall operate in a state of pure democracy until Constance returns restored.'

'God, whatever . . . ' The sopranos had had enough.

'Oh, do sit down, Lewis,' bossed an alto.

The door slammed yet again and their regular accompanist waddled past with her head down. 'Evening, Mrs Coles.' Mrs Coles was the local piano teacher, credited with annihilating the musical enthusiasm of the children of Bridgeford for generations. 'Have you heard?' She did not reply. She never did. Mrs Coles spoke to Constance, or she did not speak at all.

The next ten minutes were completely taken up with the democratic process: Maria was shouted down for asking for 'Summertime' – no more solos; Lynn's request for 'Oh Happy Day' was thrown out – *absolutely* no more Jesus. After a lot of noise and in an atmosphere of unhappy compromise and profound ill-will, they all agreed that the first half of the evening should be spent on early folk. Most of the hall was disgruntled; Lewis was triumphant.

And, then, as always happened, once they started to sing their divisions were forgotten. By the end of 'Scarborough Fair' they were all smiling at one another across the circle of trust.

They were on the second verse of 'The Skye Boat Song' when the door opened and a new woman slipped into the room. Tall and narrow with short-cropped, very black hair, she crept quietly across the hall towards them. She was dressed for comfort – boyfriend jeans, T-shirt, black buttoned-up blazer. And with her shoulder-bag strapped tightly across her person and flat sporty shoes, she came across as not so much a local coming to a community centre, more a tourist out on a very quick day trip who didn't quite trust the natives. She slid into a seat between Judith and Lewis. He smiled and held out his songbook for her to share. She nodded and read along, but did not really sing.

And then it was time for the break. Even before the applause had quite finished, Lewis was on his feet again and holding up a hand.

'Just one more announcement, everyone, before you get your refreshments: I would like to introduce you to our newest recruit.' He pointed to the woman sitting on his right. 'Everyone, this is Tracey. Tracey, this is everyone. We're neighbours,' he added, with a swagger. You could see it was a big thing for Lewis: not only had a seriously cool person chosen to live in his fifty-yard radius but that seriously cool person had turned up at his choir and at his bidding. He looked around with a self-satisfied smile – as if he too was somehow now seriously cool. Or a bit cool. Or, come on, surely, at the very least, not as uncool as some had previously thought him to be ...

Tracey looked uncomfortable at the great gush of welcome.

'Blimey.' She pulled a face. 'I feel like a mail-order bride.' The gush stopped. Ooh dear, that was awkward – a mail-order-bride joke in front of Lewis, of all people. Just that bit too soon ... Annie jumped up and stepped across the circle with her hand extended. 'Great to see you again. We're old friends,' she told the group, steering Tracey towards the tea table.

'I don't *think* so.' Tracey looked nervous.

'Annie.' She put her hand to her chest. 'You remember. Rosie's mum.'

'Um ... No ...'

'They were in church choir together.' Annie started pouring from the catering pot; Tracey stood and watched her. 'Rosie and Billy ... You must remember. Little cassocks ... Tea?'

Parenting – with its open-door policy to such a wide age range – can often cause this sort of social confusion. After all, women can be born twenty or thirty years apart, yet have children at exactly the same time. And just because they are in the same mothering boat, some of them sometimes can make the mistake of thinking that they are together in all sorts of other boats too: the boat of age, for example; the boats of clothes or food or interior design; the boat, disastrously, of a good night out; sometimes even the boat of life. Or at least, the older ones can. The younger ones tend to be all too aware of the differences between them.

'Ah, yes. The church choir ... sorry.' Tracey was coldly polite. 'I'd forgotten that little phase.' She held cup and saucer with both hands, tense with subdued hostility, then very deliberately stepped back a couple of metres and looked at the floor – a physical representation of the vast generational divide between them.

'I know.' Annie chirruped on regardless. 'Sometimes, looking back, I think that's all my girls did in their first eighteen years: take

35

things up with a passion and then drop them again with a thump. Rock cake? At least, I think it's a rock cake. Rosie's twenty-two now. I guess Billy's the same.'

'Oh no,' said Tracey emphatically. 'No, he's . . . Well, yes, I guess he is. Twenty-two! Sort of, technically, twenty-two. Not *actually*. I never think of him like—' Tracey took a nibble of the bun and tucked the rest under her cup.

'None of us does, with our own. She's living with her boyfriend already.' She sipped her tea, dropped her voice – 'Tastes a bit better if you dunk' – and went on: 'Yes, one of the Williams boys: have you come across them?'

'Er, no.'

'Very nice family, but I still can't quite believe she's "shacked up". Always our babies.'

'It's not that so much. More, well, he's spent a long time lying on the sofa and it feels like that ought to be factored in. They might have stopped the clock for that bit.' Tracey looked over her shoulder for someone else to talk to.

Annie carried on. 'Is he on a gap year? Thanks, love. I'll do the washing-up.' She took a cup from Maria.

'Less a gap, more a ruddy great hole.' Tracey scanned the room. Everyone else was deep in conversation. She surrendered. 'He's working now, though. Just started, actually, in a bar . . .'

'Oh, Tourism, Leisure and Hospitality,' Annie approved. 'Excellent industry for young people. Is he on a trainee scheme?'

'Nope . . .'

Annie went back into the kitchen and started filling the sink. 'Have you come across the Hendersons at all, over in Priory Lane?' she called through the hatch. 'Nice couple. In hotels.'

'And no again. Look – er, Annie – I don't really *know* people. I never actually *come across* anyone. Just to save you the bother of asking. It's just not how I roll. So, general rule of thumb: if you know them, I don't. OK?'

'Oh dear, that is a shame. Well, you've got us now.'

'It's not—' Tracey started, and then shook her head. 'Never mind.

Anyway, Billy's not in the "industry" as such. More running the bar down at the Square for a bit—'

'But it's just getting on that ladder, isn't it?' She was back in, wiping down the Formica tabletop. 'Might be worth getting in touch—'

'—with two mates.'

'Oh, yes?' Annie perked up.

'Mm. Curly and Squat? Lovely boys. Now I don't know if you've come across them at all?'

'So, let's get back to it.' Judith clapped her hands. Still chatting together, they all drifted back to the circle of trust.

'What do we fancy to finish up with?'

'I know.' Annie, shaking the water off her hands, was the last back to her seat. 'Something a bit modern – end on a high. Let's show Tracey here what we're made of.'

'How about some ABBA?'

'Judith's favourite.'

'Go on then.'

Mrs Coles began, they started up. They hadn't done this one for a while and while Judith was particularly audible, and quite heart-felt, on being 'nothing special' and 'a bit of a bore', the rest were a bit rusty. The sopranos were horribly warbly and the altos, having for-gotten the words, were sharing their reading glasses and losing their places. Tracey sat with her arms crossed, rolling her eyes, flaring her nostrils, very clearly having nothing to do with any of it. Towards the end of the first verse, they were starting to lose their way al-together. Even Lewis seemed to be aware that something was amiss.

And then it happened.

So I say . . .

As the volume began to build and Mrs Coles' fat fingers bashed out the first chords to the first chorus:

. . . thank you for the music

Tracey – despite herself – started to sing. It didn't seem to be a particularly joyful or even a voluntary act. She looked quite shocked, almost violated, as if her voice was forcing its way up through her chest and out of her mouth, like sudden vomit or an alien baby. She sounded strong from the first, but soft, like she was keeping a hold of it, still had some control. But then her sound started to build and that full, distinctive throaty mezzo filled the whole hall almost at once. And then it built some more. And suddenly it burst through and up and out at the top of its own strength and the sound of the Choir was at once transformed. Lewis held out his lyrics for her, but she couldn't see them. Tracey had stopped fighting; she was possessed, lost, somewhere inside the song. Her eyes were closed, her fingers were snapping, she rocked in her seat. Her mouth was so wide that the light kept catching her tongue stud. All the others could do was cling on for the ride.

For gi-ving it to . . . me.

The rest of them leapt to their feet, cheering and whooping, but there was no time for any of that stuff. Without any sort of democratic discussion whatsoever, Tracey had gone back to the beginning of the *ABBA Gold* track list. She was off, unstoppable. Nothing was going to get in her way until Waterloo had been fought and lost.

At the end of it, they bellowed for their own encore, roared their own appreciation. 'That was amazing,' called Maria.

'Just what we need,' Pat muttered to Lynn, 'another bloody diva.'

'Tracey, before you go, we must get your email,' shouted an alto over the din.

Tracey, who was sitting still, stunned by the sound of her own voice, slowly came blinking back into the room. 'Oh . . . no . . . Christ, no . . . I don't think . . .'

'Don't worry. We know where you live. Well done, Lewis, for bagsying this one. Why don't we say that everyone has to bring a new person next week: friend, family member—'

'Total stranger dragged in off the street.'

'Unsuspecting passer-by by means of a sack over its head.'

'—to double our numbers. And need I remind you: we are DES-PERATE for MEN!'

'Speak for yourself, love.' Some of those sopranos – so predictable you could set your watch by them.

And the basses were no better. 'Am I not man enough for you any more?' That was, of course, absolutely hilarious. On some obscure historic point of principle, basses were required to find everything said by basses to be absolutely hilarious.

'You're all too funny for words. Just a few notices before we go ...'

Everyone got up. There was a loud scraping of chairs.

'We're singing at midnight on Saturday at the anti-superstore protest on London Road,' Annie shouted over the noise. 'Usual protest programme – the one we did when they demolished the cottage hospital, closed the youth club, "We Shall Not" etc., etc. Sign-up sheet here.'

The Choir were picking up their bags, shoving in their lyrics, making plans for the week ahead.

'We've also – do you all minding waiting until I've finished, please? Not much more. Thank you – we've also been asked to run the hot-soup stall for the sit-in for the protesters on Friday night, ten p.m. onwards. A big issue for everybody – excuse me, Lynn, if I could just get to the end of the sentence – an honour to be asked. I've done a rota of half-hour slots. All who can come, put your names down. Thank you.' Annie waved two sheets of paper at the hall and went to put them on the table by the door.

'Can I just add,' bellowed Lewis, even though the hall was nearly empty now, 'we're just weeks away from the Talent Show – our major fund raiser of the whole year. I hope you're all perfecting your acts.'

'Night,' called the last ones to leave.

'Night.'

And the singers drifted out into the darkness, huddled into their coats, clutching music to their chests, bracing themselves against the cold air.

Outside on the pavement, Tracey stood awkwardly watching Lewis as he steered Katie towards their specially adapted car. 'Can I help you there?'

'We're fine, Tracey, thanks.' Together they pressed a series of buttons and made a sequence of moves – like well-trained synchronised swimmers – at the end of which Katie and her chair were tucked up in the back. 'Just turn up next week, that's all you have to do.'

'We're both so thrilled you came,' said Katie, quite firmly. 'We know you're going to love it,' she added, in a manner that would brook no possible argument. 'Night, all,' they both called out, and drove away.

Annie, always the last out, turned off the lights and locked the door. 'Oh, good,' she said to Tracey, who was staring after the car and chewing her lip. 'So glad I caught you.' They fell into step together. 'You're a terrific addition to the team, I must say.'

'Oh, ha, very kind.' Tracey still seemed distracted – altered – by the last hour. 'Yeah.' She was seized by a shiver of retrospective pleasure. 'Thanks. But I shouldn't think I'll be taking it up again any time soon ...'

'What? You've already taken it up!' Annie laughed. 'You've just got to wait till next week, that's all. Don't worry, it'll fly by. And there's Saturday midnight, too, don't forget.'

'Um, well. Busy then. Obviously. And all that cheesy stuff, ABBA and all that – it's not really my sort of thing ...'

'Isn't it? That's odd.' Annie clicked at her car and it came obediently to life. 'You seemed to know it all well enough.'

'Yeah, but, actually I'm more of a rock chick?' She had the grace to look embarrassed even as the words emerged from her mouth.

'Ooh, that does sound jolly. And we're happy to turn our voices to anything, you know. By the way,' she opened the door, 'I was thinking about Billy in the second half there . . .'

'Billy?' Tracey stopped walking and frowned. 'Really? Why would you do that?'

'I've got a few ideas.' Annie settled herself behind the wheel. 'I'll get some options together for the next time we see each other.'

'What? No. Please, don't bother,' Tracey called into the car door.

'It's no bother.' Annie tucked her coat in. 'In fact, it's a pleasure.'

'Eh? A *pleasure*? Why—'

But Annie had already shut her door.

4

The train pulled away into a dank, colourless Monday morning that promised nothing much. Annie gripped the lapels of her padded jacket with one hand and waved with the other. She seemed to spend half her life right here these days – waiting, for one train to bring James or the girls home; watching, as another one took them away. There was her family pulling off in their exciting different directions – well, they all went off in the same direction really, but then some of them got off at the next stop and changed. It was a very good service. You could easily get to anywhere you fancied from here. And there was Annie, always there – the first and the last thing they saw, at the end of their journey and the beginning. A star, that was what she was. Not a twinkling or a shooting one or anything – ha – but a star of sorts: reliable, steady, the light that an Elizabethan sailor could depend upon to guide him home. Navigational, that was it. Yes. The lodestar of the Miller family was Annie. She waved again.

The morning rush was over. There wasn't a soul around now; only their cars remained. She moved through the packed car park and up the steps. The best thing about being out of the house so early on a Monday was there was just time for a nice breakfast before she went in to her job at the library. Normally it took for ever for Annie to walk the length of the High Street, with all the stopping and chatting that was generally involved – it seemed to be the last place on earth where she was not actually invisible – but she couldn't fit all that in today. Between the station and the Copper Kettle lay a social dodgeball course that many might find daunting: a run of charity shops being opened up for another quiet day, each by a very nice woman whom Annie had known for years. Fortunately, she was a social athlete in peak condition.

'Morning,' she tossed at the Oxfam shop – head left, body forward, speed up. 'His cold better?' A question came flying out of the Red Cross. 'Just put her on the train.' She caught and lobbed it back without a break in her stride. 'Loving it, thanks.' By the time she approached the café she had learned as much as she needed to – one grandchild had colic, another was overdue, a daughter's holiday was a rip-off – and done it in record time. She had also nearly bumped into Sue's ex a few times – clutching what looked like an onion – but fortunately Bennett seemed as reluctant to chat as she was. And at nine o'clock on the dot, she reached for the door and it gave its happy little tinkle that she loved so much, the tinkle that Annie knew to mean 'coffee and a bun with Sue'.

However early Annie was, Sue would always be earlier. The two of them had been meeting here every Monday morning for nearly sixteen years – ever since their girls had both toddled off to nursery. There she was, already with a cappuccino, scribbling in a notebook at their usual table under the window. 'Menopause Corner', Sue called it – she was extremely gung-ho about middle age, like she'd been waiting for this her whole life. Annie was a good five years her senior and did rather wish she wouldn't say that sort of thing. It just flagged it all up, somehow. When Annie was with any of her other friends, time just fell away. Everyone she had known since they were twenty-eight still looked, to Annie, as if they were twenty-eight, and when she was with them she felt twenty-eight too. Sue had been a wonderful friend to her in every way for ages, but she didn't half make her feel every one of her fifty-nine years. Annie moved between the tables, bent to kiss her friend and sat down with a plonk. She felt older already. 'Oof.'

'How was your weekend?' asked Sue. 'How was that brilliant daughter of yours? List her latest triumphs. Share them with us, the mothers of mere mortals.'

'Er ...' Sue always talked about Annie's girls like this, and Annie never knew quite how to respond. Jess wasn't brilliant at all, if she was honest, but it rather went against the grain to reject compliments directed towards one's own offspring, however undeserved.

Sue leaned across the table, looking closer into Annie's face. 'Oh. Not so good?'

'Of course, it was lovely.' Annie sat on her hands. It had not, in fact, been one of Jessica's better visits home, but she didn't want to go over all that now. And anyway, it was just a phase, Annie was sure of that. 'She's on great form.'

'Something's up.' Sue put the lid on her pen, closed the notebook – full of lists, Annie noticed – and put both back in her bag. 'What,' she put her elbows on the table, linked her fingers and rested her chin, 'is it?'

'I'm worried about choir,' said Annie, staring out of the window. It was true, actually: she was. Jess was just having a bit of a blip; choir, though, seemed to be in its death throes. 'I just don't know if we're going to survive while Connie's out of action. We were supposed to do all our protest songs down at the superstore sit-in on Saturday, and only Lewis and I turned up. And the night before that, we were doing the hot-soup stall and that was me on my own for hours on end. I didn't get home till about two. It was bloody knackering. Nobody turns out for anything and we've got this competition coming up and that's a huge thing for us. Absolutely crucial. We've reached crisis point. It's like the decline and fall of the Roman Empire all over again.'

Sue looked a bit bored.

'Well, all right then, it's like the BAAS.' That made her sit up. 'It's the Bridgeford Art Appreciation Society all over again.'

'Blimey.' She gave a low whistle. 'Not that bad, surely.'

'OK,' Annie conceded. 'But if it doesn't grow, it's going to die, and that would be heartbreaking. We've been going for years. Every member is supposed to deliver a new person tomorrow and, I tell you, I'm stumped.'

'Hmmm.' There was an awkward pause. Sue looked lost in thought; Annie held her breath. Please, she thought, please don't offer your own services. Sue and a good tune were, famously, strangers. Her voice was the last thing they needed. But then suddenly, Sue grabbed her notebook and pen, wrote CHOIR??, threw them both back in her bag and Annie was able to breathe again. This was exactly Sue's favourite sort of problem. She was diverted, energised.

'What about that woman – oh, you know, whatsername, lives near the school ...'

They were both becoming slightly forgetful at exactly the same time – which was rather cosy in itself – but even more comforting was the fact that they tended to forget completely different things. They were like two radar, positioned either side of the same area, which together combined to give total coverage and which had their own secret code of communication, limited to a sequence of blips and bleeps.

'Clue?'

'Big.' Sue measured a width with her hands.

'Jackie.'

'Yes.'

'Moved.'

'Good.'

'Quite—'

'—vile.'

Annie unwrapped her scarf and shrugged off her jacket. 'We have already got one newcomer.'

'Yeah?' Sue took a gulp of coffee and put the cup back in the saucer with both hands. 'Who?'

But now that she was out of sight, Annie had forgotten her name already.

'Clue?'

'Legs.'

Sue took one foot from its shoe and rubbed her bunion reflectively. She shook her head. 'More ... '

'Hair.' Annie made a cutting motion round her ear.

'Tracey.'

'Well done, old girl! After all, we haven't even glimpsed her for years.'

'Still got it ... ' Sue tapped her temple. 'What was it with her, can you remember? There's some reason she sticks in the mind. What was the rumour ... ?'

They both sat for a moment, raking through the fallen leaves of their autumnal memories, and then gave up.

'It's gone,' said Annie. 'Now, who else can you think of?'

Sue gave a little jump. 'I know! I do believe I've got it: what about Bennett?'

'Bennett?' That one came out of nowhere. 'You mean, your Bennett?'

'How many other Bennetts do you know?' She took a sip and wiped the foam off her top lip.

'Fair point.' Annie couldn't quite tell if this was a serious suggestion or just an excuse to get on to her pet subject. Divorcing couples were always like this, in Annie's experience: couldn't live with each other, couldn't stop talking about each other either. She and James had lived in quiet contentment for over thirty years, and his name hardly came up from one coffee to the next. Sue had moved out because Bennett was boring her to death, yet she had been a tiny bit of a Bennett bore ever since. 'But isn't he terribly busy?' He'd looked very busy this morning, striding across the street. And, desperate though they were, Annie couldn't quite picture Bennett fitting in, somehow.

'Busy? Busy?' Although their separation was, as Sue kept saying – over and over – very amicable, Annie thought that Sue didn't always sound all that amicable when she talked about him. 'Busy being redundant, you mean?'

'Well, more busy looking for a—'

'Busy living on his own?' Sue laughed a not very amicable laugh.

'I suppose that can—'

'Busy watching me and the children move out into a squalid little rental while he stays behind in the house?'

'You've all been so amazing about that. I've said it before, I'll say it again: you've been too generous, Sue. I don't know how he dares—'

'I think he's got time. Also, you know, he used to be a cathedral chorister. He might even be an asset.'

'Gosh, eek, he's probably too grand for us.' They'd had classically trained singers in the Choir before, with what can politely be called 'mixed results'. 'I mean, is he terribly good?'

'Extremely. Highly trained. Over many years.'

Annie felt a desperate need to head this off. 'Really, honestly, I think we're beneath him. We don't even sing in harmony these days. In fact, quite a lot of us don't even sing in tune.'

Sue looked even more determined, delighted almost. 'I think it will do him good.'

Another tack: 'Why do you even want to do him good? After everything he's done to you? You're an absolute saint. I wouldn't bother putting any fun his way.'

'Well, you can't be married to someone for a quarter of a century and just stop caring about them.' She took her pen and notebook out of her bag again. 'I'll be cosseting and worrying about him and running around after him for ever, I should think. He seems to expect it of me.'

Annie watched as she wrote TELL BENNETT HE'S JOINING THE BLOODY CHOIR!!! and underlined it three times. She was pressing so hard, the pen pierced the paper.

'He'll be there.' She sighed. 'Now. What else is bothering you?'

At that moment, the waitress came to their table. And, oh good, it was Jasmine White – her little favourite. Annie had a passionate interest in her children's generation. She felt a bit responsible for all of them somehow, not just the three she had brought into the world.

And the newly grown-up whom she had known and watched and cared about since infancy were a source of endless fascination. She valued every glimpse of them, like an instalment of a long-running drama serial. Especially Jazzy, for some reason. Even though everyone else had given up on her years ago – she did have her tricky moments, that was certainly true – Annie still had that soft spot.

'What can I get you, Mrs Miller?' Jazzy leaned over and wiped the oak table, readjusted her mob cap, took her order pad out of the pocket of her long flowery apron and waited.

'I think I'll have a cappuccino and . . .' Annie shut the menu and looked up, 'I might have a Danish, please, Jazzy. Special treat. What about you, Sue?'

Annie watched as Jazzy wrote down *2 x cappuccino, 2 x Danish* and then sketched a plump little woodland creature on her pad while she waited.

'Oh, go on then, I'll have the same, thanks. Two old bags like us. Who cares if it goes straight to our hips?'

Jazzy took their menus and let through a flicker of irritation.

'How are you, love?' Annie just felt sorry for the poor girl, that was what it came down to. She had watched in horror as the mother had left and come back and left – over and over, the whole time Jazzy was at primary school. It was quite touching to see her now holding down a job at the Copper Kettle – putting on that dreadful uniform – when she could be out of her head in some dive somewhere like her feckless parent. 'How's your grandmother?'

'Same as last time, thanks, Mrs Miller.' She picked up a dirty cup. 'No better, no worse.'

'Well, she's lucky to have you . . .'

Jazzy was staring at them both. The sun was coming out, and the light wasn't doing anybody any favours. Annie was pretty sure she was in decent repair but Sue was looking particularly furry there this morning. And the badger-like white stripe down the parting of her black hair . . . Annie could see the horror and fascination on Jazzy's face. That's it, she thought with a tug of sympathy, not just for Sue but also for herself and every other woman who might one day find herself approaching the age of sixty. That's our choice: total invisibility or being gawped at like something on *Nature Watch*. 'Oh, it's all much better than it used to be. We've got great carers now. I don't have to do anything like as much any more.' Jasmine turned to get their order.

'Aha. And do you still sing, love? I will never, ever forget your solo in that nativity play at St Ambrose as long as I live. Do you remember, Sue?'

Jazzy turned back slowly.

'Oh, we all blubbed, the lot of us. Every single parent. "Away in a Manger", wasn't it? You were brilliant. So much better than my useless lot.'

Jazzy's mouth was gaping. She shut it.

'Yes, and you had a veil that slipped further and further down your nose and all we could see was your little mouth.' Both the women were laughing.

'But it didn't matter because your singing was so mesmerising,' said Annie.

'Oh yeah,' Jazzy joined in, although Annie could tell she couldn't remember any of it and knew there was nobody else to remind her. Not one member of her family had ever once turned up to watch Jazzy in anything at all. The rest of them had all clapped her twice as hard, to make up. 'What year was that again?'

'Now, let me see . . .' Sue began.

'Year Two.' Annie did not particularly want to keep all the information for the Official History of Bridgeford Schooldays in her own head, but it seemed to lodge itself in there anyway. She remembered everything about everyone. Her total recall of the exam grades of others was particularly freakish, as well as being completely useless. She was just like one of those men who could spout every result from every football match from the past fifty years. Except the whole world seemed to revere a bloke for his sports statistics; everyone thought they were so clever, so witty, the height of some incomprehensible cool. Nobody admired a person for knowing the sort of stuff Annie knew. She didn't even admire it herself. She wouldn't mind at all if she was not the sort of person to be having that conversation right there, right then. She would love not to say what she was about to say, but there was nothing for it. The information had bubbled up. If she didn't let it out it would burst out anyway. 'Definitely Year Two. Pat did the costumes. The wise men had nits. Rosie was a donkey.' There. She'd said it.

'My little darling just sang like one!'

'I'll just get your coff—'

'Anyway,' Annie burst in, seizing the moment. 'How would you like to join our choir?'

'Your choir?' Jazzy looked at her like she'd suddenly started spouting Swahili. 'Choir? Oh, hang on, was that what that thing was the other evening? All those old people outside Budgens?'

'That's right,' Annie was polite, although Sue was snorting away. 'Yes, we were outside Budgens.'

'So that's a choir?' Jazzy had a sudden coughing fit. 'Tempting, very tempting.' Then she tucked the menus under her arm – 'I think I might just stick to the solos, though, thanks, Mrs M' – and sped over to the coffee station.

5

There was a chap in the office, back in the days when Bennett had an office, who went off on his stag night with his friends one day and the next woke up alone on a roundabout in the middle of a foreign city he couldn't quite recognise, with no wallet, wearing only his underpants and with no idea how to get home. He had stood, this chap – he was in Marketing, Bennett seemed to remember, and not a particularly serious sort of person – in the middle of the department on the Monday morning telling them all about it as if it had been the most brilliant, hilarious joke. Bennett had thought that a trifle odd at the time. How could anything so obviously unpleasant be considered even vaguely amusing? And looking back, he found it even odder. Now that his every day was spent in a place he didn't recognise, since his own life had turned itself in to a never-ending replay of that one, terrible stag night, he was qualified to declare that there was nothing about the situation that could be passed off as comedy at all.

At least, he thought as he marched down the High Street through the dark evening, he had his clothes on; that was something. He may have been stripped bare emotionally – 6 p.m. was always something of a low point; self-pity seemed to get the upper hand – but, thank God for small mercies, he wasn't trying to find his way around Bridgeford in his boxers. Indeed, it had been a policy decision made by him at the beginning of this career break that from Monday to Friday he would wear a suit and tie at all times. He felt for his jacket button and closed it. He knew how he was looking and that was really rather smart.

But, while he did have his wallet – very nice, brown leather, present from Sue the Christmas before last – he did not actually have any money. Well, he did – there were his savings, of course, loathe though he was to dip into them – but he didn't have a salary. That was the thing. And as he had, at the moment, no idea of where any future salary might be coming from, he was forced to be very careful about all further expenditure.

And although he had lived in Bridgeford for over twenty years, it really might as well be a foreign city. Since they'd moved in to Sue's – their – dream house, he had spent all his time in an office miles away, working to pay for it. For half the the year, he left in the dark and returned in the dark. While she and the kids lived and learned and worked and made friends right there in the community, he only did so by proxy. The 'friends' he himself had made were husbands of friends of Sue, fathers of their children's chums at school, and in the past few weeks he hadn't heard from any of them. He could only put it down to the injured-party confusion.

He turned into Priory Lane, the solitary tin in his plastic carrier bag banging against the side of his knee. His trouble was that, while he didn't really live in Bridgeford in any real sense of the word, he couldn't obviously be said to live anywhere else either. He walked down the drive, round to the back door and into the kitchen. Lined up on the work surface were the other components of that night's meal, which he had purchased, each independently, throughout the day: the solitary onion (from his 9 a.m. sortie), the pasta (12 noon) and the garlic bulb (3.15). He put the tin of tomatoes in its place, arranged everything in order of usage, and gazed upon his work.

It was a shame he'd had the olive oil and the Parmesan already. He wouldn't have minded another outing.

The message light on the phone in the corner was winking at him – not unusual at this time of night. There was always someone out there who wanted to chat through his double glazing. He pressed Play, and the voice of his wife filled their kitchen.

'And, by the way, Annie is begging that you join her hopeless little choir. Just because that Constance who you've never even heard of is practically half dead – I mean, what's that got to do with you? I said to her, "You have got to be joking. Do you actually have any idea how high-brow he is?" I said, "Excuse me, but you do know that a cathedral choir and a community choir are two rather different animals?" And I said, "Do you not realise how busy Bennett is these days?" She certainly ought to. She's spotted you striding about Bridgeford in your suit. I mean, we all have. Not used to having such highly qualified, distinguished menfolk in our humble midst on a weekday. It's all anybody talks about. "What's Bennett up to, nearly knocking me over, in such a hurry?" Talk of the town, you are. So she should realise, really, you don't have time for all this, before dragging me into the middle of it all as if I haven't got enough on my plate. And I said, "How can he say he'll be in the Coronation Hall every Tuesday at eight p.m. when he's bound to be out having dinner with old clients and for all I know young new girlfriends, it's none of my business what he's up to and certainly not my place to—"'

The machine beeped, its space exhausted. Bennett knew how it felt. He sank down the side of the kitchen cupboard on to the floor and hugged his knees. It took him about ten minutes of very deep – almost painful – thought, but eventually, he reckoned, he got there. It was hard work, his head was throbbing, but by the end of it he was pretty sure he was having one of his glimpses into possible motive or plausible explanation and it was this: however unlikely it might seem on the surface, he was reasonably confident that what Sue actually wanted was for Bennett to join Annie's choir.

He sprang up. Pasta and tomato sauce could wait. What he

needed right now was the greatest piece of choral music known to mankind. He started singing to himself as he ran down the spines of his record collection until he got to V.

Gloria . . .

There you are, Nicolo.

. . . *in excelsis Deo*

He slipped the vinyl out of the sleeve, held it between the flats of his hands and blew on it.

Et in terra pax . . .

It had been years, but at last the needle was back in the groove.

. . . *hominibus bonae voluntatis*

And Bennett was going to start tuning up.

6

Tracey couldn't quite tell what was going on with Billy tonight. All last week he had left for the bar at 7, but now it was getting on for half-past and he didn't seem to be showing any signs of moving off the sofa. She started taking items out of the fridge with a view to cooking herself something. Was he going to be in? Should she offer him some? If she did offer him some, would he take it the wrong way? Was he just concentrating hard on a rerun of *Bargain Hunt*, listening hard to The Bloodshitters, or was he genuinely a bit subdued tonight? And if so, was that because he had got the boot from this job already, a mere eight days in? It would be sad, but not the shortest chapter in his professional history.

'I was just going to knock up some—'

The doorbell rang. They both froze and stared at one another.

'Wha's that?' asked Billy. She remembered now, he'd been out last week, missed the Big Moment.

'It's the doorbell!' mouthed Tracey, in case someone could hear her.

'No way,' said Billy, at normal volume. 'How do you know that?' He was properly impressed.

'Rang last Monday too,' she whispered, tiptoeing towards the window.

'Last Monday? Too?' Billy turned down his mouth in a struggle to comprehend. 'So, like, twice?' He shook his head. 'Man, that's mental.'

They stood at the sill together and peered down into the street. Tracey clocked the situation at once – slightly flyaway, if-it-wasn't-blond-it-would-be-white hair, a navy raincoat, brown suede boots. 'Oh, hell,' said Tracey. 'It's that madwoman from that singing thing I went to last week.' The bell rang again, Annie stepped back to look upwards and they both, as one, ducked down. Tracey was curled, foetal, against the wall. 'She's the mother of someone you were in church choir with all those years ago. I mean, so sodding what, but she seems to think it makes us blood brothers.'

Billy took another look over.

'Can you believe it,' Tracey hissed up from the floor, 'that she and I have got kids of them same age?'

Billy looked at Annie, then back at his mother. 'Yeah.' He shrugged. 'S'pose.'

'But don't you think it's amazing,' she tried again, her voice a little higher, 'that that's even possible?'

'Not really.' He was standing at the window now, dangerously visible to all of Bridgeford. He screwed up his face. 'What you on about?' There came a noise from the street, and Tracey watched, helpless, as Billy gave the thumbs-up and called out: 'I'll be right down.'

'Ouch ... Ufff ... Hang on, I can do it, just get my foot down here ...' Annie's voice bounced up the stairs ahead of her.

Tracey looked around at the state of the room.

'Oops ... Don't be silly, just the corner of a pedal, all my fault ...'

She was at the bikes, so about halfway up.

Tracey stepped over a cereal bowl, put the volume up on the music, took *Bargain Hunt* off mute.

There was a twang of strings as the guitar toppled over, and then a just about audible 'Ah, so you're a rower . . .'

It took a decent amount of time for Annie to navigate the passage and make it up the stairs. There was plenty of time for Tracey to make it look something closer to presentable, but she didn't. Instead, she took up position on a little island of space in her living-room floor and patiently waited. Eventually the unwelcome guest appeared, a little puffed out, and picked her way across to another little island in front of her. They stood, face to face. To Tracy's great satisfaction, she noticed that just to the left of her feet was a neat little stash, next to Billy's rather elaborate bong.

'Ah, there you are. You're on my way, so I just thought I'd stop and give you a lift to choir tonight.' Annie had to shout to make herself heard over the noise. 'I can do it every week, if you like. Save you getting the car out.'

Tracey was, for a moment, stunned. Choir . . . every week . . . save her getting the car out . . . What was she, like, 102? It was hard to know quite where to begin.

'Nice of you, but I'm not going to be able to make it tonight, I'm afraid,' she bellowed back, stretching one foot around the bong while stroking it gently into a place where Annie couldn't help but see.

'Oh no, that's a shame. Lewis and Katie will be disappointed. You know, I'm not sure that poor little girl has any other social life. We all kind of owe it to them, I think, to keep it going. Why can't you come?'

Billy, of all people, turned down the music and flicked off the telly. 'Yeah, Mum.' He strode over between them, knelt down and carefully scraped up every precious little particle of dope. 'Why not? You're not doing anything.'

'And what about you, Billy?' Annie carried on looking at Tracey.

There was a rustle of cigarette paper from somewhere near their feet. 'Are you working at the Square tonight?'

'Nah,', He licked something as he spoke. 'That's over now. Didn't work out.'

'Sorry to hear that.' Annie sounded genuinely disappointed. 'How about Curly and Squat? Don't tell me they're out too?'

''Fraid so ... Hey, you know them – the lads?'

'Oh, well, know *of* them ...' Annie winked at Tracey, valiantly ignoring the elaborate rolling that was going on beneath them.

Billy was pleased with that answer. 'Yeah, ha, legends.' He seemed inexplicably pleased with Annie in general. 'You probably have met Squat, y'know – lived in the wheelie bin by the library for a bit last summer ...'

This situation was in danger of spinning somewhere out of Tracey's control. In the space of two minutes, they all seemed to have gone from perfect strangers to old family friends. And that was weird, because Tracey and Billy didn't go in for old family friends.

'Anyway, is that the time?' she said forcefully, moving her guest back towards the door. 'You don't want to be late.'

'Sure I can't tempt you?'

'Go on, Mum.' Billy sank into the sofa, examining each end of a large spliff. 'You won't miss much here.'

'*Billy* ...'

'There you are! Come along. That's lovely. We will have fun. She was brilliant last week, your mum. And while you're between jobs, Billy, you might want to look through these.' Annie rustled in the bag on her shoulder and produced a sheaf of leaflets. 'I dug out some stuff for you on charity missions to Africa. There's one in Malawi, here, in an orphanage. And then this, in Rwanda, is an amazing school that needs young men just like you to—'

Tracey strode over and grabbed Annie's arm. 'Look. I'll come to your choir; I'm coming to your choir. See? I'm getting my coat on. But I'm sorry, I don't think Billy is at all interested in going to

Africa. Are you, Bills? He'll have another job round here in no time. Won't you, Bills? He doesn't need Africa. He doesn't need anywhere. He's doing perfectly well where he is, thanks very much. So let's just go, shall we, and cut the poor bloody kid some well-earned slack.'

Billy blew a perfect smoke ring, smiled contentedly, made a peace sign of his fingers and put both feet up on a chair.

7

Tracey leaned against the wall, hugging her bag close to her chest, while Annie sped around the hall with a dustpan and brush. The rain drummed its rhythm against the skylight as Annie started to sing.

A B C D, E F G

There had been a children's party in there that afternoon. Half the piñata was still all over the floor.

H I J K, L-M-N-O-P

And there was junk food everywhere. Annie's knees clicked as she bobbed down to flick out a Monster Munch from under the skirting. There was a hall rule that if you rented the space you were responsible for clearing up your own mess, but that had lately been forgotten. By some sort of unwritten agreement, the system seemed to have boiled down to this: Annie was now responsible for clearing up the lot.

Q R S T U and V

A drip fell through the roof to the floor with the tick of a metronome and Annie's tune slowed in keeping. Tracey was not joining in with the warm-up or the clearing up and it wasn't until Judith walked in that Annie had support with either.

W X Y— Hello, Jude

She sang.

How are yooooou . . .

As the other members arrived, shook out their wet umbrellas, draped their jackets over the radiators, exchanged meteorological facts of limited significance, Annie and Judith busied away at the floor, the kitchen, the chairs. It was only once everything was ready and they had both taken their own seats that they realised quite how many new recruits had turned up.

'Look at you all!' cried Annie.

'It's amazing.' Judith clapped her hands. 'Just wait till I go to the hospital tomorrow and tell Constance about this. She'll be thrilled.'

'Have we ever had this many men?' said Lewis, with some pride. 'The Town Hall darts team and then some.' The basses gave a happy roar. There was no reflective cool from this lot like there was with Tracey, but Lewis still looked pretty pleased with himself anyway. Then Annie shrieked: even Jazzy was there, pinned to her seat by Maria's forceful grip. And as if that wasn't enough excitement for one evening, a damp gust whooshed through them as the door opened yet again.

'Here's another one!' cried Judith. 'Come in, come in,' she beckoned, 'into our circle of—'

'*IT'S THE CIR-CLE OF TRUST,*' sang Maria. She let Jazzy go and got up, gyrating – a short, stout cartoon lion.

They all stared as the new man walked towards them. The darts players stopped cheering; indeed, all the basses suddenly shut up. The men of the Bridgeford Community Choir tended to be much of a muchness; the latest addition, however, seemed to be of a different order. Where they brought sweaters, this one brought tailoring; where they brought Hush Puppies, he brought black Oxfords. He strode across the hall with a long, lean ranginess; they sat clutching at their paunches as they might clutch their ageing animals in the waiting room at the vet. His features were neat and regular and hard to object to, but of the sort that preferred to work individually rather than pulling together as a team. Swinging from his right hand was a battered old leather music case.

'Don't panic,' said Lynn as he took the seat next to her. 'The rest of us just call it a circle. We're not all potty.'

'Thanks for coming, Bennett.' Annie waved across at him. Bennett nodded a firm sort of nod and sat, holding his case on his knee.

Lewis beamed around the room. 'I think we should save the introductions till the break. For now, let's just put our voices together' – he adopted the smooth tones of a Radio 2 DJ – 'and make us some beautiful noise here tonight. Why don't we start with what we all know to be Connie's favourite?'

'Oh, bless her,' said a soprano.

'Mrs Coles, if you will do the honours . . .'

Mrs Coles started thumping away; Lewis tapped his foot and they began. It was their *Sound of Music* medley.

It went off very well, on the whole. All the new people enjoyed themselves, with just a few exceptions. Bennett didn't seem to feel comfortable with the clapping – although he did pat his case a bit here and there – nor, despite clearly being white, British, middle-aged and middle-class, did he seem to be completely au fait with the words. Tracey sang, but quietly and politely and with a distant sort of look about her – quite a different performance from her astonishing ABBA of the previous week. And Jazzy refused to open her mouth, just sat there beneath a cloud of dark curls bigger than her skinny body, riveted to the screen of her phone. But still, when the time came for the break, the applause was healthy and there was a definite buzz in the room.

Annie should, at that moment, have approached Bennett – welcomed him formally, had a chat, caught up. Instead, she grabbed Tracey's hand and pulled her over to the tea table.

'Well, Billy's a lovely boy, I must say.' Annie poured tea into a row of white china cups. 'What a charmer.' She gave Tracey the milk jug. 'Perhaps you could . . .'

'Thanks. Yes. He is. Which is just one of the many reasons I don't want him to go off to the arse end of bloody Africa and catch AIDS and Ebola and get kidnapped and DIE.' Tracey kept missing the cups and sloshing milk all over the table.

'Oh, but it's marvellous, Africa, for sorting some of our young out, especially the boys. There you go, love.' She wiped up the puddles with one hand and with the other gave a cup to Maria. 'A lot of our lost young local lads have gone off there and come back transformed.'

'That's the great thing about the Third World.' Tracey chucked what possibly might be flapjacks on to a plate, any old how. 'It's one big character-enrichment programme for the youth of Bridgeford.'

'Well, I'm not saying the Africans don't get something out of it, too.'

'And what about me, eh?' Tracey picked the plate up with an absent air. 'What am I supposed to get out of it? Death by loneliness?'

Annie stopped and stared at her.

'Oh.' Tracey came to. 'Did I say that out loud?' She picked up a cup. 'Forget it.' And she swished off to sit with Lewis.

♫

Lynn and Pat chose not to leave their seats during the break; they had evolved a system whereby others brought drinks and snacks to them. Bennett, lodged between them, unclaimed by Annie, still clutching his case, stayed put. He didn't seem to know what to do with himself or where to look, but more often than not, he seemed to look over at Tracey.

'I know who you are,' said Pat, leaning in to him. That made him jump. She got out her crocheting. 'I taught your children to swim.' He relaxed a bit. 'How are they getting on, then?'

'Um, well, their crawl's pretty good, I think.' Bennett's voice was surprisingly rich, coming as it did from such an anaemic exterior. 'Butterfly less so. I don't know if that fits in with your assessment.'

'Oo-er,' said Pat. It obviously wasn't quite the answer she'd expected. 'Let me ... It's a while ago now ...'

Lynn gave him a long look over her Argos catalogue. 'I don't think she gives much of a stuff about their swimming any more, love. I think it was more of a general polite enquiry.'

'Yes, of course.' He twisted in his chair. 'Well, Casper is an estate agent, and ...'

It would be hard to judge whether Jazzy would have anything to do with Katie in any other social situation. Jasmine was famously one of Bridgeford's scarier teens – very much of the 'Yeah? Like, hello? What the fuck you staring at?' school of social intercourse – and it had been a long time since anyone of her own age had made any attempt to have anything to do with her. But, either because she was getting that little bit older or because there in the Coronation Hall they were such a tiny minority, the two girls had instantly bonded. They were both bent over phones, sharing pictures of cats; Jazzy leaned in to the wheelchair as they giggled together.

'Long time since I've seen her like this,' muttered Lewis. The muscles in his cheek twitched with something too emotional to be a smile.

'Sweet,' agreed Tracey, looking at him sideways. 'Has she got plenty of mates her own age?'

'It's not easy.' He spilled some tea and dabbed at his denim shirt. 'Do you know that guy over there, by the way?' He nodded towards Bennett.

'Nope. I do wish people would stop asking me that. I don't *know* people, all right? Jeez.' Tracey collected a few tea things. 'Why?'

'Certainly knows you. Or you've got yourself an admirer.'

Tracey looked over sharply, and then Judith was clapping her hands and calling everyone back to the circle. It was time for introductions. All the regular members were to take it in turns to stand, give their own names and introduce their guests to the group. Judith began, but with an apology: she had hoped her boyfriend might come along but sadly, at the last minute, he couldn't find the time.

'Well, it is hard, isn't it, finding time,' Pat stage-whispered to her crochet needle, 'when you're a figment of the imagination.'

'Fantasist,' mouthed Lynn, shaking her head and tapping her temple. 'Total bloody fantasist.'

Lewis jumped up and went through his lot from the council. There was a good bit of banter at this point: basses always like a bit of banter; they like jokes by other basses and they like a bit of banter.

And then it was Annie's turn.

'Hello, everybody. I'm Annie Miller. I've been in this choir – gosh – for most of my adult life, I think, and this is my guest, Bennett St John Parker.'

'Ooh-ooh-ooh,' sang everyone in unison, as if it was a quiz show and Bennett the jackpot. 'Good evening, Bennett St John Parker.'

Bennett hugged his music case in close. 'Actually, it's just Parker. I don't really use the St John.' He pronounced it 'Sinjun'. 'And just Bennett is fine.' Annie grimaced and mouthed a 'Sorry' across the circle, but his gaze slid down and away and the next member took the floor.

'My name is Maria, as in—'

'No. Don't. Please.' Pat held up her hand in the stop sign.

'—*I just met a girl called*—'

'Every. Single. Time.' Lynn shook her head.

'And this is my new recruit, Jazzy. I know Jazzy because I'm one of the carers for her lovely nan, aren't I, Jazz?'

The girl with the phone flicked back her voluminous hair, looked up and blinked a thick black fringe of false eyelashes. Clearly her expectations of the evening had been a little unrealistic: her make-up was more O_2 main stage than Bridgeford circle of trust.

'Hi, Jazzy,' chorused everybody.

'Yeah,' Jazzy frowned. 'But, hi, um, listen. What is that, "recruit"? Is it, like, someone who only ever has to come here like once?'

'Hah. The opposite, love. They've got you now. I was only a bit older than you when I got roped in,' cackled Pat.

There was a hoot from Lynn. 'That'll be you, Jazzy – sitting there crocheting your blanket, specs on the end of your nose.'

'OH. MY. GOD-uh,' groaned Jazzy, flinging herself back against the chair and making like a corpse.

'Anyway,' cut in Lewis, 'on to the second half. Does anyone have any requests or suggestions?'

'I think Bennett St John Parker might,' said Lynn. She seemed rather taken with Bennett St John Parker. 'He's brought his music.'

'No, no, it's fine.' His complexion, until then pallid as a vampire, started to pink. 'I haven't. Well I have, but it's not quite suitable. I got the wrong end of the stick.'

'We do anything round here, Bennett. We are a broad church.'

'Ha! Oh, yes. A *very* broad church,' scowled Lynn. 'Apart from when it comes to *Jesus*, that is.'

'What have you got there?' Pat took his bag and started pulling out music. 'Requiem ... requiem ... miserere ... requiem ... '

'Blimey,' said Lewis. 'Expecting a massacre?' He was smiling, but quite clearly put out. Neither Bennett nor Bennett's music – or his voice or his name or his clothes or, by a short and obvious leap of prejudice, his politics – were Lewis' cup of tea. Like a pack, the rest of the basses took his side.

'You want to lighten up a bit, Bennett Sinjun Doo-da.'

'What can we all sing to give our friend here the strength he needs to carry on?'

'I know.' Annie tried to broker a peace. 'Let's do our Eurovision medley. Everyone likes a bit of Eurovision, don't they?'

'Oh, I shouldn't think so. Europe? I can't imagine he's very fond of your Europe, are you, Benjy? Johnny Foreigner? *Pop* songs? That's not your scene, is it, Mr Sinjun?'

'It's Bennett.' He was starting to get tetchy, stuffing papers back into their case as one who was about to leave. 'And yes, thank you, it just so happens I rather like it.'

'Then don't go, not yet,' pleaded Annie across the circle. 'Just sing with us for a bit, please?'

He sank back into his chair. The basses calmed down, Judith

handed out the lyric sheets, Mrs Coles fiddled with her music and they began.

Con-grat-u-lations . . .

Bennett was quite visibly crushed. He was still an unearthly pale colour, still clutching his case, still rigid in his formal suit, yet from somewhere deep within his cadaverous frame came the most extraordinary sound.

'Oh my goodness, as I live and breathe,' said Pat, too overcome to actually sing.

Lynn was fanning herself with her lyrics and gazing at Bennett with awe. 'Oh my God,' she gasped. 'Oh. My. God.'

'We've actually got one. At last, we've got—'

'—a tenor!' panted Lynn. 'I thought it would never happen.' She touched his leg, to convince herself. 'Our very own church-trained tenor.'

Somehow, Bennett was not put off. He looked nervously at the hand on his thigh, but his voice remained strong and pure and dominant. When they came to the final cheerful chorus of 'Making Your Mind Up', the cheers and applause were all for Bennett.

As everyone got up, scraped their chairs, gathered their belongings, Lewis shouted out the notices: the countdown to the County Championships in May; the Talent Show coming up on the twenty-eighth of February. Annie needed help with the Evergreens' lunch on Wednesday . . . But nobody really listened. The door was open and they were drifting out into the night.

'That was brilliant. Night, all.'

'See you next week. Can't wait.'

The rain had stopped. Spirits were high. So high that nobody noticed that Tracey was not walking out with them. Indeed, such were the thrills of the journey through the Eurovision hits of the twentieth century, nobody had noticed that Tracey slipped out sometime around 1972.

8

Annie sat slumped on the pale blue sofa, still wearing her navy mac. It had been a day of dreariness and disappointment and she was thoroughly drained. There was a selection of remote controls lined up on the cushion beside her. She picked up the biggest, pointed it, pressed and hoped for the best; the television screen stayed dark.

For the first time ever, not one mother, carer or child had turned up to her Monday After-Lunch Pre-school Storytime down at the library ... She tried another remote. Fifteen years Annie had been running that story slot – and for the ten years before that she had turned up every week as a mother with a pre-schooler – and nearly all of that time it had been a busy, thriving part of the library service. Now it was gone; over; redundant ... Ah, there was sound, but no picture. She picked up another. And for that to happen in the wake of Connie's accident and the crisis with the Choir ... Damn: the sound had gone away again and there was still no vision. Oh yes, all those new recruits had been dragged in, but how many of them would last the course? And not a single member had turned out for the sit-in the other night ... She prodded a few other buttons – Channels, Menu, Play. Interactive? What did that mean? She didn't want to interact. She wanted to be passive just for once in her life. Was that never to be allowed? Would she never be able to sit there, slack-jawed, while someone else did the work? It felt, sometimes, like the end of days.

Perhaps she was supposed to press two buttons at once, was that the answer? She reached for her mobile and dialled James's number. She'd never hear the last of it, but still. That was odd ... No answer. Where was he, then? She was sure he had said he was at the flat tonight ... Well, it couldn't be all the remotes in one go, could it? She was sure she would have noticed if the others held four whole things up every time. It certainly seemed to be the end of Bridgeford ... She started smacking the controls with the flat of her hand, trying to get all the buttons all at once. Or at least the end of Bridgeford as she knew it ... 'AAAARGH.' She hurled the remotes at the wall. 'HOW THE BLOODY, BLOODY HELL DO YOU PUT THE BLOODY TELLY ON?' Her cry rang around the empty house. She fell back, exhausted. Perhaps it was actually the end of the world.

Annie shook her head, stood up and scratched out that thought. Apparently, she had to stop being a drama queen. Jess had been home again at the weekend and impressed a number of facts upon her mother, loud and clear – so loud and clear that she was sure the neighbours could hear it all, that Pamela two doors down was probably taking notes – and the ones that stuck most vividly in Annie's mind were: 1. Jess had a tattoo saying B.I.T.C.H. on her ankle and that was cool. 2. Annie was a drama queen. 3. Jess did not know the difference between a stupid word and a stupid acronym. 4. Annie was annoying.

She took her coat off, hung it up and went through to the kitchen, rubbing at the tears and feeling aggrieved all over again. She still hadn't recovered from her night out serving soup for hours on her own in sub-zero temperatures, and her resistance was understandably low. The thing was, if a person announces she's going to drop a bombshell and then drops it, then the other person in the conversation – the one in whose face the bombshell has just exploded – was almost entitled to get hurt. And cry, yes – why not? She wasn't going to apologise. That was, to be fair, the whole point of the bombshell, wasn't it: impact? You can't lob a grenade and then just roll your eyes and mutter, 'Drama queen' at anyone unfortunate enough to lose a limb. She opened a few cupboards and banged them shut again. She couldn't think of what to eat. She had hit a crisis with food, as well as everything else. It was the end of days, the end of Bridgeford, the end of the world and, on top of it all, it was the end of dinner.

After all those years of what felt like feeding the five thousand every night, she simply did not know how to even begin to go about feeding just herself and James. The two of them, for so long the least important members of the household (in Annie's view), didn't seem deserving of actual cooking of proper meals. Back in September, when Jessica – the youngest and last to desert them – went off to college, she had decided that that was it for weekday dinners: the kitchen was closed. She could do a kilo of pasta, or she could do no pasta at all; a shepherd's pie as long as a cricket pitch, or nothing whatsoever. James had argued at first, said he would do it all from now on. There had been a bit of a row about it, in fact – was Annie being a drama queen then? No, she didn't think so – before he saw her point of view. And as it turned out, he'd had to stay in London a lot since then, on this tiresome, tricky case, so Annie was on her own more often than not anyway.

She wandered over to the shelf of cookery books and stroked along the row of cracked spines. Annie loved her cookery books. If this, their bashed-about, well-loved family home of thirty years, were to go up in flames, she would make straight for the— Or, actually, would she? All the family photo albums going back over a century were in the sitting room, after all. And the little mementoes of the girls as babies – curls, teeth, lawn linen smocks – were tucked away for safe-keeping upstairs. Then there was the doll's house: she couldn't possibly lose the doll's house. It had been handed down, from her granny to her mother to herself to her girls, and if her own little granddaughters – not as yet conceived but still the focus of constant, whirring, low-level mental preparation – if they did not get to play with that doll's house then Annie's heart might actually break. But could she even manage to carry that through the flames? A firefighter probably could; definitely two. OK, here was the plan: send the crew straight to the landing for the doll's house, perhaps dive into the sitting room on the way back through, so leaving Annie free to rescue the cookery books ...

Because, of course, these were heirlooms too.

Her finger stopped at Marguerite Patten's *Pressure Cookery*. She plucked it out: 'First published 1949'. That was a fascinating social record, right there, of British attitudes to domestic cooking of the twentieth century. Annie never used a pressure cooker these days – technology had moved on and her memories of childhood meals made in one were not fond – but for her mum it had been a life-saver. Annie knew – she had heard it all often enough – about her mother's earlier years, working in a lab – the only woman who went past Reception – living in a bedsit, putting on a cheap one-pot meal when she left in the morning that she could eat alone as she pored over her work at night. The book fell open in her hands: 'Creamed Tripe and Onions', obviously a favourite because of the splashes on the page. It wasn't just a social record either: this was her mother's own personal history. She traced the stain on the page with her finger and felt a shiver of connection: that wasn't just any old splash, it had been splashed there by a brave, determined, trail-blazing, post-war proto-feminist; that was no bog-standard tripe juice – it was the tripe juice of her darling, much-missed mum.

And here was the bulging file of hand-written notes that her mother had collected throughout her life, including the recipes for the simnel cake, which Annie had enjoyed every Easter as a child and made every Easter as an adult, and the delicious Christmas pudding, which she hoped would continue to serve her family for generations to come.

Annie adored and admired her mother. She was proud to be the daughter of one who, in her childhood, was branded – often with derision – a 'women's libber'. She was thrilled to be the mother of three daughters herself. She was nowhere near as clever as her own mum, or as wildly talented as her amazing girls, but still she loved to think of them all as a human chain, with Annie in the middle, receiving ideas, and things, from one generation and handing them carefully, tenderly, inspiringly, to the next, onwards and upwards, higher and higher, towards the light of total gender equality. So how bloody come she of all people now had the total embarrassment of this wretched girl with B.I.T.C.H. scrawled all over her in indelible bloody ink?

The phone rang. That was bound to be Sue. They hadn't spoken since Saturday morning – practically a record – and Annie was longing to have a catch-up, but she was not, under any circumstances, going to let on about the tattoo. Absolutely not. They shared everything, had done for decades, but this particular horror must stay in the family. This was one secret Annie would keep till the grave – or at least till the summer and Jess turned up in town with a skirt on. She took a deep breath, steeled herself, picked up the phone and cracked.

'She got a tattoo!' It came out as an almost bestial wail.

'Hello?' It sounded like a caller from the moon. 'Am I speaking with Mrs Miller?'

'Yes, you are.' That was a relief. And this was a nice young man, she could tell even at that distance. She trotted to the fridge and took out a carton of soup. 'How can I help you?'

'My name is Ravi—'

'Hi, Ravi.' She fumbled about in the drawer and found her granny's old pinking shears. 'Call me Annie.'

'Well – er – Annie, I was wondering if you were satisfied with your current broadband provider.'

'Oh, Ravi,' she laughed. 'You've got the wrong member of the family.' She snipped the corner off the carton. 'Don't ask me. I wish we weren't provided with any internet at all.' Ravi, all the way over in wherever he was, was clearly a little stumped. 'It's just changed everything, and not for the better. Don't you agree? The way I see it, there was human progress, going along on a nice straight upward trajectory since – I don't know – since Georgian times, practically, and then along comes the internet and everything goes off, loopy, completely haywire.'

'But are you happy with your price plan, Mrs Miller?'

'I'd pay to get rid of it, Ravi.' She tipped the soup into an enamel pan and lit the gas. 'Pay to get rid of it. I honestly don't think family life has ever been the same since. It's all quite wrong, you know. All this worldwide snooping, not to mention the horrors of Googling a recipe and never holding a photo in one's own hands. And as for mobile phones – well, don't get me started. You know babies now – little tiny babies – would rather play with one than pick up a picture book. Doesn't it break your heart, Ravi? Certainly breaks mine.' She foraged in the bread bin for a roll or two. 'Anyway, I know, I'm a dinosaur, save it all for Menopause Corner . . . ' Ravi made a noise like a choke. 'Time to change the subject. Why don't we talk about you?' By the time Annie had warmed her chicken and mushroom, unearthed some cheese and returned to the sofa with a tray, she had established that Ravi was calling from outside Delhi and dreamed of studying Medicine. Before she had finished eating, they had together decided that Biochemistry might be just that bit more realistic – he could always convert later – Annie would research some suitable courses and funding options and he would call back at the same time next week.

'Mrs Miller, I don't know how to begin to—'

'My pleasure, Ravi, really.' Annie felt altogether calmer than she had done half an hour ago. 'There is one thing, though, you could do for me. Would you happen to know how on earth I am supposed to turn on a television?'

9

Tracey, in the back seat, waited for her moment. She sat acquiescent as Annie took the keys out, trilled, 'Here we are. Back in a sec,' shut the car door and trotted through the neat front garden, and then she went for it.

'Shit.' Child lock. And weren't Annie's kids all, like, barristers or prime ministers or something? 'Un-bloody-believable.' She scoped the house – Annie had got to the doorstep – began to climb over the handbrake into the front and then heard a thud. A very bossy thud and a crisp little click. 'Shit, *shit*.' Central locking. She looked over just as Annie, fob in hand, whipped round, turning her back. Tracey fell back into her seat again, defeated.

For the past few weeks Annie had turned up to collect her every Tuesday and – as promised – saved her 'getting the car out'. She had also saved her from a good few nice evenings in, several glasses of wine and a firm grip of her own identity but – partly because Annie was so impossible to argue with, mostly because Billy, irritatingly, always took Annie's side and, all right, a *tiny* bit because she did like the singing – she went along with it anyway. This evening, though, was different. Tracey really, really did not want to have anything to do with this evening. And Annie clearly knew that, or she wouldn't have bothered to lock her in.

She tore at a hang-nail with her teeth and ducked down to get a proper look at what was going on in that house. Annie was only picking up that Bennett, but it seemed to be taking for ever. Don't say even *he* doesn't fancy this gig? If it was too tragic for tragedy king Bennett St John Parker, it was definitely no place for Tracey Leckford. They had not, so far, had any sort of conversation but, on cursory examination, Tracey had come to the judgement that Bennett had the personality and character strength of the average glass of Bridgeford tap water. Now, watching the charade playing out before her, she wondered if there might not be just a little bit more to him.

The downstairs lights were all blazing, and – bizarrely – the house didn't seem to have any curtains, so Tracey and the rest of the neighbourhood could watch and enjoy what was going on like a bit of slapstick from the silent era. Annie pressed the doorbell; Bennett, in his suit and bent over a saucepan in the kitchen, jumped as if given an electric shock. Annie rang the bell again; Bennett vanished behind the kitchen door. Annie tiptoed across the manicured lawn – she was actually unembarrassable – and pressed her face to the kitchen window.

'Come out now, Bennett.' Tracey could hear her from the car. 'I can see your shoes. And you're burning the sausages.'

Bennett came out as bidden, clutching a potato masher. OK, so he didn't quite have the bottle to stand up to Annie, but then he was only human. He was at the front door now, still clutching his masher and clearly still trying to wriggle out of coming. 'Good luck with that, mate,' Tracey muttered and settled down to await his surrender.

She drew her eye away from Bennett's pretty detached Edwardian villa and looked around at all the other pretty villas in the road. It was a nice neighbourhood round here, much better than Tracey's own. The houses obviously dated from that era when small-town life was an upper-middle-class aspiration, a mark of arrival; these days people only lived here because they couldn't afford anything else. Of course, anyone in their right mind would prefer either smart city life or gorgeous rolling acres. Well, Tracey certainly would anyway, and she presumed the whole world felt the same. Small towns were just a compromise – a mark of not having got anywhere near where you had been aiming for; a sign of falling by the wayside of life. Her own area was entirely populated by people who couldn't afford anything else. 'The squeezed middle', politicians called them and they were right, almost literally: their estate was just that, squeezed right into the middle, between the car park and the back of the leisure centre, and it wasn't where you would choose to be at all.

The passenger door opened and Annie guided Bennett into it. 'You know each other: Bennett, Tracey?'

Bennett climbed in. 'Oh yes. I think we've met before, haven't we?'

'No. We haven't,' replied Tracey. 'But hi.'

Their next stop was at the social housing behind the High Street. Tracey and Bennett waited silently, obediently, while Annie nipped out and up to the door of a ground-floor flat. They could quite possibly have run away here, but this wasn't really the sort of country where you would want to run much, at least after dark. And anyway, before they could even think about it Jazzy came flying down the path and into the car, leaving Annie to hurry along after her.

'Jazzy!' Annie almost bounced into the driving seat and pulled on her strap. 'Your mum's back!' She beamed over her shoulder as she pulled out. 'How amazing.'

'Yeah.' Jazzy clicked her seatbelt in and stared out of the window. 'And? Do I look like someone who even *gives* a shit?'

Tracey glanced sideways and thought, with a pang, that she did rather: she looked like she both gave it and was rather deeply in it, too.

'She seemed very perky.' Annie pulled out and headed for the ring road. 'Is she on good form?'

'Oh yeah. *Great* form.' Jazzy was speaking into the window, hunched right down into her seat. 'Not even a junkie any more, apparently. Cured.' She clicked her fingers. 'It's a fucking miracle. And how long do we give that, eh? About a week? Till I get home one night and find her off her bloody skull.'

'We must all help her.' Annie settled into the slow lane of the dual carriageway and started to bang on about how to solve the problem that was Jazzy's mum. 'Now then ...'

There seemed to be nothing, in Annie's world picture, that could not be solved with a healthy dollop of Neighbourhood Watch – not even chronic addiction. Tracey, cringing in the back seat, could see that Jazzy was quite close to losing it. She leaned across and changed the subject.

'Nice to see you and Katie getting on so well.'

Jazzy uncurled herself slightly. 'Yeah. She's sweet. I like Katie.' Then she half turned with a jerk. 'I'm not here for long, though. You do all know that, right? I'll be off soon. Got plans, me.'

'Oh. Sorry. I didn't realise ...'

'Yeah.' She flicked her hair back. 'My nan says it's good to come for a bit just for the experience, but I'm not to waste myself here for ever. Can't hang around with these tragic deadbeats, can I?'

'Of course you can't. Where are you off to, if you don't mind me asking?'

'Going solo, aren't I?'

'Ah.' Tracey felt a tug somewhere in her chest. It caught at her breath. 'Of course you are.'

'She's got the most marvellous voice,' Annie chipped in. 'I first spotted her when she was seven – the St Ambrose superstar she was, when my girls were there.'

'Yeah.' Jazzy nodded, conceding the inarguable. 'So. Auditions coming up. Shouldn't take long. My nan says if that Adele can do it, they'll be bloody delighted to find someone decent.' She pinched her nose in apparent illustration of the nasty pong coming from the direction of Adele's talent. 'My nan hates Adele.'

'Good luck with that.' Tracey was hunched down now, talking into the window on her side.

'Aw, ta.' Jazzy was gracious. 'By the way,' she put her hand on Tracey's leather sleeve, 'I wasn't including you in that. You're not a tragic deadbeat.'

'Oh? Too kind.'

'It's true actually. You're cool – well, quite cool, you know, considering . . . ' She glared at the front of the car, rolled her eyes, made an L with her fingers and then fell into a deep and sulky silence.

Tracey lay back against the leather upholstery and listened to the conversation in the front.

'So how is everybody, Annie? How's the gang?' Bennett was asking. Tracey got into the brace position. Here it came: an avalanche of smugness and boasting. After all, her kids had to be perfect – otherwise why would she get her kicks poking her nose into Billy's business? But:

'Oh God, Bennett, it's so awful,' she heard Annie wail. She sat up straight and pricked up her ears. 'It's Jess. She's gone and got a bloody tattoo.'

♫

'We're very early,' moaned Tracey as they pulled in to the car park. 'You're always early. What are we supposed to do now for half an hour?' She peered out at the monolithic Victorian hospital with modern knobs on. 'You're not going to make us clean all that, like you do the Coronation Hall?'

Annie got out and unlocked the back doors. 'And you do help *such* a lot with the Coronation Hall.'

Ouch – that was rather sharp. Tracey got out of the car without meeting Annie's eye.

'I thought,' Annie locked the car and led them all towards the entrance, 'we might do a bit of chatting on the ward before we start.

Or do you object to visiting the sick like you object to everything else?'

'Yes,' Tracey was about to say. 'Obviously.' She honestly couldn't think of anything worse.

But Bennett cut in: 'Of course. Lovely idea.' And after that she thought she had better shut up.

The four of them headed for the entrance, Annie and Bennett striding ahead, Tracey and Jazzy mooching along behind. Parkway Hospital serviced several towns and Tracey was struck, as she followed her in, how few people Annie said hello to now that they had crossed the town boundary. Since Tracey had joined the Choir, they had bumped into each other quite a lot around and about – that was, if Tracey didn't see her coming first – and it was no exaggeration to say that Annie knew absolutely everyone and absolutely everyone knew Annie. But there they were, a few miles down the road, and it was quite a different story. 'Hey, Annie,' she called to the back of her navy raincoat. 'You know what you remind me of? A French pop star. Mobbed at home, a nobody abroad.' Tracey giggled. They walked past a family huddled beneath a noticeboard. 'Look, they're all ignoring you. Don't you know who zis ees?' she asked a passing stranger in a cod French accent. 'Eet's *Annee Mileur*. Eet's ZEE Annee Mileur. De Breej-fod.' She caught at a swing door before it swung right in her face.

When they got to the ward, though, Annie was back on home turf; Tracey could see that immediately. The vast, cheerless space was crammed with ladies of a certain age and Annie was on close terms with at least one in three of them. Their little group moved from bed to bed like the party of a visiting dignitary and they chatted to them all. Tracey met a woman who had given Annie her job at the library all those years ago, and set up the children's book group which Billy had loved – she was in with her osteoporosis. There was a good sort with nine kids who'd been a school governor for decades – her uterus was playing up, apparently. Hard to blame it. Someone who cleaned the church every Friday had broken her hip and was worrying about the aisle carpet. Annie promised to go and sort it all out and Tracey did wonder how on earth she would find the time for that and all the other stuff she seemed to do, but she didn't say anything. Obviously. Christ, she might have ended up hoovering it herself.

Tracey kept her distance then, not wanting to get too embroiled, and leaned back by the door looking down on them all. And two things struck her.

The first was that, in their various different ways, they were all Annies, these women: doers of their bit, thinkers of others, busiers of bodies. They were all Annies, and they were all knackered. Who was going to take over from them all, when they couldn't do it any more? Was Annie really going to run the lot?

The second was: at least they were not alone. They were ageing and they were knackered but, clearly, they still mattered. Their beds were surrounded by cards and flowers and home-made cakes. The primary school had done a frieze for the retired librarian; the Sunday school had made a little garden in a box for the church volunteer.

And then an image swam up before her: of herself in here, in, if she was lucky, several decades' time; of one card, from Billy, on her bedside table and nothing much else. Or perhaps even no card at all. Did Billy actually know that that was life's cycle – that love and care and nurturing were a two-way thing; you got it, you gave it and then, by rights, you got it back again? Of course, Tracey had no contact with her parents from one year to the next, but that was different. She and Billy, they were good, they were best friends. They had it sorted. Didn't they? And Billy had picked up on all that. Hadn't he?

The Choir was holding its Tuesday session on a hospital ward at the request of Connie's family. Judith had been keeping her informed of all developments but still Constance was, they were told, terribly frustrated at not being able to hear them in person. Also, her recovery wasn't going quite as well as expected and it was hoped that this would really buck her up. Most of the Choir had arrived now, and were gathered around the nurses' station ready to perform. There was only one thing missing, and that was their leader.

Constance was not on this ward just yet – not quite well enough, apparently – and was coming down from another wing especially. The Choir old guard were excited to see her – only Annie and Judith had been allowed to visit so far; the family was keeping things very low-key – and the new members were agog. When Connie was talked about at practice – which she very often was – it was with the sort of rapture only reserved for the most extraordinary humans of a generation. She was, they had all been told, charismatic, inspirational, dynamic, life-changing ... And among those who had not yet had the privilege, expectations were, quite reasonably, high. They shuffled their lyrics, chattered away, craned their necks to witness her arrival. Each member had developed their own mental picture of Constance and was eager to have it confirmed. But there was bound to be at least a modicum of disappointment; some were expecting a sort of mature Beyoncé, others Mrs Thatcher, a couple Joan of Arc and one the Queen of Sheba. However extraordinary this Constance was, it would be hard for her to tick every single box.

'Here she comes,' clucked Judith in the voice of a nursery nurse. 'How are you, Connie? On the mend?'

A bed was wheeled in with two nurses on either side and Connie's husband bringing up the rear. Beneath the sheet, attached to the mobile drip, was a tiny, grey-haired creature – very pale, worryingly gaunt – who was either deeply asleep or even unconscious. A sense of shock rippled through half of the Choir: they weren't prepared to see her so ill; a muffled, unanimous disappointment ran through the rest: they weren't prepared to see her so ... so very ordinary.

'She's doing so much better, aren't you, darling?' her husband shouted at the bed. 'And this is a sight for sore eyes, isn't it, eh? Just the ticket.'

'Look at you, love.' Annie stepped forward and kissed a white cheek. 'I can't believe it. What an improvement.' A few singers exchanged glances and raised eyebrows. 'Now what do you fancy hearing first? You're in charge!'

'Oh yes,' chuckled her husband. 'Isn't she just? We're all in our place, aren't we, nurse?'

An inner circle continued a group conversation around Connie's bed – speaking for her and about her, yet at no point acknowledging that she was not speaking herself. Loved ones do this with the very sick: interpret words that are never said, emotions that can only be guessed at, wishes that may or may not be there. It's not so dissimilar from that rather touching anthropomorphic thing that besotted owners do with their pets: 'He wants ...', 'He hates ...', 'And he looks up at me as if to say ...' It is just one way of coping with the unspeakable truth that your best friend in the whole world is a labradoodle, or your partner on life's journey might be about to get off at the next stop.

'I think we all know what *you* want, Connie,' laughed Judith.

'Goes without saying,' nodded her husband. 'She's not called Constance for nothing!'

'*Sound of Music* medley it is,' agreed Annie. Mrs Coles lifted her hands above the keys of the portable piano, and they began.

Connie's nurses, bent beside her prone form, clapped along, beaming; her husband wiped away a tear. A couple of patients on the ward were not best pleased with the intrusion. It was time for *EastEnders* and they put in their ear plugs and swivelled round their TVs, but there was no need for the Choir to take offence. As Annie loudly whispered, they were, after all, 'non-Bridgeford' – as if, on a variant of dogs and whistles, their music could only properly be heard by ears from a certain postcode.

Good-bye

Good-bye

Good – byyyyye.

'Oh, she loved that,' pronounced Pat, on the basis of no evidence whatsoever.

'Aw, bless, look at her,' agreed Lynn. 'It's all been worthwhile.'

'Well, I think we've definitely got our opener for the contest then,' nodded Lewis. 'That's all sorted.'

'All right then, Connie.' Annie approached the bed, but addressed her husband. 'Time for one more set. What's it to be?'

'Need you ask?' he chortled, leaning over his wife to wipe away a trickle of spit.

'Of course,' chipped in Maria. 'We'd better do a round or else there'll be trouble.'

In the last few weeks, the Bridgeford choir new and old had really started to merge together, to form a cohesive whole. The meeting with Constance, though, split that whole right down the middle. In fact, it started to fall to bits. The new members, alienated as they were by this odd little pantomime, did not know quite what to think, but did know to question their own sense of belonging. Then Jazzy muttered, 'Fuck. They're all bleedin' mentalists,' just that little bit too loudly and several, including Tracey, gave her a look of comradely relief.

Lewis set about arranging them all into groups. If the regulars started off with the melodies, the newcomers could come in in their wake.

Summer is a-coming in

Although Annie, Pat, Lynn, Maria and Lewis were giving it their all, their all was not quite enough. By the time the meadow had blossomed, the attention of the younger and newer members had drifted somewhat. Jazzy and Katie were over their phones; a newcomer called Kelly was explaining the secrets of chakras to a puzzled Tracey; and the lot from the council were gossiping in whispers. Bennett alone seemed to be disengaged from his surroundings, eyes fixed on the far window, one finger tapping in an absent sort of way.

Bullock leapeth, buck doth skip now

Those singing, about to start the round again, looked at each other nervously.

Loudly sing cuckoo!

Surely the rest of them would come in. Wouldn't they? They

wouldn't just leave them to sing a round on their own ... Would they?

Spring the wood anew

The council lot all had their diaries out – there was a fortieth coming up, it was going to be totally massive – and they were no longer really whispering. The singers had reached the point for the next group to enter. Lewis raised his hand in signal, swept it down like a baton and

Summer is a-coming in

one voice sang, alone. Fortunately it was strong and pure enough to carry the part on its own, but still it was a shame that it was not accompanied. Bennett had looked as distracted as everybody else, but it didn't matter because he was already prepared. It was drilled into him. He had been prepared for all this for most of his life.

10

The bells had stopped their pealing and given way to the chimes of the hour. It was ten o'clock. Bennett had walked past twice, in the manner of one frantically on his way elsewhere, but this was it. If he was going in, he had to do it now. The last few stragglers headed under the arch and he scurried into their wake.

The woman by the door, handing out the service sheets, had a familiar face and gave a smile of recognition, but Bennett could not quite place her. Living without Sue was, he was starting to think, rather like living with early-onset dementia. So many of the small details of their life together were – by whose arrangement: his, hers, mutual? – under Sue's jurisdiction. When she left she had, of course, taken them all with her. It was fair enough, as they were all in her head, but he did often find himself wishing she had left him a helpful little folder, like landladies did for holiday rentals: a starter information pack for the rest of his own life. It wouldn't take her a moment to jot down a few names for him – who did what to the house, who lived where in the street. A Who's Who of the Miller family would be particularly useful: he had never quite got to grips with the names of anyone, and wasn't quite sure, talking to her independently, who on earth Annie was nattering on about. (He did think Jess was the Miller dog, but dogs didn't get tattoos, as far as he had heard, and he certainly couldn't imagine how they could pull it off without owner's permission.) And then there was the problem of Tracey. Bennett knew full well that they had met before – he had a niggling worry that in fact they were really old friends – but how, since when, where from? He would love to ask Sue, before there was any sort of awkwardness, but – he didn't know why – he just had a hazy glimpse of the very stony ground on which any such enquiry would almost certainly fall.

So he went about his business in the sort of vague, benign state that his poor senile father had adopted in his later years. Bennett just wasn't quite convinced he was getting away with it. He nodded and smiled at the woman in the church – he hoped with the amount appropriate to whatever their relationship might be – took a prayer book out of politeness and grabbed the hymnbook with both hands.

Of course, Sue would never have been with him here, whatever the state of their marriage. She had fallen out with organised religion years ago – he could not now remember its crime; several institutions and many individuals had committed crimes against Sue over the years and it was hard to keep a track of all of them – and made it clear that if he must persist in going, Bennett could go alone. And although he had rather fancied it, several times, he never actually had. Now he hovered in the aisle, wondering where to sit. There were so many empty spaces – perhaps everyone had fallen out with organised religion – and far fewer clumps of families than there used to be. There was more of a fine scattering of isolated individuals all over the church. He chose a pew that was close to several worshippers but near to none, because he really didn't want to stand out. But then, on closer inspection of those around him, he didn't really want to fit in either. While he was on perfectly good terms with the Church, and enjoyed a distant, respectful, nodding relationship with God, today he was only here for the music. He looked up at the numbers on the board, looked down at his hymnbook and felt the first stirrings of excitement.

When Bennett was a little choirboy, he knew the numbers of all his favourite hymns off by heart. They all did, all the trebles, just like they knew the Latin of their anthems inside-out. They communicated in numbers and archaic languages in the robing room as if this was perfectly normal behaviour, because, for them, it was. As other boys could trot off the numbers of engines – train-spotting was still a thing back then – or the categories of dinosaurs or the batting average of Sobers, it was just what happened in Bennett's gang. Like any other gang they dressed the same – in their case, long red cloaks with white cassocks, starched clean ruffs and extremely neat haircuts – and they had their own argot – 'Quis the descant in the Adoramus?' – and the years that Bennett spent with them were among the happiest of his life. He simply belonged. He wished, he really did, that he might find some sort of future singing with the Bridgeford Community lot, but he was starting to lose hope. He could see now that what he loved about his old church choir was not just necessarily the sort of music they sang, but the structure, the rigour, the hierarchy that that music seemed to demand. It had all been so reassuring, somehow. And while Bennett had certainly enjoyed singing again and didn't even mind the songs – he was really rather partial to all those pop songs, frightfully catchy – he simply could not bear the state of permanent chaos around it all. Still, it had helped remind him of who he was, or at least who he used to be. He needed to get back in a proper choir – join another gang – and he was here to check this one out.

The vicar announced a hymn number from the back of the church and they all stood. Bennett did have a wish list – one that hadn't changed since before his voice broke. It included 'Your Hand O God Has Guided', 'Dear Lord and Father' – obviously – and 'Lord of All Hopefulness', of which he liked either version, the older or the more modern, poppy one, which used to make the choirboys feel incredibly with-it, like one of The Osmonds. He stood with all the others and found the words.

'You Are So Good to Me' was a new one on Bennett, and represented something of a stylistic change. And as the Choir, dressed in jewel-coloured sweatshirts and jeans, came jiving down the aisle singing about dancing in the street, shouting from the roof and a love that set them free, he began to think there had been a few other changes too – perhaps more than he had bargained for.

The service was not, from Bennett's point of view, a success; although he could quite accept that others in the congregation were happy as could be. The hymns were all a little too modern, unfortunately – one seemed to be about refuelling jet engines, which was rather an odd business – and he wasn't entirely comfortable with all the clapping and unnecessary arm movements and so on. At one point it all got terribly energetic, reminiscent of Sue and her chums in front of Jane Fonda on the TV, back in the day. But the lowest point of a pretty low hour was the sign of peace. Last time he went to church, that entailed a nice curt nod to or brisk handshake with those closest to you. So Bennett was understandably a little taken aback to find himself swept up in the warm embrace of total – and rather aromatic – strangers: kissed by women to whom he had not been formally introduced, scratched by the whiskers of – extremely – strange men. 'Splendid,' he heard himself saying into the anorak of a big burly chap. 'Jolly good,' to a rather frisky little woman who wouldn't let go. 'Excellent. Let's press on, shall we?' as he peeled her off him. It was the closest physical contact he had known for many weeks, and it left him a little shaken.

He collapsed into his pew and, instead of taking communion, reflected on how the universe had shifted without him even noticing. Was everybody else across all these changes? Was the shifting universe something else that Sue had taken on, on their joint behalf, so that he should not be bothered? If so, he would say that he rather wished she had not. If she was always planning to cast him back out into this unrecognisable universe, it would have been helpful to him to have been aware of some of its features. How on earth was he supposed to get a new job or start a new relationship if even his dear old Church of England had turned in to something totally unrecognisable?

Twenty-five years ago, before he retreated into his life of hard work and busy family, God was part lord, part father, with a background in the military. He was in his heaven and all was well with the world. Now, it seemed, He had been rather sidelined for Jesus, who had grown up into quite a different sort of chap altogether, apparently. They had spent half the service telling him, in song, that he was beautiful and lovely and the centre of their being – not the sort of stuff they used to go in for in Bennett's day. As for that one where they kept calling him, over and over, 'my king of love' – well, that was very rum. He had always been led to believe, by the women in his office, that there was a big chap with a deep voice called Barry Someone who was the King of Love. But now it was Jesus? How was one to keep up? Anyway, the point was that this new, latest son of God seemed to make everyone in the congregation very jittery and over-excited – as big Barry Someone had also done, if memory served, with the women in the office – and Bennett had to concede that this was not, after all, the solution to his problem. This church was not his gang.

Bennett was finding it hard to cut his meat, and not just because it was the texture of a good pair of brogues. Although he was tucked so far in to the kitchen table that it pressed on to his chest, every time he cut the food, he hit his elbow on the washing machine behind him. He could see, with his ever-expanding grasp of motive and explanation, why Sue had brought their table to this new house, but he was not yet qualified to determine whether she might be regretting it. Still, it was very nice of her to include him in the family Sunday lunch – even if he was sustaining a number of repetitive strain injuries in the process – and he was grateful to be there.

'So,' said Sue, chewing energetically. 'How's the job-hunting going?' She poured on a bit more gravy. 'Whenever the children start to get worried about my future, I say to them, "Don't."' She held up her hand to halt all discussion. 'I say – don't I say this, kids? – "Your father is cleverer than the rest of us put together."'

Casper rolled his eyes while shovelling food indiscriminately into his mouth. He was still in his muddy kit after the morning's rugby and was looking enormous to Bennett. Surely he wasn't still growing now he was in his twenties? Bennett wondered if perhaps the children shrank a little in his imagination now that he wasn't seeing them every day: his mind's eye returned them to smaller incarnations and happier days.

'Well, I'm not sure about ...' Bennett tried to shuffle in his seat, but there wasn't enough room. It was getting very hot in this little kitchen. He wasn't sure the four of them had ever been crammed into so small a space before; there was certainly more room, as far as he could remember, in the family car.

'He will be buried in job offers, you mark my words. Buried.' She took a gulp of water.

Araminta, pretty in a new top that Bennett hadn't seen before, put her fork down after three mouthfuls. She hated it when Sue went on the warpath, retreated into herself often before Bennett had even realised what was happening. In fact, over the past few years, Bennett had learned to use her as a barometer. He could be a little obtuse in picking up the changes in Sue's emotional weather, but Araminta was finely attuned. She now had a pleat of long fair hair and was examining it for split ends – a classic signal that Bennett was in for a serious drubbing. He must be on his guard.

'Well, the recession—' But the truth was that his job-seeking had lacked a little energy of late. He had started off enthusiastically enough. He could remember that quite clearly: firing off emails (he was pretty sure about that, didn't just send them, oh no, he was definitely firing them off) and fixing up meetings.

'There isn't a company in Britain who wouldn't be desperate to get your father on board.'

And he had rather expected, like Sue, that it would all be sorted out quickly enough. Contacts in other companies had always rather given that impression, when the situation was purely hypothetical.

'Not. In. Britain.' Sue was thumping on the table.

But nothing had happened. And quite quickly it seemed that he was more caught up with the minute details of his own day-to-day existence than he was with the larger question of his own future. The planning, shopping for and composing of his own meals, which had begun as a way to pass the time, had turned somehow into a raison d'être. He enjoyed his little forays to the High Street throughout the day, had started to use more ingredients in order to get out of the house more. And he had even been known to strike up conversation with young shop assistants of his own, independent acquaintance. Now he thought about it, life really was rather pleasant.

'So which one are you going to choose?'

'I'm sorry?' He was still thinking about young shop assistants.

'Job offer?' She looked at the children and beamed. 'We're dying to know. Which is it to be?'

'Well.' He completely panicked. He mustn't lie, of course he mustn't. 'It's down to two, at the moment.' Oh dear. He seemed to have lied. It was just that Sue was making it all sound so easy, and she was so sure. For a moment there, Bennett himself had become convinced that job offers were things of such abundance that even a low wretch like him must surely have picked up at least a handful. 'Yep, think I've narrowed it down to the two . . . ' And when those words came out, well – he did enjoy hearing them. Pathetic as it may seem, it was rather nice to find himself a success again – to be admired rather than pitied, a focus of celebration instead of resentment. Just the once, for a change, he wanted to be congratulated.

'I knew it! Didn't I say? Isn't that exactly what I predicted? Credit where credit's due, I said . . . '

Bennett put his knife and fork together and slumped. Araminta took his hand under the table, and gave it a little squeeze.

' ... at least two by now, I said. Must admit I was hoping for even more, but still, two's enough and I did say two. Even you, Bennett, must admit that I was bang on ... '

His eyes met his daughter's in a moment of loving complicity.

' ... I'm really quite pleased with myself about that. Two – that is exactly what I said. Anyway, come on then. Who are they?' She waved her knife around the table. 'Surely you can tell us.'

He sensed danger.

'Yeah, come on, Dad.' Araminta nudged him. 'We won't sell it to the *Actuary Daily News*. Promise.' She wasn't being deliberately mean to him, he knew that. She was a darling girl – she just couldn't help herself.

'Or put it on *Actuarial Entertainment*,' joined Casper.

None of them could.

'*Tonight, live from the Actuary Red Carpet* ... '

The real joke was that Bennett had never, ever wanted to be an actuary. He was not from that sort of stock, not at all. His father was a bishop, his mother did good works. He had been brought up to help and to serve, but helping and serving did not, in his wife's opinion, keep any of them in the style to which she rather fancied becoming accustomed.

'They say they won't.' Sue shook her head as she piled up the plates. 'But you'll leave here and the paparazzi will be banked up on bleachers up and down our humble little road ... '

And now he was, once again, just an object of ridicule. In a moment of boredom last week, Bennett had found himself, much to his own surprise, casting his eye over a dating website. He would never go on one, he was sure about that, but he was curious about the sort of person who did, what they were looking for in a man, what they were offering about themselves. One of the many things he was interested to learn – well, there was a lot that was extremely interesting. Who knew people said those sorts of things? That shifting universe, up to its tricks again – was the way they all went on about their Good Sense of Humour. He was baffled by that at the time and sitting there, enduring the torture of his hilarious family in full comic voice, he found himself even more so. Why on earth would anyone want to live with anybody who thought they had a good sense of humour? He watched them all, bent double with laughter at his expense, around his kitchen table and shook his head. If Bennett Parker was ever going to embark on any relationship ever again, it would be with someone who could prove to him that she had no trace of humour whatsoever.

11

Tracey sat in the corner of the sofa, hugging her knees, glued to
Bargain Hunt; Billy was at the table, poring over forms, poking at
a calculator, a pencil behind his ear and a pen in his hand. 'Can
you turn it down a bit over there, Mum? Can't hear myself think.'
His phone gave a whistle. 'See?' he said. 'That's Annie downstairs
and we didn't even hear the doorbell.' He leaned over, scribbled
something on the corner of a scrap of paper. 'Do you mind letting
her in?'

'Eh?' Tracey was mystified – cross and mystified. 'Yes, I do mind.
She's only coming to drive me to choir like I'm bloody six. If I go,
I shall walk down in a bit.'

'Not "only" – she's come to see me too.' He leapt up, hitched up
his jeans and called from the stairs, 'She said she would last time I
went into the library.'

They came in together, chatting – her only child and this other,
trespassing woman. Tracey heard the word 'visas' and suddenly felt
unnaturally cold. Billy walked over, picked up the remote control
and killed the sound.

'Evening,' Annie sang.

'What do you mean,' Tracey was outraged, pushing herself up and out of the sofa with both hands, 'you *went to the library*?'

'Uh,' Billy went back to the table and rifled through bits of paper, 'I went to the library. Time was, Mum, when you were all for me going to the library.'

'I was all for you going to the library to take out and read books in order to contribute to the broadening of your mind,' she retorted. She had not used this tone of voice with him for years – if ever. 'Not for this kind of stuff. It's probably all out of date, anyway, knowing that place. If you want to do something for charity, why didn't you just say so? We can go and see some people – *proper* people – who actually know what they're talking about. Don't bother with the library unless you want to change the habits of the last decade and actually read some bloody books.'

Annie reached into her basket. 'So I've brought the books you asked for, Billy.' She was, at least, a bit sheepish for once; Tracey would give her that. 'That one's got the best overview of the Rwandan genocide, and the one I was telling you about, *Is That It*?'

'Cool.' Billy leapt over and nearly snatched them from her grasp. 'This,' he explained to his mother like she was the village idiot, 'is by a guy called Bob Geldof? He did this thing that Annie was telling me about called Live Aid?'

'Did he now?' Tracey drawled. 'Wow, Billy. That must have been ama-zing.'

'Oh, I'm sure Tracey knows all about Live Aid, Billy. I don't think we need to—'

'Well, she never told me about it.' Billy shrugged. 'She never talks about anything like that. It's all heavy rock and new stuff round here, the indie-er the better. She hates old music and all that, don't you, Mum?'

'Ah, well, I'm not so sure she does actually—'

'And the way she throws out old food when there's nothing wrong with it. Don't think she's ever even heard of the starving in Africa . . .'

For what seemed a lengthy interval, Tracey stayed on the sofa, staring from one to the other with her mouth open. Then she leapt up, stormed across the room and grabbed her coat from the chair. That, she thought, wrenching the belt around her waist, it should come to this. This – this miserable domestic inter-generational conflict – was exactly what she had been trying to spare them both for the last twenty-two years. And here was Billy, the lucky spared child, firing the first shots. She slipped her feet into her shoes. During all that time, with no support – moral or otherwise – and often in the face of considerable provocation, Tracey had been determined to keep the peace. She threw a few cushions around the place, in search of her phone. Her childhood had been a torture – *torture* – of instructions and commands, moans and misunder-standings. For years, she had been mocked and derided about her clothes, her records, her friends. She found the mobile and chucked it into her bag. She had been forced to listen to lectures on how much better the music had been in the old days, how much worse the food, how terrible their each and every day in their separate offices and how she, Tracey, did not know she was born. And as a parent she had made a point of never saying anything like that to her child, not ever – until now.

'Just listen to yourself, Billy Leckford.' Tracey headed for the door – 'You don't know what you're bloody talking about' – and battled her way down the stairs. 'You don't even know you're bloody born.'

She slammed the door and stood alone on the dirty, narrow pave-ment, waiting for the angry tears to subside and the shaking to stop. She wasn't going back in there to talk to that ungrateful little sod for a bit – he could stew. And she certainly wasn't going to be trapped in the car with that mad meddling old bat. She stood with her arms tight round her chest, looking up and down the street, first one way, then the other, trying to decide where to go and what to do. Then she tied her shoulder bag round her coat and set off for choir on foot.

♩

The WI had been in the hall all afternoon, enjoying a Great Bridgeford Bake-off, and the atmosphere was toxic with the acrid smell of burnt oats. Annie ran around trying to help the kitchen back on the road to recovery – honestly, the WI? You would think ... – but there was only so much she could do without some very powerful oven cleaner.

Leave it open, leave it open

she sang to the tune of 'Frère Jacques' as Judith came beaming in.

Yuk it stinks, yuk it stinks

she trilled happily as she trotted over to the chair stack. Judith seemed to be in a particularly good mood tonight.

You seem very cheerful, you seem very cheerful.

Annie, scrubbing away at the counter, studied Judith through the hatch, with a raised eyebrow and a curious smile. But then Lewis was among them:

Got bad news, got bad news.

'Oh no!' wailed Annie. *'Now* what?'

Mrs Coles had now been admitted to Parkway Hospital as well, with a nasty chest brought on by a late night at the Anti-Superstore Rally. She was on the same ward they were singing in the other day, the one that Connie would soon be moving down to; at least they would be together. But the tone of the evening was a little subdued as everyone came in, heard the bulletin, took their seat and wondered aloud where on earth they were going to find another accompanist – and in time for the contest, too. It was yet another blow. Only Judith seemed cheerful despite it all.

Maria was the first to spot why. 'Judith! What is this on your finger? It's as big as the Ritz!'

Judith flashed a stone the size of an ice cube on her left hand, and blushed almost prettily. 'Got engaged ... At the weekend. Oh, thanks ... Oh, bless you ... Oh, you are kind ...'

'Oh yeah?' said Pat to Lynn. 'Good thing we were all born yesterday.' And then to Judith: 'Can I just have a look at that, please, love?' She beckoned towards the ring with an imperious manner, clearly intending to sink her teeth into the stone to check it was real. Judith looked panicked and Lynn rather nastily amused. The situation was teetering on the brink of unpleasantness when a new voice broke through the air.

'Excuse me.' She was tall and auburn-haired, and tapped towards the circle in vertiginous heels. 'I'm here for the Bridgeford Community Choir.' She flicked her long curls back. 'I do hope I'm in the right place?'

Several men were instantly on their feet, but Lewis – moving at a speed of which nobody hitherto knew he was capable – was the first to the chair stack. He shoved Maria along and made a new space, right next to himself. 'Come through, come through.' He ushered her over. 'Do, please, introduce yourself.'

Her name was Emma and she lived about ten miles away, had been a member of her local operatic society for many years but found that there had been an influx of new people, with new ideas – didn't they all just *loathe* it when people got new ideas? – and she just wasn't getting the parts she deserved any more. 'And then I thought: That's it. I've had enough. It's their loss,' she said brightly. 'So here I am, to seek musical pastures new.'

'Welcome, welcome,' said the basses.

'And why us, exactly, out of all the choirs in Britain?' asked Pat with narrowed eyes.

'Hmm. How did we get quite so lucky?' added Lynn.

'I have family in Bridgeford.' Emma directed her answers to the friendlier side of the circle. 'They told me all about you. I don't know if any of you know my sister, Bea—'

'Not Mrs Stuart?' Jazzy turned her nose up, poked out her tongue and said to Katie, 'She used to come to the caff.'

'—and my mother . . .'

'Pamela?' Annie's smile was a little frozen. 'Ah yes, lives two doors down.'

'There we are,' concluded Lewis. 'Bridgeford enough for me. Shall we begin?'

'Surely you want me to audition first?' Emma laughed. 'That was the other thing that went wrong at my old place, by the way. Can you believe it?' She held both hands up and out like a Hindu goddess. 'They *stopped auditioning.*'

'Oh, we never—' Annie began.

'Of course,' cut in Lewis. 'What was I thinking? Please. Go ahead.'

Emma leapt to her feet; coming as she did from the operatic tradition, she didn't just sing her Gilbert & Sullivan, she acted it too. That sun, whose gaze was all ablaze, was quite real, at least to her. It was somewhere up near the cobweb that Annie couldn't reach, on the strip lighting – she kept pointing at it. Pat sighed and took out her embroidery, Lynn picked up a cruise brochure and Jazzy, who quite possibly hadn't heard any operetta before, got the giggles.

Somehow the Choir had assumed that Emma would be treating them to just the one song. They were quite taken aback when she became one of three little maids from school, broke through the chairs and started shuffling round the hall. Katie started giggling too; the two young girls had their heads together and were whispering. The others, though, were less subtle. Emma had, it seemed, by taking herself out of the circle, made something of a tactical blunder. Once she was out of their direct line of vision, everyone lost interest. Of course, they could still hear her – pert as a schoolgirl, she was, apparently – but really, if they weren't allowed to sing themselves, then they had the more pressing business of Judith's engagement to be getting on with.

'Where's it going to be, then – this "wedding"?' Pat was still openly sceptical.

'Do you need a choir?' asked Tracey. 'With a bit of practice we could do you a mean "Lean on Me".'

'You could make the cake.' Jazzy elbowed Katie.

'That's the thing.' Judith sighed, her left hand to her face. 'It might have to be abroad . . .'

Going to abroa-oad and she's
Going to be ma-a-a-rried . . .

Maria drowned out Emma for a moment.

'Oh, shame,' Annie was a bit sad, 'not to do it in Bridgeford, really, when you've lived here all your life.'

'And where we would have been able to witness it really happening with our very own eyes.' Lynn and Pat exchanged knowing looks.

'*Three little maids from school.*' Emma was kowtowing to herself.

'Quick.' Lynn gave Lewis a kick. 'Stop her now before she starts doing the bloody *Ring Cycle*.'

'Don't call us,' muttered Pat.

'That was terrific,' said Lewis as Emma came back towards them. 'We've had a chat and we *think* we can offer you a place.'

'Oh my *God*,' squealed Emma, hands over her mouth. 'No! Really?'

'Really.' Lewis was warming to the role that Emma had assumed for him. 'You nailed it out there. That performance gave me goose bumps. You're coming with us.'

'Oh, I am *thrilled*.'

'We've got an important competition coming up. This is a crucial moment in this choir's history and we need all the talent we can get. Emma,' he patted the chair beside him, 'you sit here and share my lyrics. We're going to start with our celebrated—'

'Oh fuck . . . Please, no . . . Jeez . . . I can't take it, I'm dying here, literally . . . Bury me now,' whimpered Jazzy.

'—*Sound of Music* medley.'

At break time, Annie rushed over to the tea table as usual, only to find that Bennett had beaten her to it. He had his glasses on the end of his nose and was inspecting the urn.

'I think there's a loose connection in here, Annie. I'll take it home with me tonight and have a look.' He took off his specs, popped them into his top pocket and turned to the row of cups. 'I'll pour, you do the milk.'

Lynn grumbled over to the table. 'I'm getting mine, as nobody else seems to have thought.' She piled in the sugars. 'By the way, did you get anyone to help with the Evergreens' lunches?'

'No, just me at the moment,' said Annie. 'I have to take the morning off work every time now. I can hardly cancel it, can I? They haven't got anything else to look forward to, poor old loves.

'And they've earned it, anyway. They all did their bit, didn't they? Bit of quiche on a Wednesday, least they can expect. Trouble is, none of this lot do their bit or any bit at all. Who's going to serve *our* quiche on a Wednesday and give *us* a drink through a straw?' She flicked her head at the room behind her. 'Not that rabble, that's for sure. It's the same down at Outpatients in the afternoons,' she went on, through a slurp. 'You know, I've been doing the teas there since Mrs Thatcher was on the throne.' Annie laughed, but Lynn was deadly serious. 'There's just nobody out there to take over. I think I'll be stuck doing it till I collapse on the job.

'Useful place to collapse, at least.' Annie filled the pot again.

'You have got to be joking.' Lynn picked up a cup to take back to Pat. 'They'll kill you soon as look at you in that dump. I must say, I've got my worries about poor Constance. I know I'm alone, and I don't like to be the one to spread gloom and misery, as well you know, but *I* didn't think she was looking too bright the other night.'

Tracey handed a cup to Lewis and sat down next to him. 'It's all getting way out of hand now.' She took a sip. 'Leaflets, fund-raising and now bloody visas. I mean, visas? Actual visas?'

Lewis looked sympathetic.

'It's plain ridiculous.' She shook her head. 'And it's not just that he's applying for permission to clear off as far as possible. Oh no, that's not upsetting enough for everybody, nowhere near. So in the meantime, just to twist the knife a bit while he's waiting, he has chosen to remove himself into temporary accommodation right at the top of the moral bloody high ground.' Her voice was rising again. 'He's only just found Africa on the map and now he's lecturing me – me! – on food wastage when he's never eaten a pizza crust. It's all *her* fault.' Tracey looked over at the small, slight, busy figure of Annie, smiling and chatting as she passed round the ginger biscuits she had knocked up for them all before her long day's work in the library. 'That bloody woman is an absolute menace.'

Lewis wasn't really listening to Tracey's woes. He was watching Katie and Jazzy – absorbed in each other's company, busy taking selfies – and clearly trying, subtly, to listen in.

'She just turned up. Not a word for four and a half years and then there she is on the doorstep.' The girls put their heads together and beamed. 'But I'm sorry, I still don't trust her.' Jazzy gave the thumbs-up and snapped again. 'I just don't bloody trust her and nor does my nan.'

'But she *is* your mum.' Katie stuck her tongue out and Jazzy pulled her eyes down. 'You got your mum back. I mean, how lucky is that? If I had could have just one wish . . . '

A flash of pain crossed Lewis' tired, middle-aged face. Katie's mother had died in the accident that had left Katie in her wheel-chair. She almost never talked about it – when her spinal cord was severed, a part of her personality shut down too. But there she was, with a friend of a few weeks' standing, being as open as could be.

'Yeah, well, yours sounds like she was lovely.' They mock-throt-tled each other. 'Mine's just some random junkie mentalist who turns up every four years. The stuff she's got up to – honest, even if I told you, which I can't because it's just so crap, you still wouldn't believe half of it.'

'I still say you have to give her a chance.' They blew kisses at the camera. 'I mean, what else can you do? If she says she's clean then you've got to believe her.' Katie used her firm voice – the one that nobody ever bothered to argue with. 'It's not like another Jazz's mum is going to turn up. This is the only one you've got.'

Jazzy went behind the chair, put her head on top of Katie's and grinned. 'It's weird knowing you.' Her phone flashed. 'I've never been mates with someone worse off than me before.' She made a face like a goldfish. 'It's actually well rubbish.'

There was a scrape of chair leg as Lewis got up and rushed out to the car park. Everyone should carry on without him, he called; he was perfectly all right – just needed a bit of fresh air.

The men's voices were a little tentative against the backing track blaring out from the boombox. Even the hitherto unembarrassable basses looked, well, a bit embarrassed.

I'm up all night to get some

The women, peering down their noses and through their reading glasses, replied in their best, politest Julie Andrews sopranos.

Katie and Jazzy – driven half mad by the endless repetition of 'The Lonely Goatherd' – had had enough. Lewis was always on about people power and true democracy: well, that meant that they had a say, too. Earlier, on Jazzy's afternoon off, they had decided to take matters into their own hands. It was time for some proper music, and to have a bash at dividing up into parts.

It was going OK so far, although none of the men looked very comfortable with their solo lines and Bennett, in particular, seemed to be squirming, contorted with some physical or psychological discomfort. But when the room came together for the chorus, there was strength, harmony, even a little foot-tapping from – almost – everyone.

We're up all night to get lucky

'You know what?' said Pat, putting away her specs. 'I'm not sure we are.' She reached for her bag.

'I'm not sure we ever were,' added Lynn, with a tone of regret, as she rose and picked up her mac.

We're up all night to get lucky

They were trying it for the second time now, and – perhaps because it was new to them, perhaps because it was song at its most virulently infectious – it was starting to really take off. The men on one side were singing across to the women on the other – goading, baiting, bouncing in their seats, dancing with their arms.

We're up all night to get lucky

'Up all night with indigestion more like,' shouted Pat over her shoulder as she stomped off to the door.

'Owph.' Lynn ran to keep up with her. 'Don't. You'll set me off.'

We're up all night to get lucky

But with their leaving, something was released in the room – as if they were ballast and without them the Choir could at last take flight. By their third run-through, they were all up and bouncing around in the centre of the circle of trust. They couldn't help themselves; the music was irresistible. Jazzy was dancing with Katie's wheelchair, Maria and Lewis were jiving, Annie and Bennett were grooving back to back.

We're up all night to get lucky

'I must say, it isn't *quite* what I was expecting,' Emma shouted at Lewis' rear as he twerked in her general direction. 'I take it this is something of a one-off?'

We're up all night to get lucky

And in the middle of it all, up on a chair, singing to the maximum capacity of her powerful lungs –

Up all night to get lucky.

– was Tracey.

♫

When they finally had to accept that the session had come to its end, the applause seemed to go on for ever.

'Don't forget the Talent Show,' bellowed Lewis over the noise. 'All in a top cause. We're raising funds for the coach to take us to the Championships. We need notice of your acts NOW for the programme. It's a big week next week: Connie is even now working on the set for the competition so that we can at last get CRACKING. Goodnight, everybody.'

'Night.'

'That was brilliant.'

'Can't wait for next week.'

'Well, that was certainly different,' smiled Annie as she finished up in the kitchen. '*Tum tum ti-tum ti-tum lucky*. What fun.'

'Hey, Dad,' Katie called over her shoulder to Lewis. 'Are you all right driving home on your own? Jazzy says she'll walk me back.'

Lewis' delight was so extreme it almost winded him. He slumped against the car and managed to splutter out a forced, casual, 'Yep, fine by me.' Tracey – who was until that moment still singing, who wasn't so much walking but more shimmying her way home – caught it, bit her lip and looked away.

12

You could always just tell when it was Saturday morning, even without opening your eyes. The traffic made a different noise, for a start – less impatient, not as uniform, none of that everybody-having-to-do-the-same-thing-at-the-same-time military precision that you got on a weekday; instead, there was a pleasing individuality to all those engines out there – a sort of auto self-expression. Tracey enjoyed that. She also enjoyed the conversations that floated up to her window from the pavement below. People liked each other on a Saturday morning, in ways they quite forgot midweek. Their children were less annoying, their partners more attractive . . . Tracey turned over in bed and sank into a long and lazy stretch.

It was always her favourite day, hands down. She was aware, of course, that this was just a hangover from her youth. She knew she loved it because it meant wearing her own clothes, hanging round the Rimmel counter in Boots, parading with a gang of girls up and down the High Street, baiting gangs of boys. It was the only day of the week when she didn't have to account for her whereabouts. Wearied by the demands of Monday to Friday, the army of adults at school and at home – the ones who combined to make her life an imprisoning misery – even they seemed to take the day off, too. None of these privileges meant so much to her any more – hey, it's great being a grown-up, you can just hang around that Rimmel counter whenever you fancy – but she felt the pleasure of them just the same.

By the same token, she hated Sundays – yes, yes, you could go shop your head off on a Sunday these days, but you couldn't then, so it didn't count. A Puritan air hung around the Sundays of her youth: walks were taken, rooms tidied, lawns mown; her parents sang along, actually sang along with their own hymnbooks, to *Songs of Praise*. If it wasn't for the Sunday-night music charts on the radio she probably would have topped herself before her fifteenth birthday.

She got out of bed, pulled her old kimono around her and went to open the blind. Look at that – it wasn't even raining, for the first time this week. She nodded at the sky with satisfaction. That was Saturdays for you, in a nutshell – unlike the other days, your Saturday could be relied upon to deliver. Lewis and Katie were already up and on their way out. She stopped for a moment and watched them as they bumped their way over to the disabled parking space and started the necessary manoeuvres to get into the car. Tracey remembered now, they were off swimming this morning; she would pop round for a cup of tea this afternoon. It was so odd that they had all lived so near to each other for so long. How had she never noticed them before?

Trotting down the stairs in slippered feet, Tracey thought of all the things she did not have to do that day – go to work, go food-shopping, get in the car . . . there was no end to the list of irritants that she did not have to suffer. Though she would go into town later on – just to see how things were settling down with Jazzy and her mum. She poured some coffee into a filter paper and switched on the machine. Not all the Saturdays of her life had been quite this perfect. When Billy was younger, he kept taking stuff up in an enthusiastic sort of way, and for a good few years there were all sorts of sporting nonsense involving early mornings and clean kit and Tracey standing outside in the cold. It was really pretty grim for a bit, but he gave it all up soon enough, bless him. She could now say, with pleasure and not a small amount of pride, that most Saturdays he did not even stir before nightfall.

It was only once the toast had popped up and the coffee machine ceased to gurgle that Tracey noticed there were other noises coming from elsewhere in the house. She cocked an ear as she spread her butter and marmalade, and then took her breakfast into the living room for a closer listen. It was coming from the stairs, the stairs down to the front door, the ones that nobody had ever gone up, ever, other than Annie Miller. She couldn't be breaking in, could she? Not on a Saturday ... Annie Miller was, like teachers and parents, exactly the sort of person whom one should never have to encounter on a Saturday. She opened the door, and there was Billy.

'Bills! Hello,' she said through her toast. 'Thought you were a burglar, or a choir nutter.' She took a slurp of coffee. 'Late night? Haven't gone to bed yet?'

'Been up for an hour,' called Billy cheerfully from behind a bin bag halfway down.

'Why?' Tracey was aware of sounding rather stern; parental, almost. He was peculiarly alert; not even hungover. 'Billy, what on earth ...?'

'I was just looking out that old rucksack—'

'Rucksack?' She didn't like where this might be going. 'What possible use could you have for a rucksack? Would you mind, Billy, telling me exactly what is going on?'

He stood up straight, with the rucksack slung over one shoulder and an armful of Warhammer, and began to pick his way over their domestic rubble towards the top of the stairs.

'Who knows, Mum?' Now Tracey was aware that he sounded a bit sarky; cheeky brat, even. 'Perhaps at some point in the next sixty years I might go away for a night or two, somewhere out of the dump that is Bridgeford, and need something to, um' – he looked around him wildly, clearly trying to take the imaginative leap towards what someone who went somewhere might reasonably be expected to take – 'put a ... a – I dunno – a shirt in.'

'Fine. Good luck. Enjoy.' She turned her back to her son and took her breakfast over to the table. 'And you're taking all your Warhammer with you, too? Packing all your favourite toys when you run away from home?'

'TBH, Mum, twenty-two-year-olds don't tend to "run away from home" so much. They tend to more, like, "move".' Billy emerged into the room and spread his reclaimed stuff all over the table – all around Tracey's sacred Saturday morning breakfast. 'And I just found all this and it was, like, Wow, this is seriously not cool having that on the stairs just doing nothing. There's some little dude out there who would love this stuff, and there's Mr William Leckford Esquire who could make a few quid by selling it.'

'Selling it? Selling it? Who are you, then, all of a sudden: Donald Trump?'

'Hey, did he sell his Warhammer?' He opened the still-intact boxes and examined the contents. 'And isn't he like really rich? Cool. Oh, yeah, talking of rich ...' He looked up and straight at Tracey; her breath was arrested by a sense of impending doom. 'Been meaning to go over all this with you. I think it's time I got the low-down about Dad's allowance and all that. You know, no reason, just like to get across it, you know what I mean?'

'Billy Leckford,' Tracey rose and so did her voice, 'what is it with you today? You, mate, are seriously harshing my Saturday-morning mellow.' She stormed off up the stairs and slammed and locked the bathroom door.

Tracey took another gulp of air and then sank again into the soapy water. 'Be sure your sins will find you out.' That's what her mum and dad were always telling her in that boring, predictable, sad-sack parent kind of way. She shuddered, these days, when she reflected on how she herself had been brought up, and 'Be sure your blah-di-blah' was just typical: never once did they sit down with her, examine her choices, help her through her own behaviour. Instead, they just spouted this kind of stuff – lifted off the nearest tea-towel – and hoped for the best.

To be fair, it had almost worked. She didn't enjoy any of these pithy aphorisms, but she had believed them. The evidence was there to back them up. When Tracey lived with her parents, her sins did find her out, more often than not. But then she was being constantly monitored and her sins were of the low-level variety, the nicking of the last chocolate digestive, the failure to clean out the guinea pig: pretty harmless and of little consequence.

But in the past twenty-two years, she had lost faith in it entirely. For over half her life now Tracey had been living with sins of a different stature altogether. Her sins were her lies and those lies were enormous; colossal great things; lies the size of magnificent buildings – that was what she lived with. In fact, so big were these lies, so spacious and capacious, she didn't just live with them, she lived *in* them. It was perfectly nice in there: comfortable, quiet. Perhaps it got a bit boring, occasionally; other people might find it lonely, but Tracey was fine.

Sometimes she read, in interviews and magazines, about 'impostor syndrome': it afflicted people who were so successful – High Court judges, CEOs – that they couldn't quite believe it; they lived with the constant fear of being tapped on the shoulder and told they were in the wrong life. It amused her. Because there was Tracey, who was meant to go much further, who should never, by rights, be living this life of anonymous under-achievement, who was an actual, genuine impostor, and she had no fear whatsoever of being found out any more. Everything, every landmark on her biographical landscape, was untrue – who she was, what she used to be, who Billy was, where he came from – it was all lies, all of it. But somehow, and this was perhaps because of the very scale of it all, nobody had ever tapped on her shoulder. Contrary to her parents' wisdom, and almost to her own amusement, she had never been found out at all.

Until today. She came up out of the water, took another deep breath, and stayed up. Tracey loved everything about her sweet little boy, but the quality that had been so useful to her over the years, and of which she was most particularly fond, was his overwhelming incuriosity. She really shouldn't berate him for suddenly asking difficult questions now, just be grateful they had never entered his brain before. And all was not lost, not quite yet. He had only made a simple enquiry, not suddenly turned into Sherlock. The situation could be retrieved, she was sure of it.

Leaping out of the bath, Tracey grabbed a towel, dripped her way over to her bedroom and quietly shut the door. She stood silently for a moment, listening out for Billy's movements, working out what he was up to. He was back on the stairs again, she reckoned, whistling while he foraged about, bringing up more stuff. She shook her head – talk about impostors: who was this stranger in her house?

It didn't matter. The coast was clear. Tracey burrowed to the back of her wardrobe and pressed the buttons that opened her safe.

13

There must be a stage in the history of all great institutions when they somehow develop instincts and survival skills all of their own; when they come to life, throw up their hands in despair at the mess their members have wrought and seize control of their own destiny. They must at the very least have one hand on the tiller as they navigate the course from one generation to the next. Otherwise, how to explain the continued existence of, say, the House of Commons, or any of our organised religions? Surely they are only still with us despite, rather than because of, the competence and common sense of man.

Looking in at the Bridgeford choir at this critical moment in its history, it seems to be exhibiting the behaviour of an organism all too keenly aware of its own mortality, even as its own members are sleep-walking towards oblivion. On this particular Tuesday evening, Lewis and Annie were in the middle of the circle; Lewis was doing the talking, Annie looking suitably grave.

'... what we were hoping for, I'm afraid. Until the weekend, Constance was, as you know, making an excellent recovery and was, apparently, hard at work on the set list even on Saturday morning. Sunday, though, saw a little dip and sadly she hasn't been able to do as much as she had hoped since then.'

'Poor love,' said the altos.

'We'll manage,' said the basses.

'So when *is* she going to get round to it then?' the sopranos wanted to know.

'Listen to me.' Lewis obviously felt the need to turn this from an announcement to a rallying cry. 'The underlying trend is UP. She WILL be better by the end of the week. She may even be WITH US for the contest ...' He continued in that vein: they were in good shape, things could not be better ... And most of the singers seemed happy to take his word for it; the institution itself, though, could clearly see right through him. As he adjusted his blinkers and blathered on, the Choir was busy at work on a variety of alternative futures for itself.

And it was doing very nicely. After all, against all the odds, Tracey was still there. She was sitting in the circle of trust with the rest of them and rolling her wide brown eyes at Jazzy as Lewis spoke. Despite the constant irritation of Annie's presence and her monstrous interference in Billy's life, Tracey did keep coming, week after week: Annie repelled her, but somehow or other the Choir kept drawing her in.

And Bennett was there, too. It wasn't an easy gig, not only being the sole tenor but being a damn fine tenor, too: the basses gave him a hard time, the sopranos made far too much of a fuss of him. But he had stuck it out anyway and was sitting quietly listening to the latest health bulletin with a worried frown.

And just as Lewis' speech entered its final cadence, in walked Emma. She was back for more, and this time she was not alone. The hall fell silent as everyone assessed the vision that swaggered towards them: two men, both mid-forties, dress smart/casual. They had, as far as anyone could tell, absolute lashings of their own hair; their BMI was, quite remarkably, just fine. They clearly came from another town. They possibly came from another world.

'Hmm,' said Maria, to nobody in particular. 'Who do we have here?'

'I hope you don't mind' – Emma beamed – 'taking in two more refugees from my old place? We all feel the need to move on, and you were so welcoming to me last week. I was hoping you could find space ...'

'Well, I don't think we need to audition *them*,' said Pat, sucking her cheeks in.

'Great,' said Emma. 'Well, this is Edward and this is Jonty and Jonty just happens to be a pianist too in fact he was the pianist at the Operatic weren't you Jonty I don't suppose you've brought some music with you here tonight oh you have, how fantastic, oh it will make such a difference won't it to be accompanied instead of just wandering about all over the place so does anyone have any suggestions or shall we leave it to Jonty over there, oh listen, not a bad sound at all, shall we get cracking?'

'Uh, hello, hello, and steady on. Woah, there. If I could just hold you back for a minute.' Lewis was back on his feet, holding up a cautionary hand and looking most concerned. 'Good-evening, Emma. Welcome, Edward, and welcome ... um, J ... J ... brjzsh.' He choked a little. Lewis had a private, unofficial list of names that he could never comfortably say out loud and, as it happened, 'Jonty' was near the top. He would always be polite, of course. He would never be outwardly unpleasant. But he would not, under any circumstances, let the word 'Jonty' cross his lips – unless it was to condemn said Jonty to the guillotine, or to order the placing of his very smug head upon a very sharp stick. 'We do have a programme already for tonight, thanks for your input—'

'Not. Again,' Jazzy groaned.

'We have to practise our *Sound of Music* medley for the upcoming County Championships. While our leader, Constance, cannot be with us, not tonight anyway' – he walked over to the piano and put the sheet music upon the stand – 'she has asked that this be done.'

'Then who are we to argue?' smirked Jonty, with a wink to

Edward. 'Here we go then.' He chortled as he opened the overture. 'Haven't heard this for a while.'

'*I* bloody have,' said Jazzy.

Even Lewis would have to admit that Jonty was an extremely accomplished pianist – worth two Mrs Coles and then some. They hadn't heard even one of the many wrong notes they were used to hearing by now. But nor could they quite catch any of the emotion that they might hope to hear, either. There was no sense of joy in those hills, no beauty in that edelweiss, no love in the love songs: instead, there was just a deep and nasty sarcasm.

Annie was arranging the cups in their saucers and Bennett was pouring when Tracey came up to the table.

'Are you all right, Bennett? Couldn't help noticing you looked a bit tense in there this evening . . . ' She piled sugars into Lewis' cup.

'Well . . . Actually . . . ' He offered up the plate of Katie's brownies. 'I am getting worried, thank you for asking. I really think it's time to give the Choir a proper definite structure.' Annie started clattering the crockery. 'Oh. Of course,' he carried on, 'Constance will be back any day now, and obviously we shouldn't commit to anything definitely until she gets back.' Annie nodded and calmed down a bit. 'But it really is a terrible mess.'

'Come, come, Bennett, that is a little negative,' Annie retorted. 'We've got a lot of new members and it's bound to take a while to settle down. It's just a bit hit-and-miss, that's all. Last week, if you remember, was a great hit.'

'Yes. Yes.' Bennett seemed to be drawing some moral strength from somewhere. 'Last week was fine, but other weeks are a total waste of our time.'

'Bennett St John Parker!' Annie was outraged.

'I'm sorry. But it can't go on like this. Either we go in for this championship and we do it properly or we don't bother at all. Our opponents will already know their stuff backwards, you do realise that, don't you? And we haven't even picked our songs. We're heading for disaster here. A total wipe-out. What do you think, Tracey?'

'What do I think?' Tracey had been watching it all with open amusement. 'I think I'll have another brownie please, ta. Katie's improving. They're not bad for once.'

♫

As if to prove Bennett's point, the second half of the evening took the Choir to whole new depths. There was none of that letting their hair down that they normally went in for after the tea break. This Jonty already had control of the piano; he was now determined to seize control of the content. He ran a few arpeggios, asked over his shoulder: 'Everyone knows this, surely?' and launched into the waltz from *The Merry Widow*.

Emma moved around the circle handing out song sheets while she and Edward sang up and along.

'Oh, lovely,' purred Pat, putting away her needlework. 'This is more like it, eh, Lynn?'

'Gorgeous,' oozed Lynn. 'Ah, to be back where we belong.'

'What? Eh?' Jazzy was in outrage. 'What's going on?' She flicked her lyrics sheet. 'Hello? Can someone sort this out, please?' They all looked down at their words.

Love unspoken, faith unbroken

'This cannot be happening,' she shouted. 'Oi. You. You taking the piss? Jasmine White just does not' – she waved her index finger in front of her face and shook her head – 'do this kind of stuff.'

Love me true

'I mean, have I gone mental OR IS THIS BY ACTUAL DEAD PEOPLE?' Jazzy shouted up and alone:

WE'RE UP ALL NIGHT TO GET LUCKY

'Owph. Dear,' whispered Judith to Tracey. 'Is this what true democracy sounds like?'

Let your heart sing this refrain

Emma and Edward warbled.

UP ALL NIGHT TO GET LUCKY

belted Jazzy over the top of them.

'A Franz Lehar/Daft Punk mash-up?' replied Tracey thought-fully. 'Yes, I should think it probably is.'

'Sounds to me more like a coup,' said Maria with authority. She knew a political takeover when she saw one. 'A violent, bloody coup. There's a foreign power over there, Lewis my lad, and it's got its tanks right on our lawn.'

The applause, when it came, was muted and polite. Lewis hardly had to raise his voice to be heard. 'I hope you've all got the Talent Show fund-raiser in your diaries. In the hall at St Ambrose at eight p.m. on the twenty-eighth. All welcome. Plenty of room for all our fans. Be there or be a no-mates. And after that's over, THEN we,' he looked angrily at Jonty, 'we *the members* will sort out the champ-ionship. Goodnight, all.'

'Night.'

'Night,' called Annie from the kitchen, where she was gathering up all her stuff. 'Don't lose hope, everybody,' she called through the hatch, in her cheerful voice: 'Everything has a habit of turning out for the best.' Her phone was trilling from the bottom of her basket but as soon as she found it, it stopped. She pulled down her read-ing glasses from the top of her hair and held the screen at a distance. 'Hmm. Jess. That's very odd.' The humans had all gone now, but she often talked to the tea urn. 'Jess never calls me these days. What can that be about ... ?'

14

Bennett emerged from the butcher, twisting the plastic bag around the primary ingredient of that night's supper. He was thoroughly preoccupied this morning. He had promised Annie he would go to the Talent Show, and actually he really wanted to go to the Talent Show. The problem, though, was that he had sort of, somehow or other, given Annie the impression he might perform something himself and he really was not sure whether he did in fact have a talent. He could sing, of course, but only really in a choir, and best of all in harmony. Bennett had never been one of nature's soloists; he was pretty sure about that. He was rather rusty on the piano, though he had started playing again for the first time in years. So what else was there? He was unusually strong at mental arithmetic and his sweet peas always came up a treat, but neither of those was really a performance art. Of course, it was always hard living without his loved ones but he especially felt it when he could do with some trusted, caring counsel on tricky intimate questions like: what was particularly special or entertaining about Bennett Parker? Because the more he turned it over in his

123

own mind, the more he was starting to suspect that the answer was: not much. He turned towards home, and there in front of him was Sue.

'Oh. It's you.' She raised an eyebrow, gave a little smirk then gushed a quick, warm 'How are you, love?' over her shoulder to someone else. 'Lamb chops, then?' she snarled at Bennett; a kinder 'Aw. How's he getting on?' oozed towards an elderly lady tottering out of Boots.

Bennett looked down at the bag. They were lamb chops, indeed, but would a 'Yes' be the right answer, or might she, in this instance prefer, a 'No'?

'I've been thinking of you, all of you.' Sue gripped the arm of yet another complete stranger. 'How did it go?'

He suspected there was no right answer to the lamb chop question; he was on a straight course to unpopularity either way.

'Look at her!' She chucked an unknown baby under the chin. 'That cannot be another tooth!'

'Yes,' he declared. 'They are. I am having,' he held up the twisted plastic, 'lamb chops.'

'Gorgeous! Are they new?'

'Well, I hope—' Oh. Someone was showing off her shoes. Eventually, Sue turned back to him.

'So suddenly we're Masterchef.' She gave a glint of smile.

It was the wrong answer. 'Hardly—'

'What a fascinating insight into how the other half lives.'

He knew from experience not to join in, and yet: 'There are only four of them.'

'Only four?' She laughed. 'Well, I'm so glad I bumped into you. Now I know that you're a gastronome to whom money is no object, I think it might be time *you* had *us* to Sunday lunch. It's not easy for me, coming up with anything decent in that poky little kitchen we all have to squash into. So let's say next Sunday, twelve thirty.'

♩

Annie was, for once, the first to arrive. She sat trembling under the window in Menopause Corner as Sue thumped open the door and stomped over towards her.

'Oh, thank God you're here. She's pregnant,' spluttered Annie. 'She's gone and got herself bloody pregnant.'

'Ooh-ooh-ooh.' Sue was instantly cheered. 'Clue?' She sat down with a force that made the floor shake.

'Jess. My Jess. She's having a baby.'

'Little Miss Perfect?' It sounded to Annie like the beginnings of a hoot coming out of Sue before the gravity of the situation hit her. 'I mean, not Jess of all people? Golly.'

'All that work,' huge dollopy tears rolled down Annie's cheeks, 'to get to that university and she goes and throws it all up in her second term.'

'You poor darling.' Sue took a manky tissue out of her pocket and wiped Annie's face. 'That's tough – especially as she's never given you a moment's trouble till now.'

'Huh. Apart from the tattoo, of course.' Annie sniffed. 'Let's not forget that little drama.'

'Tattoo?' Sue cocked her head and froze, a squirrel at the crack of a twig. 'I didn't hear about a—'

'Sorry. I couldn't face telling anybody. I thought it was just a blip.' The tears rolled out again. 'I didn't know it was part of a whole new lifestyle package.' Annie was waiting, damply, for some wise counsel or calm comfort. She blathered on: 'One week a law student, the next an inked-up single mother.' Normally Sue's mental weather was on display all over her face, which, for some bizarre reason, was looking rather sunny. 'What next, do we suppose – drugs? A cult? Terrorism?'

'Humph.' Sue had at last accumulated enough dark thoughts for a cloud to cross her features. 'But the point is: you're all sorted, aren't you?'

'What do you mean,' Annie dabbed at herself, 'sorted?'

'I mean, this might not be the best thing for Jess, but it's great for you, isn't it? Like a promotion, or being fast-tracked at the airport.

Oh, yes, typical Annie Miller.' She reached into her bag and took out her reading specs. 'Fallen on her feet again. Everyone else munching on the happy pills, moping around their empty nests, searching high and low to find where they might have left their own identity ... And there's you, straight into grannyhood without passing Go.'

'Are you mad?' Annie whispered. 'She's not even twenty. This is not what I wanted for my daughter.'

Sue studied the menu through the glasses on the end of her nose. 'Well, it's her life. She's got to make her own choices ...'

'Choices? Choices? The only choice she seems to have made is to get herself so thoroughly rat-arsed that she was incapable of making any proper choice at all.'

'Tea for two, please, Jasmine. And who is he, the father?'

'He's not a father. He's, I don't know, some passing bloke at a party – facing the right bit of wall at the right time, as far as I can tell. No question of him having anything to do with it.'

'See? Miller's Luck. I can't think of anything worse than having to share my grandchildren. I worry about it all the time. Can't get to sleep some nights. Especially now we're in our own little economic downturn. Supposing we stay broke and the in-laws are loaded? Then where would we be? The other day, I bumped into, oh, what's her name ...'

'Clue?'

'Porridge.'

'Tina.'

'... and she's a terrible case. Her other one gets called "Granny Big House" and she's saddled with "Granny Fish Tank".'

'Granny Fish Tank?' Annie shuddered.

'It's not even an aquarium.' Sue squirmed out of her jacket. 'She's only got a bowl.'

They held a moment's silence.

Sue started up again: 'And as for that every-other-Christmas lark ... Our little sproglets tucking into some stranger's turkey purée? Absolute hell. From here on in you and James will have total, unimpeachable grandparental control. Granny and Grandpa

Big House, always and for ever. No competition.' Sue shook her head. 'Bastards.'

Jazzy unloaded the tea tray on the table in front of them. As Sue poured, Annie turned towards the window and set about repairing her face.

'What does James think about it all?'

'Well, desperate, obviously. Completely desperate. I mean, I haven't seen him since she told us—'

Sue let the teapot down with a thump. 'Haven't *seen* him?'

Annie jumped and turned back to the room. 'Well, he's in London all week these days—'

'Is he just? And what's his excuse for that, exactly?'

'Oh, you know, it's this case ... been going on for ages ...' She took a sip of tea.

'"Case"? Is that what he calls it ...'

'Sue. Stop it.' Annie gulped too quickly, scalding her throat. 'You are ridiculous sometimes ...' She had forgotten what a risky business it could be, confiding in Sue; how sometimes you could end up with your troubles doubled rather than halved. 'Just promise me you won't tell anybody any of this. Please.' She would give the Church Fête Committee meeting a miss on Wednesday and call James; they could have a proper chat about the whole business. He would know what to do and say. And while they thrashed it out, she might just set about spring-cleaning that doll's house ...

The banknotes beneath her crinkled as Tracey rolled back on to her duvet and pulled her pillow over her face. They had found her out; her sins had finally found her out. She had counted her money several times now, yet the total stayed the same. She had to face the truth. The safe, her own private safe, the safe that had been buried beneath her old maternity clothes for the last twenty-odd years, had been raided. There was nearly three hundred quid missing, and while she was going in for this truth-facing lark, she might as well accept another thing: this had happened before. In fact, for a while now, since – coincidentally – around the time that Billy's dope-smoking moved from occasional to habitual, money had been somehow escaping from the only private place she had in her house.

Tracey's world of deceit – that sounded like a theme park; perhaps they would open it one day, in honour of her spectacular crapness – was a multi-layered thing. Once the basic sin had been created – the original, as it were, big bang, ha ha – the lies had then been deposited upon it like the geographical layers of the crust of the Earth. What she needed to work out was: once he had broken into the safe, how many layers had he excavated? How much did Billy now know?

If, as she strongly suspected, he had been going in there quite often, he could know the following:

1. That cash appeared in there on a frequent but erratic basis.
2. That cash was then taken out on a regular-as-clockwork monthly basis.
3. This always happened about twenty-four hours before the same amount fetched up in Billy's bank account.
4. That amount was, or was at least what he had always understood to be, his allowance from his father.

But did he? To get from points 1 to 4 would require methods of deduction – not exactly Holmesian but still active and reasonably sharp. Billy could not, at the best of times, even by devotees such as Curly, Squat and his dear old mum, be described as particularly active or especially sharp. So if, as was possible, his approach to the safe was like his approach to most things – that is, employing the memory and perception of the average goldfish – well then what could he know?

1. That cash appeared.
2. He helped himself.
3. He got away with it.

Tracey took the pillow from her face and started to sit up. That was all, wasn't it? He may only know that—

'Aaaargh.' She shoved the pillow in her mouth and flung herself back down on the bed. How could she not have noticed this before? Every time he had opened that safe to get to the cash, he had to actually pick up and actually move her actual vibrator.

It took a while, but Tracey did gather herself together. She was being silly. So what? It was no big deal. Sex toys were not a sin. She wasn't a nun in the Vatican; she just happened to have the sex life of a nun in the Vatican. Who knew what was stashed under Billy's bed? She had never had the nerve to look. And on the matter of her lies, all was not quite lost. Billy hadn't quite got all the way down. There was still, at the bottom, the final layer, the Mariana Trench of deceit that nobody had quite reached, not yet. But he had picked up enough material to be going on with, that was for sure.

The doorbell rang. That would be Annie, come to collect her. She flung up her window, signalled that she would be right down, bundled up the money and returned it to the safe. Perhaps this was her penance, she thought, as she placed the Magic Wand back on top of the cash. There were all her sins, and there – in Annie, the Choir, the *Sound of Music* medley – was her penance. She sighed and grabbed her coat. At least she didn't have to get the car out.

15

Hell is gone and heaven's here

The Bridgeford Community Choir Talent Show was an annual fund-raising event that had been a fixture in the social calendar for many, many years – possibly more years than its public demanded. The need for funds, of course, had not diminished – it is a fundamental economic principle that in local civic life the need for funds can never diminish – but the talents on offer seemed, sadly, never to change. The St Ambrose Primary School hall had seemed quite buzzy at the beginning of the evening, but now that the singers were up on stage for the opening act, the paucity of the audience was more apparent. The Choir had an unbroken view to the crayoned frieze of THE FOUR SEASONS displayed along the high back wall.

And step and click.

Maria had insisted on free entry for all senior citizens, under-eighteens and the unemployed; the scattering of people out there on the chairs seemed to consist only of senior citizens, under-eighteens and the unemployed. Other members had argued that they ought to pay at least something for a decent show, but Maria had been firm: she knew this lot and if they didn't get in free, they wouldn't bother coming at all.

Now SCREAM

And at least there was someone there to watch them, even if they did look a bit bored.

And clap and turn.

Some went the right way, but just as many didn't. There was a bit of a muddle while they all caught up with each other. They had practised, but for whatever reason it hadn't quite gone in. The truth of it was that, despite the much larger numbers and more consistent attendance, they still weren't functioning quite as a proper choir should. That telepathy they had once enjoyed had long been silent, and there still wasn't the confidence to attempt proper harmony. It turned out that there was more to a choir than just enthusiasm, and their lack of progress was causing a group frustration.

Let me-ee enter-tain you

The applause was thin; if it expressed any emotion at all, it was relief.

'Thank God that's over,' said Lynn as she stomped off the stage.

'I'm up first,' replied Pat. 'Save us a place.'

As the stage was being prepared, Annie came and sat next to Tracey.

'By the way,' she said as she settled herself down, 'I meant to ask you earlier. Any chance you could help down at the protest next week?'

Tracey kept her eyes to the front. Pat's act so far seemed to involve her sitting on a chair on her own with her bag by her feet. This represented no great change from Pat's normal position. 'Sorry. Too busy,' Tracey said out of the side of her mouth. 'Do you think her act is going to be sitting there having a moan till someone brings her a cup of tea?'

'Oh no, she's doing her Knitting Nancy,' replied Annie. 'She does it every year. Anyway, you're not going to be too busy for long, are you? I mean, Billy's off in a couple of weeks, after all. And although they're supposed to be all grown up, you certainly find you have more time on your hands once they've left.' She pressed her lips together and turned her mouth down. 'Believe me.'

'Yes, well,' hissed Tracey, 'if it wasn't for you I wouldn't have to worry about it, would I? You—'

And then Pat was bellowing to them from the stage: 'So, first of all you take your wool. Any thickness will do . . . ' The first act had begun.

Pat's knitting was average in most respects, apart, mercifully, from its speed. And Lewis and Maria's double act – a joint rendition of 'Your Knee Bone's Connected to Your Thigh Bone', delivered while Maria bandaged Lewis up from head to toe – seemed to go down a storm. The under-eighteens, especially, were very amused. So then it was time for Judith, who emerged from the cupboard to the right of the stage and climbed up the steps wearing apparently nothing but a swimming towel.

'As many of you know,' she smiled, and ran her hands through her frizzy ginger hair, 'I have felt an almost overwhelming affinity with the French film star Marion Cotillard—'

'Never heard of her,' heckled Lynn.

'—ever since I discovered that we actually share the same birthday.' She let the towel drop to the floor, revealing a Lycra swimsuit clinging tightly to her ample form. 'You will no doubt remember that last year I did an excerpt from her Oscar-winning Edith Piaf biopic *La Vie en Rose*.'

'Seem to have blocked that one out,' said Pat.

'And tonight I would like to re-enact for you some of my favourite scenes from one of her greatest dramatic films, *Rust and Bone*.'

'Is that a sex film?' asked a senior citizen.

'When I cover a Cotillard, I prefer to do it in the original French, so I would like to ask Kerry to come up on stage and provide tonight's narrative description and simultaneous translation.'

Kerry had joined the Choir as one of the lot from the council, but she and Judith were firm friends now. She beamed with pride as she took her position stage left.

'So Stephanie is, like, this killer-whale trainer in the south of France . . .'

'*Allez, allez, allez.*' Judith started to gesture wildly with her arms, throwing imaginary fish into an imaginary pool. '*Et voilà.*' She smiled and applauded her imaginary whale.

' . . . and she has developed an incredible empathy with this orca. At least, I think it's an orca . . .'

Judith stroked its pretend-nose, pulled back from a splash, laughed and bowed to the audience.

'But today is no normal day at the whale display . . .'

'*Non, non.*' Something very bad was happening on stage, very bad indeed. Judith was flinging herself around, falling down, sliding about, screaming. '*Non, non, non. Sauvez-moi!*'

'This is MENTAL.' Jazzy was standing up, filming it on her phone. 'It's gonna go viral, this is.' The rest of the audience, though, was subdued, squinting at the stage in silent puzzlement.

'Aaargh!' roared Judith, clutching at her leg and losing pretend-consciousness.

Pat passed Lynn a bag of Murray Mints and checked her watch. 'I wonder,' she mused to herself, 'if this will ever end . . .'

They paused for a scene change, assembling a collection of school chairs into a bed, upon which Judith lay down with eyes closed.

'It is after the whale attack, and Stephanie is now in hospital. She has been in a coma for many days, and does not yet know the seriousness of her injuries.'

Judith started to wake, moan quietly and feel around the bed.

'When she finally comes round, she is alone. There is nobody to warn her that she has lost both legs.'

'*Ah non. Qu'est que c'est—*'

Tracey could stand it no longer. She slipped out of the hall on to the balcony and took a few good draughts of clear night air. That was a right collection of prize nutters in there. For twenty-odd years she had deliberately avoided getting to know anyone in the vicinity, for her own, very good, reasons, but even just observing them from a distance she had always suspected they all had a communal screw loose. Now she knew for sure they did, and yet somehow she found herself right in the middle of them. How did that happen? Through the window she could still see Judith, now writhing all over the floor, clearly none too happy with her sudden leglessness – Tracey could hear the Gallic wailing even out here. She turned round, put her fingers in her ears and gazed out over Bridgeford. The lights were all glowing beneath the network of satellite dishes. Everyone seemed to be in for the evening. Tracey looked down at the cosy scene, imagined the kettles being put on, the cheap entertainment being beamed in from all over the world, and felt a surge of irritation. All the organisation that had gone into this so-called talent show, all the efforts of the performers – Judith let out a blood-curdling scream and a torrent of awkward French – the desperate financial state of their own community choir, and there was the rest of the town down there, sunk into its armchairs, with its backs to them.

Occasionally, Tracey found herself having to visit other places during a normal working day. She would alight in the high street of a Home Counties market town, or the corner of some small provincial city that rather fancied itself. She would watch, with detachment, its inhabitants going about their business. And she would want to laugh. The self-importance with which people strutted about their own territory was amusing, of course it was. The way they hurried to and from jobs that didn't really matter, rushed in and out of shops for things they didn't particularly need, ran around in the frantic rearing of children that were never to amount to anything: it was all just part of the human comedy and their own seriousness was, in itself, the biggest joke of all.

Yet somehow, here tonight, it didn't seem so funny. Of course, the chaos of the evening still did have an indisputable dark humour; that nobody could deny. But she, Tracey, had changed. She knew these people now; they had identities; she understood them – well, some of them. She had got used to them, put it that way. She even found, to her surprise, that she cared about a few of them, too. And if Billy really was about to clear off and leave her, she didn't have anybody else in the vicinity to care about. And that meant that she was no longer a critic sneering out from the stalls at the human comedy that was Bridgeford. She now had a part – OK, a bit-part, but definitely a part – in it. Everything felt different. She turned back to the hall, where Judith was bowing and generously applauding Kerry for her efforts. *'Merci, merci, alors, trop gentils ...'* They might be prize nutters, thought Tracey, but they were her prize nutters. And they needed sorting out before their comedy turned very black indeed.

Bennett came out and leaned on the railing beside her. She rolled her eyes at him; he raised his brow at her and together they turned to look out at the view.

'You're right. We can't go on like this,' said Tracey, continuing her train of thought out loud.

'I thought you'd never ask,' he chipped in.

She looked at him sideways. 'Was that a joke?'

'Um ... sorry ... yes, I think it might ...'

'Didn't have you down as the joking type.'

'I'm not, usually,' he admitted. 'Or, um, ever. I think that was a bit of a first.'

'You might want to think twice before having another go.'

'Sorry. Yes. Of course. I do apologise.'

Tracey couldn't quite make this Bennett chap out. He was like no other man she had ever met – and not in that way. It was her observation that you generally only found two sorts of bloke getting involved in communal activities. The loser types, who joined in with great unembarrassed enthusiasm – like Lewis, say. Oh dear, she thought with a pang. Poor Lewis. And then there were the Bennett types – suited, booted and successful, a bit of gravitas – who only got involved out of some moral or historic duty and did so with a perfected air of swaggering yet rigidly detached irony. There weren't any of those in the Choir – that nice GP was a member, apparently, but far too busy to ever turn up. Bennett was the only one who looked the part – but, disconcertingly, he never acted it. There was no swagger, no detachment, and he seemed to be genetically incapable of processing any sort of irony. She couldn't work out quite what he was doing there.

'You wouldn't have a kitchen table for sale, would you?'

'Not on me.' She stared at him. 'Was that another joke?'

'Absolutely not, not at all. I do actually need, rather urgently in fact, a second-hand kitchen ta—'

Tracey held up her hand to stop him, to seize control of their dialogue. 'Back to the beginning: this choir cannot go on like this. This "democracy" lark – it's just another word for a bloody shambles. Everyone in there is making a complete arse of themselves. Seems to me they're all just willing Constance to get better and haven't noticed that week after week she never does. If we really want it to carry on – with or without her – then we need to get organised. Have a structure. Another leader: one person in charge with the authority to tell us all what to sing and when to sing it.'

'I quite agree.'

'Good.'

'And it should obviously be you.'

'Me?' Tracey reared back in alarm. 'Oh, no. No, no, no. I was just suggesting ... I'm not—'

'Of course it should be you.' He looked straight at her with his strange pale eyes. 'You've got the voice and so on ... ' He paused and seemed to consider what he was going to say next. 'Listen. I hope you don't mind me asking this.' Tracey started to feel nervous. 'The thing is, I'm just hopeless with this sort of thing. And I don't want to offend you, not at all.' She stepped back a bit further, pressed into the wall. 'But I know I know you from somewhere.' He gave a little chuckle. 'I mean, I'm hopeless but I'm not that hopeless. The thing is, I just can't remember from where.'

'Ha. Well, I've got good news. You're not hopeless at all. I remember everything and I know for a fact we have never met. So there you are. You can relax.'

'Honestly? But—'

The door of the hall clanged open. 'Hope I'm not interrupting,' trilled Annie.

'Not really.' For once, Tracey viewed Annie's arrival with relief.

'Thought I'd just have a breather before the next act. It's going well, don't you think?' Annie looked down at her list. 'Now that Judith's turn is over we'll be trotting through.'

'What do you think, Annie?' Tracey's hands were trembling. She clasped them behind her back. 'We were just saying it's about time that someone took control of the Choir. We need a leader.'

'Ooh.' Annie frowned. 'Hmm. Gosh. Connie will be back soon, I'm sure. And what about the pure democracy? I think the members rather like the—'

'What are you lot plotting out here?' Jazzy shut the door behind her and felt in her pocket for a cigarette. 'You having Judith put away? Very sensible, Mrs M. She's a serious mentalist.'

'Jazzy, I don't think that's on.' Annie was smiling but her tone was firm. 'You can't smoke on primary-school property.'

'Really? You used to be able to.' She looked around her with a nostalgic air. 'It's where I started, come to think of it. Right down there, on Sports Day.'

Tracey stepped forward, removed the cigarette from Jazzy's fingers and stubbed it out. 'What about your singing voice? What about this career you're always talking about?'

'I was enjoying that,' whined Jazzy. 'And what *about* my career? Nothing wrong with a bit of smoking. Have you never heard of Amy Winehouse?'

'Yes. I have. And I know she's not doing too well.'

'Yeah, but that's not the fags' fault.'

'Why aren't you performing a solo out there tonight, anyway?' asked Bennett. 'We're all very keen to hear you.'

'My solos are for bigger gigs than this.' Jazzy smiled smugly. 'I've got some auditions coming up in the next few months. I'll keep myself pure for them, thanks. Me and Katie are doing a little double act instead. We've been practising.'

The second half was altogether more successful than the first. Bennett, to popular surprise, took himself off to the piano at the back of the hall and played Poulenc's Novelette in C Major. The instrument was not in perfect condition, but Bennett's playing was sublime and the beauty of the piece moved some of the audience to tears. As the final chord died away, they leapt to their feet in ovation.

'Who knew he had that in him?' said Pat. 'And proper music, too. I do like a bit of proper music.'

'A lovely addition,' agreed Lynn. 'And I've just flogged him my old kitchen table.'

Jazzy and Katie's rendition of 'Cups' was not in the same league, but just as moving none the less. Partly because they had clearly been working hard on it and there is nothing like young people trying their best at something – from the Olympics to their homework – to make the older generation just melt inside. And partly because they performed it rather nicely, albeit a little slowly. But mostly because all of that upper-body movement was not easy for Katie and she was pushing herself to her limits up there with every single member of the audience willing her on. Whether she liked it or not, the applause was so deafening at the end that they simply had to do an encore to shut the crowd up. And that meant that there was no time, after all, for Lewis and the lads from the council to do their *Full Monty* routine.

'What a shame,' they all agreed.

'Maybe next time.'

But before the Choir could get up for the joint finale of 'Those Were the Days', Edward – to everybody's surprise – appeared on stage holding a mic, which was attached to a neat, portable sound system.

Time, to say goodbye

He slid his little round glasses, which so many of the ladies found rather adorable, up on to his hair, revealing crinkling blue eyes and angular cheekbones, and then undid another button on his deep-blue shirt.

Paesi che non ho mai

Pat gasped and clutched at her bosom. 'Oh.' She looked over her left shoulder. 'That's *Italian!*' she mouthed helpfully. '*Italian!*' she added, over to the right.

Edward's honed and polished baritone sang down to the hall with a tone of entitlement, its notes tossed out like alms to the poor. A small fortune had gone into that voice; it was obvious to anyone.

Con te partirò su navi per mari che, io lo so

They could hear every lesson, every practice, all those exam grades and recitals and parental applause ... They could hear some natural talent too, to be fair, but it was quite buried beneath the rest of it. Still, you get what you pay for, and clearly it was worth every penny. The audience – well, everyone bar Lewis – was properly impressed. Their own choral rendition of Mary Hopkin was redundant. Edward alone had already taken the show to its climax.

'Oh, bravo!' cried Pat, leaping to her feet in ovation. 'Bravo!' She blew a kiss at the stage. 'Brav-o. Marvellous, that was.' Her hands kept clapping towards the stage and Edward, but she was talking to Lynn and the rest of the sopranos. 'Bloody marvellous.'

Annie was counting up the takings on the table at the door as Bennett wandered past. 'How much did we make?'

'Not a huge amount.' Annie tried a bright smile.

Tracey was leaning against the wall, arms crossed, waiting for her lift. 'If we can top it up with a decent grant from the government, we might get a new box of teabags.'

'Still, on the whole, it was a very good evening.'

'Weirdly enough,' Tracey admitted, 'it was, rather.'

'Quite damp out there, Bennett – can we drop you off at home?'

For once, Annie didn't seem to have anything cumbersome to transport, and her front seat was free. But Tracey and Bennett went straight for the back automatically. It was rather a nice feeling, this, Annie thought as she brought across her seatbelt: driving home after a fun evening out. Like all those disco pick-ups with the girls. She looked at them in the rear-view mirror as she pulled out into the road. 'So did we all have a lovely time?' She had to stop herself asking if there were any nice boys.

'I'm sorry you didn't sing, Tracey,' said Bennett, as if Annie had not spoken. 'I was hoping—'

She flicked him away. 'So, what are we going to do?'

'We must,' Bennett thumped the middle armrest, 'elect a leader forthwith.'

'Gosh,' said Annie in to the rear-view mirror, 'steady on. I'm sure we don't need an *election* as such—'

They ignored her. 'OK, but should we stop at leader? What about treasurer and secretary and events manager and so on? It's ridiculous that the same poor dogsbodies have to do everything for everybody—'

'Oh, I don't really mind,' called Annie, presuming herself to be all the dogsbodies in question. She didn't know who else they could be referring to. There weren't any others as far as she had noticed.

'Good idea.' Bennett whipped pen and envelope out of his pocket and set about drawing up plans on the back of it. 'And I am quite sure you are the person to do it.'

'Really? Me?' asked Annie, flattered. 'Well ...'

But apparently he was addressing Tracey: Tracey who hadn't been there five minutes and couldn't keep a civil tongue in her head half the time; Tracey who couldn't even raise one child without making a total hash of it; Tracey whose son had to be taken under Annie's wing – and God alone knew how there was any room left under Annie's wing – before he could amount to anything at all; Tracey who couldn't even pour milk without missing the wretched cup. *That* Tracey?

'I was thinking about it in the second half there, and what with Billy being packed off to the other side of the world,' Tracey shot what Annie believed her daughters would call 'evils' at the driver's seat, 'and work being quiet, I've decided that yes, all right, I'll give it a go.'

'Fantastic. I'll propose you. And you are the best musician, after all.'

Annie looked back, to check again that they weren't talking to her. They weren't.

'Oh, come on,' scoffed Tracey. 'You're quite the musician yourself.'

Hello? Annie thought. I'm here too. You know, the one with actual perfect pitch? The well-known local tuning-fork? Remember?

'I'm happy to go for treasurer,' said Bennett. 'Get the finances in order straight off. They're all over the place.'

Apparently, they did not remember. And apparently nothing meant the same as it used to any more.

'Brilliant.' Tracey sounded quite fired up. 'OK, this is me. Thanks, Annie.'

Annie drew in outside Tracey's garage, feeling extremely put out.

16

There was an interesting percussional effect whenever Annie knelt down these days. She stood up and went down again, to have a proper listen. C-r-r-r-r-r-r-r-r-r: there it was, like that satisfying first crunch into a fresh Hobnob. She could have done something with that at the Talent Show, if she had noticed sooner. Ow. It did hurt rather. James would have to put the doll's house back up on a table somewhere at the weekend – she couldn't be doing this every five minutes, her knees couldn't take it. Now she was down, she had better stay down.

Last week she had sorted out all the bedrooms; tonight it was the turn of the nursery. She reached in and started to take the furniture out, piece by piece. There was the little baby, flung to the back there. She rummaged around for the pram, put the baby in, covered it with a blanket and popped her into the wooden painted garden for a sleep. A sense of calm came over her. Back in real life, those were some of her happiest moments – getting on in a busy way with domestic tasks while an infant snoozed somewhere. It had a time-less essence of purpose and usefulness to it; a William Morris–style organic beauty. Now then, did these walls just need a wash, or a full repaper?

The phone rang; she leaned back, picked it up off its base and tucked it under her ear.

'What you up to there?'

'Just sorting some stuff out, love.' She lined up the little fireplace against the wall.

'Great. Can I order a skip? Are we at last having a clear-out of The Museum?'

'No. I said sorting, not chucking.' It worried her sometimes, how James always wanted to throw things away, destroy all evidence of the miracle that was their family. While she devoted so much time to preserving, cherishing, cataloguing for the future, he was never happier than when he was lighting a bonfire or filling a bin. Was he trying to wipe the slate clean? Did he want to somehow create the impression that their wonderful history had never happened? 'How are you?'

'Busy.' There was a rustle in the background. 'And not really sleeping. You know. I must say, it all takes some getting used to. I just wish I could get through to her, but she won't pick up or reply ...'

'Not to me, either.'

'It just wasn't what was expected, I suppose ...' His voice sagged under the weight of his disappointment.

'Sue says we're lucky. It's Miller's Luck.'

'And how does she come to that conclusion?' A fridge door opened with a suck. 'Sue has the most extraordinary talent to work up jealousy of almost anything if you give her long enough. How would she feel if it was Angostura, hm?'

Annie sighed and put a wooden pink blancmange on the little table. He knew full well what the girl was called, but he flat refused to use it. Personally, Annie thought Araminta was a lovely name and, if she had been married to anyone else on earth, she might have given it to one of her daughters. She would have gone even crazier than that – the wilder the better. Partly because, at that moment of birth, her babies had all seemed so simply extraordinary that an extraordinary moniker was the least they deserved. And partly because she had never quite got over being called Ann. She wasn't even called Anne, for heaven's sake. And the 'ie' she walked around with now, well – that was pure absurd, extravagant affectation on her part. The fact that her own parents had taken one look at her and said, 'Ann' had always rather hurt. Was one simple e too much for her? Did they actually doubt whether she could carry it off? She was never going to be extraordinary after that. She was done for.

'Bet she'd be pretty bitter' – James had kept the Angostura puns running, very happily, since for ever. It was interesting that he always wanted to clear perfectly useful stuff out of the house as quickly as possible, when he could keep a rather bad joke going for eighteen years – 'if her daughter was mixing with the wrong sort.' There was at that moment a tap, then a sort of slurp.

James was from the Annie's parents' school of baby names: the plainer and more straightforward the better. Even the battles for Lucy, Rosie and Jessica had been pretty intense; each had at least one unnecessary syllable, in James's opinion. She put a curled-up black cat in front of the nursery fireplace and as she did so her heart gave a private, shy little bounce. It might not be long before we're all picking names again; there was a thought.

'Anyway,' sighed James. Annie thought she heard a thump then a snap, like the breaking of a bone. 'I suppose I'd better be getting on.'

'Must you, darling? Really?' She had flaked out on the Parish Council AGM this week to talk properly to her husband, and as far as she was concerned they had barely begun. 'Now what's so urgent?'

'Sorry, my love.' Something in the background was at the point of a rolling boil. 'It's this case. Won't last for ever. I'll call you tomorrow. Have a lovely evening.' James blew a kiss and hung up.

Annie stared at the phone for a bit, frowning. There was a quiz programme on the television when she was growing up called *Ask the Family*, which she used to love – mostly because she was pretty brilliant at it. She used to sit at home with her mum, both of them shouting their answers at the screen, bouncing on the sofa with glee. If they had gone on it, they would have won, Annie was sure of that, but it could never happen. Each team was made up of that traditional post-war social construct, the family of four, and for some reason she was just a member of an anachronistic, inadequate, rather woeful family of three. Annie never found out why. All she did know was that her parents produced one, unextraordinary baby, gave it the plainest name they could come up with in the time available, and stopped right there. She had always felt a little hard done by because of it – deprived of a sibling, denied that crucial extra syllable and, most painful of all, precluded from ever going on *Ask the Family*. She opened up the doll's house kitchen and repositioned the little Aga.

Annie could answer most questions on that show, but the round she was best at was the Mystery Sounds – when they played the audio of regular, everyday things and you had to identify them. She had an almost perfect record, in fact – aural memory was, apparently, one of the few areas in which she was not completely ordinary – and it was for this reason that she felt, right now, rather perplexed.

For the last thirty years, James had rented, for almost nothing, the little attic of a distant relative's house in Clapham. The idea was that, when work was intense, he could stay up in town and not wear himself out with the commute; the reality, though, was different. When the girls were at home, he actually came back every night. Annie would take each nightly menu as seriously as a dinner party; the conversation didn't just flow, it overflowed, and James just couldn't bear to miss out. So what had happened? Now there were no children at home, he was suddenly staying up all week and had almost no time to talk to her, even.

It was years since Annie had been to that little bedsit, and she couldn't quite picture James in there now, or imagine what he might be up to. But she knew what she heard and she knew she was right about it. A packet had been opened. Something had been butchered, she was almost certain with a cleaver – a lobster was split or a chicken spatchcocked, she couldn't quite distinguish between the two. And an egg had been broken.

And therein lay the mystery. Annie had known James for so long, and in such depth, that he was just another part of her. It had been decades since he had surprised her, and she liked it like that. Who wanted a marriage of shocks and surprises? Not Mrs A. Miller, thanks awfully. So she knew, like she knew the bald patch on the back of his head and the varicose vein behind his knee, that he was completely incapable of splitting a lobster, let alone spatchcocking a chicken. She knew that it had been many, many years since he had cracked an egg – in fact, could not at that moment recall him ever having done so. And last time he was even seen opening a packet, indeed, he was a much younger man, with no varicosity in sight. There was a lovely set of miniature copper saucepans somewhere that her godmother had given her for her tenth birthday – now where had they got to? Annie opened the roof of the doll's house and rooted around to see what was hidden in the attic.

And as she did so, she reflected on the past half-hour – all those clues, all her solutions, and where these things had got her. And it seemed to come down to this: if James wasn't cracking that egg and spatchcocking that chicken, then who the bloody hell was in there doing it all for him?

The phone rang again and she relaxed immediately. He was calling back, coming clean, had more to say. Really, she could be mad sometimes. As if James, of all people . . .

'Hi, love.'

'Mrs Miller, it's Ravi.' There was the sharp clatter of a call centre in the background.

'Ravi! How lovely to hear from you.'

'I just wanted to say: thanks to you, I've had a bit of good news . . .'

17

Bennett reached into the pocket of his apron and took out a few pegs. He stuck them in his mouth then took them out, one by one, to fix the corners of a sheet to the line. The day was cold but the sun bright and the breeze brisk. He stood for a moment with the light on his face and watched the wind catch the linen and toss it up against the blue sky. It brought to mind a *Swallows and Amazons* sail, and with that little memory his heart gave a skip. Smiling, he bent to pick up the wash-basket and busy off back to the kitchen. Heavens, was that the time? The morning was running away with him. So many jobs left to do . . .

He tightened his pinny, ran cold water in the sink, tipped out a bag of potatoes and set to with a peeler, humming. Last week marked his fourth month of unemployment and, he worked out, the longest stretch of consecutive time that Bennett had spent at home since his boyhood. He was eight when his parents first sent him to boarding school, he was to turn fifty in a couple of weeks, and for that whole chunk of his life, home had been just another place he visited sometimes. Like every other location in his life – the school dorm, chapel, the holiday cottage they always took in

Devon; then university, then the office, and the offices of others, the holiday house they always took in the Dordogne – it was a fixed point in his universe, which he knew very well but to which he did not really belong.

Those first few terms away at school, he would come home so excited, desperate to know everything that had happened without him, wanting to bury himself in its day-to-day business, roll around in domestic facts like a dog trying to change its scent. But he soon gave that up. After they put on the Christmas bazaar without him – he used to love that Christmas bazaar, especially the lucky dip in sawdust; could it really not wait? – and had the cat put to sleep – he didn't really love the cat, at least not as much as the bazaar, but still the lack of consultation was the final proof that he was no longer considered quite 'inner circle' – he came to accept that home life went on very pleasantly without him.

As an adult it was the same. In fact – he counted the number of peeled potatoes with the point of a knife – it had been even worse. At least, as a child, he had managed eight years as an important player in home life; but for the past twenty-five, he had only had a walk-on part. He walked out first thing in the morning, walked back in quite late at night, and hovered around getting in the way at weekends. Looking back, he saw himself rather like a human in *Tom & Jerry* – faceless, anonymous, occasional; a pair of legs saying irrelevant things. Crucial, in that without the provision of a nice house neither Tom or Jerry nor Sue or the kids would have any sort of life at all; but at the same time unnecessary because all the important action went on in his absence.

He dropped the potatoes into the saucepan and lit the gas, then opened the oven for a quick check. A satisfying sizzle and delicious aroma assaulted his senses. Basting the meat, he licked his lips: chicken, lemon and thyme – that was happiness, wasn't it? He put it back in the oven and went over to the fridge to check on his syllabub. A perfect set. Araminta was going to love that – more happiness. How much happiness did one chap have the right to expect? Time to pod the peas, which he might do sitting down at the new kitchen table. Good to take the weight off – what a busy morning. He slipped his feet out of his shoes and got popping.

What a shame that the 1950s housewife had become quite such a maligned species. Of course, he understood why. It wasn't that he wasn't a feminist, oh no. If Araminta came to him and said she wanted to keep house for some chap he would be furious. She was as good as – no, much better than – any boy. She had a great future ahead of her. If she should ever, in this endless series of national testing, actually ever finish taking – and doing brilliantly in – exams she could go out into the world and claim it. He was really thinking more of himself. He, Bennett, would really rather relish the life of a 1950s housewife.

Of course, he might still be in some post-traumatic psychosis. He had, after all, suffered major unhappinesses recently – separation from his family, the humiliation of unemployment. And yet he found in his new life so much minor happiness – the cooking of a meal, trotting about the High Street, watching the sheets dry off in the wind – and moments of an unfamiliar pride that seemed to compensate for so much. He didn't miss his work at all. Indeed, he found more passion and involvement in the Anti-Superstore campaign and the Bridgeford Community Choir than he had ever felt in any professional projects. There were the elections coming up, and the competition after that – so much to look forward to. Admittedly, he missed Araminta with a permanent biting pain, like a stitch in his side, but what else was he lacking? His relationship with Casper was a happy, less passionate thing, which could be picked up or rested down with ease at any moment, so that was fine. That just left Sue – he put his shoes back on and took the peas over to the side – and the question of how much exactly he was missing her.

He stood for a moment, bit his lip and then suddenly remembered: he had quite forgotten to do the carrots.

Sue noticed it as soon as she was through the back door. 'What. Is. That?'

Bennett was prepared. It might look like a literal kitchen table, but it was in fact a metaphorical diplomatic tightrope, too. For the past two days, he had thought of little else. He had game-played it every which way he could think of and he faced this *dénouement* with total confidence. This kitchen table was conflict-proof.

'Where did you get it?' Sue ran her hand over the surface: good, but not mint condition.

Araminta was beside him with her arms wrapped around his neck. 'I bought it off someone called Lynn.' Second-hand – no store of which she could disapprove.

'Lynn.' She looked up sharply. 'Lynn? You mean Shopping Lynn?'

'Well, Lynn, I don't know, um, oldish Lynn ...'

'Exactly: Shopping Lynn.' She rolled her eyes at his ignorance. 'So what's she doing now, poor Shopping Lynn? Now you've turned up and taken her table?'

'She'd already bought a new one,' Bennett shot back, rubbing his daughter's back. 'This was in her garage.'

Who could possibly object – a table from a garage? It was wartime thrift, it was make-do-and-mend, it was housewife economics. Winston Churchill, Margaret Thatcher, even Susan St John Parker herself could only approve.

She sniffed. 'What on earth did you choose a white one for?'

'Oh.' Bennett looked down at his table, deflated. 'It was the only one she had.'

♫

'So.' They were all squashed round the table now; Sue was surprised it was so small and had already mentioned this a few times. Bennett needed to change the subject. 'I met your old swimming teacher.'

'No way! Which one? Not miserable old Pat?' Araminta shrieked.

'Old Patters? Fabulous.' Casper struck the table. 'She still on the go?'

'What is she, like, a woolly mammoth?' More hooting.

'Well, Mum did say you'd have a new girlfriend by now.' Shriek, guffaw.

Bennett had a flicker of curiosity as to whether they got on this well all the time, or just when he was here. Then he noticed Sue's face.

'How do *you* know *Pat*?' Her smile was bright, but her voice chilly.

'The Choir—'

'You're actually *going* to that?'

'Well, yes. I thought it was your idea . . . '

'It was.' Sue pierced a carrot with her fork. 'To go just the once. I didn't expect you to want to go back.'

'Casper,' he tried another subject, 'how's work?' He was a natural for estate agency, his boy – charming, sunny, keen, brilliant with people, could talk anybody into anything. Bennett often wondered if he was really his child.

'Lots coming on the market, that's for sure. All of Bridgeford seems to be selling up. Where to find the buyers from, though – that's the question . . . '

Sue looked bored. She was against Casper's choice of work, still grievously disappointed that he hadn't gone to university. As she so often pointed out, all of Annie's children had gone to university. Talk to him, Bennett, she was always saying. Tell him, just tell him. And Bennett did have a go, but his heart wasn't in it. If he had a son who actively wanted a job and was desperate to earn his own living, well, that seemed to him something of a minor miracle. He was hardly going to meddle with it, try to make water out of wine. Why would anyone do that? And besides, Bennett was now finding his son's line of business really rather interesting.

'There is a lot of uncertainty about, what with the new superstore and—'

'Sorry,' Sue interrupted. 'What was that?'

'Well . . . ' Bennett reached for more potatoes. Very nice meal this was – slightly more successful than the one Sue made the other week, in his opinion. 'I've been going down to the sit-in most days and got to know all the protesters down there, and they were saying—'

'You've been WHERE?' Sue put her knife and fork down. She seemed to have lost her appetite.

'Good on you, Dad,' Araminta cut in. 'And this is yu-um, by the way.'

'The latest commission we got this week was,' Casper inter-rupted, looking around the table, 'promise you won't tell anyone: the Copper Kettle.'

'NO!' Both parents were equally shocked.

'I go there practically every day,' wailed Sue. 'Everyone who is left in bloody Bridgeford goes there every day.'

'Yes, well, he's selling up, the old guy.' Casper seemed rather excited about it. 'And if we do get that huge retail park, he might as well. The best thing for all those shops in the High Street is to get planning permission to go residential. That's the future for all town centres, I reckon. The old CK will make a very desirable prop-erty.'

'But they can't do that.' Bennett was outraged, really properly outraged. 'That's where Jazzy works. That's a disaster. Oh God. That poor girl. It's just one thing after the other. What is she sup-posed to do now?'

'Jazzy? Pat? Lynn? THE PROTESTERS? Well, get you.' Sue's face was bright red now, her neck all hot and mottled. 'Aren't you just the Bridgeford socialite? You'll be throwing a bloody party next.' They all roared at that one, although Sue's laugh was more of a sharp-edged cackle.

'Oh. For my fiftieth, you mean?' A vision of a little drinks do started to form in his mind. He saw a few of his new friends, a couple of acquaintances, some nice wine ... perhaps a bowl of nuts?

'DAD! You HATE parties! Have you gone COMPLETELY INSANE?'

'Oh yes, go on, go ahead.' Sue waved her arms about. 'Hey – get the caterers in.' She was radiating heat like a three-bar fire. 'Put a sodding marquee up in the BLOODY BACK GARDEN. Make it FANCY-FUCKING-DRESS, why don't you?' She grabbed a tea-towel and stormed off through the back door. Bennett felt quite shaken, but his children, he noticed, had barely reacted. Casper reached for another helping and Araminta returned quite calmly to her spit ends. Was this what she was always like these days? Perhaps it was nothing new. Perhaps – he couldn't quite recall – this was what she always used to be like back in their day.

'Anyway,' Araminta sighed, 'what's all this about a clothes rail?'

Bennett started to clear the plates; he was unsure how to answer. 'Well,' he parried, 'it's just a clothes rail.'

'Didn't go down too well.' She flicked her eyes towards the garden – where Sue was marching up and down flapping a tea-towel at her face – and up to the heavens before returning them to her hair. 'Seen as a bit permanent.' She put on her mother's head-mistress voice. '"Moving on", that's what she said.'

Bennett was rather loving – almost luxuriating in – this us-against-her intimacy; it was such a beautiful part of their relationship and they hadn't done it for so long. But he was simul-taneously determined to put the record straight.

'But it's not! Not at all!' His voice was raised in excitement. 'With the easy-glide light aluminium telescopic bar system, it can be erected or dismantled at a moment's notice—'

'Dad.' Araminta gave him a baleful look. 'Stop. Enough. You're being really, really boring.'

Sue came back in, restored. Her colouring had returned to normal and she was even smiling.

'I forgot that I've got some top-secret news too, that you mustn't tell anyone.' She plucked a potato as the bowl passed her nose on the way to the sink. 'Annie's Jess is ... pregnant!'

'That's nice,' said Bennett, turning the tap on. He'd been think-ing of getting a pet. 'Puppies.'

Sue laughed, joyously. That was clearly more like it: Bennett getting everything round his neck as usual. She much preferred that. All his sins were immediately forgotten. 'Jess is not a dog, love. She is Annie's youngest, whom you have known literally since the day of her birth.'

They were all in fits.

'Aha!' Bennett reached for the washing-up liquid, so pleased to be innocently amusing for once. 'That makes more sense. I really didn't quite get the whole issue with the tattoo—'

'She told you' – oh dear – 'about the tattoo?' Sue was red again.

18

Tracey needed to get over to the printer on the other side of the room, but it was hard to navigate, with Billy and the contents of the Leckford stairwell all over the floor. She leapt over a few bin bags and landed where Billy was sitting. He had a packet of labels in his lap, a permanent marker in his hand and his tongue out the side of his mouth – evidently he was deep in unfamiliar concentration.

'Sixty quid?' she spluttered as she read his childish handwriting. 'You're trying to charge sixty whole quid for a rowing machine as old as the Ark?'

Billy looked up, lost and baffled. 'Not enough? They were loads more on Amazon, and that was without delivery . . . '

'They were probably new, love. Also,' she sounded like a nursery teacher, 'people don't come to garage sales for commercial prices. They'll be expecting a bargain, you see.'

'Ah.' His face cleared, and he lifted his marker. 'Sixty p, then? That more like it?'

She stared at him for a bit, hoping to discern a trace of irony, a cheeky glint in his eye, then surrendered. No glint, cheeky or other-wise; irony-free. Sixty pounds, sixty pence – hey, sixty grand, sixty million – who cared? What was the difference? None, apparently, if you never had to think about earning it.

'Tell you what,' he conceded, in the firm tones of an experienced chap blessed with a remarkably sound business sense, 'I'll put it up to one pound thirty, because the lava lamp is a fiver.'

Tracey stared at him for a bit, wondering – not for the first time – what on earth went on in that pretty head of his. Still, he wasn't going to be her problem for much longer; he was Africa's. Poor Africa – drought, disease and now Billy Leckford. It was, as so many so often said, a beautiful but benighted continent. She would feel a bit guilty, if it wasn't all meddling Annie Miller's fault.

Tracey picked up the lyric sheets and put them in her bag. She was feeling – what was she feeling? Not nervous, of course, and certainly not excited. Christ, no, definitely not excited. Jittery, perhaps. Yes, she was feeling jittery. Bennett had sent her an email – man of action he was, all of a sudden – telling her to pick a song to suit everybody, adapt it and prepare to teach before the election in the tea break. And much to her own surprise, she had found herself – possibly for the first time in decades – actually doing what she was told. She felt she had no choice. This time next week, Billy would be on his way, her stairs would be empty and so, she had to admit, would her ... well, her ... what was the word she was after ... something like, she wasn't sure ... Was it, possibly, 'life'?

She grabbed her coat, called goodbye to Billy, who was too busy to look up – another man of action, she was surrounded by them all of a sudden – and headed out of the door.

19

Uh. Stomp. *Uh*. Stomp. *Uh*. Stomp. *Uh*. Stomp.

One of Jonty's many innovations was the introduction of warm-ups from around the world. He had a book of them, of which he was rather proud. Tonight, they all had their right arms raised by their right ears and were marching in a circle, right foot first, around the hall while reciting a deep, chesty chant. It was, Jonty informed them, a bonding ritual favoured by the herdsmen of Lapland; so far the people of Bridgeford were not terribly keen. Annie winced every time her right foot went down. The gang from the council were making fun of the whole thing. Pat and Lynn were sitting it out – they refused to leave their handbags unattended, because frankly you never knew, and it was tricky being a Lapp herdsman with a bag on your arm – and Jazzy was refusing in solidarity with Katie, even though Katie was being wheeled around and chanting with the rest of them. Tracey was doing it but with a half-hearted, eye-rolling, lip-curled surliness that broadcast her own displeasure. She was wearing skinny jeans and a skimpy grey T-shirt that rode up her back as she marched.

Uh. Stomp. *Uh*. Stomp.

Meanwhile, Lewis was sitting slumped in his chair, staring vacantly into space. He was a busted flush; a spent force. The glorious era of true democracy was finished and all he was left with were the shattered pieces of his utopian dream. Bennett was in the corner, receiving the names of candidates for the forthcoming break-time elections.

Uh. Stomp. *Uh.* Stomp.

The rest of them all turned to the centre, pointed their antlers at one another, gave one last guttural, Lappish sort of *Aaaagh,* found their places in the circle and settled down.

Lewis had tried to start the session with the latest health bulletin from Constance, with one last entreaty to give her another week, but he was howled down – howled down quite loudly, indeed. Having introduced people power to the singers, he now had good cause to regret it. They had embraced the concept all right, but this was the wrong sort of people power entirely. This, this *mess*, was not what he had ever had in mind. There they were, clattering off in the grip of some pathetic, misguided self-determination that could only end in disaster, when what they should have been doing was exactly whatever Lewis wanted them to do.

Jonty played the opening chords of *Sweeney Todd*, and Lewis shook his head in despair. Then Bennett shot a sharp look across the hall to Tracey and she leapt to her feet.

'Actually' – she walked over to the piano and put the music on the stand – 'I thought we might try a slightly different style tonight. If nobody minds.' She passed around the lyrics and stood in the middle. 'And if we can just rearrange the chairs a bit, it would be great to try a bit of harmony.'

There was a lot of excited approval as they separated into their voice parts, and a sceptical scowl from Lynn. 'What's all this, then? Modern, is it?' Then she looked down at the lyrics and let rip a squeal of delight. 'Oh, look. Oh, hooray! Oh, he's back!' she shouted across to Pat.

'WHO'S THAT, LOVE?' bawled Pat. They were finding it hard to judge the new distance between them.

'The Lord! We thank Him at the end of the first verse. Oh, I am pleased.' She settled back into her seat with a satisfied wriggle. 'I was worried for a moment there, I don't mind saying. But now,' she announced, to general indifference, 'I am pleased.'

People get ready . . .

Tracey sang through the first verse with soul and passion.

. . . there's a train comin'

By the tea break, she had taught half the song in three parts. And there was a beautiful harmonious sense in the room that not only were they all on board, but for once they were travelling in the same direction.

'OK,' said Bennett, taking to the centre of the circle and twirling his specs in his left hand. He was wearing a maroon cardigan for a change, which – deliberately or by happy coincidence – gave him a politico-back-room-boffin sort of air. 'Two pieces of major political news this evening.'

Lewis harrumphed: 'Oh yes – you defecting to UKIP? You know the way out . . .'

'The first is that next Tuesday there is going to be a significant event down at the London Road site. The protesters are expecting the developers to move in sometime that afternoon, so anybody who can be there, please, please join us. This might be our last chance to fight back. It is a crucial day for the future of Bridgeford, and anyone who can be there should be there.'

Lewis couldn't argue with that, so he sulked instead.

'And the second is: tonight is the night for the election of new choir officers. Polling is to take place over in the corner there, on top of the pre-school's fancy-dress box.' Bennett looked grave. 'Ballot papers are available from Pat, our returning officer – thank you, Pat, for giving up your break this evening.' Pat looked important. 'And the eagerly awaited results will be announced by Pat in the meeting next week. Is that right, Pat?'

'I think so, love. I'll have to take them home with me. I can't really count all of them tonight and I didn't bring my proper glasses.'

'We'll have Dimbleby and the pundits on the telly before that, though, won't we?' shouted a bass. 'Live from the count? *Election Special*?'

'And have those pinkos from the BBC all over my nice kitchen?' Pat shuddered. 'I should very much think not.'

'And what about the exit polls?'

'I urge you,' Bennett, still solemn, raised his hand and his voice to quell the hilarity, 'to ignore all exit polls. They are not to be trusted.'

'Remember April '92.' Lewis was now almost on the verge of tears.

'Here,' Jazzy cut in. 'That's enough. We're not all bloody ancient.'

'Thank you, thank you. Shall we settle down now.' Bennett's voice was louder still. 'Refreshments are available and the polling booth is now ... OPEN.'

He came and sat down next to a less-than-impressed Tracey. 'Great. Masterful. Well done,' she said, rolling her eyes.

'Thanks,' he replied sincerely, before whispering out of the side of his mouth, 'Just to tip you off, there is competition ...'

'Oh. Yes. Good. Of course.' She nodded, and then dropped her voice to a hiss. 'I thought you said there wouldn't be anybody.'

'It's fine. Nothing to worry about. Emma has nominated Edward for leader, and Edward has nominated Emma for treasurer, that's all. Don't panic. They don't even live in Bridgeford ...'

'Right.' She looked over to the fancy-dress box, where an orderly queue was forming.

'Real democracy in action.' He patted her arm. 'The best man will win.'

Annie was pouring tea with her shoulder to Pat and the polling booth. These elections seemed to be going on despite and without her; she was emitting an atmosphere of short shrift.

'So I've heard your news,' said Maria as she took a cup. '*One gran, one gra-a-an.*' She did quite a good Bob Marley. '*Trust A-nnie Miller to be just one gran.*'

'How did you hear that? Maria, keep your voice down. Please. It's a secret.' She piled some Jammie Dodgers on a plate.

'From my years as a health professional,' said Maria, helping herself to a handful, 'I know that babies don't stay secret for very long ... Oh, hello, Tracey. You've got my vote.'

'Thanks, Maria. Can I take one for Lewis as well, ta.' Tracey piled in some sugars. 'I thought you'd go in for secretary, Annie. That's your sort of thing, isn't it? Admin, notices, lists ... knowing what everybody's up to ...'

'Did you? And where did you think I'd find the time for that?' Annie hissed, slamming down the teapot. 'Has it ever actually occurred to you that I don't *want* to do every boring little thing around here for everybody?' She picked up a tea-towel and dried her hands. 'That I'm not, in fact, a control freak? That I only do it because nobody else will, and if I don't do it *everything will fall to pieces*?' They stared at one another, Annie and Tracey, eyeball to eyeball – on the brink of social catastrophe. But then Annie saw her girls from the altos in the queue just behind Tracey, and as if nothing had happened she set about chatting with and pouring for them.

Jazzy barged up next to Tracey. 'Let's have a selfie, seeing as how you're practically famous. Smile.' She held up her phone and the flash went off. 'Everyone's voting for you, you know.'

'Even me,' chipped in Lynn, on her way back for more biscuits. 'We haven't all had our heads turned.'

'Jazzy, love,' said Maria through a Jammie Dodger, 'how's it all going at home? Your mum settling in, is she?'

'Um, yeah, think so.' Jazzy nodded and looked thoughtful, which didn't happen that often. 'It's all going OK, ta. You know, I think we're fine.'

Meanwhile, over at the polling station, Edward was resting his bottom on the table and regaling a delighted Pat with some quite long anecdotes. She barely seemed to notice when the ballot papers were returned to her. Her bag was open and, from time to time, without counting, checking or even looking at them, she shoved another batch in.

'And what are we doing for the second half?'

'More of the same, surely.'

'Yes, Tracey, get back there. Let's finish what we started for once.'

There are some songs that – by some extraordinary chemical reaction or miracle – work for just everyone. And that night, in the Coronation Hall, Curtis Mayfield's 'People Get Ready' was one of them. With the voices of the Bridgeford Community Choir, under the direction of Tracey Leckford, it turned into something wonderful. Section by section, one by one, different background by different background, they all climbed right on board. *I'm ready*, sang the pop fans; *I'm ready*, sang the opera lovers; *I'm ready*, sang the voices that were trained to praise their Lord. Together they stood, hips slowly rocking, bodies gently swaying, voices aiming up to heaven.

This time

It was that gorgeous, rounded, completed sound that only harmony can create.

This time

Every gaze was focused on Tracey and still it was not possible to sing that word without a smile.

This time ...

They sang as one voice, moved as one body.

... I'm ready.

The roar of applause could be heard all over Bridgeford.

'There's our opener for the contest, then.'

'I feel sorry for the opposition.'

'Oh, Tracey, amazing.'

'Night, Trace. And thanks, wow, really thanks so much.'

'Best ever, Tracey. Until next week.'

'I think I'm right in saying,' said Bennett, wrapping his mac over one arm and tucking a brolly under the other, 'that what you did in there is commonly referred to in modern parlance as "nailing it".'

'Hey, Bennett, listen to you. May I be the first to welcome you into the twenty-first century?' Tracey bobbed her head in deference as she walked backwards away from him. 'And thank you very much. I really enjoyed it.'

'You should start planning next week and come up with a full set for the Championships. If you want to talk any of it through, do get in touch.' He held up his hand in farewell and set off towards Priory Lane.

Tracey turned, gave a little jump, clicked her heels together in mid-air and fairly sprang up the hill towards home.

20

If, a year or two previously, you were to cast a dispassionate eye upon the London Road site of the proposed new Bridgeford superstore, you would not have thought it likely to be the focus of any fuss. It was a wide, open space, yes, but nobody could argue it to be a thing of beauty. It had been hanging around aimlessly on the side of the main road for ages, like it had missed the last bus and was too knackered to walk. It had never been developed, but had ceased to be green years ago. When it came on the market, it was of no use or interest as anything to anybody, apart from the odd stray dog or a particularly unambitious bit of tumbleweed.

But look upon it on the day that the developers were to come face to face with the protesters and you could look dispassionately no more. Sure, it was still a rubbish bit of land, but that was no longer the point. The Gaza Strip is, underneath it all, a rubbish piece of land, but it matters. To the people who are on and around it the Gaza Strip matters enormously. And yes, the wider world cares about it very much too. And OK, no lives were in danger there in Bridgeford, no rockets were being fired or bombs being dropped and the wider world could not have cared less. But still: to the people who lived around it, the London Road site had come to matter enormously, too.

Nobody was as surprised at the depth of passion of the Anti-Superstore protest as the Anti-Superstore protesters themselves. Who knew they gave a monkey's what happened to that bit of dirt over there? They certainly didn't. That little core of eco-warriors, sitting around that fire, giving it the odd poke? They weren't even eco-warriors before the planning permission went in. That man in waterproofs, who got up to shake Bennett by the hand? That was the assistant manager of the bank in the High Street. He had never been known to opine on the environment, or indeed any other subject, before this blew up, but there he was. He had taken a week of his precious annual leave to be down there for this crucial moment.

The ever-wise Joni Mitchell once warned us, in exactly this context – paradise, you may remember, and parking lots – that *you don't know what you've got till it's gone.* Well, it was Bridgeford's good fortune that, in this instance, they realised just before it was about to go. As soon as the land came under threat, indeed: that was when the concerned citizens realised what it meant to them; that it was the only barrier left between Bridgeford and the rest of the world; that they could stand at the bottom of their own high street and see straight through and over it and beyond it. If they angled themselves one way, they were rewarded with a scene of rolling downs and enclosed fields, a doily of white sheep on the green. And if they swivelled to the other, they got the pylons and developments that were bursting out of the next big town. And if that was filled in, well, then what? What would Bridgeford look out on then? They would see nothing but a structure in the ranch style indigenous to some tranche of Middle America. And a petrol station and, rumour had it – rumour was now well into overdrive – a multi-storey car park. These developers thought they were actually going to pave paradise and put up a parking lot, did they? And meld their town into the next one and take away its very edges? Oh no, they weren't. Not if Bridgeford could help it.

There were more people turning out right then today than ever turned out for the Remembrance Day parade or to support the football club. The original little band of protesters had put out its social tentacles and gathered all sorts of different interest groups together: there were members of the church, the running group, the chamber of commerce, the Round Table, the bowls club, the Girl Guides and, of course, the Community Choir. They were all bound together in pursuit of the one cause, and passions were running high.

'Here, Curly, so you definitely reckon there'll be trouble? We're not wasting our time here?' There were some bystanders, it was true. Curly Jenkins, Billy's friend, had been present throughout the history of the protest, not because he cared one way or the other but because he had to set up a car-washing place somewhere or his mum would be after him, and when he fetched up down here, nobody asked him for rent or threatened to throw him out. Unfortunately, nobody ever asked to have their car washed either. That was often the trouble with eco-warriors, even novices like these: on the whole, they didn't drive their cars into battle. But Curly hadn't worked that bit out – and anyway he wasn't really bothered. As long as he could say to his mum he ran a car-wash service, then she'd get off his back. He had high hopes for today – riot shields, petrol canisters, bit of a laugh – and had imported a few mates for the afternoon to enjoy it with him.

And Jazzy's nan, in her wheelchair with a flask and a packet of sandwiches in her lap, was here to make a day of it too. 'Park me here, Angela. There's a good view here. That's it. Hello, love. How can I help you?'

Chrissie from 'News from Your Neighbourhood' was crouching next to her with a mic in her face. 'And over here is one of the town's more senior residents. Tell me, what brings you down here to the protest today?'

'Well, love, when you're my age, it's just nice to get out, isn't it? A nice day out. And there's no steps or anything, perfect disabled access, you've got to hand it to them, wheeled in no trouble. Oh, it is nice to see so many people. I don't get to see so many people any more ...'

'And why are you so against the building of the new superstore?'

She started to fiddle with the greaseproof paper around her sandwich. 'Oh, I'm not against the superstore, love. Oh no. I'm really looking forward to that. Have you looked at the prices in that place in the High Street? Robbery.' She bit into her cheese and pickle. 'Daylight bloody robbery. And they never have my diabetic chocolate or my magazine.' Chrissie held her mic back from the loud chewing. 'Be nice to get some proper service, too, for a change. Owph, that woman in there, such a cow. I know you're the radio but I don't care who hears me.' She bent towards the microphone. 'JACKIE CRAIG, YOU'RE A RIGHT— Oh, she's gone. Hello, Maria love. How are you? You going to sing us all a song, are you? That will be nice.'

The atmosphere was carnival that afternoon. Katie was running a bake stall and doing a roaring trade; acquaintances were catching up with each other, filling in the gaps of years. Everyone was pleased to be there and when the singers started up their by now well-worn protest programme, those who could joined in, and those who couldn't clapped and swayed along. They were all deeply engrossed in 'If I Had a Hammer' – banging out the love between the brothers and the sisters – and had mostly forgotten what on earth had brought them there, when Lewis shouted over the music: 'OK, EVERBODY. ON YOUR GUARD. THEY'RE HERE.' The singing stopped. 'THE ENEMY IS UPON US.'

21

'Coming up shortly, "News from Your Neighbourhood" and all the latest developments over at Bridgeford's London Road. It's been quite busy down there. But first let's just enjoy a moment of calm . . . '

The evenings were lightening and the gunmetal sky above the damp, clogged motorway told Tracey everything she needed to know about the day she had missed. It had been and still was grim out there. But inside, her car was filling up with the gentle beauty of one of the greatest piano intros in music history.

When you're weary . . .

She pitched her voice at a minor third above Garfunkel's and indicated to move into the central lane.

. . . feeling small

And then suddenly, just as quickly as she started it, she was losing it. Her own sound caught in her throat, she lost sight of the road for the mist in her eyes.

Tracey had been doing so very well right up till that moment but just two little words set to three simple notes and she was a goner. What was it with music? What exactly was its power? How come smart-arse scientists were capable of splitting atoms yet were unable to explain how music could conduct electricity through the souls of men? If Art Garfunkel came up to her in the street and suggested she might be feeling small, she wouldn't put up with it for a second – there would be a bit of 'Er, excuse *me* . . . ' She might possibly bop him one. But since he had just happened to mention it so melodically, and on this night of all nights, Tracey was defenceless. All she could hear was the truth of his words. Small was exactly how she was feeling – very small, totally inconsequential and rather lost.

It was another good reason why a person should never listen to the radio at all, of course, be it local or national, naff or not. You had no control. It was emotional Russian roulette. You just turned it on, caught a couple of chords and a killer line, and anything – any past love or hate, any ache in your heart that you could kid yourself was healed – could shoot out of there and slay you in an instant.

I will lay me down.

This was one of the first songs she ever taught Billy, 'Bridge Over Troubled Water'. When he was an infant – and the two of them together combined to make up one indestructible world – it was the lullaby that she used to get him to sleep. 'Can I lay me down now, Mamma?' he would ask when he wanted a nap. There was a tight squeeze in her chest as she thought about it; her breath was short. The rock and metal thing had not started by then, but she still had extremely high musical standards from her very first days as a parent. None of that nursery rhyme rubbish, certainly not. Billy never heard a nursery rhyme until he had been thoroughly indoctrinated against such musical inanities. All that hard work, all that parental dedication, and for what? So that one day he could just pack his bag and walk out of her door.

She gulped and blinked away the tears. *Dave at Drivetime* was really rubbing the salt in with this one tonight, and yet still she didn't turn the radio off. Her CDs were all over the seat, but Tracey hadn't actually listened to them for a while now. For some reason, hard rock and loud shouting weren't quite working for her these days; she seemed to be rediscovering the sensual pleasures of harmonic singing. She found the note and wrapped her voice up and around Garfunkel's once more. It wasn't quite the same, sharing harmony with a disembodied voice – a bit like telephone sex, she would imagine, getting your rocks off without looking each other in the eye. But for the frustrated and alone, it gave some sort of comfort. They were on to the final verse now, Tracey and Art, and could do with a bit of help to carry them off to the climax. Hey, Paul, fancy a threesome? It's only pretend, after all . . .

Now last week in the Coronation Hall, that was the real thing. When Tracey was conducting 'People Get Ready', and all those eyes were gripping hers and those hips were moving in time with hers and those voices were all doing their own thing and yet together making one big beautiful thing, well, that was the beginning of a serious, meaningful relationship. So really – and she must just keep telling herself this until she believed it – she was lucky. Billy may be leaving her, but at least the Choir was there to take his place.

Tracey looked up to see that she had parked in the High Street outside the supermarket even without even noticing, so often had she made this exact journey over the past years. And now she was here, she realised she didn't need to be. They would go out tonight, of course they would, their last night together after twenty-two years; it was a huge night for both of them. But her baby bird was flying off at 6 a.m. tomorrow, so she was actually all right for bread and milk for once. She was probably all right for bread and milk for the rest of her life.

' . . . Over LIVE to London Road, where there has been a lot of action. Chrissie, fill us in.'

Hello, what was this? Tracey leaned over and turned up the volume.

'Well, Dave, demonstrators end today with the upper hand after the dramatic personal intervention of a Mr Bennett Parker from Priory Lane.'

No way! Tracey hooted with delight.

'He lay down across the site entrance, while the Bridgeford Community Choir sang "He shall not be moved". The developers, faced with the sight of Mr Parker in a puddle wearing what looked like a rather expensive suit, didn't seem to be able to agree on how to proceed. At five p.m., they withdrew. His actions just show quite how high feelings are running over this local issue. Developers are tonight said to be reviewing their tactics.'

'Thanks, Chrissie. It's all kicking off in Bridgeford, then. Meanwhile, preparations for the St Ambrose Summer Fête hit a snag when—'

Well, well, well. She turned the radio off and smiled to herself. A straggle of commuters came up the steps from the station and pressed down the High Street to their homes. It isn't quite kicking off in Bridgeford, Drivetime Dave. Right here it is quiet, even by our dozy standards. Guess you just had to be where Bennett 'Trouble' Parker was, eh? Hang out with the rebels. Tracey wished now that she had taken the afternoon off work to go and join in. She turned the key in the ignition and looked over her shoulder before pulling away. If they did go ahead and build that wretched retail park and close down this nice little place, of course, she would probably never come down here again in the week. Instead, she would have to go off and do battle with lots of other people, from lots of other towns, around some ghastly giant superstore in order to buy food just for herself. She drove off, through the fading light, feeling – as Art Garfunkel had so neatly put it – small.

Tracey moved up the stairs with a heavy heart but a lightness of body. She had no carrier bags this evening, for a change, and her shoulders were not clenched, braced against the violently loud music that assaulted her on a normal night. She opened the door to see Billy, a list between his teeth, tightening the straps on his rucksack.

'Umph.' He took the paper out of his mouth. 'Hey, Mum. How was work?'

'Yeah, a blast. We had such a laugh. So quiet in here, I thought you were out.'

She walked across the cleared floor and put her bag on the table, next to his ticket, passport, wallet.

'I've packed the iPod. Here, are you going to be all right without our music? Only just occurred to me . . . '

No Bloodshitters? Hey ho, she would have to struggle on somehow. 'I'll sort myself out. Don't worry about me. Now I do have to pop down to choir but I'll make it quick and then we'll go out, shall we?' She reached into the fridge and took out an opened bottle of white. 'Where do you fancy – Indian for old times' sake?'

'Oh, sorry, can't. It's my last night, so I'm out with the lads. Curly and Squat. Off for some beers.'

Tracey hugged the bottle to her chest and stared, hard, out of the window with her back to her son. By employing the maximum amount of self-control available, she could just about hold herself together. Just give it a moment, for her pounding heart to subside and her throat to reopen; wait for this chill to pass. It could have been worse. Imagine if those words had been sung, not spoken. By Art Garfunkel:

It's my last night . . .

– and in a minor key –

. . . so I'm out with the lads

Then she would be writhing on the floor, weeping tears of blood, flaying at her own flesh. As they had come out of the mouth of a young man who – face it – still had stuff to learn, then she could afford, or at least try to afford, to ignore them.

The young man himself certainly displayed no awareness of the impact of his short but devastating speech. He was just settling down in front of the TV, putting his feet up on a kitchen chair, about to enjoy some final quality time with his games console and a post-apocalyptic world.

'Thought you'd be busy with your singing thing anyway.'

'Yes, of course. I'll probably have quite a bit of stuff to sort out. We get the election results tonight. And I do want to have a proper catch-up with them.' Her voice brightened automatically as she spoke. 'Apparently this afternoon my friend Bennett lay down in a puddle and it was on "News from Your Neighbourhood".'

'Hey. Mum. Enough.' Billy kept his eyes on the screen as he pulled a virtual hooker out of a car and shot her dead. 'You're not going to go like completely lame while I'm away, are you?'

22

It was results night for the Bridgeford Community Choir's elections, so it was never going to be a quiet one. The Coronation Hall would anyway be buzzing – the members would be walking a little taller, speaking a little louder, behaving in that exaggerated way we all do when we are at a crucial moment in our lives that will be recorded in our own memories until the memory itself starts to fail us. So throw into the mix the afternoon's events at the sit-in and the excitement had to go off the scale. How could you quantify the energy in the room that night? The scientific instrument capable of reading those sorts of numbers was yet to be invented.

'Come on, Bennett. Tell us everything.'

Bennett stood, bashful, in the middle of his admirers. He was looking as clean and smart as usual; he had changed his clothes since the afternoon.

'It was just brilliant.' Maria was still excited. 'Most fun that's ever been had on the London Road, I can tell you.'

Annie poked her head through the hatch from the kitchen. 'Did you see him on TV? He was actually on the local news!'

'I can't believe I missed it.'

'Why wasn't I there?' wailed Tracey. 'Born too late for Woodstock; stuck in the office for Bennett versus Capitalism.'

'I know: act it out for us!'

Judith, who in a filthy boiler suit with a beanie on her head was still showing off that eco-warrior sort of look – and giving off that eco-warrior sort of smell – cleared a few chairs back and pulled Bennett over into the space. 'OK, lie down,' she instructed. And to the rest of them: 'Imagine a deep and rutted puddle.'

Bennett lay, hands crossed at his breast like a knight in a tomb, and his fellow-protesters arranged themselves around him in a half-moon.

He shall not, he shall not be moved

'And try and imagine I'm a bulldozer,' Judith continued.

Jazzy and Katie spluttered into laughter.

'People power,' shouted someone from the council.

'Hallelujah!' called Lewis, elated. 'It's the Bridgeford Spring.'

Spirits were high, they were all singing, at top volume, clapping along. Pat, Lynn and Maria struggled to their feet and began to lead half the members round in a conga.

'*Ben-nett, Ben-nett, Ben-*nett,' they chanted, kicking a leg out on the final 'nett'. '*Ben-nett, Ben-nett, Ben-*nett.'

The door opened and smacked against the wall. Emma and Jonty led the way and Edward – greatcoat slung over his shoulders, bundles of music in his arms – swished in behind them. He let the door slam, took position in the centre of the hall and clapped his hands.

'Good evening, everybody. Exciting moment for the future of the Choir, so those of you who are lying on the floor pretending to be dead might want at this juncture to rise.' His voice dipped with that cadence most regularly associated with the more pompous wing of the English clergy.

Bennett rose and, with the rest of the Choir, scuttled around and back into place as Lewis drew himself to his moderate height and intoned: 'They will rise, *Edward*, when they choose to rise and not a moment before.'

Edward smirked. 'Thanks for that, Lewis. I'm well in my place. And oh look, they seem to have risen. Sit down now, there's a good chap.' He made a suggestive little flap with his hand. 'So here goes. I would like to ask Pat to come forward with the resu—'

'Hang on.' Lewis was up again. 'Who are you to ask Pat to come forward? Why are you suddenly in charge of things?'

'Ooh.' Edward jumped to one side in mock-fear. 'I'm so sorry, Lewis. Quite forgetting my place there. What was I thinking? You're so right. Why don't you ask Pat to come forward and announce the election results?' He gestured to Lewis that the floor was his, crossed his arms and waited.

'All right then.' Lewis looked, and clearly felt, horribly ridiculous. 'I will. I would like to ask ... obviously ... Pat ... to ... so, you know ... results.' He sank back into his chair and studied his knees, while Pat heaved herself up and waddled into the centre.

'Thank you very much, *Edward*. I haven't got the exact numbers with me, I'm afraid. I put the bit of paper out on the kitchen table so I wouldn't forget it and what did I do? Anyway, I can remember the gist of it. So I, as returning officer for the Choir elections, can tell you that Bennett got the most votes for treasurer and Edward for leader and hereby duly they are hereby elected as, um, those things.'

At first there was a stunned silence in the room, broken only by a subdued 'Well done, Bennett'. But then Emma, Jonty and a number of sopranos burst into such warm applause for Edward that the rest of them had no choice but to join in. Tracey, clapping politely, bit her lip and caught nobody's eye.

'Thank you, all who voted for me,' boomed Edward, taking to the centre of the circle. Emma passed him a music stand and he snapped it open. 'Just a bit of business before Jonty's new warm-up – a few little parish notices.' Emma passed him a baton.

'We've never had a baton before.' Lynn gave a jump of alarm.

'Oh, I like a baton,' Pat shot back as she returned to her seat. 'You know where you are with a baton. I'm pro-baton.' She nodded smugly. 'I've actually always wanted a baton, just never said so.'

Lynn looked at her sideways and shook her head. 'I hope you know what you've started.'

'I love his shirt,' Maria muttered, to no one in particular.

Edward called for silence. 'The first, I know you don't need reminding, is that we only have five weeks until the County Championships.' He poked the baton in the Choir's direction. 'Obviously, this is not going to be easy. I know that you saw that I was the person to deliver you that victory.' Tracey raised an eyebrow, crossed her arms and looked off sideways. 'With that in mind, I have planned an ambitious programme for the night, which frankly not all of you' – the baton poked out again – 'are going to be able to cope with. So,' he shrugged off his coat, somehow indicating that he had arrived at the least interesting point of his speech, 'if any of you find it too challenging then you might want to think about whether you want to get involved at all.'

'What? No!'

'That's not what we're about.'

'See?' said Lynn to Pat. 'Now look what you've done.'

Annie stood up. 'Edward, if I might just explain, fill you in on the history of our little group. I've been coming for decades, and my mum came for years before that. The Bridgeford Community Choir have been going, in varying strengths and numbers, but still continuously going, for over fifty years. You see, Edward, we sing for friendship. We are a community within a community. And we have never, ever, not once, barred anyone from entry or tested them on their vocal strengths.'

There was a smattering of applause; a muttering of 'Hear, hear'.

'I know, and it's what makes you so very, very special.' Edward unscrewed the top of a bottle of vitamin water and took a glug. 'I think I can honestly say I don't think I have ever heard a choir quite like this one.' Emma sniggered; Jonty played a few Hammer Horror chords. 'But OK, if that's the way you want it. Only I thought I heard something about actually winning, rather than just turning up.'

Annie rose again. 'Actually, Edward, we have already won, three years ago, without any censorship or exclusion, under the guidance of our beloved leader Constance.'

'Then if that's the general standard we're laughing, aren't we? Right. Let's get started.' He tapped his baton on the stand. 'Tonight's warm-up comes from the Eskimo people of – of . . . Jonty?' he shouted over to the piano. 'Where are these particular Eskimo people from again?'

♩

Annie poured out two cups for Lynn. 'How are you feeling about the election result?' she spoke quietly. 'I must say I was rather surprised. I wasn't aware that Edward was a popular choice.'

'We should all be extremely surprised, in my view.' Lynn splashed some milk around. 'God knows what we were singing in the first half there but if everyone wants to get up at the competition and sound like a load of tom cats out on the piss, then they've picked the right man for the job.'

'I think it was Tavener.'

'Is that what he calls himself? I call him a bloody racket. Be Sondheim next, you mark my words. Then,' she drew herself up to her full five foot two, 'I'm warning you: I might have to consider my position.'

♫

'Hey, Maria,' said Jazzy, without looking up from her screen.

'How are you, love? It was nice to see your nan this afternoon. I do miss seeing her every night. And you, of course.'

Jazzy looked up and smiled. 'We're fine, ta. My mum's doing

really well. She's got it all running like clockwork and my nan's hardly complaining at all.'

'You do know, don't you,' Maria settled herself on the next chair and adopted a bedside manner, 'that it wasn't easy for the GPs down at the practice to get your nan's care sorted at home.'

'Yeah.' Jazzy walloped an angry bird. 'So?'

'And they were a bit worried when your mum dismantled everything like that. We've all been a bit worried.' She shuffled in her seat. 'Has she talked to you about it? Only, if she were to ... Well, I'm sure she won't for a minute but if she were for any reason—'

Jazzy put down her phone, crossed her arms and looked at Maria head-on.

'—to need to move on again, well ...'

'Well what?'

'Well, it will be hard for us now, under this new system, to get it all back in place at the level you've been used to.'

'Really?' Jazzy went back to her phone. 'Then it's good she's not going to move on, isn't it? It's good that we're being a proper family and she's really got her act together at last and everything's fine. Isn't it?'

'Yes.' Maria patted her on the shoulder. 'That's great. It's all anyone wants for you. So how are you enjoying the new music tonight? Different, I thought ...'

'Crap. The music is crap and the singing is crap and the contest will be crap. I'm not coming back here again. And I didn't vote for that stupid wanker. Wish I hadn't bothered. What's the point of bloody voting if you end up with someone you don't bloody want?'

'Political apathy in a nutshell.' Lewis shook his head sadly.

'Here, Katie.' Jazzy took an earphone and put it in her friend's ear. 'Let's listen to something decent before this lot send us mental.'

Lewis passed a biscuit to Tracey and sat down next to her. 'You OK? I'm sorry you're not the leader. It doesn't feel right, this regime. It beats me why all those people would have voted for him.'

'Oh, yeah, whatever.' Tracey dismissed it all with a brash flick of her right hand, and with the heel of her left quickly rubbed away a tear. 'I only put my name down because Bennett talked me into it. And anyway,' she gulped and sniffed, 'as from tomorrow my life is changing for good. Six o'clock tomorrow morning and Billy is finally out of my hair.'

'It's actually happening?'

'Yep. And I was just thinking in the first half – during, I must add, the strangest piece of music I have ever had the misfortune to sing, what was all that atonal crap? – that I don't have anything to keep me in Bridgeford any more. Everything is about to open up for me now. I can feel my horizons pulling off into the distance; my world opening, oyster-like, before me.'

'Lewis,' called Jazzy, 'Katie needs the toilet.'

Bennett slipped into Lewis' chair as he vacated it. 'It's all completely ridiculous, I don't know what happened, I am so terribly sorry.'

'Congratulations, treasurer.' She bent her head in deference. 'And don't worry about it. I've enjoyed myself here, but this stuff you're doing now, it's not my scene. I'm going to have a look at what other choirs there are out there, look for the one that suits me, not just the one that's closest.'

'Oh. No.' Bennett looked stricken. 'You can't, please don't do that.'

'Yes I can.' Tracey jutted her chin at him. The whites of her eyes were palely pink. 'And yes I will.'

Edward rapped his baton on his stand. 'That's enough chit-chat, everybody, thank you very much. On to the lighter end of our competition repertoire and – I know you're all going to love this – it's a vintage bit of Sondheim.'

'Thank you and goodnight,' called Edward, clapping in the general direction of the Choir before collecting his music. 'If you can all take your music home with you, practise hard over the next week and learn your words, please.' His own words were drowned out by the scraping of chairs and the disgruntled mutterings of friends.

'Just one notice before you go,' Bennett called, with a new loud authority. All the other noises ceased. 'I'm having an open house on Saturday week for my birthday, all welcome, from seven o'clock to ... um ... silly o'clock! Hope you can all make it. Flyers with details are on the table by the door.'

'Well done, sir.' Another stranger patted Bennett on the shoulder as he waited to cross the road.

'Thanks. Got to show them, haven't we?' Bennett hadn't known such popularity since he was the ice-cream man at the St Ambrose Summer Fête. If he was honest, and took all confectionery out of the picture, he had never known such popularity ever. He took to the pedestrian crossing, and waved at the waiting driver tooting his horn in admiration. He had never been one of those popular sorts of chap. Indeed, since he had first grasped the fundamentals of the English language, Bennett had understood that 'popular' was an adjective used only ever in relation to others.

'Good on you, mate,' shouted a man out of a van.

So the fact that, for the first time in his life, it could now be justifiably applied to him was really – he bounced in his shoes – quite extraordinarily pleasant.

'Here he comes,' said the lady in the newsagent: her face was very familiar, but her name and basic biography? Bennett didn't have a clue. 'Our hero. There you are, love – packet of wine gums on us.'

'Oh, how lovely, thanks. I just want to pick up some stationery, if that's OK. Back in a sec ...'

And the fact that this sudden popularity had hit right now he found rather interesting. Last Tuesday, in a matter of minutes and for the first time in his life, Bennett had found himself contravening, in quick succession, every edict of acceptable behaviour that his parents had ever taught him. He had got his best clothes dirty – that puddle had, he feared, cost him a good suit, but he still didn't regret it; he had challenged authority: in this particular debate he was on the opposing side of the council, the planners and a major FTSE100 company, yet he felt perfectly comfortable over there; and – most significantly for the elder Parkers – he had, that most evil of upper-middle-class crimes, drawn attention to himself. And boy, had he drawn attention to himself. He was all over the local news and he was the talk of the town and the fact was it was all very bucking up. Clearly he had been leading his life according to a set of outmoded values. He should have disobeyed his parents years ago.

He wandered down the aisle full of notebooks, diaries and writing materials and felt happier still. The role of treasurer was an excellent and genuine excuse for some brand-spanking-new stationery and oh, how Bennett loved stationery. It was a passion that belonged to his old, pre-revolutionary – pre-popular – self; it was founded on his enthusiasm for a new term, his passion for exams; it spoke to the most successful side of him, the swot. He picked up a ledger that was not what he was looking for, looked around him furtively, flicked the pages and inhaled deeply. Virgin paper – couldn't beat it. He shivered and exhaled like a horse.

'I saw that,' said a voice behind him.

Bennett jumped. 'Sweetheart.' He kissed Araminta on each cheek. 'What are you doing here?'

'Same as you.' She gestured to the pens. 'God, Dad. How dare you come in here without me? You're supposed to share your interests with your kids, you know. And since stationery is your one actual interest in the whole actual world, you could at least have called. I'm at a difficult age.' She pouted and leaned in to him, wagging her finger. 'And from a broken home now.'

'I'm so sorry, it was just—'

'Dad. Stop. Joke.' She flicked him away – 'Don't care' – and reached over to stroke a notebook. 'Anyway, we've got something else in common, haven't we? You little rebel, you. We couldn't believe it when we saw you on the news. Ha. You should've heard Mum. She seems to have changed sides all of a sudden. Smell that.' There was a new brand of perfumed gel pen; they sniffed together in happy unity. 'Suddenly she's all for one of those hypermarkets the size of a planet. So bloody predictable.'

'Is she? Really? Is that how you think of her – predictable?' Bennett had long ago decided that Sue's responses and opinions had the predictability of a roulette wheel. To find that his daughter had, all the time, some formula by which she could find actual patterns in the behaviour was simply astonishing. The girl was a marvel. Was there anything she didn't know? He lowered his voice. 'Do I know that lady on the till over there? She gave me some free sweets. What's her name?'

Araminta sighed and flicked through an address book. 'Dad. Such a dork. Carol. Babysat us for literally a thousand years. I know,' she pointed at the shelf: 'pick a colour.'

What, just like that? In his old life, Bennett had been known to spray around decisions of great import as fast as he could articulate them; it was what had made him – or at least he had always it assumed that it was what had made him – such a highly valued colleague. Although, do highly valued colleagues actually get made redundant? There was a chilling thought. Back to the stationery: for the new, more thoughtful, domestic-goddess Bennett, however, a decision of that magnitude – picking a colour, of all things – well, that could take him hours. He just took the plunge like a madman and, all caution to the winds, went for the tan. She overruled him, grabbed the navy, held her hand out for some money and took off for the till. 'Hey, Carol,' he heard from the other side of the shop, and drifted off again into his choice of ledgers for choir accounts.

'Right.' She was back. 'This is what we're going to do. Whenever you find out the details of someone you'd forgotten you knew – i.e. everybody; do you recognise me every time or have there been a few narrow squeaks? I won't forgive you, FYI ... Anyway, you find the letter ... see, N for Newsagent, write in the details: Carol, ex-babysitter, and in brackets any relevant info, e.g.' – she carefully formed the letters in her pretty handwriting – *'free pack of wine gums.* See? And then, with a bit of luck, you might just stop making a total arse of yourself everywhere you go.'

He took the book from her hands and gazed at it in wonder. 'So, a sort of starter information pack, you mean? For the rest of my own life?'

'Well, I suppose.' Araminta slumped, swung her arms low and groaned with what Bennett considered to be disproportionate despair. 'If you absolutely must be a *total* drama queen about every-thing ...'

'This will come in very useful for my party planning. You and Casper are coming, aren't you? Next Saturday, seven o'clock till silly o'clock. I'd really love you to—'

'Aaaaagh!' Araminta folded into the shelving with her hands over her eyes. 'DAD. What did you just say? Jeez. Hell. What has got into you? Silly o' .. ? Where did you pick that up from?'

Bennett couldn't remember now. It might have been someone in the basses – silly o'clock? That did sound very like someone in the basses. He had been making a conscious effort to update his vocab-ulary, to try to fit in that little bit more, and listened out for phrases and sayings that he perhaps ought to be using, rather like a German spy parachuted into the Home Counties during the war. And judging by Araminta's response, not quite as successfully. Perhaps he ought to write them all down first, then run them past her before using them. Oh good, he would need another notebook. He turned back to get that tan one, then noticed she was looking very serious again.

'But, hang on, who else will be there? Like out of your gazillions and bazillions of actual mates?'

'Well, there's all the Choir, and all the protestors, and the woman in the butcher's is always very friendly—'

'Oh, Dad. Dad, Dad, Dad. You've gone and ruined it now. Do you see?' He didn't see. He'd slightly lost the hang of things somewhere around the tan notebook. She tutted and let out a sigh of disappointment rather like her mother's. 'Are you quite sure she isn't just being friendly because she's the woman in the butcher's? See, what happens when you take away the meat, or the singing, or the protesting, hmm? That's what you've got to ask yourself. Like, is the woman in the butcher's still friendly when she's not getting rid of her chops and you're not giving her your cash?' Bennett felt unaccountably sad for a moment. There was so much in that little speech that he wanted not to know, that he wished he could go back over and unhear. He sensed, lurking within, a very unwelcome subtext – a suggestion that perhaps he was not after all the popular fellow he thought he was. Fortunately Araminta's attention was suddenly taken up with something else. She was moving off, fast, past the greetings cards and pressing herself up against the shop window. 'Oh, look.' She pointed over the road to the Copper Kettle, where Casper and another chap were nailing a notice to the wall. 'It's actually happening.'

'For sale,' he read. 'With planning permission for change of use. Potential for one desirable four-bed house.'

A small crowd was already gathering before they had even finished hammering. There were quite a few young mothers with buggies, and a couple of old people on mobility scooters. Lewis was holding Katie's wheelchair and bending over her shoulder talking. Maria, in her carer's uniform, driving past in her little blue car, slowed down to stare. Jazzy emerged from inside, took up position beside Katie and looked up at the notice without expression.

Bennett felt Carol at his elbow. She stood with them, hand at her neck, mouth open in horror. 'Oh no, that's all we need. They can't do that. That really would be the end.' She turned to Bennett. 'So what are you going to do about this one?'

$$\downarrow$$

'What was that?' asked Sue loudly.

'I said,' Annie had to raise her voice just to make herself heard, even though she didn't really want to; this was highly confidential information, 'I'm starting to look forward to it now I'm getting used to the idea.'

The hammering started up again, just outside Menopause Corner's window.

'You were right—'

'Sorry?' Sue cupped her hand to her ear.

Annie suspected she had heard perfectly well, but just rather liked the sound of the sentence. 'YOU WERE RIGHT. I do feel rather lucky, now. It's been miserable since Jess left and James started this, um . . .' – oh hell, she had walked right into this one – 'this rather engrossing . . .'

'Ah, yes.' Sue's voice dripped with meaning. 'The engrossing *case.*'

Annie stumbled on. 'I mean, Jess won't be able to look after a baby, will she? She couldn't look after a pet rock. Bloody useless.'

'Sorry?'

'I said, JESS,' Annie obliged, 'is BLOODY USELESS. And a baby does fill a house somehow, doesn't it? Do you remember when we used to run that playgroup in your front room? I miss it all.' She sighed and looked over to a table in the centre of the café. There was a crowd of mothers from the primary school gathered around it and she knew exactly what they were doing because she had done it herself so very often: they were planning the Summer Fête.

'Who's that man over there in the middle of it all?'

'Oh, that's um – tsk, whatsisname.'

'Clue?'

'Head.'

'Tom Orchard.'

'And his wife.'

'Gorgeous baby.'

Sue looked over but didn't agree – she had never been heard to compliment the babies of others. Well, she had jolly well better be nice about my new one, thought Annie. Our new one. OK, Jess's new one. Annie already felt so bonded to the little foetus. Every time she thought about her – it was definitely a girl, Annie was never wrong – her internal organs gave a little flip. She was something special, this baby. How could anyone not be nice about her?

The noise from outside brought her back to the room. 'WHAT is that wretched banging out there?' Peering out, she saw Casper with a hammer. 'For sale? No!' And then when she saw Sue's impassive face: 'You knew? Before me?'

'Sorry?'

'You heard.'

'Well ...' Sue conceded. 'I was told to keep it a secret. This is Casper's career, you know.'

'Hmm. And yet the news about the baby seemed to get out and I can't quite think how ...'

'It's so hard in this town. I mean, Bennett – Bennett of all people, a man who would not know a piece of gossip if it fell on his head and knocked some sense into him – even he had somehow got wind of Jess's tattoo.'

Annie bit her lip.

'I SAID, BENNETT KNEW ABOUT JESS'S TATT—'

'All right, all right, keep it down, I heard you the first time. It just slipped out. It's funny now that I see him once a week, without you. I mean, he's a nice guy, isn't he? I know you don't mind me saying that, it being so amicable between you. He's very popular down at the Choir, you know.'

Sue put a couple of sugars in her tea.

'In fact, he's just been elected treasurer!'

'Marvellous.'

'It was completely brilliant of you to suggest he joined – so nice and kind and thoughtful. He's really coming out of his shell. He's got a fabulous voice, hasn't he?'

'If you like that sort of thing. Jazzy, could I have another bun over here?'

'And so much *energy*. He's been quite the local superstar down at the protest. He's a real asset. I really think he's turning his life around, and it's all down to you. I'm sure he's grateful. You're going to his party, I take it?'

'Sorry?'

'Sue. Joke's over. The banging has stopped.'

'Yes. I noticed. But I thought you said Bennett was having a party.' She was very red all of a sudden. A thick white whisker shone, luminous, against the colour of her chin.

'He is. For his fiftieth. Rather a huge affair, it sounds like. I somehow got the impression it was all your idea.'

24

Tracey swung out of the car park on to the roundabout and soared straight past the slip road of the motorway. It was the first Tuesday of the rest of her life – in the first full week of the new normal – and the new reality was that she was free. Perhaps for the first time ever in her forty-four years, she was not supposed to be anywhere and it didn't matter what she did. There was nobody at home tonight, there would be nobody there for months, and it could well be that there would be nobody at home ever again. She had no demands to meet before the next morning and really, if she didn't show up at ONS Systems ever again, then so what? After a bit they would stop paying her; they might promote a junior; the world would reliably turn. Perhaps sometimes, during a coffee run, catching the whiff of a skinny latte, they might be struck by an involuntary memory of that Tracey Leckford and wonder aloud what had become of her. But then again . . . To be fair, she had gone to quite a lot of trouble to make herself appear as boring and distant and anonymous as possible, so why should they? She would remain for ever a mystery that nobody could be arsed to solve; a jigsaw of a remote, bleak landscape – with too much cloud – that would never come out of its box. It was a beautiful evening. She wound down her window, inhaled deeply of the lead-filled air and took an A-road directly away from Bridgeford.

This early, milky dusk of spring was rather magical and of the sort that Tracey had been deprived of since – when? Well, since her youth really. Before Billy, she had been locked into a relentless schedule that meant this time of day was all about sound checks, make-up and nervy rows – no time for standing and staring back then, that was for sure. And certainly, during the past two decades of single parenthood, this had been the point of maximum stress upon her strained schedule. Belting home to give Billy his last bottle, then to read his story, to have the last hour and then the last hours before she put him to bed; to relieve babysitters and collect him from clubs, her heart thumping against her ribs with the fear that something would happen on the road and she would be – sin of maternal sins, horror of infant horrors – late. Never in all that time would she have had the mental presence to look out of the window, witness the new green on the trees, keep an ear out for the birdsong.

And then in the last few years, when she should have been through all of that, she had a new and different worry: when she got home, would he even be up yet? There was an ever-present dread, as she had been slogging away earning their living, that her fit and able son had spent the working day snoring in his boxers, smelling rather ripe. And dangling off the side – of the worry, that was, not the rather ripe boxers – were the accessory fears that he was suffering from fatherlessness or clinically depressed or just born bloody idle to the marrow of his bones. Each of those theories held its own particular horror and, driving home on autopilot, she would wrestle with them individually, determined to prove them wrong and that no aspect of the disappointment that was the early-adult Billy Leckford could be pinned on her, his only parent. And yet, by the time she got back, her guilt was so overwhelming that immediately she started clearing up after him and indulging his every whim. She roared through a pretty little riverside village at break-limit speed, until an electronic sign flashed with fury. Taking her foot off, she drifted over a little bridge into a lay-by on the other side and parked. From that distance, with a fresh perspective, Tracey had to admit that the past five years of her relationship with Billy did take on the appearance of a right old mess.

She pulled her jacket around her, got out of the car and wandered down to the water's edge. Her son had been in her thoughts every waking minute of every day since he had left. She longed to hear he was happy and useful and at last embarking on the journey to becoming the person he ought to be, and yet ... If he was, would that be because of Tracey, or despite her? She sank on to a bench and hugged herself.

Nothing seemed to make any psychological sense any more. If there was a defining fact that she could take away from her years of parenting it was that one: nothing makes any sense. When pressed, she might add the supplementary wisdom that you just never know. And beyond that, there was nothing else to give. There were her parents – cold, repressive, occasionally downright mean – who had never expressed anything but a tetchy disappointment in their own daughter; and there was Tracey, who had worked non-stop since her sixteenth birthday and until now had never sat at the water's edge at dusk in springtime. And there was Tracey again – loving, loving to the point of madness – who, on the birth of her son, quite willingly and literally surrendered her own identity; and there was Billy, a dope-smoking lump. And then on top of all that, wind-up of wind-ups, there was bloody Annie Miller, who seemed to be the only person capable of bringing him to some sort of life. That might even be the worst aspect of the whole business. All those brilliant teachers, his own brilliant mother, and yet the first signs that there might just be some human intelligence locked away in there were made for and received by Annie. How much humil-iation exactly was Tracey expected to take? Were there any plans to stop it at any point, or was she to spend the rest of her life just suck-ing it up?

A mother duck swam out of the reeds and a fleet of little

ducklings dropped into the water and followed her. She had that earnest, smug, know-it-all demeanour of new mothers of every species; that triumphant air of one who has just changed for ever the future of the planet by bringing forth the most magnificent specimen that the world has yet known.

'You bloody wait,' snarled Tracey.

A little one swam in the wrong direction; at one imperious quack it returned to its mother immediately.

'That's the easy bit.'

There was a cascade of what sounded like duck laughter.

'You won't be laughing when they're six foot two and shooting cyber-hookers.'

The whole family turned its back on her and swam upstream.

'Or flying off to sodding Rwanda and leaving you,' she called after them. 'You think it won't happen, but it will.' It was getting dark, and cold. Tracey looked at her watch. Ten to seven – not long until choir rehearsal. Not that she actually cared . . .

Bennett charged headlong towards the Coronation Hall, his briefcase clutched to his side and a bit between his teeth. A grave injustice had taken place, he had uncovered it and now he owed it to the world – or at least to the Community Choir – to bring it out into the open. But he couldn't do that without Tracey. And though he had tried her number several times, just to make sure she was coming, she hadn't actually picked up. He was sure, though, that she would be there. Wouldn't she? Of course she was only teasing when she talked of other choirs in other towns. She couldn't really mean it. Why would she do that? He picked up speed until he almost ran into the hall.

Annie was sitting alone on the only chair in the middle of the room, clutching a large ledger and a pen. 'Ah, Bennett.'

'Annie. You're sitting.' He felt disorientated, looked about him, wobbled a bit. 'No tea urn?'

'Huh. No point. Hardly anyone's coming. I'm afraid the situation can be summed up in one word: kettle.' She opened the book, and put a tick in a column. 'So glad you're here, anyway.'

'Of course I'm here.' He got himself a chair. 'Hey, nice notebook.'

'Thanks. From that place in the High Street.' Annie loved stationery too. She held it out for him to stroke and for just a while there they were alone, with the book, in a mutually contented silence. 'I got so many messages from people saying they weren't coming, I thought I might as well go with the flow and accept that I'm secretary.' Opening the back of the book, at the page marked *Apologies*, she started to read. 'Lynn says she's had it up to here; according to the basses there's something big happening down at the council – though I'm not sure I believe them; Jazzy says – well, I'm not going to repeat what Jazzy says, really, that girl's language, bad as her mother, but she's definitely given us up ...'

'And what about Tracey?'

'I haven't heard from her.' Annie looked up. 'Anyway, what about Tracey?'

'Well,' he leaned over and dropped his voice, 'I have reason to believe—'

'Am I pleased to see you two!' squealed Annie as Lewis came in, pushing a downcast Katie. Bennett had never seen Katie without a smile on her face before; she looked quite a different girl.

'We're here all right,' said Lewis brightly. Then, pointing at his daughter's head, he mouthed: 'Bad day.'

And after that, there was a trickle: Pat came in, stood in the middle waiting for a chair, sighed and then actually got one for herself. Judith and Kerry arrived holding hands and sat, heads together, talking in low voices. And then Edward, Emma and Jonty swung in. The piano was opened, the music stand erected and the baton raised.

'Good evening, all,' boomed Edward. 'I hope you've been working on your Tavener.'

Still free as a bird, Tracey glided past an industrial estate at a responsible 38 mph. She had been driving in this particular town for a good three minutes, yet its name had already escaped her. They were all so similar, these places, and their differences were so slight – it was a wonder, really, that anyone bothered to name any of them at all. Each had, somewhere at its heart, the architectural evidence of the settlement it had once been, when it was at a distance from all other towns and its identity was important – this evening she had come across an abbey, a windmill, an ancient grammar school, the railway. Each was now cursed by its own particular eyesore – this estate, other retail parks, warehouses, shopping malls. And then, all together, they had been swamped by so many miles of modern identical housing that there was almost nothing – just a field here or a dual carriageway there – between them. What were once the towns of England had somehow leaked, congealed together, and now formed one giant smear across the centre of the country. It was too late to separate them off now. House names and numbers she could see the point of; street names, very sensible. But really, place names? In this day and age? No point.

She waited at a pedestrian crossing beside a town sign thanking her for her visit and boasting of its German twin. Some sort of social group drifted out of the Methodist Hall and over to the other side. It was hard to tell what exactly they had in common – they were all walkers or historians or bird watchers or brass rubbers. Why people had to bind together in order to enjoy activities that were perfectly pleasant solitary pursuits was a mystery to her.

The thing about Tracey was that she had always had the opposite take on small-town life. She alighted on Bridgeford, all those years ago, not to meet people or join things or become a cheerleader for some bogus, delusionary civic pride. She had handpicked it as the perfect place in which to bury herself in anonymity, raise her child without any unnecessary interference. She drove on and without even reading the signpost turned left on to a minor road.

Of course, the thing about the new normal was that she no longer had to stick in Bridgeford. She could live anywhere, do anything. Any of these towns round here would do. It didn't really matter which one, as it was almost impossible to tell them apart. Or she could fetch up in a city this time, or change her name – she was good at that. Her life seemed so small, looking back on it. Even with the embellishment, the little flourish, of her commute she was still confined to the space of this one little area, just going hither to work, thither to home. If she pulled back a bit, got some distance and perspective, she could now see that she had been enjoying the physical liberation of a battery hen. And all those years – her best decades – they all looked so short: sliced and cubed and shaved as they were into terms and holidays, days and evenings; phases marked by the changes in Billy while she herself remained remarkably unchanged. It could all stop now. She could do what she liked, go where she fancied, be whoever she wanted; fill every hour with more excitement than she was used to in a month. The words 'free' and 'bird' once again came to mind. But – in the way of real life and its intolerance of metaphor – she was only as free as one of those birds whose fuel light was flashing. Pulling in to a small petrol station, she stopped to fill up.

This was not the right place to lift Tracey's spirits, but it was exactly the one to prove her point. She looked around her and through the window at the man sitting there in a little booth, in a shabby little shop, on the built-up outskirts of – she didn't know where she was any more – Nowhere-that-Mattered. Poor, poor bloke: if she was a battery hen, he was a beetle in a matchbox – even lower down the hierarchy of species. How do we end up trapping ourselves like this, erecting unnecessary boundaries and then hiding behind them, making our lives such narrow, scrunched and little things? She returned nozzle to pump and headed in.

The door chimed like an ice-cream van. 'Hello there,' called the man from the till. He was one of those smiley sorts of people. 'Lovely evening.'

Tracey had that sinking, pitying feeling she always got when faced with the blind, wilful misinterpretation of a glass as half full. She handed over her card and for politeness' sake agreed, although she couldn't see how he could possibly tell.

'Summer be with us in no time.' He passed the machine for her PIN, and she noticed all the photos he had put up around him, of people and activities, sun and sea, a child in a mortarboard.

A homely, middle-aged woman came out from the back, leaned against his chair and called out to a young teenage boy to stop stacking the shelves now and get down to his homework.

'I'll sort him out, babe.' The man tore off the receipt and gave his chair up to his wife. 'There you go, madam. Have a good evening.'

'Drive safely,' added his wife, with a smile.

Tracey backed over towards the door and then hung around the magazines for a bit, observing. A few years ago she would have looked at a couple like that, automatically thought 'old' – and then thought of them no more. Recently, though, around the time she herself hit forty – funny, that – she had developed a sort of X-ray vision that could pierce through the ageing process to the younger person buried within. She watched as he kissed his wife on the cheek and promised to bring supper through in a bit, and she saw – past the bad clothes and unkempt hair, beneath the middle-aged weight and eye bags – the attractive young couple that they once were. A boy, with the open features of the woman and the height of the man, lugged a box of cat food over and dropped it behind the till. His dad mock-throttled and chided him for being a little devil in that way a parent would only ever do to a child who wasn't a little devil at all, and together they went through a beaded curtain to the back.

Setting off the ice-cream chime again, Tracey returned to her car. Poor buggers, she said to herself, shaking her head: not just one beetle in a matchbox; there was a whole family of them squashed in there. She sat for a moment, watching the woman and her next customer sharing a joke. And then, because she couldn't quite think of what else to do, she drove out of the garage and back towards home.

♩

'OK, OK.' Edward was holding up his baton like a truncheon. 'There's something not quite right in there. Let me listen to all the parts separately. Sops, from the top.'

Pat, Lynn and Katie sang well enough, although in this instance they were completely drowned out by Emma. Edward listened to them, ear cocked, frowning, and then tapped his stick down. 'It was much better last week. Who are we missing?'

'Quite a lot of people,' said Annie in a secretarial tone. 'But I think it's probably Tracey you're thinking of. Very strong mezzo. I don't know if she's coming back.'

Edward sighed, pointed at the altos and concentrated as Annie, Maria, Judith and Kerry did their bit. 'Not bad,' he begrudged. Maria preened. 'Especially you,' he singled out Annie. 'The rest of you, try and do what Annie's doing. Remember you're supposed to be part of a chorus, not drowning each other out. Pat, we don't need that trill on the D-flat. I think Tavener knew what he was doing.'

And then it was the men's turn. There were only two of them. Bennett and Lewis began their phrase and were immediately stopped. 'Uh-oh.' Edward sucked his teeth. 'Bennett, you're fine, but you' – a quick baton-thrust – 'can I just hear you on your own.' Jonty played the chord again and Lewis started up alone. He tried dipping his voice until it was inaudible, then strengthening it with a false and flaky attempt at confidence. All the time, Edward winced, Katie fought back tears and the rest of them shifted uncomfortably in their seats.

'Well.' Edward put his baton down in a gesture of resignation. 'That was quite something. Are you sure you're free the night of the Championships?' He laughed. 'Nothing on the telly that night?'

'Yes,' Bennett spoke up, 'he is sure he's free.'

'In fact,' said Annie, 'we're all sure he's free.'

'Hear, hear.'

'But perhaps,' added Bennett, chin thrust forward, 'you would prefer us to vote on it?'

Pat slid down and into her chair.

♫

At the end of the session, Bennett sidled up to Edward as he gathered together his papers. 'What are we going to do, do you think?'

'Do?' Edward stood back while Emma dismantled the music stand.

'About our numbers. A lot of our best voices weren't here tonight and they might not be coming back.'

'What a shame.' Edward handed Emma his baton. 'Oh well, can't be helped. But fortunately I have a long list of singers from far and wide who seem to be desperate to join. I'll hold auditions at the weekend and perhaps try and fit in a separate rehearsal to get them up to scratch. And there are a few professionals who owe me a favour; I can bus them in if need be. Don't worry.' He patted Bennett on the shoulder. 'Really. I've got it all in hand.'

'Ah. I thought you might have. I wonder, though, if you could explain one thing to me. Why, when you are going to end up with a choir that is nothing to do with Bridgeford, did you ever want to take over the Bridgeford Community Choir? Why not just start your own?'

'Fair question,' Edward conceded as he leaned down to fiddle with the base of his stand. 'It's an established name, for one thing.' He collapsed it at the top. 'But more importantly, it's got a back story. Oh, they love a back story, these judges.'

'And what is our back story?'

'Well, everyone knows Bridgeford is a right dump, and they love all that stuff. You know, "bunch of losers climbs out of miserable little hell-hole for one night, blinking into the limelight" sort of thing. Can't go wrong.' He shuffled his papers. 'And then there's old whatsername – er – Permanence, in her irreversible coma.'

'Constance. Her name is Constance. And where on earth did you get the idea that she's in an irreversible coma?'

'Believe me,' Edward chuckled, 'they're going to be absolutely bloody creaming it over Constance in her coma. Ten points to us right there, thanks very much.' He then gripped Bennett's shoulder – 'You can stay, though, and that's a promise. You sound like you come from somewhere else altogether' – gave him a pat and swept out of the hall.

Bennett stood for a moment, looking after him. And then called across the room: 'Lewis, could you possibly give me a lift?'

Tracey was now wildly enjoying her avian liberty on the front stairs, with the vacuum cleaner. It was high time, really, that she gave it a going-over – once every twenty years seemed about right for a spring clean. And if she was going to put the property on the market, it needed to look its best. And also, if she was completely honest, she had found herself by the middle of the evening at something of a loose end.

She wondered vaguely, as she ran the brush along the stair rods, if the Bridgeford Community Choir might have noticed her absence – after all, much to her own surprise, she had to admit that her attendance had been unbroken all year. Still, they couldn't have been expecting her to turn up, after that ghastly election nonsense. Not that Tracey gave a damn about it, of course; she had spent a very busy and profitable week not caring two hoots about any of it. She smacked the wood-attachment along the skirting board. Why, at this juncture in her life, when she was at last at liberty to do whatever she wanted, would she saddle herself with a load of provincial losers and gallop headlong towards humiliation? If there was one thing that her self-esteem could reasonably do without, it was to enter a singing competition and face certain defeat; to emerge from two decades of grief and try to lay her own ghosts by creating a few more. She must have been mad to even put herself forward; that was hardly the right approach to her new freedom. And whatever was she doing spending her time with people like Bennett Bonkers

Parker and the like? It was obviously a temporary madness at a time of great upheaval.

She now felt a bit sorry for herself that she was ever dragged into that terrible underground world. It was only to be nice to Lewis – there you go, Tracey being nice again, and where did it get her? – that she ever went in the first place, and it was only ever a timid politeness that kept her going along at all. So there was that one strange week, when she had led them in 'People Get Ready' and had allowed herself to somehow believe that what they were all feeling was something along the lines of the real thing. Of course she should have known better. It felt like a beautiful moment, but even as they were at it they were all planning to dump her. It was nothing but a one-night stand, followed by the boot. And wasn't that just the story of her life?

She was quite sure they would not be thinking of her; she would no longer think of them. Unwrapping the new feather duster she'd bought on the way home – oh yes, Tracey Leckford still knew how to enjoy herself – she smacked a generation of cobwebs from the ceiling.

Bennett took a pace back from the doorstep and looked up. Annie had dropped Tracey on this road, and Lewis had said this was the right number, so it must be. He had of course driven past thousands of times – and spent a significant percentage of his life waiting for the lights to change right outside – but the house would have held no significance for him then. It wasn't the kind of place he expected Tracey to live in. The paint on the window sills was peeling and the gutters could do with a good clear-out. The black front door, though, looked hardly used. He rang the bell and reflected on how a woman like that could end up in a place like this. What, he wondered, and not for the first time, could possibly be her story?

A cloud of human form took shape behind the frosted glass but the door didn't open.

'Who is it?' demanded Tracey, in the manner of a border sentry at a war-torn frontier.

'It's Bennett,' he shouted at the door, feeling rather self-conscious in front of passers-by. He leaned in a little further. 'I say, might I possibly come in?'

'No,' she snapped back. 'You can't.'

'But I need to talk to you,' he pleaded through the keyhole. 'I can't shout it out here in the street.'

She put the chain on and opened the door a crack. He saw half a snub nose, a bit of a full mouth and one reddened eye.

'OK. Say it. And then go.'

Bennett pressed himself up against the doorframe and began. 'It's amazing news: you did win the election after all.'

'Bennett, for God's sake, do I look like a person who gives a toss about your stupid bloody election?'

'Um, I can't really answer that. I'm not looking at you. You're behind a door.'

'I meant' – she did sound jolly cross tonight; the whole conversation was starting to resemble a scene from his marriage – 'in general. Do I in general look like the sort of person who gives a toss?'

'Well ... ' It was rather a philosophical question, that one: the importance of appearance in the reflection of character, the old book/cover debate. 'I don't know how—'

'Sorry. My fault. Forget I asked. Tell me whatever it is you have to tell me and then leave me alone.'

'You won.'

'No. Edward won. Goodbye.' The door started to close. Bennett, much to his own surprise, stuck his shoe-tip in it.

'You did win. He only got twelve votes, you got all the rest. You won.'

The door opened a little bit more.

'And how do you work that out?'

'I've seen all the votes, and counted them.'

'Oh, right. So, like, some Deep Throat sent them to you in a brown envelope? Or did Julian Assange put them on Wikichoir?'

'No. I found them. In Pat's wheelie bin.' Bennett was so proud of this; he had been longing to share it.

'And you just happened to be ferreting about in Pat's wheelie bin, did you? Or is that a routine thing with you – going through all the bins of Bridgeford on a regular basis?'

'Oh no,' he said cheerfully. 'Just that one, just the once. I knew she was lying and I had to prove it.'

'Oh, Bennett.' She sounded a little sad as she unhooked the chain and opened the door. 'You are such a monumental twerp. Supposing someone had seen you?'

'It was fine. I was wearing Casper's balaclava!' He didn't want to show off – that would go quite against the grain – but it was jolly hard not to. Going through that wheelie bin in the dead of night in heavy disguise had been peculiarly enjoyable. And the fact that he had uncovered such a monstrous case of electoral malpractice made it even more so. The only thing that could have made the whole enterprise more exciting was if someone had been there to enjoy it with him. That was why he was so desperate to tell Tracey.

'Hang on. So you dressed up like a bank robber and climbed into an old lady's wheelie bin to take out a few bits of paper to find out who really won the election to be leader of' – she gave a trumpet fanfare and raised her voice like a town crier – 'the Bridgeford Community Choir?'

'YES!' he carolled. 'I DID!'

In his head, that had been the point at which Tracey had flown into his arms and he had swung her around and, well, various other bits and pieces. But she didn't.

Instead she said, 'Wow!' but in a voice heavy with sorrow and regret. She shook her head. 'Bennett.' She gave a heavy sigh. 'How ...? Who ...?' She stopped, thought, tried again. 'What do you think you can do with this information?'

'Tell everyone, of course.'

'And when they ask how you found out, what will say then?'

'I'll say,' he started to explain again, patiently, slightly surprised that Tracey hadn't grasped the whole narrative the first time, 'I climbed into Pat's wheelie bin wearing a—'

'But you can't do that, though, can you, Bennett love, hm?' She sank against the door jamb, seemingly depleted and defeated.

'Why not?' Were there legal implications that he had failed to consider?

'Because they'll just think you are a total weirdo.'

'Ha!' Was that all? 'Ha!' Bennett began to laugh. That was what she was worried about? 'Ha ha!' Tracey thought Bennett might worry about being thought a weirdo? 'Ha ha ha!' One day, he might tell her his life story, starting with his butterfly collection and the boy next door. 'I promise you, if there is one thing that I am really quite used to—'

But the front door had closed – gently, firmly – in his face. Which was doubly annoying, because he had really wanted the chance to remind her about his party.

25

Annie put a tray of home-baked biscuits in the middle of the table and sat down. The five of them had not been in the same place together since Christmas – she could hardly believe it of them, they were once all so tight – and before proceedings properly started she just had to take a moment to savour it. She always enjoyed looking at her family as a whole, rather than individually; they were much more impressive with their resources pooled, in Annie's view. All three girls had made it to the same level of good university, which sounded like a great achievement. After all, what were the chances? But the truth was that none had done quite as well as she should. Individually, they were all nice-looking girls rather than beautiful – each with her similar cut of straight, light brown hair; round, friendly face naturally given to cheerfulness; expensively regulated teeth. *En masse*, though, they seemed so much more. Somehow they bounced off one another, were amplified by each other. It was as if the very volume of them created a sort of optical illusion – a con-trick on the beholder. Anyone would look at them and think: Well, if three separate lots of DNA have all chosen to fall like that, then who are we to argue? OK, we're convinced: they're lovely. That was how Annie had always thought of it anyway, from her position as an only child. She had long thought that siblings gained some sort of knock-on from each other that she was missing out on. And that people looked at her and thought: Hmm, medium height, slight build, general air of beigeness ... yes, all right, we get it: one was enough.

She felt so much better, around the table with the rest of them – she was a working woman, an active volunteer, the mother of fine girls, the wife of a good man, the architect of this unit that was a building block in the future of the world. Only with them did she really feel important; only with them did she feel herself.

'So,' she began. They had gathered all the girls together on that Saturday morning to thrash out this whole business about Jess and the baby. Neither parent had spoken to her since she had told them about the pregnancy, and they were quite unable to bear the situation a moment longer. Annie in particular wanted to go over all the important stuff: what week number, how much folic acid, how many – dread thought – vodka shots. They needed to get her to a doctor and choose a hospital, and they felt they really could do with the moral support of the older girls. James, like a love, had driven up to college at 9 a.m., fished Jess out of her fetid bed and brought her home. It was time for a family summit, and Annie was dreading it. So it was a relief that before they could even begin, a natural, happy, irrepressible family conversation had spontaneously come to life.

'You will *never* guess who I saw last week with a ring through her nose.'

Annie sat with her chin on her hand and watched them. They were so lucky, to have these shared, entwined histories; that whenever they saw each other, for the rest of their lives, they would be able to communicate without explanation or translation.

'So are you going to call him or let him stew?'

But the best thing was the way they all had their roles. Although to the casual observer they were all much of a muchness, they had a strong sense of their own positions – oldest, youngest, cleverest, naughtiest, most popular, most dippy, and on and on. A good-sized family was a microcosm: when you looked out on the real cosmos and couldn't see how you could ever fit into it, you could always retreat back into that little version and know your own place.

'Of course you'll get it. Why wouldn't they hire you?'

Annie and James exchanged a look across the table, and a smile.

'Anyway, what is all *this* about?' said Rosie, her face screwed up with worry. 'We've never had a "family summit" before. You're making me nervous.'

'They're getting a divorce, obvs,' yawned Jessica. 'What else can it be?' She reached over, fingered all the biscuits until she found a chocolate chip and took a bite. 'It's all a bit tacky, IMO.'

Annie had sort of taken it for granted that she'd had all her shocks to be going on with and was not armed to deal with another one. The very D-word nearly winded her.

'DIVORCED?' Lucy shrieked. 'DAD. FUCK. SHIT. What have you gone and DONE?'

But not enough to deafen her to that: how very interesting, she noted, that they assumed him to be the guilty party.

'LUCE!' James shouted. 'Stop that at once!'

'But I don't see why,' continued Jess calmly through her munching, 'we had to come all the way home for it in the *total* dead of night. A phone call would've done the trick.'

Rosie had flung her arms around Annie's neck and was sobbing energetically.

'Really. Girls. Stop this.' James took control as Annie stared aghast at the chaos around her. 'Of course we're not getting a divorce.'

'We're not?' Annie thought she might as well check, just while they were on the subject; it all sounded so certain.

'Annie! For God's sake. Your mother and I are very firmly together.'

'Except,' she didn't add, 'you never come home.'

'Fine,' said Jess, rising. 'I'll be off then.'

'Sit down!' James shouted. 'We have a crisis and your mother' –
he pointed at Annie – 'the woman to whom I am married, and I
thought it would be better for everybody if we all got it out in the
open and talked it through. Jess,' he gulped; Annie's heart went out
to him. He looked quite old and extremely knackered, 'has something to tell you.'

Jess, who was now texting, looked up through the curtains of her
hair with her mouth hanging open. 'Do I?'

'Yes!'

'What?' She frowned, looking genuinely baffled.

James shook his head in despair. 'Jessica is having a baby,' he
announced to the room. 'There.' Then he put both hands flat on the
table, and looked at them.

'FUCKING HELL.' Lucy's shriek was back. 'You silly, stupid
COW.'

'Oh, J.' Rosie started crying again. 'You're NOT!'

'No.' Jess spoke calmly through the mayhem, like everyone else
was stupid. 'I'm not. Is this really what all this is about? Christ. You
lot. Pathetic.'

'WHAT? You rang me up,' countered Annie, her voice rising to
the level of all the others. 'You said you were pregnant. And then
you disappeared from all contact. Were you lying? Was it a JOKE?'

'Well, yeah, OK,' Jess, bored again, grudgingly conceded. 'I was
pregnant and I did mention it.' Her sisters started up again but she
just shrugged. 'And now I'm not. Big deal. None of anybody's business. And I might have said I was pregnant but I never said I was
having a baby. Honestly, Mum, what is it with you? Did you seriously think I would?'

Annie slumped. Her hands were shaking, her mouth dry. She
had bred a monster. She had done everything she possibly could
have done to bring these girls up to be wonderful and at least one
of them was, before their eyes, revealing herself to be an absolute
monster. Having grown-up children was like living in a horror
film half the time. There she was, in her normal life, in her everyday kitchen, and these bizarre creatures who on the surface

seemed so familiar suddenly come out with the most terrifying and unexpected things: Jess tilting her chin at them – James's chin, originally – and flippantly dismissing the existence of their grandchild; Lucy, from that mouth that was so like her mother's, swearing at the top of her lungs. They all seemed to be flickering in and out of an alternative universe. Annie could hardly bear to watch.

'You can sort of see,' sneered Lucy, 'how the confusion came about. I mean, pregnancy does often lead to babies, after all, doesn't it? It *is* one of the many awkward side-effects.' She climbed out of her seat and then collapsed back down looking suddenly exhausted. 'Oh, J.' She shook her head, in sorrow. 'You are such a fuckwit.'

Lucy was doing very well for herself in the City these days, which both parents were delighted about, but for some reason the higher she rose in the business, the lower her language sank into the gutter. In the world that Annie had been brought up to join, bad language had a completely different social significance: stockbrokers spoke like royals and swearing belonged to dockers. Still, that was back when Annie was an actual person, one who vaguely mattered, instead of this unconsidered wisp of a thing she had become – a wife one decides to divorce or not; a mother one chooses to inform or not; flesh and blood that is rendered invisible whenever it leaves the town boundaries.

'Well, it's all sorted now, isn't it?' Jess had that shifty look on her face that Annie associated with matters of homework and its non-completion. 'D-rama. Not.' She waved out the palms of both hands, waggled those – now retired – pianist fingers, then added: 'Mum. Stop snivelling. I'm going to be a lawyer, remember? You wanted that as much as me, didn't you? I've got years and years of studying ahead of me. Did you want me to have a baby?'

'Of course not.' Annie sniffed. 'Of course not.' Tired, ageing, barren Annie just wanted tired, ageing, barren Annie to have a baby. That was all.

At some point she lost her bearings and her grip on the rest of the conversation but as suddenly as that enormous scene had blown up it was over. James had taken himself off to the pub – in search of some male company, she suspected, and it was hard to blame him – Lucy and Rosie had nipped into town, Jess had gone round to see Araminta. And that left Annie, collapsed over the back of a kitchen chair; a smashed-up, defeated boxer against the side of the ring, facing up to a career in ruins.

26

Bennett's experience of parties was really not extensive. He had attended a few, of course – but not as many as he had wriggled out of going to. They had, as a family, thrown one or two, though he had always managed to excuse himself from the actual planning and scheming and inviting. And then, at the do itself, he had always found a way of travelling through the evening well below the social radar: standing behind a barbecue with a flipper was a solid approach, or hovering around a drinks table, opening and filling. Packets of crisps were a useful diversion and Sue never actually complained if he just vanished into the kitchen and did the washing-up – that was a solution that seemed to satisfy all concerned. His trouble tonight was that none of these coping mechanisms would be available to him.

He put the hired wine glasses out in carefully straight lines on his new kitchen table. The man in the shop had asked him how many guests he was expecting, and he had answered frankly that he didn't have a clue. But that was the thing with an open house, wasn't it? Anything could happen. The new Bennett had rather liked the wild danger of the idea, when he was back in the planning stages; but then the old Bennett popped up, rather nervous, when the off-licence chap looked into his eyes and asked if anyone at all had replied and if he had any idea how many people he had asked.

He counted the packets of crisps and deliberated on the best time for their opening. It would be fine, as he kept telling himself. In Bennett's experience life never turned out to be as extreme as the imagination might lead one to expect – neither as bad as might be feared nor as splendid as might be hoped. Although he was apparently popular these days – and the latest rumours, that the superstore was not now going to happen, could only increase his position – he was pretty confident that his popularity was not so extraordinary that the house would be swamped and the police would be called. And some guests were definitely coming. The children, for a start – although not quite guests, still very welcome – and most of the Choir, he was sure, because why wouldn't they? – and if the protesters had indeed won their case then they would be in the mood to celebrate. He had not after all invited the woman in the butcher's – Araminta had put him off, and also the mince she sold him last week was a rather off-putting grey – but he thought she wouldn't make much difference either way.

The phone rang. Hugging several packets of crisps, he went to answer it.

'Dad. 'S me. Crap news . . .'

♩

Annie, punch-drunk, was still slumped against the kitchen chair, experiencing an acutely painful mixture of bereavement and embarrassment. 'She lost it.' That baby had been so real to, and so loved by, Annie that she was left in a state of sad and empty shock. There had been times, over the past few weeks, that she had loved that baby more than she loved her own daughters: she was pure and unspoiled and had the world at her little pink toes; she was all promise and potential, with no disappointing reality. 'She lost it.'

The doll's house was all ready now, total refurb top to bottom; she even – God, how mad was she? – had more furniture on order, due to arrive next week. She put the back of her cold hands to her hot cheeks. What a complete fool she had been. 'She lost it.' The details of it all were still unclear and Annie hoped they would remain that way. Of course, so many first pregnancies didn't make it past the three-month mark that Annie was amazed that possibility had never occurred to her. Indeed, she was amazed by the appalling, blinkered, mad-old-bat approach she had adopted to the whole thing since the beginning. She had made so many assumptions – that Jess would go ahead with it, and would come home to her parents, and that she, Annie, would become its – her – principal carer – and recast her own future accordingly. Sue was completely right: she had invested everything in this baby as if it were a copper-bottomed empty-nest-avoidance scheme. She wouldn't have to unearth her old identity or discover a new one or rekindle her marriage or travel the world. Instead, she would live another eighteen years beholden to a school timetable and feeding someone else and worrying always about someone else and hoping piles of hopes for somebody else and never giving very much thought to herself. And the worst of it was, she had thought that would be a good thing. Her mother would have been horrified.

It was late afternoon now: the sun had moved round to the kitchen window and illuminated the mess still spread all over the table. She got up and began to gather cups and plates. One lingering problem was that the whole of Bridgeford knew about it and she was going to have deal with that. Pat was already knitting. Why had she confided in Sue, of all people? She was a more efficient information service than 'News from Your Neighbourhood'. Oh, well. Annie grabbed a cloth and wiped the table down. 'She lost it.' That was what she would have to tell everyone. And what could they say to that? 'She lost it.' It was just another repeat of an old pattern. 'She's sleeping through the night.' 'She just gets on with everyone.' 'She missed it by one mark.' 'The school said she would get in but she wouldn't apply.' This was just the latest: 'She lost it.'

The dishwasher was half full from the simple supper of the night before. Annie stacked the rest, looked at it and thought about what needed to be done for the evening meal. All three of them might hang about for it. There could even be an attempt at a vaguely cordial gathering before they all scattered once more, so all this stuff did need cleaning now, probably. Yes. 'Let's get it on,' she said to herself aloud, turning back to the sink. And then, absent-mindedly rinsing the first plate, suddenly heard herself singing:

Oh baby

Dancing with her hips, she went back to the lower plate rack.

Let's get it on

There was no need to get up in the attic and find the original 45 to sing along to. Annie had left her own body. She was now completely possessed by Marvin Gaye.

Sugar

The Annie/Marvin hybrid ground its pelvis, dancing with a mug held tight and close, before coaxing it into a tight place on the middle shelf.

Le-et's get it o-o-on

Annie remembered every note of the funk instrumental, which was pretty amazing considering the word 'funk' had not even crossed her lips for decades. But then this was 1973, wasn't it? Back when Annie was Annie and the only music in her life was hers and hers alone. She thrust her arms in the air, brought her hands down through her hair on to her neck, and caressed herself there while grinding her hips to the rhythm of Marvin's voice in her head. Then she grooved back to the sink, and wondered if everybody's life was like this. Did they all have their own musical identity buried somewhere back in time, beneath a mound of compromises and the choices of their loved ones? Perhaps it was just her. Only she was foolish enough to let it happen.

Annie had cherished and curated all those physical things like she was a warden in a museum: the smocks, the photos, the drawings, the toys. But the very essence of herself – that had slipped away from her somehow. And it had left no trace. If she were to suddenly die, or just fade away – and it scared her how bloody lovely, how very peaceful, those words now sounded – her family would be able to look through the Miller Collection and see which child she was holding when, which holiday she had booked and which cake she had made for what. And they would never know, because they had never asked and she had never thought to tell them, what had ever gone on in her head before it was full up with them. Or that for hour upon hour of year upon year, she had sung alone in her bedroom and dreamed of fame. They didn't have a clue. To be honest, Annie had forgotten all about it herself, until that moment. The idea – so shocking, so, well, vulgar – had been rubbed out by her own mother with such vigour that only the merest trace of it remained. And her girls didn't even know what music she used to listen to, what she would be listening to now if it wasn't for them, because she simply never listened to anything. There wasn't a music-playing gadget in this house that she knew how to use, other than the radio. It was pathetic. She was pathetic. Or, at least, she had been pathetic. She picked up a couple of teaspoons and drummed out the irregular beat while Marv crooned the backing track.

Ooooh – oooooh

Her eyes were closed, her hips were rocking, she was twirling the cutlery round in her hands, humming the electric guitar part, when her happiness was disturbed.

'God. Mum. What are you doing?' Jess was back. *'So* embarrassing.'

'I'm embarrassing?' Annie swung her hips and sang like Marvin. *'I'm* embarrassing?' She span around, rinsed a plate, stuck it in the dishwasher, thrusting her hips. 'How very amusing . . . '

'I hate it when you don't act your age.'

'That bothers me, Jess.' She wriggled up to her, sang in her face. 'That really bothers me. Grr. So bloody sexy, this. When Dad comes home I'm going to snog his head off.'

Jess gagged in a theatrical fashion and Annie stopped singing. She felt so much better.

'Anyway, how was Araminta?'

'Had to go out. So annoying. Her gran's like dead or something *super*-boring and Sue's dragged her off there. She's really pissed off.'

Annie stopped still and stood with her head on one side. 'Sue's mother's dying and she didn't call me?' It didn't make any sense. Sue rang her if the tumble drier broke down or she was off to have a smear. So why wouldn't she ring her if her mother was gravely ill?

'Is that what it's come to? People round here can't even snuff it any more without your permission?' The only time Jess used her 'interested' voice to her mother was when she was taking the piss. 'How does that work, then, in practice – they come round and you issue them with a little chit, or what?'

The truth hit Annie with such a sudden force that she dropped the plate she was holding. It smashed on the floor.

'Mu-um. What's got into you?' Jess wailed. 'What the actual f—?'

'Bennett's party.'

'Eh?'

'It's Bennett's party. In just under an hour. I'd completely for-gotten. I was never going to go because you're all home. She's out to ruin it. That's why she's taken the kids away.' Her voice rose. 'And I bet NOBODY ELSE IS GOING.'

'Man. I'd forgotten quite how exciting it gets round here.' Jess yawned and padded over to the fridge. 'What's for dinner?'

'I don't know, love,' replied Annie, distracted, reaching for her phone, flicking through her mental Rolodex, wondering how many people she could rouse. 'Whatever it is that you decide to make.'

♩

'So.' Bennett forced out one last chuckle, shook his head. 'I think that's probably the last of my funny stories from the world of work.' He twisted his hands in his lap. 'It was lots of fun.'

'Sounds it,' said Lynn, who had not yet cracked a smile as they sat either side of her old kitchen table and looked at each other over a field of unused wine glasses.

'Anyway,' he carried on, 'does anything funny happen in your line of business?'

'No.' Lynn didn't even try to think one up. 'Never.' She helped herself to more crisps.

Rather surprisingly, given his background in mathematical probability, Bennett had not considered this situation among all the possible outcomes of the open-house invitation. He had worried, in times of low spirits, that nobody would show; he had worried that too many might come; he had hoped for more nice people than not. But at no point had it occurred to him that just one person would turn up. Or that that one person would be Lynn. Perhaps his conscious mind had reared back from it, as the probability was that this was the worst-case scenario.

'What about sad things? Perhaps it's more sad things that happen to you?'

'Not really.' She looked at her watch. 'It's only Outpatients. Malingerers, half of them.'

Lynn had arrived at 7.31, and it was now gone 8.30. She had very politely not remarked on the sixty-five glasses, or the remarkable absence of anybody else, and he was grateful for that. They were conspiring in the pretence that it was a perfectly normal social situation being played out here – just two lucky people with plenty to drink and a nice, wide range of vessels with which to drink it – but then how did they ever stop that? At what point would she feel free to get up and go, or he able to declare the party at its close? They might sit here for the rest of their lives, existing on crisps and dry white, pretending to each other that everything was fine.

'What about just interesting stories? Not so funny, not so sad, but a bit, well, interesting?'

Lynn sighed heavily and had a think. She had clearly made a great effort with her appearance tonight, which made Bennett feel a bit worse. The price tag was hanging out of the back of her black sleeveless dress and her make-up seemed to be on the thick side. He had always rather assumed there was a Mr Lynn in the background somewhere, but surely if he existed he would be here. Bennett felt nervous again as his mathematical brain threw up another statistical possibility. He hadn't been alone with a woman other than Sue since the 1980s. The kitchen was suddenly fraught with danger and unwelcome difficulties.

'Well, there was a man who—'

The doorbell rang. Bennett could have wept. He jumped out of his chair and ran through the hall. As he opened the door, Jazzy, wearing not very much at all, almost fell through with Annie and – oh! Something somewhere deep within him danced a little jig – Tracey behind her.

'I've been KIDNAPPED,' Jazzy shrieked. 'We're not all SAD ACTS, you know. Some of us have something to DO on Saturday nights. ACTUALLY.'

'Yes, that's why you were already in your pyjamas. Your nan said you were stuck at home doing nothing, so stop fibbing.'

'SHE STOLE ME FROM MY HOME.' Jazzy turned round and slapped the air around Annie. 'SHE'S NUTS.'

'That's ENOUGH,' Annie shouted back and kicked her up the bottom towards the kitchen. 'Look. Free drink. Count yourself lucky. And pull your knickers up. Hi, Bennett.' She kissed him. 'Sorry we're a bit late. Happy birthday.'

'Thanks, Annie. I'm very glad to see you. Is James coming?'

'Well, I haven't bloody asked him. Jazzy,' she called as she marched through to the kitchen, 'pour me a big one.'

'And happy birthday from me.' Tracey kissed him too. 'Not a relaxing journey. Jazzy kept screaming for help, saying she'd been abducted and climbing out of the car. I had to sit on her.' She flung her jacket on the hall table, headed for the sofa in the lounge and slumped down on it. 'Could do with a lie-down after all that. Any chance of a drink?'

The doorbell rang again. 'Oh.' Tracey jumped up. 'That'll be Lewis and Katie. I'll go and help.'

'It's all right,' said Maria, coming through behind the wheelchair.

'I arrived at the same time. Can't stay long, mind.' She was in her tight green carer's uniform. 'I've got an enema round the corner at nine thirty.'

'Thank God you're here, Katie,' said Tracey. Katie beamed. 'Jazzy's in a right strop. Talk her down for us, will you? You're the only person who can get any sense into her. She's in the kitchen.'

Bennett left the door open after that, and took up position at the drinks table in the kitchen, from where he could see all the arrivals flooding in. The basses were all here now, in a gang – they were the sort of men, Bennett had noticed, who had to be in a gang. The phrase 'life and soul of the party' came to mind and brought a temporary heaviness of heart. But then Judith and Kerry walked in with their arms around each other, followed by the nice chap from the bank, and behind them was another gang – female and young enough to lower the average age. Which was good, as next in was Pat with ... good Lord, wasn't that the woman from the butcher's? He couldn't quite tell without the white coat. Bennett worried that it was a rather random selection of people, now that he could see them all together like this. Was that how you threw a party – did you almost literally fling anybody you could find at one particular venue – or was there a bit more to it than that? He was just starting to tense up again when the most beautiful girl in the world just strolled into his kitchen and flung her arms around his neck.

'Dad.' She kissed him, 'I made it.' Then, turning to the room, she announced: 'Hi, everyone. I'm Min.'

'What are you doing here?' said Bennett. And as an afterthought, 'Who did you say you were?'

'I'm just your daughter.' Araminta stepped back to shake his hand. 'No reason you should remember me. But for future reference – in the notebook, under D.'

Everyone laughed and the whole house relaxed.

'I just didn't know you called yourself Min.' She looked slightly different to him here tonight, among these different people, under a different name. He felt a bit baffled. 'And I thought Grandma was sick.'

'Not sick enough, sadly. I have grave news.' 'Min' turned her mouth down. 'The old trout's got years left in her. So,' she brightened, returning to the guests, 'as we have established, I'm the daughter he'd forgotten he had. But who are all you lot? Hey, Dad,' she elbowed him, 'is this your gang?'

Tracey noticed how much better-looking Bennett was all of a sudden. He was clearly much happier when Min was about, and the set of his face had lifted and altered accordingly, but that wasn't all. Now that one could see the exact replica of his features playing about in the prettiness of his clever, funny, lively daughter, he was a completely different proposition. It was a realisation that Bennett didn't actually have to be Bennett. That with this face he could have a different destiny, that there was an alternative in there somewhere. All he needed was a new, open confidence, a casual, relaxed air and a different attitude. Tracey smiled as she watched him. What was she thinking? If Bennett had all those things, then he really wouldn't be Bennett, would he? But still, he had already moved along to a place that was somewhere just that little bit closer to handsome.

'We could do with some music, couldn't we?' Tracey called over. 'Where is it? Let's see what you've got.'

'Ah. Oh dear. I did think I'd thought of everything. Um. I've only got a record player, over there I'm afraid. Terribly old-fashioned.'

'Not old-fashioned,' she told him firmly. 'And stop apologising. Just say it's retro.'

'Would retro be a good thing?' He looked a little disbelieving.

'Cool.' Tracey marched over to the records stacked tightly along the bottom bookshelf and started to pull a few out. 'Take my word for it.' She was enjoying herself doing this. Not looking at the actual sleeves – that made her heart sink; they were hardly going to get a party started with Bachs CPE through to JS – but fingering through them. She had grown up into a world of cassettes, and then CDs; vinyl had started to bow out gracefully just as she was bowing in.

So the joy of arriving at a bloke's house and evaluating him through his record collection was one that only really belonged properly to the generation just above her. Tracey had watched them all doing it – elder siblings in the houses of friends; sophisticated young girls-about-town in sitcoms and dramas – but she had been denied a long and happy adulthood of getting to act it out herself. It was like all those other things that she had watched and read about and heard of and considered to be such obvious entitlements of grown-up life – the very basics of her birthright – yet which had never fulfilled their promise, like going to the moon or dating Warren Beatty.

Her fingers moved past Weber and on to a different-looking section altogether. Aha, she thought. This is more promising. We seem to have left Classical Gloomsville and moved on to—

'Oh.' Bennett was beside her. 'You've found my Eurovision collection?'

'Your—?' She span round and looked at him. 'Your *what*?'

She suddenly felt cold.

'Yes.' He was smiling and friendly – in deep pretence that the conversation was nothing out of the ordinary. She wondered vaguely if he had been trained for this sort of thing by MI5. 'Eurovision. One of my specialist subjects.' He filled her glass. 'Araminta always says I should go on *Mastermind*, but I don't think she would really like it if I did.'

'I wouldn't,' Tracey replied, glugging it back. 'There's bound to be some obscure little act that passed you by.'

'Oh, there isn't. I know there isn't.' He tapped his head. 'It's all in there. I started,' he was getting chatty now, 'when I left choir school. I had nothing in common with all the non-choristers out there in the world. They were all interested in pop song instead of Evensong—'

'Funny, that ...' She looked around her for a getaway. He had her trapped against the shelves.

'I thought so.' He shook his head, rueful. 'Anyway, in a vain attempt to fit in, I set about becoming the school's top expert and

225

statistician of all things Eurovision.' He gave a sad little chuckle. 'It was my bid to be cool.'

All right, she thought. He wants an ordinary conversation, I'll give him an ordinary conversation. Two of us can play at that game. 'Well, come on. The suspense is killing me. Did it turn you into the Fonz?'

'Oh. Well, I don't know what a fonz is but it didn't make me cool, if that's what you're asking. In fact,' he looked into her eyes, 'for a bit there, back in Fourth Year, I thought it might ruin my life.'

'That's a bit extreme.' She wasn't biting, she didn't think it was fair to. If they were going to have a Eurovision Ruined My Life-off, she was going to win it, hands down. 'Did you give it all up then, in Fourth Year?'

'Oh no. I couldn't, for some reason. It's been an obsession of mine ever since.'

She took a deep breath, pinched together her trembling hands. So here we go: the great unmasking. Of all the people Tracey had felt nervous around over her twenty years living the lie, she had never suspected that it would come down to Bennett. Never once. Still, let's get it over with.

'Everyone from Matt Monro through to, well, to be honest,' he gave a shy smile, 'my absolute favourite – actually, I had a real crush on this one ... Teresa V ... '

He smiled and, feeling rather pathetically chuffed, she waited patiently for the penny to drop. He went back to his records, took one out, held it and stared. He looked down at the cover, then back up at Tracey. He cocked his head, furrowed his brow, looked down again, back again, shook his head. He opened his mouth to speak, then shut it again, frowning.

I don't believe it, thought Tracey: I just *don't bloody believe it*. The penny does not seem to be dropping. The penny is defying gravity. All these years. All this time. All that subterfuge, and name-changing and hair dye and never getting close to anybody because she could never bear to say the truth. She had lived her whole adult life as an enormous great lie and for what? There was only one person alive who even remembered her, and he was too blind or too dim to know her when she was right in front of him.

Then: 'Dad,' said Min. 'Music. Get your act together. Come on, not all that old stup—' She looked over his shoulder and saw it at once. 'Hello. That's you, isn't it? I mean, long blond hair and all that but still, it is you, isn't it? Are you Teresa V? How exciting.' Although she did not, Tracey thought, sound very excited at all. Indeed, she sounded thoroughly unimpressed.

'But – but – how . . .' Bennett was still struggling at the back of the class there. Clearly nobody had ever told him that hair colour was optional or that sometimes, some people – people other than Bennett, for example – were capable of change.

She put a hand on his arm. 'I promise, I'll tell you everything. But later. Let's get this party on the go first.'

♩

Annie had been dancing for hours and was now collapsed on the sofa, content to sit and watch the others like a Jane Austen chaperon. It was nearly one in the morning, and most people were still in Bennett's front room and bopping away. Including, of all things, Bennett – and, strangely, that was not quite the unpleasant sight she had been expecting. Of course it was natural that his great musicianship gave him a sense of rhythm but oddly, in all the years that she had known him and Sue, she had never once known them to dance. Had Annie just never been there, or had he simply never done it in decades? It was rather a sad thought. Because she had danced with him a lot tonight, and much to her surprise it had been an extremely enjoyable experience indeed. James, of course, never danced. It was, Annie was fond of saying, his one fault. She might update that little wifely statement now, though: he was developing, or she was starting to notice, faults galore.

She was just getting her breath back. The neighbours, who were very much anti-Bennett in the very amicable war of the St John Parkers, had come round to complain at midnight but even they were still there, dancing and drinking with the rest of them. It was actually a rather brilliant party. The young ones had got them all up dancing with that lovely 'Happy' song that seemed to please all ages, and then Lewis of all people had taken over the iPad; his playlist was older but still suited everyone.

Oliver's Army are on their way

There was plenty of life to this party – the basses were inevitably the loudest, but Judith, Kerry and their lot were coming close. The young ones were still going around Katie in her chair. Bennett went from one group to the next, pouring yet more wine.

. . . here to sta-ay

But the soul of it was definitely Tracey. She had been up on the coffee table on and off since about ten past ten, singing at the top of her fabulous voice – as if she was the artiste and the tracks were just backing. She was clearly loving it but then so was everyone else. Her knowledge of all the lyrics from every genre from 1965 to 1990 seemed to be absolute and her performance honed. The party roared its approval as Elvis Costello finished and 'Midnight Train to Georgia' came on.

Ooh-ooh LA

We don't really need Gladys Knight, thought Annie. We've got Tracey. No wonder she left the Choir. This girl wasn't a chorus member; she was a soloist and performer through every fibre of her being. Her voice was knocking a hole through to the house next door. How peculiar life was, that a woman with all that charisma and talent was a paralegal in a tech company. She must have wanted for a mentor. Every time one of her girls had taken up a musical instrument Annie had anticipated a glorious career for them and researched it all just in case. If only she had known Tracey earlier, she could have used all that expertise on her. What a shame. It really was a shame.

Oh he's leaving (leav-ing)
On that midnight train . . .

Annie sank into the sofa and her mood sank with her. It was the worst thing about drifting over the age of forty: you suddenly got a view of yourself as a finished product. Her own next stop was sixty, and she had long ago got used to living with a long list of Things Annie Miller Would Never Be or Do. Her focus now was more on what the girls might be or do, and that kept her going. But someone like Tracey she could really feel for. To have so much possibility and to hit the age when you have to face up to the fact that you are never going to get the chance to realise it – it was a shame.

The neighbours started slow-dancing, and so did lots of other suddenly close couples whom Annie was not aware were even previously acquainted. And so did Judith and Kerry. Pat and Lynn were either side of Annie like a shot.

'Well, well, well,' one bellowed into her ear, 'are you seeing what I'm seeing?'

Annie ignored her.

'I wonder what her' – she made inverted commas in the air – '"fiancé" makes of it?'

'Just as well he doesn't exist, really, isn't it? Otherwise he might be a bit put out.'

They cackled at each other and Annie removed herself to the kitchen.

At about 2 a.m. the dancing stopped and the singing began. Araminta had, like her father, a talent for the piano but, unlike her father, she also had a working knowledge of popular music. While she banged away at Beatles classics, the rest of them gathered around, arms linked, heads leaning on the shoulders of others, and belted them out. When they were halfway through 'Hey Jude', Tracey – who had been down on the floor and singing along with the rest of them – leapt back on to the occasional table and took control. Within seconds she had them all divided into three groups, doing their own parts while she improvised over the top.

La, la, la, la-la-la laaaa

Min kept changing key, going higher and higher and louder and louder, and the singers spiralled up and up on to a plain of delirium that many of them had never known. They danced, they beamed, they hugged, they swayed. Bennett's front room was a bubble of ecstasy, until someone said, 'Shit. It's three o'clock in the bloody morning,' and popped it.

There was the normal clapping and cheering – but this time, for once, it was actually appropriate – and appreciation of Min on the piano. And then the spotlight turned to Tracey.

'Wish you were our leader.'

'We'd actually be in with a chance if it was you.'

'Never mind that, we might even enjoy ourselves again.'

'Well, I voted for her.'

'So did I.'

'She should have won.'

Bennett, his forehead damp and his eyes large, stood up tall and raised his voice above the crowd.

'Yes. She should have won. And she did.'

'Dad. You and your wild parties. Is it like this every Saturday night?' Araminta had folded herself into the large armchair, like she used to do at the end of the school day. 'Women all over the place. It's like the *Playboy* Mansion.'

There was just the one woman, but his daughter had inherited her mother's talent for wild exaggeration – it was possibly her only flaw. They both stared at Tracey, out cold under a blanket on the sofa.

'So what's the full story with her, then? She's a bit too cool for Bridgeford. Where did you find her?'

'I found her at choir, but that's not how I know her. I know her, it turns out, from when she had that album out years ago. She was in the Eurovision Song Contest, you know.'

'No. Dad,' she wailed and thrashed about in pain, 'don't. It was bad enough that *you* owned it, but I was hoping it was nothing to do with stupid Eurovision. You're breaking my heart. So she's not cool enough even for Bridgeford. She's actually as lame as you?'

Bennett pondered for a while, trying to ascertain how that lameness might be quantified. 'Quite possibly,' he said after a moment's reflection, 'even lamer. She wasn't just sitting at home with a pencil and a score sheet and a file with the records of all previous years—'

Araminta buried her head in her hands. 'That's it, as much as I can take. Somewhere out there must be my real birth father.'

'—she was actually in it.'

They both stared at the sleeping beauty with the tongue stud and the leather jacket over her feet. 'So was she very famous?'

'Well, yes and no.'

Bennett lowered himself on to the piano stool and told Araminta what he knew. And as he told her, he reflected on the extraordinary turns that life takes if you give it long enough; how even if you have a full cast list of all the people who are ever going to appear in the story of your life, you can never really predict who is going to have a minor part, who will never even make it into the final cut, and who will, eventually, take the lead.

'Tracey Leckford isn't famous, no. It seems to me she's gone to great lengths to be as anonymous as possible. But Teresa V – of the eighties girl band Teresa and the Miracles – well, she was really getting quite well known. There were a few of these bands back then – schoolfriends from provincial towns, going to London, making it big.'

'Oh, Dad. Like you would know. Are you telling me you used to follow that kind of stuff?' Araminta was sceptical.

'No, of course not.'

'Course not.' She nodded and held out her hands, palms uppermost. 'Too lame.'

'Far too lame. But I became aware of her when she did her Song for Europe, and did all my usual mugging up.'

'OK. So did Teresa and the Miracles do Eurovision?'

'No. Just Teresa. Teresa V, she was called. She was very pretty –

I mean, still is, but in a different way. She had this full fair hair that came past her shoulders and she wore this sort of floaty sort of, pastelly sort of ... Well, you saw that photo.'

'Dad. Stop. Hopeless.'

'Sorry. Anyway, some big-shot producer persuaded her to dump the group and do his song. It was called "The Island Was a Dream".'

'Sounds dodgy. Is that famous?'

'Only for being one of the worst things we've ever entered, and getting one of the lowest scores in British history.' He still shuddered when he remembered that dark night of the national soul.

'And was that the end of her?'

'Hey.' Over on the sofa, Tracey was coming round. Groggily, she raised herself on to an elbow. 'Don't mind me, you lot. "The *end* of her"? That's a bit much ...'

'Oh,' Araminta was out of her chair and kneeling beside her, 'you're crying. I'm so sorry. Did we upset you?'

'Talking about me like I'm a corpse? Of course not. Carry on.' She sniffed a bit. 'Probably a bit pissed, that's all.' Then she fell back on to the cushions and the tears came in a rush. 'It's just that I haven't heard my life story put together like that before. It's sort of a bit shit, isn't it?'

'Well, I don't know,' Araminta soothed. 'I'm sure it's not. I mean, that was all a while back. When was your Eurovision? Like thousands and thousands of years ago, surely? What happened after that?' She stroked Tracey's hair. 'Loads of good stuff ...'

'Well,' Bennett had passed Tracey a tissue and she looked down at it as she chose her words, 'the rest of the group wouldn't have me back. So I went solo. And that was a disaster. And then I got pregnant. And my parents wouldn't have me back either. And that, looking back on it, was a bit of a disaster, too. And, apart from Billy, I've been basically solo ever since. And now he's buggered off and left me so I'm completely solo—' Self-pity overcame her.

'Hang on.' Min made a wind-it-back gesture with her fingers. 'Billy? Billy Leckford? As in Famous Dopehead Billy Leckford?'

'The very same.' Tracey blew her nose. 'See? A bit shit or a bit shit?'

'Well, er ...' Min screwed her face up.

'... yes.' Tracey finished for her.

'OK. Yeah. Defo. Quite a bit shit.'

As one sobbed and the other comforted, Bennett went over to his album collection, found the one he wanted without needing to look, and put it on.

You were on the island

But the island was a dream

Araminta was holding her nose. 'Blimey, what a stinker.'

'Yeah,' said Tracey, groggy but almost sober. 'Bloody terrible.'

'Well the funny thing is,' said Bennett, beating time with his finger and singing along, word-perfect, 'I absolutely love it.'

'She lost it.' Annie looked down at her Danish to avoid Sue's eye.

'Oh, love, no.' Sue sounded genuinely sad, as if something had been stolen from her personally too. 'What happened?'

'She just came home at the weekend and told us.' Annie shrugged. 'She lost it. It's perfectly common, after all.'

'What a shame. So no point asking about your weekend, then. It must have been grim.'

'Not entirely, no.' Annie looked up. 'I went to Bennett's party on Saturday night and that really took my mind off everything.' She leaned in conspiratorially. 'Didn't get home until silly o'clock. That shocked them all, I can tell you.' The truth was, nobody had even noticed. She had slipped into a sleeping house, beside a sleeping James, and the next day nothing had been said.

'Silly o'clock? God help us.' Sue rolled her eyes.

'It was fantastic. Best I've been to for years. Singing. Dancing. It was a complete blast.'

'And this is definitely my Bennett we're talking about?'

'How many Bennetts do you know?' Annie took a sip of

cappuccino, then shook her head and laughed. 'I went round the next morning to get my car – I'd had far too much to drive home – and there were still bodies on the sofa in the sitting room. It was like being a young person.'

'Bodies! Whose bodies?'

'Well, Araminta was one' – she watched as Sue tried to swallow that down without choking – 'and Tracey was certainly in there ...' Much to Annie's fury. She didn't know why she hadn't thought of that one, staying over. Perhaps, just possibly, if she hadn't come home at all, someone might have picked up on that.

'Hang on. Tracey? What Tracey? Clue.'

'Hair.'

'Ah. Yes. Hair. And legs. Hair AND legs.'

'Oh, yes. Legs. Definitely legs.'

'More coffee, ladies?' asked Jazzy. 'Laugh on Saturday, wasn't it, Mrs M? Tell you what, though, got some dirty looks going home in my pyjamas.' She and Annie giggled together. 'Do you think Lewis has even come round yet?'

Sue, reddening, charged in and took the conversational lead.

'So how's your mum settled down this time then, Jazzy?'

Annie winced. Sue had a certain approach towards those less fortunate than herself that could often lead to conflict. She couldn't help it. This imperious Justice of the Peace/lady on the board/pillar of the community/expert without portfolio manner had been bred into Sue as herding is bred into a collie. Generations of ladies in hats had peered over mahogany desks at generations of wastrels, pointed out to them the errors of their ways and directed them towards the better path. Sue just happened to be the latest in their line. The fact that, these days, there was a whole class of highly educated caring professionals to save her from poking her nose in did not seem to have occurred.

'Brilliant, thanks.' Jazzy leaned over and wiped the table, hard. 'My mum's doing great.'

'Well, it's nice she's made a positive start, but it's a bit early to say that, don't you think? She's hardly been home five minutes.'

'Two months,' snapped Jazzy. 'She's been home nearly two months and . . .'

This was not going to end well, but there was nothing Annie could do about it – she was no match for either of them. So she tuned out, and then in to the conversation on the table next door. If she knew her Bridgeford social classifications – and Annie certainly did know her Bridgeford social classifications – that was the St Ambrose Summer Fête Committee, meeting yet again. They did take it seriously, this lot. Annie couldn't remember exactly, but she was sure that they had done all those things without any committees at all; it had just been a question of Annie and Sue getting on with it.

There was clearly some huge issue going on; voices were starting to rise. 'So do we have the Elvis impersonator or don't we? It's a perfectly simple question.'

'But Melissa, I definitely booked him,' said a pale and nervous creature. 'I know I did. I'm just not sure he's actually going to come.'

'Does anyone know a Colonel Tom Parker impersonator?' drawled a skinny woman with a beautiful toddler on her lap. 'He'd be able to sort it out.' She laughed at her own joke, and her little girl giggled with her. Nobody else did though.

'Shut up, Georgie. This is serious.' The woman with the schedule in front of her slapped the table with impatience. She was so puffed up with the importance of her job, and the importance of herself, that Annie couldn't help but smile.

They all looked perfectly ridiculous, sitting there so steamed up about such a silly little thing that didn't really matter. And as someone who had spent decades of her life getting steamed up about silly little things that didn't matter – fêtes and events and schemes and lunches and now the Choir – she was jolly well entitled to think that. If you pulled back from it, pretty much everything looked meaningless and inconsequential next to the bigger things around it. There was always something more important to worry about than that which was costing you your sleep. Their little fête – just one afternoon, with or without Elvis – looked absurd next to the Choir. The Choir, after all, was a permanent fixture – open to all generations, of any class. Yet the rest of Bridgeford did not care whether it lived or died. But then Bridgeford was just a tiny, inconsequential dot on the landscape of Britain; Britain looked so small next to America; America was dwarfed by Asia. Perhaps somewhere out there in the universe was a world much greater than ours that even now was looking down upon us, shaking its head and smiling a patronising smile.

And then Annie looked at her own family: smaller than any of it. How much time and worry and thought and love and caring – days and weeks of desperate, non-stop caring – had she squandered on silly little Jess and her non-baby? And what wider resonance did any of it have? None at all. If Annie, or any other member of the Miller family for that matter, were to flap their wings in the jungle it would have absolutely no effect on anything, anywhere, ever. All the hours she spent in the service of others and yet the world simply refused to change. Perhaps she had been missing the point all along; living with the wrong end of life's stick.

Jazzy was stomping off and Sue was very red. 'Some people just need to face reality, that's my view. And some people need to show them how.'

'What about you?' she asked casually. 'Will you and Bennett be getting back together again, do you think? Is it all still on trial or is it permanent?'

'Permanent. Definitely. We're getting divorced. I'm never going back there. God, it's a relief to be out of it.'

'But, do you mind me asking, because you've never really told me: why?'

There was a pause while a different waitress came over with their new cups of coffee, and Annie reflected for a moment. From the point of view of her own sterile marriage, she had been studying Bennett for the last few weeks and had started to wonder why any sane woman would ever want to let him go. He could sing, he could dance, he was a wonderful dad and had the manners of a nineteenth-century gentleman. She spent a lot more time enjoying the company of Bennett these days than she did that of the absentee James. She had even developed a rather illicit envy of married life with him. Was he really such a terrible mate? At least he came home.

The waitress left them.

'I mean, it's not going to be easy in the long run. It's a tricky age to suddenly find yourself on your own again.' It was something Annie seemed to dwell on rather a lot at the moment: how she was soon to be sixty, and how much she did not want to be on her own again.

'Are you joking?' Sue spluttered, mid-gulp. 'I can't wait. Cannot bloody wait.' The cup thumped back into its saucer. 'It will be such a relief. You have to remember: I made the big mistake of marrying a younger man.' She shook her head in self-pity. 'He's not like us, Annie.'

'How do you mea—'

'He's not all old and fat and wrinkled and falling to bits ...'

'Oh.' Annie gasped and brought a hand to her throat.

'... he's all,' she made a moue of distaste, 'I dunno ... frisky' – the word shot out like spit – 'and ... Well, you said it, don't you even listen to yourself? *Energetic.* I mean, singing? Dancing? Bodies? Really, God. Help. Us.'

Annie was aghast; chilled by the horror of what she was hearing.

'As soon as he started talking about redundancy, that was when I realised: I don't want some younger, *energetic* bloke hanging around, tarnishing my golden years. I want to eat what I want and when I want it. I want to go to bed at eight o'clock. I want to sleep in a fleece.' With each point, she banged on the table, as if demanding a new charter of basic human rights. 'I want to watch *Countdown* and I want watch it ON MY OWN.' She polished off her Danish and, through the mouthful, let out a bitter laugh. 'Of course, it's not that much better now, with the kids. They seem to have inherited his *energy.* Still, they'll be gone soon. Can't think why you're always moaning about your empty nest; I'm counting the days. Where's that bloody girl got to? I want another bun.'

28

The heavy door was wedged open. It was a beautiful spring evening, one of the first since the clocks had changed, and nobody wanted to shut it out. Inside, everyone was in their place already, and feeling fraught. It was like those last few minutes before a surprise party – exciting, yes, but not without its tensions. They had all arrived at choir early so that when they challenged Edward they did so together as a united front. And now they sat in their rows, too nervous to talk.

Jonty, tinkling on the piano, sent sideways looks over to the singers; he could sense something was up. Pat, though, was quite unaware of what was about to break. Insensitive as ever to the emotions of others, she sat with them, stitching her tapestry, chatting away.

'Quite some party that was, Bennett.'

Nobody else spoke, but she didn't seem to notice.

'Lynn and I didn't leave until nearly one, did we, love? What happened after that? Did I miss anything?'

Nobody replied.

'Shame Edward didn't make it. I bet he can dance.'

The minute-hand on the hall clock passed the top of the hour and some of them dared to hope Edward wouldn't turn up at all; that he had heard what was going on and had already packed it in. A few shoulders relaxed, conversations broke out. Then a car drew up and almost instantly the hall door thwacked back against the wall.

'Evening, all,' he boomed as he crossed the floor. 'Aha. A better turn-out tonight.' He flung his coat away, flourished his baton and looked around him. 'Excellent. This I can do something with. Let's get started.' He raised his arms and looked over to Jonty.

Bennett got to his feet.

'We won't get started actually, Edward.'

'Sorry?' He looked amused.

'You're not starting anything around here.'

Edward laughed and called over his shoulder. 'OK, hold that, Jonty. Apparently we're not starting.'

Jonty giggled.

'What are you up to, Bennett?' Pat was just wrapping her needles up in her canvas and bending over the needlepoint bag at her feet. 'All that protesting's gone to your head.'

'I am seeing that justice is done.'

The evening sun broke the clouds and shone through the high windows; it held the men in sharp relief against its beam.

'Woo, justice eh? Big stuff.' Edward crossed his arms and blew out his cheeks. 'Justice. Wow.'

'I have here,' Bennett produced a jiffy bag full of votes, 'the EVI-DENCE,' and strode over to the tea area, 'that the election for the leadership of the Bridgeford Community Choir was rigged.' He shook out the contents and spread them all over the table.

'Boo.'

'For shame.'

'Cheat. Cheat. Cheat,' chanted Lewis and friends, stamping their feet. 'Out. Out. Out.'

Tracey sat hunched with her face in her hands.

'How did you get your hands on them?' shrieked Pat.

'I retrieved them,' Bennett was now in full Henry Fonda mode, 'from your' – he pointed at Pat, built his voice up to the final flourish – 'WHEELIE BIN!'

'Here!' Pat was outraged. 'You can't go around doing that sort of thing. Poking around in someone's wheelie bin? That's creepy, that is. You're a pervert, a horrible *pervert.*'

Edward was bent over his music stand in hysterical laughter. 'You went into her wheelie bin?' He wiped the tears from his eyes and tried to get the words out. 'Well, you're not a weirdo, are you? Hello, Mr Normal. What about recycling – do you like a bit of that too, eh?'

'Er, not really, no.' Bennett was immediately sidetracked.

'Oh yes, nothing like a nice rifle through someone else's wet waste, is there?'

'Actually that's not at all my thing.' He had completely lost his momentum now.

'I might bring mine in for you next week as a special treat, seeing as you've made such a complete arse of yourself here tonight. So get back to your seat and we'll all pretend it never happened. Now then. Warm-up. From th—'

'No.' Annie jumped up. 'I'm sorry, Edward. Bennett's methods may have been a little comic—'

Bennett frowned and turned his mouth down, affronted.

'—but the injustice he uncovered is one that we take very seriously. We are, indeed, very proud of him and what he has done in the interests of the Choir. In fact, I think Bennett is a hero.' She blushed. 'Only because of him do we know the truth: that TRACEY won the election and NOT YOU.' There was loud cheering. 'And now we would very much like to ask you to leave.'

Tracey uncovered her eyes and watched the drama unfold.

'Out. Out. Out.' They were all on their feet now, clapping and stamping. Lewis and the lot from the council were loving it – fists clenched and faces contorted in anger at this enemy of democracy. This was the sort of people power Lewis had been wanting all along.

'Look here, there might have been a *minor* discrepancy, I can't believe there were many votes in it, and we've done so much work now for the contest—'

'OUT!' They were loud and united and strong and immovable.

'Why don't I take us through to that and then hand over to Tracey afterwards and—'

'OUT!' They were the entitled ones now: entitled to send Edward and his horrible smug friends packing.

'Come on, *Jonty*.' In this particular context, that name tripped off his tongue with ease. Lewis tipped up the chair and unseated him while he was at it. 'On your bike, now, there's a good chap.' Jonty scrabbled around on the floor, struggled to his feet and scuttled out. Edward gathered his stuff and followed briskly. 'And you can take that baton with you.'

Emma hurried after them. Pat got up and then, trying not to draw any more attention to herself, discreetly sat down again.

'Excuse me. Can we help you?' Lynn asked her.

She looked around a room of cold stares, got up again and left.

'OK then.' Annie beckoned. 'Tracey – come forward.' And to much noisy enthusiasm Tracey took up her place in front of them all. She looked different tonight. Her hair – worn in such a severe crop when she first joined them – fell softly, almost to her shoulders. The trademark skinny jeans were still on, but now teamed with a cobalt-blue shirt, short-sleeved and hanging loose. As she raised her voice, they could all see that her tongue stud was no longer there.

'Thanks, everybody. Thank you for voting for me. I just hope it wasn't under false pretences. You see, I've been thinking about you all, and who likes what song and who hates which style – Lynn with her hymns and Maria with her musicals and Lewis with his folk and the girls with their new stuff ... And I think there's only one way to keep all of you happy; one way to make sure that all those different traditions get a look-in, with all of you enjoying yourselves at the same time. We should just become a pop choir—' Lynn started to protest but Tracey wasn't having any of it. 'That's what pop music is, Lynn – popular, something for everyone. What do you think?'

There was cautious approval among the older members, raucous appreciation among the young. 'Look. Let's just give it a go. If you don't like it, you can throw me out of office. Lewis can personally defenestrate me.'

'Oh, no I wouldn't ...' Even Lewis had had enough political excitement for one evening.

'I know you won't. Because you're all going to LOVE it. Jazzy, pass these around, will you? We need a set of three songs for the Championships. This will be our first. You should all know it and you can't not like it: it's called "Lean on Me".'

Lynn was first in the queue for the tea.

'Well, that was dramatic, wasn't it?' Annie asked her. 'How do you feel about it all? You've been friends with Pat since I can remember.'

'Fifty-five years.' She shook her head and took a cupcake.

'Aw,' Annie sympathised. 'That's going to be hard. I'm sure you can be still.'

'Bloody hope not. Relief to see the back of her. I've been trying to dump that miserable old cow since the early nineties. You know those friends who are well past their sell-by date but you never get round to chucking them out?' She turned round, leaned her bottom against the table and sipped her tea.

Annie looked up. 'Yes,' she said. 'Yes, I think I do.'

'She was mine. I remember on my mum's larder shelf there was a jar of pickle left over from the war. It sat there looking at us till the day she died, and very nasty it was too. Could've killed someone.' Lynn sank into her cake and carried on through a mouthful of crumbs. 'At least once a week for the past ten years I have been reminded of that pickle. Quite past it, very nasty and extremely dangerous – you know what I mean?'

A queue was building up and Annie didn't have a chance to answer. But she looked very thoughtful as she reached for the milk.

Tracey sat alone against the wall, marking up her music. When Bennett handed her a cup of tea she looked up, smiled and put down her pencil. 'Thank you for that. You stuck your neck out there. I appreciate it.'

'Enjoyed myself.'

She hugged her mug with both hands and blew across the top. 'Told you they'd call you a weirdo.'

'And *I* told *you* I wasn't bothered.' He sat down, leaned right back in his chair, stretched his long grey-flannelled legs out and balanced his mug on his thigh. 'What are we going to do about a pianist – any ideas?'

'I was just mulling that over. I could do it myself, of course. Not from the piano but if I brought my keyboard and set it up here.'

'I didn't know you played.'

'Hmm, well, not all of us bob up like a performing seal at the first sign of an audience. Some of us are a little more shy and retiring.'

Bennett looked at her sideways. 'Was that a joke?'

'Yes, Bennett. It was. Sorry, forgot who I was dealing with. The other option I was considering was: your lovely Min.'

'Araminta?' His face softened. 'She would be brilliant. I'll ask her tonight. Anything else I can do?'

'Actually, I wouldn't mind some help with choosing the song list. I've got various ideas but I could do with a sounding-board. Could you possibly come back to my place tonight when we're done here?'

'Oh. Hmm.' Bennett sucked his teeth and thought about it for a bit. 'I should think I can manage that.'

Lewis came over. He took Bennett's elbow and led him away, keeping his back to the hall. 'Here, Bennett. A quick word.' He was talking out of the side of his mouth like a police informant. 'Well done on all that, by the way. I didn't know you had it in you.

Electoral malpractice strikes at the very heart of democracy and we must all be vigilant.'

'Indeed.'

'Now then. On another little matter. I'm not telling everybody until I've heard a bit more, but the rumour machine down at the council was in overdrive this afternoon. Apparently the whole superstore project is on the verge of collapse.'

Bennett jumped and shouted, 'Wha—'

Lewis shushed him. 'Keep it down,' he whispered. 'The thing is, apparently there's been a change at the top. Bit of a rethink. And there's going to be a dramatic U-turn in company strategy. They won't be building any more of those vast places until further notice.'

'But that's great!' Bennett was loud again.

'Well, yes and no, Ben; yes and no.' He was so quiet, Bennett was straining to hear him. 'But I don't think that's how we want to spin it, do you? I think it might be a bit – well, more useful, somehow, if everybody thought they had won an important victory, rather than just, you know, being the spineless creatures of wilful corporate self-interest . . . Do you get my drift?'

'That it was all down to the protesters, you mean? And the rally and the sit-in and the, well, the lying down in the puddle?' Bennett looked thoughtful.

'That's right.' Lewis slapped him on the shoulder. 'You're getting me, aren't you? I knew we'd be of the same mind. That superstore brought Bridgeford to life. We don't want it dying on its feet again.'

. . . need somebody to lea-ean on.

'Thank you very much, everybody,' Tracey shouted over the warm applause. 'That was a great start. Need I remind you that we haven't got long to get this all together now, so full attendance from now on, please.'

'Thanks, Tracey.'

'Great evening.'

'Promise to learn the lyrics by next week.'

'Night, all.'

'Well, that was a night and a half.' Annie had one last look round the kitchen and hung up the tea-towel. 'Can I give either of you a lift?'

'We're fine thanks, Annie,' replied Tracey. 'Bennett's coming back to my place to talk through the programme. We can walk.'

And Annie watched them as they left together.

♩

They were already talking through the various possible song ideas as they went through the front door and up the clean and vacuumed stairs.

'Can I get you something?' Tracey turned the light on, had flung her coat on the nearest chair and was just going towards the fridge when there was a loud clatter from above, in her bedroom. She and Bennett froze and stared at each other.

'Is there supposed to be someone else in here?' he whispered.

She shook her head, slapped her hands over her mouth to stop herself screaming. Her throat was tight with panic.

Bennett grabbed the post at the bottom of the banisters, swung on to the stairs and sprang up them. Tracey heard scuffling, thumping, crashing; an 'Ow' of protest, an 'All right, keep your hair on', the split of a kick.

'Oh my God.' She couldn't swallow the scream a second longer. 'Bennett!' Then suddenly he was back before her, a bit ruffled but still in one piece, the bearer of two trophies: in one hand Curly and in the other Squat.

'You two? What the hell ...? You little shits. Why were you ...? You were in my safe. Weren't you? *You're* the little buggers that have been nicking stuff. It was you all along.'

'You actually know these characters?' Bennett, incredulous, twisted the unclean head of one and stared at it like it was a ventriloquist's dummy.

'Bennett St John Parker,' said Tracey, all polite, 'meet Curly and Squat.'

'Curly?' Bennett lifted a strand of Curly's long lank locks with a mouth-wrinkle of distaste.

'Yes,' sighed Tracey. 'Curly. Because he isn't.'

'I see.' Bennett turned to the short, stout, pug-faced character in his other hand. 'And I'm guessing Squat because he is?'

'No.' She sat down at the table with a thump, suddenly very tired. 'Squat because he does.' Bennett looked baffled. 'He's called Squat because he squats. Pretty much anywhere. Has done for years.'

'Tell you what, though, Trace,' chipped in Squat, in the manner of a chap trying to change the agenda, 'if you were after a lodger for Billy's room, I might be interested.'

Tracey rose out of her seat. 'If I decided to get a lodger, SQUAT,' she put her face right into his, 'I would select a decent working person who actually paid me some money instead of a LAZY SCROUNGER LIKE YOU WHO FUCKING NICKS IT OFF ME.'

'All right.' Squat, flinching, sounded a little hurt. 'Just a suggestion.'

'So,' said Bennett, 'shall I call the police or will you?'

Tracey reached for her phone and a chorus of protest started up – a load of rubbish about cautions and probation and promises and new starts. 'Oh yes,' she cut in. 'Of course. I believe every word. Lucky for you lot I was born five minutes ago, eh? Sure I'll let you off.'

They smiled and relaxed, winked at each other. 'Thanks, Trace, you're cool. We always said you were the coolest.'

'Yeah?' Then a memory seized her, about the hiding-place of her vibrator, and a realisation floored her – of the now wider knowledge of its existence. And suddenly she was roaring at them with an uncontainable fury. 'That's interesting because that's not how I see it. You see, I think I *was* a bloody idiot, and now I'm not.' She reached for her phone again. 'In fact, I might even frame you, while I'm at it. Bennett, I think there's about a grand missing from that safe, isn't there? Round about ... Oh, and my grandmother's jewellery. I think I'm missing all my grandmother's jewellery. Bennett, was there any really, *really* expensive jewellery in there? Sort of like the Crown Jewels, but massive?'

Bennett, with the nervous look of a person trapped with a madwoman, shook his head.

'Well, that means these two bits of scum must have nicked it, then.' She gave a low whistle. 'Valuable stuff, that.'

There were more protests, and wriggling and pleading. It was not a pretty sight. She dialled a 9.

'No, Trace, PLEASE.'

'I can't think of any other option.'

She dialled another 9.

'TRACEY. DON'T.'

'Unless ...' She looked thoughtful.

'What?'

'No, you'd never do it.'

'Anything!'

'You sure?'

'Tracey, just put the phone down, and we can talk.'

She put the phone down and talked. 'You join the Bridgeford Community Choir. At least until the County Championships.'

'Oh no. No way.'

'Oh. Sorry. I made the mistake of thinking you were completely and utterly desperate.' She picked up her phone again.

'All right. Bloody hell. What is it anyway? A load of sad old people?'

'Yes. Basically. That's exactly what it is. But the good news is that it won't be just a load of sad old people when you've joined, will it? It will be young.' She pinched Curly's cheek. 'It will be vibrant.' She patted Squat on the head, wiped her hand on her denim. 'And you know what? I've just had another FANTASTIC idea.'

'Fuck me. She's really off on one.'

'All those little gits that hang out on the war memorial taking the piss – your brother's in that lot, isn't he? And your sister, Curly. I think they're going to join in too, don't you? I've had this sudden premonition. I think they are all going to join in and if they don't I am telling the police such stories about you that you will find—'

'All right.' They shrugged Bennett off and straightened their clothes. 'Calm down. We get it. Our lives are over. You can shut up now.'

'As a matter of interest,' said Bennett tentatively, pouring wine into two glasses, 'why exactly do you choose to keep cash in a safe instead of a bank? I know our financial institutions are at a particularly inglorious moment in their history, but still . . .'

Tracey sighed, slumped on to the table and rested her head flat on her forearms. 'It's Billy's allowance from his dad. I keep it in there for a bit before I put it into his account.'

'Billy's dad pays you in cash?' Bennett pulled a chair out and sat down at the table opposite Tracey, with a view to being useful. The pros and cons of various financial transactions were one of the few areas of life to which Bennett could make a sensible contribution. 'It would be more economical for you if he—'

'Don't waste your breath.' Tracey propped her head up on her hands and looked at him. The marks of a deep tiredness were etched around her eyes; Bennett longed to reach across and rub them away. 'He won't do it, whatever you suggest.'

'Oh dear, is he very difficult?'

She thought about it. 'No. I don't think that's exactly fair.'

'Then I'm sure if you told him that the system was unsoun—'

'No, I can't really do that, Bennett.'

'Well, perhaps I could get in touch and explain—' He wasn't sure what he would explain, but Tracey cut him off anyway.

'All right, all right. Look. Bennett. I can't get in touch because' – she gulped and stopped and thought and then went on again – 'because I don't actually know who he is. OK? There. I've said it. And I'll say some more. Here goes: he doesn't know that Billy exists. And I don't want Billy to know that I don't know who his dad is. So whenever I get a few royalties from "The Crappy Island Was a Sodding Dream" – you'd be surprised at the standards of advertisers in certain corners of the world – I put it in his bank account and say it's from his dad, who, for various differing reasons that I make up on the spot, loves him very much but can't actually see him. And then the bulk of that money goes back into my account for child support.' She gave an ashamed sort of giggle. 'See? All perfectly straightforward. And that, ladies and gentlemen, is my final disgraceful secret – unless you want to know about the last digestive I nicked thirty years ago. You have wormed it all out of me. Congrats.'

'Aha,' he said thoughtfully, as if he had understood any of that at all. 'I see,' he added, although he really didn't. Then a light dawned: 'So it was a sperm-donor sort of situation then?'

Tracey gave a bitter laugh. 'Nothing so romantic.' She sat up straight and looked Bennett in the eye. 'Just a normal, run-of-the-mill, routine tour fuck. You know how it is.'

Bennett was curiously flattered.

'Just after the Eurovision débâcle, I was on my final terrible tour put together by this arse of a manager to "build on that success". Ha. The Who Gives a Shit Tour, the sound guys called it. Anyway, we were staying in this dump in Leckford – you know Leckford?'

'There's quite a nice hotel there, The, um—'

'Yeah, there might very well be, but we weren't staying in it. We were in this God-awful pub, there was a bloke, there were drinks, there was sex and then there was Billy.'

'Of course.' He sounded dismissive, waved her story away, as if Bennett and the tour fuck had known each other for years, actually their parents were old friends. 'But still, you must know who he is. Surely you got his name?'

'Yes, I got his name. Don't worry, even in my wildest days I only ever shagged the ones to whom I'd been formally introduced.'

'Well, there we are, then. You do know who he is. So what was his name?'

'His name,' she sighed again, 'was Florence.'

'Have you looked him up in the phone book?' This was rather exciting. They could join up together and hunt him down. 'There can't be many Florences . . . '

'No. Of course I haven't. Because he wasn't called Florence, was he? Not really. He was called Florence like Curly is called Curly and Squat is called Squat.'

'Oh.' Bennett was rather crestfallen. 'So Florence because he wasn't?' He thought again. 'Or Florence because he did?'

'Christ knows. Florence so daft girls couldn't turn up on the doorstep with his bun in their oven, probably. It certainly did the trick, anyway.' She seemed to calm down again, smiled across the table with what Bennett thought – hopefully – might be some form of affection. 'You see, if he'd been called Bennett St John Parker I would have been able to find him like a shot.'

'Ah,' said Bennett St John Parker, walking into what was indubitably the bravest two seconds of his life. 'If he'd been called Bennett St John Parker he would never have let you go.'

29

Bennett emerged, blinking, from his long meeting with his new friend at the bank in the High Street and stood outside the news-agent, waiting for his next appointment. With the early summer sun brightening the High Street, Bridgeford looked rather beautiful to him now. The origins of a lively market town were all still there, after all – the Victorian Corn Exchange, with its pillars and clock tower, was an impressive sight if only you stopped and looked at it; the war memorial with its steps and roofing, if you could gloss over the kids and their crisp packets and their tins, was a grandiose tribute from a town united in grief. The Copper Kettle, he now knew, was once a coaching inn that had, until the building of the railway, put Bridgeford on the map.

'Can I get you anything, love?' the woman from the newsagent called out, as Bennett had known she would. He was prepared.

'No thanks, Carol. I did enjoy those wine gums, by the way.' He couldn't quite build in a reference to babysitting but still: O blessed daughter, that notebook was quite invaluable.

So when people talked about the town being a miserable dump, they were not being strictly accurate. The unusually wide high street, with a trim of hills and fields in the view beyond, was a lovely sight, which Bennett could see now, for some reason, in a way he had never been able to before. And the shopfronts were all charming – many Georgian, mostly Victorian, and all of them listed. No, there was nothing wrong with the town at all – it was the people that were its problem. The people who didn't shop here, causing more than half of the shops to be empty or to strap brash SALE signs across their leaded windows; the people who did shop here, and threw their litter all over the pavement; the people who treated the place like a transit lounge – as Bennett had done himself. And the people who didn't realise how lucky they were to live here. Bennett had been one of those, too, once upon a time.

'Hey, Dad,' boomed Casper, in his habitual state of advanced good cheer. 'What a COINCIDENCE!' Several people turned round – it was a sound of such piercing volume that a passenger might pick it up on a passing train. 'I'm supposed to be meeting my eleven o'clock here.' The boy was wearing a pinstriped suit, carrying a folder under his arm and jangling a set of keys. 'Some idiot's interested in the Copper Kettle as a going concern. HA!' Carol poked her head out of the door again, to see what the commotion was. 'That's one thing to do with your money, eh? EH? Or he could just dig a bloody hole and BURY THE BLOODY LOT.' A baby in a buggy jumped and burst into tears.

'Um, I hope you don't mind the cloak-and-dagger stuff but I am your eleven o'clock.' Bennett felt rather guilty now, but he just hadn't wanted Sue to hear about it too early on. 'And yes, I am very interested in buying it. I've been thinking about it long and hard, and I'm sure there's a good little business in there somewhere.'

For his first fifty years, Bennett had failed to surprise anyone, at any time, about anything. His was a life of such plodding predictability that the only surprise, looking back on it, was that he had managed to stick it for as long as he had.

'DAD.' Bennett looked round to see if any windows had blown in. 'Have you totally LOST the PLOT?'

Recently, though, he seemed to be surprising quite a lot of

people, rather often and in a multitude of different ways. And the surprise to him was quite how much he was enjoying it.

'No. On the contrary: I feel like I have never had a plot—'

'He came in the end, look.' A tired-looking woman stopped and showed Bennett the contents of her pram.

'I thought he probably would. Splendid little chap. Well done you.'

Casper watched this innocuous interchange with his mouth agape; Bennett turned back to him.

'—and now I feel like I might be getting a plot for the very first time.'

'But, DAD. I really shouldn't say this, entirely off the record . . . ' He adopted the covert body language of international espionage, and then bellowed, 'The SUPERSTORE—'

'I don't think that's going to happen,' Bennett replied mildly. 'According to my contacts—'

'Your CONTACTS?'

'Yes, Lewis in Planning on the council tipped me—'

Casper nearly fell on the floor. 'DAD! YOU know Lewis in PLANNING? WOW. You kept that quiet. Could you introduce me?'

'Sure. You should have come to my party. The entire committee was there.'

'Bloody HELL.' Casper was impressed with him, Bennett could see that. 'When's the next one?' Indeed, Casper was impressed with him for the very first time.

La-la-la-la, lo lo lo

Annie hummed to herself as she set up the tea urn. There was talk of a lot more people tonight, some of them very young. She had bought some hot chocolate and animal biscuits in case they weren't quite grown-up enough for caffeine.

Ta-ta-ta-ta, toe toe toe

Katie came in, wheeled by Lewis, with a huge tray of chocolate-chip cookies in her lap.

'Katie. You're back baking! Hallelujah!'

'That job wasn't right for me, I'm afraid, Annie. So it's back to college and another course. We're going to have a go at book-keeping this time. Anyway,' she spread the biscuits out on the table, 'Tuesday afternoons to myself again.'

At that moment, a line of hooded youths shambled in, arms buried in pockets, feet dragging in unlaced trainers – a study in surly reluctance. Lewis moved towards them, shielding Katie from their view. 'Excuse me. We have this hall booked. Can we help you?'

The hoods all waggled about a bit on top of the lanky bodies – extraterrestrials emerging from a space-ship, communicating in some manner peculiar to themselves. The the hood lowest to the ground, came forward as spokesman. 'Come for the singing.'

Jazzy breezed in and then stopped dead. 'Ur. Yuk.' She had the almost supernatural ability to discern between them. 'Who let you in, Squat Thompson?'

'Squat!' Annie came out of the kitchen beaming, hand extended.

'What?' said Squat, peering out with suspicion through a very narrow gap.

'Hello! I've heard so much about you. I'm Annie.' She put her hand to her chest. 'From the library? I believe we were neighbours for a bit last year. Welcome, welcome. Has Curly joined us too?'

'OK.' At some point in the past week Tracey had clearly decided to prepare for battle. Now armed with a baton, she tapped it on her music stand. 'Lots of lovely new faces tonight. First of all, a big round of applause for our brilliant new pianist, Miiiiss Araminta Parker ... Thank you, thank you ... We are so lucky to have her. Now perhaps the new voices could introduce themselves. And proper nouns please, rather than adjectives, verbs or gerunds. Starting with you.' She pointed her baton at Curly.

'You what, miss?' Curly looked puzzled. 'I don't understand, miss.'

'I am not Miss. I am Tracey. And you, in this hall, with these people, are Ashley. So you say: "Hello, I'm Ashley." God, it's like teaching English to foreigners.'

'Hello,' said Curly, mumbling into his hoodie. 'I'm Ashley.'

'Ashley? Ashley?' cackled Squat. 'Ha. Forgot you was Ashley. Classic.'

'Thank you, Felix,' cut in Tracey. 'Would you like to do the same?'

'FELIX? Fucking Felix?' In an instant half the hall was on the edge of riot.

'Excuse me?' called Bennett from the men's section. 'Does everybody have to give their birth name?'

'OK.' Tracey glared at him, hit the stand and raised her voice.

'Forget it. That was obviously over-ambitious. But you lot, just do as you're told from now on or else. Wouldn't you agree, Squat? Hm?'

'Yeah, shut up, you lot. Or else.'

'Yes, *Felix*.'

'Certainly, *Felix*.'

'So we're going to start off with the song we were working on last week, "Lean on Me". The lyrics are just coming round.'

'Here!' said a hood, reading the words. 'I like this!'

'Jolly good. So some of you lot are in the basses—'

'But I thought you'd be doing like really dead people, like ...' he paused, clearly trying to come up with the most extreme idea of a musical dead person, 'I dunno ... Beethoven.'

His mates had never heard a funnier thing. They all roared.

'Oh yes,' Bennett joined in, shouting over the top of them. 'The jolly songs of Beethoven!' He smiled, paused for effect, and then: 'What do you fancy? *"Nur hurtig fort, nur frisch gegraben"*?' Chuckling away, he smiled about him.

The hall fell silent. Some new members turned, lips curled, and studied him more closely. A whiff of danger span around the hall.

Tracey rushed on: 'We can if you're disappointed—'

'Nah. We'll have this please, miss.' The boy turned round to the others. 'We'll do this. We like this.'

'We are grateful,' said Tracey. 'Right. Let's take it from the top.'

By the time Lynn got to the head of the tea queue, there were no cakes or biscuits left. Annie's happy face was quite pink, not only from the rush of customers but also from the total satisfaction of her irrepressible primal urge to feed the hungry, growing, grateful young.

'You'd think they've never been fed,' she laughed. 'We'll all have to make twice as much for next week.'

'What's that peculiar smell?' Lynn turned around the room with her nose wrinkled. She sniffed once. 'Sort of farmyard.' She sniffed again. 'But sort of not.'

Annie reached for her bag. 'I know what you mean. Tracey's

house has it too.' She leaned in and stage-whispered, 'I think it's modern marijuana. Not quite so *grassy* as our day.'

'Eugh. It certainly isn't. More like a blocked sewer. Hell in a handcart. If you can spare a cup of tea, I would be grateful.' Lynn looked huffy. 'Oh well, they probably won't stick it here for two minutes.'

'They're with us for the contest, definitely. Do you mind pouring your own, love? I just said I'd look up a job vacancy I noticed last week that might suit one of the lads.'

♫

The Coronation Hall was alive with laughter and chat. Min, Katie and Jazzy were all sitting around the piano, surrounded by half a dozen show-offs, all of them new recruits. That was a noisy corner. Annie seemed to be conducting interviews with a few bored-looking boys in the middle – 'And Squat, have you noticed that the old nursery is currently standing empty? Room for lots of you there, although the loos are very low' – and all around them other members socialised. The stacking chairs with their dirty cloth seats had been rearranged, some into circles, others into smaller groups. Judith and Kerry sat alone, apart from the rest, one red head close to the other dirty blond, locked in intense conversation.

Bennett, tonight wearing suit trousers but no jacket, pale blue shirt but no tie, approached Tracey at the music stand. The two had not spoken for exactly a week and Bennett seemed unsure of what sort of a reception he might get.

'Well,' he began.

'Hmm?' Tracey, pencil between teeth, vigorously erased a pencil note on the music and flicked away the trace.

'They all turned up then.'

'Indeed.' She turned a page.

'Full house.'

'It is.' She looked at her watch. 'And we need to crack on. There's a lot of work to do.' She tapped her baton. 'Everybody back in your places now. We're going to do the next song.'

Bennett, with the rest of the Choir, slunk back into his seat.

'You all know this, so there is nothing to learn but your parts. I will also tell you now that we will be needing soloists for this one. If anyone fancies having a go, come and see me. Otherwise, I might just pluck you for stardom. Here goes. It's by Pharrell Williams.'

They all gasped.

'It's called "Happy".'

There was a loud cheer and whoops.

'And the lyrics sheets are coming round now. To kick off, I will do the solo, while you do your bit.'

♫

Because I'm happeeeee ...

By the third attempt, they were all up on their feet. Bennett and Lewis were dancing between Curly and his cousin Frank; Jazzy stood in front clicking her fingers and stepping her toes; behind, a line of sopranos copied her. Squat and a couple of basses were bopping round the outside of the circle.

... I'm happeeeeee ...

They all sang up to Tracey, underneath her throaty solo. They clapped when she clapped, sang when she signalled, followed her every move. Right then, Tracey knew, as they all knew, that they were completely under her spell. She had the power to make them do absolutely anything.

They finished the song amid exuberant self-congratulation. Tracey raised her voice again.

'This is going to be seriously great. Now for take four, and we're going to do it just a little bit differently.'

Tracey started them off, and then pulled back into being conductor. For every solo line over the 'happy' chorus, she pointed to a different singer without warning and made them take it. To the surprise of each of them, as well as the whole room, they all did as they were told. And that night a few lives were – just ever so slightly, but for ever – changed.

♫

A singer is one singer; singers are many singers; a group of singers is just what it sounds like. A choir, though – a living, breathing, working choir – is something else entirely. It is the singular product of a physical reaction that can only come into being under certain laboratory conditions. And no scientist alive can really tell you exactly what they all are. A good choir generally has a good leader – and Tracey Leckford, up at the front there, lost in her music, was obviously one of those.

It can benefit from a few great voices – and in the Coronation Hall right then there were certainly a few of those. Bennett St John Parker was not the only star for once. Curly's cousin Frank – a skinny figure with wide, lazy pupils and a rash of angry spots – created a sound of such unlikely untrained purity that it made the other members stare. With another chance, in another life, he too might have worn a long cassock and sung in cathedrals; as it was, he stood awkwardly in a black T-shirt, looking genuinely bewildered by what came out of his mouth.

And it can carry weak voices, with the strengths of the many making up for the weakness of the few. Not all of the new young members were as talented as Frank, but that didn't matter a bit.

Because what a choir needs more than anything is a united spirit, a communal enthusiasm, a sense of common purpose – and they certainly had all that. And so it happened that, with the weak being supported by the strong, the young dancing cheerfully around the old, the high balancing out the low, that night there was just the merest glimmer of hope that, for the first time in living memory, the Bridgeford Community singers might at last become a proper choir.

Each singer was too carried away with the song to properly notice. But Tracey, she knew. She knew that there was something happening in that hall, and that it was extraordinary. With one ear cocked, she pulled her conducting down a bit, just to test them: they carried on. She stepped away from the front and wandered down the aisle. The tune held; the rhythm bounced along. With a small, secret smile and eyes wide with apprehension, she crept up behind Araminta, whispered, 'Now!' in her ear. And the piano stopped. And ... 'Yes!'

Tracey made a fist, hissed to herself: the singing just carried on.

The piano or backing track is, to a choir, like the earth is to human-ity: take it away, and there is nothing there to hold you up. Without it, you fall or you fly. And to Tracey's delight and their own wonder, they were flying. Like skydivers in formation, they were all together; airborne. And the rest of the world suddenly felt very far away.

'Well!' Tracey laughed, quite high on the exertions of the past forty-five minutes. 'That was pretty bloody ...'

The Choir held its breath.

'... BRILLIANT.'

They all cheered.

'Who knew there was so much musical talent loitering on the war memorial? I'm just glad we got to you before Simon Cowell. So, we just have a month to go before the Championships, and to get us properly up to scratch we are going to do a performance first. Yes everybody, we have our first booking! The St Ambrose School Summer Fête has asked us to do a set at three p.m., right outside the tea tent. Now look, you lot, this is a pretty big deal. We will be singing to people who may or may not want to hear us. And we have to convince them to stay. Sorry, Felix? Did I detect something less than enthusiasm there?' She pulled her phone out of her pocket and held it up, pointed at the number 9.

'Nah, miss. You're all right.'

'Glad to hear it. So we don't have very long to prepare.'

There was a bit of moaning and a lot of muttering. Tracey tapped the stand again. 'Listen: if any of you are worried about anything – parts, lyrics, tune or the moves or anything at all – I want you to know that you can get in touch with me twenty-four/seven. You can come round to my place; I get home from work at about six on a Thursday, and if anyone needs to they are welcome to come round after that. Or you can just ring me up and we can do it over the phone.

'I will be on call at any time, like a doctor. We all need to be on top of our game.'

31

They stood, a line of separate individuals, so similar but not the same; arranged in height order like that, the differences between each and her neighbours was so slight as to be meaningless. But set the smallest against the largest, and the margin was huge. Annie stared at the little one – exposed, unprotected, defenceless – until she could bear it no longer. It was torture. She put the phone on speaker and with a practised hand swept along the table at speed, gathering them all up, nestling each within the next so that all but one was now secure, and the smallest was the most secure of all.

'What's going on there?' asked James. 'Are you chopping onions?'

'Just fiddling with the Russian dolls, that's all.' How hopeless he was at some things; she would have guessed that immediately. 'I found them in the sitting room. They just bubbled up to the surface for some reason, you know how things do.'

'I do know. Like dead bodies in a swamp. We have GOT to start chucking stuff out.'

'Mm, I agree, you know I do.' She started to unstack them again in a circle around her glass of wine. 'But not the Russian dolls, obviously. I'm not chucking them out.'

He sighed and was quiet for a bit. There was something going on there that Annie could not immediately identify – a sort of peeling noise; a fleshy, moist, peeling noise. 'Why are we keeping them, though, Annie? Seriously. Why are we cherishing dolls and children's books and bibs and beakers and bricks and bears and—'

'For the future, you know that perfectly well. For our grandchildren, and their children and . . . ' The little one was on her own again now, set apart from the others, unconnected and alone. 'What do you want them to play with?'

'Jesus. Jesus.' He sounded distracted; she wasn't sure if he was talking to her or not. There was some sort of exertion going on which, annoyingly, she couldn't quite identify.

'I mean, I can't throw out the Frances Hodgson Burnetts, can I? My mum read them, I read them, the girls read them. They're our heritage, our family tree.'

James stopped whatever he was doing and sighed. 'Annie. Should there ever be any grandchildren, they probably won't turn up until books are about as relevant as the Rosetta bloody Stone—'

She gasped. She revered the Rosetta Stone. Was he actually trying to break her heart? 'Excuse me, I know we don't see each other as much as we used to so you might have forgotten you are talking to A LIBRARIAN.'

'They'll just be – oh, I don't know, eating a story pill or putting on a story hat or sticking a story bogey up their nose . . .' Unlike everybody else's husband, hers was not technologically minded. The truth was that he was as lost in the twenty-first century as she was, but he bluffed his way around it, just like he did when they were lost on the road.

'STOP IT. And anyway, if they do then that's all the more reason to leave them *A Little Princess* with the proper cover and not—'

'And in the meantime we will be dead of asphyxiation under a heap of My Little Ponies.' He had returned to whatever he was up to. Some sort of fleshy pummelling sort of . . .

'Well, you'll be all right, won't you, as you never bloody come home any more? Perhaps you might dig me out next time you're passing.'

'Bloody hell. I do miss you, love. Even though you're a bloody bonkers old bat.'

Peace broke out. They never could row, not properly. They might push each other to the brink of it sometimes but they could never quite follow through. So they carried on chatting for a few minutes more – about the girls and the weekend and how Constance wasn't getting any better and his case was dragging him down. It was all a bit bleak at the moment and yet Annie couldn't help but notice how contented James seemed; excited even. And all the while, the sound effects got a little more bizarre. There was sipping and slipping and lip-smacking and slurping. And if she was on a panel right now, and the quizmaster put the question to her, she knew what she would have to answer: that it sounded rather like them, back in another lifetime, in a whole other world. When James couldn't keep his mouth off her, let alone his hands. When he would lay her down and stretch her out and kiss and lick and suck at every part of her. When her body was one firm, strong, beautiful wonder instead of a loose connection of just-functional parts strung together by threads of slack skin. In the days before her flesh had started to slip the anchor of its frame and her breasts to glide steadily down her ribs.

'Anyway . . . ' he began. He clearly wanted to get on.

'Yes,' she said. She really did not want to listen. 'I've got Book Club for the Visually Impaired in a minute.'

They said their goodbyes; Annie put her phone down on the table and saw that the baby doll was once again on her own. She picked it up and stroked it, watching with dampened eyes the back of her brownish, blotchy, cracked and crevassed hand.

32

On Thursday evening at 6.15, Tracey was still stuck on the motor-way, in the midst of the commuting herd, proceeding home at an infuriatingly gentle pace. She didn't really expect any of the Choir would be moved to come to her house and go over the song parts with her, but still – she had said she'd be there. And anyway, she needed to get home. There was still so much important work to be done for the Championships – like the small matter of selecting and arranging their second song; it made her quite giddy with nerves just thinking about it – she resented her tedious office work for get-ting in the way.

The volume was turned down on her now constant companion, Drivetime Dave. He had left her with no choice. Life was anxious enough without the added downer of having to listen to a load of moaning and groaning. She didn't know what Dave was thinking of. Did he actually want her to slash her own wrists on his watch?

'...and that was Coldplay there with "The Hardest Part", to help you on your way home ...'

And that was no doubt why the traffic was so slow: everyone was too depressed to press the pedal; their heartbeats had dropped beyond trace; they were sunk on to their steering wheels in a coma. 'Dave, Dave, Dave,' Tracey shouted at the radio. She now talked to him regularly, rather as if she were a mad old lady – or perhaps even because she had become a mad old lady. 'You've got a job to do. Now do it.'

'And now straight into "News from Your Neighbourhood".'

Tracey turned it up and signalled towards her exit.

'... and as I've been promising you all afternoon, we have a pretty big story for you tonight. Over to Chrissie, who is at the London Road site in Bridgeford.'

That woke Tracey up. The very mention of her town's name got her own heartbeat back up again.

'Thanks, Dave. Our main headline tonight is of course the shock collapse of the Bridgeford superstore development, and I am here tonight with all these Davids who have beaten off the multinational Goliath they thought was going to kill their town. First of all, the man who has been credited with turning the campaign around. Ben Parker, you ...'

The name didn't register with Tracey at first, although the protesters cheered loudly at its very mention. When she heard the sound of the voice, though, she was quite overcome. Moving down the slip-road, she turned into a lay-by and stopped.

'All the credit must go to the people who have slept out here, night after night, through one of the wettest winters in living memory ...'

In isolation like that, Bennett's voice had an extraordinary, almost overwhelming charm that was not quite there when Bennett himself was in the room with it. It was a soft, light, moist muscovado sort of a voice, not too deep, smooth rather than crunchy, sweet – so sweet – to listen to.

'... a joint effort by the whole Bridgeford community and I think, and hope, we have now learned our own strength ...'

It was the perfect speech of a conquering hero – modest, inclusive, free of gloat or triumph. He was the Abraham Lincoln of the M4 corridor.

' ... not finished yet. We now have to reinvigorate our own High Street, so that we never face a threat like this again.'

What a wonderful man: graceful in victory, honourable in battle, caring to all, with a beautiful voice. Tracey thought about the last time she had properly seen him, when he had made his declaration and she had practically kicked him down the stairs. She realised just how rude she had been to him ever since. And, for the first time since she was a child, she found she was blushing.

'Thanks, Ben. So, Dave, that's me signing of from the Bridgeford protest for the very last time. And I can tell you, there's quite a party just starting up here. I hope the neighbours have got their earplugs.'

'And they've got a lovely summer's evening for it, too. Thank you, Chrissie. Tonight's weather ... '

Well, there. So many of the Choir members had been sucked into the cause, there would be no visitors at Tracey's place tonight – they would all be whooping it up with the eco-warriors. Suddenly, she had the whole evening to herself. She could get to work on the second song. She could also find Bennett, say sorry, make it up to him. Her mind was already exploring the possibilities when she turned the corner into her own street and saw a crowd that – at this distance – looked quite close to being outside her own front door. She could only fear the worst. Fire? Flood? Was there a body on the pavement in the middle of them there? There was no time to fiddle about with the garage. This was an emergency. She abandoned the car on a single yellow line and belted up the road.

It was her place, she could see that now: her front door, with a good half a dozen people gathered outside. She panted along the pavement, knocked into a passer-by, went over on her ankle, stopped and swore. And then she heard the music: the three parts of 'Lean on Me' in delicate harmony, being repeated over and over. She bit her lip. Her eyes were damp. And she stayed still for a while to look, and just listen. Lewis was there, with Maria and Judith, but the rest of them – and she could see that there were four more now – were in hoodies, and the long, untied laces of their trainers were streaming over the pavement. Tracey thought she might be listening to the most beautiful thing she had ever heard. Not because the sound was perfect – there was something not quite right going on in the altos – but because it was made with such care. That was a great musical lesson being learned over there, and one that so many musicians who really quite fancied themselves failed ever to learn: it isn't just the singing, it's the caring about it, too. And that lot, out on the pavement there, well, she only had to look at them: they really, really cared.

Tracey rubbed at her face and jogged along to them, waving her keys. 'Hi, guys. So sorry I'm late. I wasn't expecting so many of you. Have you been waiting out here long?'

They greeted her, the crowd parted and her locked front door was revealed to be already wide open.

'We're not waiting,' laughed Judith. 'We just can't get in.'

'Why, what's going on?' She went in and moved up her own stairs as bodies pressed against the wall to let her through.

'Hi, Tracey.'

'Evening, Tracey.'

'Can I get you anything?'

'Oh, Trace. It's you,' said Jazzy, coming out of the kitchen with a spoon and the peanut butter.

'Yeah. Funny that. Who were you expecting?'

'Pizza bloke. Not much food in here so we've sent out for some. Don't worry.' She stuck spoon into jar. 'I found this. You needn't feel bad.'

'I don't.' Looking around, she saw the faces of pretty much everyone she had ever had dealings with in Bridgeford, plus a few she had never seen before. The only person missing, she realised with a twinge, was Bennett. 'How did you get in?'

'Curly,' said someone, pointing at him with a beer bottle. Curly, slightly shame-facedly, waved his own key.

'Christ almighty!' shrieked Tracey. 'How long have you had that?'

Curly frowned and pursed his lips. 'Let me see now. OK. Well. You remember when we started that band with Billy?'

'No!' She was still shrieking. It might be a very long time before she did anything else. 'As you were about *three* at the time.'

'Trace, Trace, hair on.' He held up a halting hand. 'We was definitely at least twelve.'

'But that's ten years ago. Ten. Whole. Years.' She shook her head. 'Unbelievable. And tell me, do you come here often?' A nasty thought then struck her. 'Oh my God. What about bloody Squat? Where is he?'

'Squat?'

'Squat?'

'Anyone seen Squat?' The happy cry undulated through the crowds in the living room and up the stairs to the bedrooms like a summer wind through high corn.

'Says hang on, he'll be down in a bit,' someone – Squat's chief of staff, perhaps – leaned over the banisters and shouted down from above.

'What? Why?' Tracey demanded. 'Why must I hang bloody on?'

'He's just having a quick bath.'

She staggered over to the sofa. Maria and Lynn budged up quickly before she fell on them. 'Who are all these people?' she muttered. 'Where have they come from?'

'You're the victim of your own success, I'm afraid,' smiled Annie, coming over with a tray full of cups of tea. 'By the way, you're nearly out of milk. All our recruits have been recruiting and half the town suddenly wants to join. It's really rather wonderful.'

'But I can see you might feel a little bit invaded,' added Lynn.

'Oh, just a bit . . .' She wondered idly whether Bennett might hear about all this and pop in later – after he'd done the media rounds, of course.

'By the way,' added Annie, 'the solo in "Lean on Me" . . .'

'Yeah. Do you want it?' asked Tracey, lifting a cup.

'GOD, no!' Annie went a bit pink. 'Not me! Huh. At my age!' She gave a little shriek at the thought. 'Jazzy, of course. She's our star, and I'm sure it's occurred to you already but I just wanted to back her up . . .'

'I made some brownies if you fancy one,' Katie chipped in.

'But now they're all here we should probably just have a rehearsal. Unless we actually want to make a total hash of it all, in which case let's just crack open a bottle.'

'Or, of course, we could do both.' The longer she kept it going, the more chance there was of Bennett turning up. Despite the numbers it seemed rather incomplete without him. Tracey stood up, did a quick head-count and assessment of the best use of the space available. If she stood on the table in the outside corner of the living area, she would get a decent view into both ends of the L-shaped room as well as the upper stairs. 'OK,' she called, heading for the fridge and taking out a bottle. 'Sopranos in the kitchen, altos in the sitting room and basses on the stairs: let's turn this chaos into a choir that will make Bridgeford proud.'

33

'Thank you ... thank you ... It was a team effort ...' It took Bennett for ever to get along the High Street these days, but he wasn't complaining. Everyone out here was a potential customer; he would treat them with respect. Even this one.

'Well.' Sue was trying to give the impression of casually bumping into him; Bennett suspected, though, that she had been cruising for a while, hunting up and down Bridgeford like a U-boat in the Atlantic. 'If it isn't our local hero ...'

'Morning, Sue. How are you?' He kissed her cheek, felt a prickle and pulled back.

'Very curious, as a matter of fact. Very curious to find out what next for our own ... our own ... our own ...'

She clearly wanted to say something deeply sarcastic but she couldn't remember the words. The new, emboldened Bennett did not see why he should come to her rescue. He stood there patiently waiting.

'Our own ...' Sue was going quite pink.

'Morning, Ben,' called Judith as she passed. 'What a night, eh? See you next week.'

'Um ... er ...' Sue went pinker.

One of his new acquaintances went past with her buggy. 'Is that a completely different baby or is he just extraordinarily advanced?' He did enjoy practising his chit-chat, and he was really rather good at it now – he didn't even sound that much like a German spy any more. He could pass for a native.

Sue now had the energy reading of a thermo-nuclear disaster.

'Why don't we have a cup of coffee?' he asked her gently. 'And I can tell you all about it.'

Sue strode purposefully towards the Copper Kettle, secure in the knowledge that she was leading him back into her territory; the café was about the last bastion of Susan St John Parker's independent power. She opened the door and ushered him in, chatting happily now. 'I never usually come here on a Friday morning – makes a change. We normally sit in the window over there. "Menopause Corner", I call it.'

Bennett intended to put the cakes and pastries in the window, to attract custom, so that table would be going, but he was sure that wouldn't bother her. Who in their right mind would want to sit somewhere called Menopause Corner, for heaven's sake?

'Ben!'

'Benji!'

'Hey, Benito!'

It took Bennett a while to get across and by the time he had finished recapping and receiving, she was sitting there drumming her fingers. 'Rosa Parks.' She got there. 'Our very own Rosa Parks. So are you going to run for office?'

After all that, Rosa Parks was hardly the right analogy but he let it go. 'No.' He sat down opposite her. 'In fact, I'm going into the catering trade.' He picked up the menu and studied it while she spluttered and hooted and guffawed and shrieked.

'You ... you ... Sorry.' She stopped and wiped her eyes. 'You, catering? Oh my God, I have to tell the kids. WHERE exactly? And, more importantly, to WHOM?' She mopped at herself again. 'If you let me know, I can tip the poor buggers off before it's too late.'

'Here.' He looked around, at the brown wood chairs and the brown wood tables and the brown and orange splodgy material everywhere. He looked at the prettiness of Jazzy, swamped in a brown and splodgy uniform with a ridiculous mob cap upon her head, and once again got the frisson of excitement he always got when he thought about how he was going to turn this around. 'I'm buying this place.' Bennett knew that he was only a beginner when it came to interior design, but he was really rather pleased with what he had done to Priory Lane since he'd had it to himself. And although he wasn't entirely sure he knew what he wanted The CK to look like, he did know exactly what he didn't want it to look like and that was what it looked like right now: something from the 1950s.

Sue was for once properly lost for words. It didn't seem to be that she couldn't remember them, more that the words with which she might describe this cataclysm had not yet been invented. So he carried on: 'The finances are all sorted. I signed the deal yesterday and in case you're worried, you will be fine. I'm going to move into the flat upstairs. If you want to go back and live at home, you can do that, or we can sell it, whichever you prefer, and—'

Jazzy was now at their table, all smiles for Bennett and a very chilly shoulder for his ex-wife. 'You missed a great rehearsal last night round at Tracey's. Went on for hours. I've got the solo.' She pointed her pen at the menu. 'What can I get you?'

'Coffee for me, please. How long are you thinking of working here, Jazzy? Is it permanent for you?'

'Did you hear that, Nan?' she called over to the next table, where an enormous old lady sat in in her wheelchair eating a giant cream puff next to a ragged, nervous woman with colourless hair the texture of garden twine and black holes around her eyes. 'And Mum? This is my friend Bennett and he says how long am I here for?'

They all had a good chuckle at that. 'Oh, Mr Bennett,' explained the grandmother. 'She's going to be bigger than Beyoncé by Christmas.'

'She's going on *The X Factor*, aren't you, love?'

'They're going to take one look at her and say, "I've got goose bumps all up me arms."'

Jazzy wrinkled her nose at them in an 'Ah, bless' sort of way and turned back to Bennett. 'Well,' she began, holding up her right hand, 'first, it's the auditions in the summer, so I'll just need the one day off for that – although there might be a bit of press afterwards. Then it's boot camp – not sure how long that lasts.' She counted up each separate stage, pulling on a different finger, as if they were just promotional rungs on the Civil Service ladder. 'Then I'm through to judges' houses: I dunno – a week? But after that it's the live shows and, you know ... ' She flicked her other hand in the general direction of the stratosphere she was off to.

That was it, thought Bennett with a pang. That was Jazzy's career plan in its carefully thought-out entirety.

'Of course I'm SO lucky,' Jazzy smiled at him, still with her shoulder very deliberately pointed at Sue, 'to have such a LOVELY FAMILY. I'm so grateful to have such SUPPORT.' She wiped Bennett's half of the table with deliberate care. 'I would like to thank them now for everything they've done for me.' She was, as Bennett believed they said in these circumstances, 'welling up'. 'They taught me that I must never give up on my dreams.'

'Down here on planet Earth,' said Sue, 'mine's a cappuccino.'

34

'Hey, Mum,' laughed a brown, blond, thin but muscular god. This wasn't the real Billy. It couldn't be. Not her Billy, anyway. This was some idealised Billy who had just popped up on the computer screen and flickered here before her. Or the A-list actor already cast to play Billy in the multi-million-dollar hagiography *Billy: The Biopic*.

'Skype, eh? Crazy. Wow.' He looked down and peered. 'You've cleaned up. Mum. *So* not cool. It doesn't look anything like home.'

Although Tracey had thought of him every hour of every day, she had found it increasingly difficult to hold on to the image of him in her mind. He had come to seem quite remote to her – like a fragment of a memory of a dream; and here he was, indeed, very remote from her: a stranger set against the clatter of an internet café in Rwanda.

'How are you, love? It is incredible to be able to look at you. Tell me every, every single thing.'

'Christ, Mum, it's amazing. It's like I never lived a proper day in my whole life until I came here.'

Tracey swallowed and tried to concentrate on everything he said, memorise it to go over later, but she could only stare at him, drink in his beauty, marvel at the miracle of his continued existence.

' . . . until we built the bridge, they had to walk twenty miles just to . . . '

Her boy: bridge builder. What a hero. They would be making the biopic at some point, she was pretty sure of that now.

' . . . running the little ones' footie team. There's this one kid . . . '

But who was good enough to play him? That was the question. Brad Pitt, possibly – bit old now, though. And nowhere near as handsome as the real thing.

' . . . soon as the materials arrive then we'll start on the new classroom . . . '

She needed to get across the next generation of superstars. After all, he was still so young, her Bills – and already saving the world.

' . . . she's got AIDS and six kids and she badly needs . . . '

All that fuss the school made about exams and qualifications and it turned out he didn't need any of them. Billy had qualities that could only be brought out by a good home and a fine soul – compassion, wisdom, generosity, empathy. She sighed with happy pride. So he was never any good at maths? He had emotional intelligence, and that was the most valuable thing of all.

' . . . I mean, that's a real single mother, nothing like you . . . '

'Well, it sounds heartbreaking, obviously. But I am still a single—'

' . . . all that money from Dad pouring in every month. And that job of yours – one long jolly . . . '

'Yes. I'm very lucky.' Tears were dripping down her face, but he seemed not to have noticed.

'I know, right. Honestly. You don't know you're bor—'

His image froze, and started to break up, and as suddenly as he had appeared before her, Billy was gone. She gripped the sides of the screen, screaming. 'No! Don't go. Don't leave me. It's not true. None of it. I have to tell you. Come back, baby. Please, please. Come back.' But the line was dead.

Somewhere nearby there was an animal in pain. Its deep, from-the-pit-of-its-belly roar filled the room, a wall of noise that came in and in, closer and closer until she feared the force of it might crush her. Tracey had heard that beast before – on a Saturday night in a dilapidated, empty maternity ward in the hours before her only child was born; those loneliest hours of her loneliest years. And now, on a Saturday night at home years later, she was hearing it again. It was back.

She flung her head on to her arms and howled.

35

By half past nine, Tracey was already in bed – propped up on
pillows, a glass of wine in her hand and sheets of music on her
bent knees. She had worked through her regular recovery programme of an ice pack on the head, a brisk walk, a lavender
bath – the one she always used whenever her world ended. And
now she was returned to her normal, calm, gloomily cynical, singular self, trying to decide how many solos she could cram into
'Happy'.

When the phone beside her rang, she immediately feared some
sort of disturbance to her finely calibrated equilibrium and considered not picking it up. But that was a luxury she was no longer
allowed. With Billy gone she could never ignore a ringing phone
ever again.

'Oh, good evening, Tracey, this is Bennett St John Parker here?
From the Bridgeford Community Choir?' He spoke up loudly and
clearly – a minor royal volunteering at the telephone exchange
during the General Strike.

'Oh, hello, Mr St John Parker,' she clipped back, stifling her giggles. 'This is indeed Tracey Leckford. How may I help you?'

'Um. Oh dear. Sorry. That sounded ridiculous. Perhaps I was a little nervous at what reception I might get.'

Tracey could almost taste the muscovado. Her tongue started to tingle; she ran it around her lips. 'Don't blame you. I was rude to you last week. I'm sorry. And hey, well done on the superstore – fantastic.'

He blathered on about the team effort and then got to his point. 'But it did prevent me from coming round on Thursday, as I'd wanted to do. So I wondered – you did mention about going over stuff on the phone?'

'Mmm. Course. I'd love to.' She twisted the hair at the nape of her neck around her middle finger and sank a little further into the pillows. 'But you don't need me, surely? You're already so accomplished—'

'Do say if this is presumptuous, but it's been on my mind for days now and I really want to know ...'

'Yes. What? Go on.'

'... if you think this would make a good second song.'

Tracey felt a clunk of disappointment, but only the most minor and quickest of clunks. Because she heard him sit down at the piano and a soft rustle as he tucked his phone into his neck. And then he started to play. How did he know? What was he trying to do to her?

I'm sitting in the railway station

A sensation – not new, but long forgotten – of intense warmth came in through her toes, spread up along her limbs, wrapped around her hips, pressed itself between her legs.

Got a ticket to my destination

She couldn't hold back a moment longer. She had to be part of it. She had to come in for the chorus. They had to do it together.

Homeward bound

Like all Simon & Garfunkel, the harmonies seemed quite shockingly natural – inevitable, even. Tracey entered at a minor fifth below him, brought her voice up right next to his tune, crossed over, went down again and rolled around beneath him once more.

Home, where my music's playing

That warmth now had her completely in its grip – her body, her mind, her musical soul. She ran a hand over herself, felt the moisture between her breasts.

Home, where my love lies waiting

And gasped as his fingers ran over the closing runs, that last tender instrumental phrase.

Silently for me.

'What did you think?' he asked her, his voice cracking a little.

Tracey found it hard to talk, but she had to. This was her moment.'I think we need to just go over that again. Properly. Don't you? Could you come over now, say? Sort of ... um, yes ... right now?'

'I'm on my way,' he said. And she could hear that he said it with his rather shy smile.

She hung up, stayed in bed, unable to move. The warmth was running out of her body like a lowering of the tide, and panic was rushing into its place. What had she done? This was absurd. Bennett's voice and Bennett were two completely different beings: one was utterly irresistible; the other, well, oh dear ...

Whatever was about to happen, though, she needed to face it fully dressed – that was for certain. Tracey jumped out of bed, reached into her laundry basket for that day's knickers and then – purely on a whim, not for any sound or thought-out reason – rustled around in her top drawer for the only pretty set of underwear she happened to own. It was a struggle to remember what false hope had led her to buy this in the first place. She pulled on the black lace, clipped up the balcony bra. Suffice to say it had proved as powerful as a portrait in the attic: for the years that this had been shut beguilingly in her bedroom, her own sex life had simply stopped, frozen in time. Crossing the room to grab just any old thing from the wardrobe, she caught a glimpse of herself in the mirror. That would never do. Even the most unimportant visitor, even for example Bennett, deserved just a bit of make-up: eyeliner, a smudge of shadow, a tiny bit of brow gel, a brush of mascara and lip gloss; blusher was the one thing she didn't seem to need tonight. But now her hair was longer, it took that bit more combing and spray and what about clips, holding it off the left side of her face? Teresa V used to use clips, she seemed to remember. And Bennett used to liked Teresa V, which was of course neither here nor there. Oh no, what a disaster, there was the bell and she still wasn't dressed. Her heart leapt. It was too late to do anything except spray scent all over her body – behind her knees, between her thighs, beneath her breasts – fling on her old silk kimono and fly down through the house as fast as her weakened legs could carry her.

She opened the door and for a fraction of a second they could only stare at one another.

Then: 'Say something,' she urged him.

'It's surprisingly warm,' he came in and, with some force, shut out the rest of the world, 'for the time of night.'

She jumped into his arms, wrapped her legs around his waist, linked her hands around his neck. He closed his mouth upon hers. Their tongues met. There was no time for the bedroom. There was no time for anywhere else at all.

He pulled away for a moment, held her face in his hands, said, 'Look at you. Oh my gorgeous love. Just look at you,' and then laid her down and lowered himself upon her.

'Thank God,' whispered a narrow, disappointing part of her brain. 'Thank God we cleared the stairs.'

She watched the morning light play on the pattern of the curtains and stroked the arm that was draped over her chest.

'What are you thinking?' he asked her.

'Tsk.' She tapped him. 'It's been a while, and I'm no expert, but I do believe that that's the first law of dating: never ask what they're thinking. But. I was thinking, how on earth did Simon and Garfunkel come into your life? How did they battle through the thickets of your requiems and your misereres and your Eurovisions and come to your notice?'

'Ah. Good question. They came to me, actually, through my requiems and my misereres.'

'Doh.'

'They did. You know, "Bridge Over Troubled Water" was written as a hymn ... My choirmaster loved them, used the harmonies as exercises in choir practice.'

'Ha!' She rolled over on to his stomach and beamed a triumphant smile. 'That's why we have to be a pop choir, see? All music leads to pop. Like I said ... So what were *you* thinking?'

'Hmm? Me? Oh. I was just thinking about a clothes rail.'

'You see! This is why you should never ask! A clothes rail? A bloody clothes rail?'

'Yes, have you considered getting one at all?' He stroked her hair, his eyes following his fingers as they moved. 'They offer the simplest solution to extra storage and I couldn't help noticing that there are clothes all over your floor.'

'A lot of those, Bennett, are on the floor because we had pre-tty nice sex last night and ripped them off each other. Should this ever happen again, would you rather we halt proceedings for a bit while we hang everything bloody up? I mean, you know, whatever turns you on ...'

He smiled and bit his bottom lip. 'I'm pretty sure there was already a layer there before we—'

The doorbell rang.

'Oh, no. It's nine thirty on a Sunday morning. This is getting a bit much.' Their bodies had been pressed together for so long that it hurt to peel them apart. Tracey had rather hoped to stay in bed all day; in fact, she wouldn't have minded staying there for the rest of her life. Grumbling, she pulled on last night's knickers and threw over a shift dress. 'I'll see them off. Be right back.' She kissed him on the mouth and skipped down the stairs.

'Morning, Trace. What took you so long?' Jazzy came through, shut the door, barged past Tracey and up the stairs. 'Annie said to meet her here. Need to go over my solo. No, I haven't had break-fast, thanks for asking.' She banged about the eye-level cupboards until she found Billy's last packet of Frosties.

'Here.' She strode past Tracey towards the fridge. 'You look a bit rough. What you been up to?'

And then there were footsteps on the stairs and Bennett stood before them, wearing nothing but Tracey's old kimono and holding her guitar.

'Oh my GOD-uh.' Jazzy stared at the apparition with her mouth open. 'What's he doing here? You haven't ... You didn't ... You had sex with him ... Oh you can't have ... Sex? With Bennett? Oh my GOD-uh. SEX with BENNETT? Christ, Tracey. That's not even funny.'

'It wasn't supposed to be funny.' Bennett frowned and strummed a few chords.

'Shut up, Ben,' said Tracey.

'Yeah, shut up, Ben,' added Jazzy. They stood there, each in their own separate minor shock, and then the doorbell rang again.

'That'll be Annie. Bagsy I'm the first to tell her. I want to be first to tell everyone. After all, I found it. So it is my thing.'

'Your *thing*?' Tracey spluttered, arms open, imploring. And to Bennett: 'It's her thing?'

But Jazzy was already down, tearing open the door and squeal-ing: 'You'll never guess, you'll never guess, quick, come up, it's actually the funniest thing ever like bloody hilarious ...'

And when they both arrived in the room: 'LOOK! They've been having SEX!!!'

'Oh, Bennett.' Annie dropped her basket and put both hands to her chest. She seemed almost crushed with disappointment. 'How could you?'

'What, is he having sex with you too, Mrs M? Cor, Dirty Ben. You are a one ...'

'And in front of Jazzy, of all people.'

Jazzy was enjoying herself enough already, Tracey was well aware of that. But she saw that this new, Jazzocentric approach took her to a whole other level of delight. 'I know right! In front of me!' She grabbed Annie's arm and shielded her own eyes. 'Oh, thank God you're here. It's been horrible.'

'But we didn't have sex in front of Jazzy.' Bennett, quite calm, was studying his fingers as he changed the chord. 'Why on earth would we do that?'

'But you let her come round, Bennett! And you let her find you like this!'

They're all completely potty, thought Tracey, staring at them with her mouth open. She quite wanted to throttle them, rather wanted to scream and really, really badly wanted a decent cup of coffee. But instead she walked to her electronic keyboard and started playing the intro to 'Lean on Me'.

'Is this what you came for?'

'That's Tracey Leckford on piano, ladies and gentlemen,' soothed Bennett. He started playing: 'Ben Parker on guitar.'

Ooh. Ooh-ooh-ooh. Oooooh

'Annie Miller on backing.'

Lean on me

'And the very wonderful, extraordinary, most talented Jazzy on vocals.'

Tracey was standing up, swaying at the hips as she played, smiling with her eyes to the others as they all sang. A sense of peace came into her lounge. Jazzy was doing OK with the solo part. If Annie wanted her to do it so very badly then Tracey would go along with it. But, without the rest of the Choir around, she did notice something else. Something she had probably known for a while, but that she was only now acknowledging to herself for the very first time. Something that did not really suit Tracey to know or to think or to have to believe. And it was this: out of all the voices she had been privileged to work with over the past few weeks, only one of them was properly extraordinary. And that one belonged to Annie Miller.

36

The Choir were gathering behind the tea tent. Tracey had insisted that, although the St Ambrose Primary School Summer Fête was an extremely informal affair, they would still observe the basic formalities of performance. This was, after all, their dry run for the Championships. It could not be more important. So they were all wearing white – well, white-ish in some obvious cases – tops and black bottoms and hanging around waiting to be put into order ready to file neatly on to the stage.

As the adrenalin pumped around, in and out of the bike shed, nearly all of the singers were at least a little altered by the experience. Tracey, radiant in crisp white cotton shirt and tight black trousers, was leaning against the post, clutching her baton and music, laughing gently with Bennett. White suited him too, and the reflection of his open-necked shirt gave his face a new, healthy pink – or something had given him a new, healthy pink at any rate. Lewis, so used to raising his voice in no end of professional and political situations, was trembling. Judith and Kerry were clinging together for support. Jazzy dug Katie's inhaler out of her kit bag and passed it to her – she looked almost blue. Squat was holding up a mirror for Curly, who was carefully tending his long clean hair. 'It's gone wrong,' he wailed and stamped his foot. 'Told you this would happen if I washed it. It's all gone WRONG.'

They all cared passionately about this gig, were desperate not to let anybody else down. But most nervous of all, clearly, was the one to whom it should feel the most natural. Jazzy kept peering round the corner to check the crowd out there, then prowling around the bike shed wringing her hands. 'Here, I could do with some of that,' she said to Katie.

Katie tried to smile around her puffer and patted the arm of her chair. Jazzy perched and put her arm around her friend. 'They did say they were coming. Mum promised. Probably just taking a while to get my nan out the house, that's all. It's not easy looking after her, as I well know.'

'They wouldn't miss it for the world, Jazz, you know that.' Katie had got her colour back and Lewis was looking at bit less worried. 'They'll cry when they hear you, I bet they will.'

'Will they?' Jazzy was round-eyed. 'Does that really happen? I mean, in real life and not just on the telly?' She thought for a bit. 'They've never actually come and heard me before.'

Annie came over and took Jazzy's hand. 'Here you are again, then. Back where you started, singing at St Ambrose.' She kept hold of Jazzy but turned to Katie. 'I first saw this girl perform when she was a tiny little speck in a gingham frock, you know. And after that she got all the solos twice a year. My lot couldn't get a look-in. So we all pretended she was ours.' She kissed Jazzy on the cheek. 'Good luck, love. I know you'll do us proud.'

'They're not here,' Jazzy mumbled. 'They said they'd come this time, but they haven't. They're not here.'

Annie held her in her arms, and stroked the mass of her long dark hair.

'Everyone else has come. Even stupid Squat's got someone out there. I'm the only one who hasn't got anyone.'

'No you're not.' Annie pulled back to look at her; she too had tears in her eyes. 'I haven't got anyone either. My lot never turn up to anything.' Jazzy looked at her, disbelieving. 'And what's more, my bloody husband is having an affair.'

A slight, rather confident, well-dressed woman with a clipboard appeared from around the tea tent and gestured for them to stop talking. 'Good afternoon to you all,' she said in a low voice, not wanting to spoil the surprise for the punters. 'I'm Heather Carpenter, the school secretary, and I just wanted to thank you for giving up your afternoon for us. There are hundreds of people out there who are all going to love you. None of us can wait. So, you know, break a leg' – she made an awkward fist, and pulled an awkward face – 'or, um, something.'

And with that Tracey came forward, put them all in order, gave them a huge smile and the thumbs-up, winked at Squat and led them out on to the playing field, beneath the bunting and the blazing sun.

They were on the second encore of 'Happy' and still nobody out there seemed to want it to end. The older generation were all sitting at the tea tables, clapping along, and a line of infants, kneeling in the front, were doing a rather messy Mexican wave. But everyone else was up and dancing; even the headmaster was getting into it: his arms were round his pretty wife and they laughed as they watched a stalky little red-haired girl twirling round with a baby on her hip. All the stalls were deserted as the whole fête came to witness its main event. The singers were completely carried away by the enthusiasm of their audience. The moves of the younger members – so carefully choreographed by Tracey – were getting more individual and extravagant. The Squat Fan Club – a loose organisation with a previously low profile – was out in force; after showing their dedicated support to the cider tent, they were now really rocking, and every time Squat stepped forward to do his four-word solo, they went wild.

As they came to the end of the song yet again, Heather Carpenter came up and took the microphone. 'Ladies, gentlemen and children, will you all show your appreciation please for our very own Bridgeford Community Choir.'

There was a roar of cheering and applause and the happy chant of, 'Squat. Squat. Squat.'

'That was their last performance before the County Championships next week. What do we think? Are they going to win?'

She put her hand to her ear as the crowd screamed its support and the Choir cheered back.

'Are you SURE?'

There in the middle of the St Ambrose playing field, the singers were locked in, secured by a wall of joyous sound. Cat-calls, whoops, screams, 'Squat's and shouting filled the air. A light breeze lifted the bunting, the flag of St George fluttered against a pure blue sky. The new local heroes soaked it all up – most were laughing, some were crying, there was a suggestion that even Curly had something in his eye. Arms around the shoulders of their neighbours, they glanced up at the heavens and then they took their bow.

'You heard them.' She smiled at the singers. 'Sounds like it's in the bag. Best of luck!'

♩

Tracey gratefully received all the slaps on the back and kisses on the cheek from people she had never seen before and soaked up all the compliments that were being showered upon her. The singers were dispersing now, absorbed by their families and friends. She watched Lynn head over to the bric-à-brac, Maria join the queue for the cakes, Squat sign autographs for an orderly queue of ten-year-old girls, Annie catch up with the teachers. 'The school said she would get in but she just wouldn't apply ...'

She felt Bennett's arm around her shoulder, the beginnings of a squeeze and a warm flutter deep inside her. He'd been brilliant up there this afternoon; she could hardly keep her eyes off him. She had watched him sing before, of course she had, but she hadn't seen him perform. Now she knew: he was the one. Not the one for her, necessarily, she still had doubts about that. But he was the one among the men in the Choir – the charisma, the star dust – and that was quite hard to resist. She scoped the fête – the old-toys stall, the books, the guess-the-weight, the tombola – searching for a corner somewhere they might duck away for a quick—

'Pa, Pa, sup-er-star.' There was the lovely Min.

And beside her, presumably, Casper: 'Good stuff, Dad.' A boy in a polo shirt, with yellow trousers, clean hair and deck shoes pumped his father's hand. 'Pretty damn good.' He was – they had already discussed this – the same age as Billy, but he was not – and they had failed to work this out before – from the same planet. He held up a hand to Tracey in greeting; she saw his signet ring and nearly got the giggles. This one had just landed in a space-ship from the 1980s. Of course it was completely impossible for her to sustain any sort of relationship with Bennett. Imagine Christmas with Casper and the Billster, passing the port, sharing the bong. Was Casper – what a name – a fan of The Bloodshitters, did we think? Or more of a Supertramp sort of cove? It was all ludicrous. Just a shame, that was all, that every time she heard Bennett's voice she was overwhelmed with a desire to rip his very classic clothes off.

'You ought to go on *The X Factor*,' chortled Casper.

'But first you've got to do the lucky dip.' Min grabbed his arm. 'His favourite,' she added to Tracey. 'Come with us.'

'I've got stuff, I just remembered . . . We'll catch up later.'

She wandered around for a bit, bought some jam and a pack of Bridgeford Christmas cards, wondering as she did so if she knew anyone to send one to. She met Maria's mother and stuck a pin on a treasure island, swerved away from a knitted-scarf stall when she saw that Pat lurked behind it like a crocodile with a killer grin. It was a joyous occasion and one that Tracey had never before attended. Seven years Billy had spent at this school, and so keen was she on her keep-ourselves-to-ourselves philosophy, neither of them had come even once.

The Upper School Dance Club was doing a routine outside the tea tent, all in a line and dancing to Katy Perry, surrounded by dads recording their every move. Billy might have liked something like that, but she would never have let him do it: he was brought up from the beginning to be different; too cool for school. How much fun had he missed? she wondered now. How much fun had they both missed, come to that? She could still see why she had done it all, but she could also now see that she was wrong.

'Dr Khan, hello.'

'Tracey, that was fantastic.' He shook her warmly by the hand. 'I'm only sorry now that I haven't made it there since Christmas. I would have loved to work with you.'

'I'm probably only standing in, I think, Doctor. Just until Constance is up and about again.'

He frowned at her and narrowed his eyes. 'Where did you hear that from? Connie's in a coma, has been since the accident. Of course, we all hope for the best, but ... '

A child grabbed his hand and pulled him along.

'I wonder, could I have a word?' said the headmaster in her ear as the dancers took their applause. They walked together across the grass. 'You've done wonders with that choir, you know. We've had them here before and let's just say – ahem – we all noticed the difference today.' He rolled his eyes.

Wow, thought Tracey. Was that an expression of – the ultimate wickedness – anti-Connie sympathy? Was this man an actual non-Connie-believer? She had not heard anything so sacrilegious all year. And it was music to her ears. 'Um, thank you.'

'Anyway, I've been looking for someone to start a choir since I came here, and after that set this afternoon I just know my children would love to learn music from you. I wonder, are you fully committed elsewhere?'

'Fully committed to a desk job, unfortunately.' A desk job in a windowless office in a climate-controlled metal box on the side of the motorway, where nobody really knows me and I never really speak. She looked around, at the pleasant Victorian architecture, the pretty new library on the edge there, a tractor mowing a field just beyond. 'But to be honest, I bloody hate it.'

His face lit up. 'Of course we wouldn't be able to pay much, but ... '

37

Annie stood outside the tube station, holding her battered old *A–Z* and blinking into the late-afternoon sun. Apart from theatre trips and the odd dash to Selfridges, she had been buried in Bridgeford for so many years that she was unsure how much of her own capital she would recognise. While Annie Miller had been suspended in aspic, London had, apparently, hurled itself into the future. It was as if someone had tipped up the country at one end and all the good stuff had just rolled down here. She stood there – bemused like Catweazle, probably looking like Catweazle, certainly dressed à *la mode de* Catweazle – and tried to get her bearings.

No wonder home seemed such a ghost town: every living person under the age of forty was doing their living up here. She jostled her way along the main road, past well-dressed workers and Lycra-clad joggers. No shops closed here, that was for sure. The street was alive with the business of choices being met and PINs being entered. Had she stumbled into a Potemkin village, or was it just another country? Next time she came up here, she would probably need a visa. And, what's more, they probably wouldn't give her one. This city had nothing to do with the rest of the country any more, and it wasn't the first time she had noticed it. It reminded her of the night of the opening ceremony of the Olympic Games, when she had sat at home – on her own yet again, funnily enough – genuinely unsure whether she was witnessing an actual national triumph or the most fantastic, elaborate CGI joke.

She made a right and a left and then stopped for a moment, leaned against a wall and took several deep gulps of air. This was it. She was going to turn that next corner, open a door and ruin her own life. Or at least let someone else ruin it for her. But it had to be done. The suffering had to stop. Tracey and Jazzy had given her a talking-to and made her come here, and of course they were right. This was emotional Dignitas – she was giving her marriage the swift, easier, honest death that she believed it deserved.

It was a tall, stucco-fronted semi-detached house that James spent his week-nights in; a lot more elegant than the square-built 1950s home he came back to at weekends. Annie looked up at the top floor – his quarters – and wondered what she was going to find. Of course, it wasn't possible to tell by just looking at the two little windows up there; there were no exterior signs of adultery, no SHAGGERS LIVE HERE graffiti on the gently flaking white walls. If she had to guess, if it was a sweepstake down at the library and she had to put her name against something, it would be 'thong'. Rustling in her bag, she found the spare key she had lifted from his cufflinks box. She couldn't say why, but for a while now, as some people dream of lottery numbers, she had been thinking thong. She let herself in, tested the silence, inhaled the scent of another person's house – faint tobacco smoke, washing powder, the charred crumbs of that morning's toast – and shut the door gently behind her. Indeed, when James had left that morning, pecked her on the cheek, said he would see her on Friday, it had even come to her in a sort of mystic vision: a red thong like a bloodstain on an acre of polished wooden floor. She began to climb the stairs. His bedsit didn't actually have a wooden floor – and if it did she was pretty sure he wouldn't have polished it – but still: the thong was the thing. It was a sign, and she had to follow it.

James wouldn't be home for at least another hour, but that did not of course mean that there was nobody else in there. She knocked on the door, to be fair – to give whoever-she-was a sporting chance to pick the thong up, slip it over her slim hips. Would their lives have been different if Annie's underwear had been different? If they got through this crisis, would she have to wear that kind of stuff? Annie believed passionately in marriage, in family, in the spirituality of home, but possibly not quite passionately enough to walk around with a skimpy bit of string slicing up her bottom. Anyway, she had lived with this affair of his for so long that this point of crisis, this coming up here and facing him down, this bloody third act of their long-running romantic comedy, now seemed to her almost banal – like she had already seen it before. She had pretty much already reached closure, so she flung open the door and calmly faced the worst.

Her vision wasn't completely prophetic. This was a bedsit – a perfectly all right sort of bedsit – with a beige carpet and an ancient chintzy sofa that looked even more battered, miserable and sunken than she did. The small double bed pressed into the corner was – she recognised it immediately – made up with the worn and faded linen of their early marriage. When Annie had given it to him years back – even darned it for him, like a mug – she could never have imagined what he might use it for. They had conceived babies under that duvet, real babies – that wasn't just sex and thongs and slurpy licking, it was an act of creation. She shook her head, blinked away the tears – honestly, the disrespect – and so it was that out of the corner of her eye she first noticed the kitchen.

Slowly turning, she took in what was before her. Where once there had been a Baby Belling, a plate rack and a sink with a curtain around it, there was now, ranged against the wall, the sort of set-up that Nigella would be happy to purr over on the telly. At the sight of it all – the aluminium work-shelf, the butcher's block trolley, the French stove – her courage failed her; her closure tore open like a wound. All that fearing the worst and here was something infinitely more terrible: she thought he was cheating on her with a slapper; in fact, he was betraying her with a cook.

There were jars ranged along the tiling, from small to large, with printed labels. She moved towards them – retching, trembling – like a detective discovering a chamber of horrors: bonito flakes, panko, stalks of lemongrass . . . It was years since Annie had been bothered to use stalks of real lemongrass. That James had found someone who did made her weep even more. And what was this on its own out here, in a dish, under a tea-towel, moist and ugly: the organ that a cannibal was saving for later? Annie sniffed it and identified it at once. That, as she lived and breathed, was a sourdough starter. Whoever she was, this thong-wearing vixen, she made her own, from-scratch, bloody trendy London bread.

She was still bent double, sobbing on to the shiny metal, when the door opened and James breezed in.

'Love! Hey, what's happened?' She saw him think about hiding his two brown bags from Whole Foods, but then he just dropped them, ignored the organic pomegranate rolling across the floor and took her in her arms. 'Tell me. What is it? One of the girls?'

She snivelled, shook her head. 'They're all fine. It's you, you bastard. You're the matter.' She reached over for the nearest jar. 'I mean, James, really, fenugreek? Fucking' – for a split second they both looked horrified: Annie never used the F-word – 'FUCKING FENU-GREEK?'

He caught her hand before she smashed the jar at the wall.

'Who is she? The scrubber with the sourdough fucking starter? WHO THE FUCKING FUCK IS SHE?'

'Annie,' his voice was all sympathy but there was in there an unmistakable Miller laugh, 'she's me, you daft old bat. She's only me.'

Later, as Annie lay naked on the floor, her head resting upon a still-full brown bag, after James had licked and nibbled at every part of her as he had once done so often, and as if she hadn't really changed, they lay together and talked for the first time in a year. He was propped up on his elbow, still stroking the length of her with the fingers of his left hand, skimming over the stretch marks on her tummy, when he asked: 'So I'm still not quite sure ... what did you think you'd find here?'

'Um ... well ...' she mumbled, 'you know, just a thong.'

'A what? I didn't hear you.'

'A thong,' she said loudly and sighed.

'Oh. Which is what exactly?'

'Don't you worry about it.' Why slice your bottom up if there's no public demand? 'Nothing you need to know. I just thought you didn't want me any more, that's all. So when did it start, then, your gastronomic adventure?'

'I want you,' he kissed her, 'more even than ever. If a chap's married to the loveliest girl in the world,' he kissed her again, 'why would he go off with a thong?'

She gazed at him happily. Bless him: he wouldn't know what a thong was if it fell on his greying, balding, beautiful, wrinkled head. 'It's not every thong as would have you ...' She bit her lip to stop herself giggling.

'I don't doubt it. I started cooking when Jess went away, and you said we weren't allowed a proper dinner any more.' He looked so downcast, her heart gave a little squeeze. 'And then you were out every night, looking after all of Bridgeford instead of being anywhere near me ...'

'Daw, love, so this is your mid-life crisis' – she gasped as he ran his hand up her thigh – 'your reaction to our empty nest?'

'No! It was my reaction to not being allowed to have a decent bloody meal unless there was a more deserving bloody child in the house. And being told I wasn't even allowed to cook for my bloody self. And I do wish you would stop saying that, Annie.' He put his hand on her face and turned it full towards him. 'How can you think our nest is empty if it's still got the two of us in it?'

She cried some more and spluttered a lot and felt a complete and utter fool. They made love again – even though she felt a bit sore, and there was some pak choi sticking into her ear. Then he drew himself away, put his boxers back on and went over to his kitchen. She watched his stocky figure marching up and down, the paunch over the ancient pants, the greying chest hair, the uncut toenails, the ... Why on earth had she thought that she had a duty to be young and toned and thonged?

'Anyway,' he said, flinging open cupboards and brandishing a knife, 'let me show you what you've been missing. While you've been cooking for all those old people and blind people and bad people and dead people ... '

'Darling,' she sat up, reached for her bag, got out her phone, 'you do exaggerate. I never cook for dead people—'

And then she saw her messages, and gasped. And she had to say, 'Love, I'm so sorry. I'm so, so sorry, but something terrible has happened. I have to get back.'

38

On her train journey home, Annie had managed to contact all the Choir members to insist that they attend an extraordinary meeting at Tracey's house at 9.30 p.m.; the only people who did not pick up the message were Tracey and Bennett. So when the bell rang at the appointed hour, it was once again a dishevelled, bemused Tracey who opened her own front door.

'What's going on?' she said to the masses who filed past her up the stairs. 'Anyone mind telling me what you're all doing here this time?'

She left the front door open and followed them up to the living room.

'Dunno.'

'All a mystery.'

'Annie said to meet her here,' Lewis was holding the handles of the wheelchair, Curly the footrest, 'for an announcement.'

Squat bounded towards the stairs before anyone could stop him – 'Might just nip in the shower' – then bellowed over the banister in a voice rich with moral outrage: 'Oi, what's that Bennett doing up here dressed like a prat?'

'They're having sex,' Jazzy bellowed back with glee.

'No WAY!' said Curly.

'Yes way!' Jazzy danced round the living room. 'They're so mad for it that they even did it in front of me! It was AWFUL!'

'Jazzy, for heaven's sake, we did no such thing.'

'Like rabbits, they are.' She turned to address the whole crowd. 'Really, really old rabbits.'

'Aha. Annie. Good evening.' Tracey gestured to the room. 'Welcome to my soirée. Any plans to tell me what exactly is going on?'

Annie, whey-faced and trembling, came into the middle of the assembly. 'Is everyone here?' She looked around. 'Then I shall begin. I have some terrible news. After all our prayers and hopes and wishes, I'm afraid that our beloved Constance didn't make it. She died, with the family around her, in her husband's arms, this afternoon.'

Lynn started to cry, Judith to pray; Maria – so used to death – shook her head in sorrow; Lewis coughed and pinched his nose. 'I'm so terribly sorry,' said Bennett, stepping forward with his hair on end and his arms tight around Tracey's kimono. 'I know how much she meant to you, and I'm so sorry.'

But the rest of the room did not seem to have any reaction at all. They looked sombre enough – although the young ones were possibly just bored – but definitely unmoved. There were nearly fifty members of the Choir now, and only a handful of those had worked with Constance; the rest did not even know her. Frank, Curly and a couple of others exchanged glances and then quietly got up to leave.

'Sit down, please,' sighed Annie. 'That is not all I've got to say. I spoke with Connie's family just an hour ago. Obviously the timing presents a few problems for us, with the contest only days away now, and the last thing I am sure any of us wants to do is cause offence to the bereaved.'

'Why would we?'

'Surely the best thing we could do now is go into this and win it for her?'

'Of course, but I was worried about how they might feel if we went along and sang a song called "Happy", and I was right to be. They would rather we didn't. In fact, they went a bit further and expressed a preference that Constance is remembered on Thursday night with a rousing performance of her *Sound of Music* medley.'

Tracey's house was for a moment suspended in silence, until a distant roar started up from the back of the room and suddenly the whole crowd was swept up in an outpouring of violent emotion.

'But we don't know it!'

'We're brilliant at "Happy".'

'If we change it all now, we'll lose.'

'If we change it all now, I'm bloody leaving.'

'We can't be singing that old crap.'

Annie held her hand up. 'I'm sorry, but our hands are tied. We are Connie's legacy. It is only right that we show our respect for what she has done.'

At a nod from Bennett, Tracey took to the middle of her own living-room floor.

'I don't think that's true, Annie.' She was calm and kind, but firm. 'I'm sure Constance did a lot for the Choir. I wasn't part of it so I really can't say. But what I can say, for certain, is that *we* are the Choir now. I am the elected leader. I choose the programme. And this is our present, our here and now, our chance. We can't go forward if we keep looking back. We owe it to all these members – and those crowds who cheered us just last Saturday, and all those people who have wished us well – to go and do our very best. For Bridgeford, for the Choir, for Connie's memory and for ourselves.'

The noise was so loud that Tracey's neighbours had every right to complain; but in fact most of Tracey's neighbours were with her now.

39

Annie was standing by the door with her pen and a list; Tracey and Bennett were pacing up and down in the car park of the Coronation Hall.

'She's the only one now, Annie. We can't wait any longer. We've got to get through that bottleneck on the ring road.'

'Try her again,' Tracey soothed. 'One more call, and if she doesn't pick up, then that's it, I'm afraid.'

A chorus of *Why are we waiting?* started up at the back of the bus and was picked up by all as it drifted down the aisle.

Annie, her face contorted with anxiety, stood with a phone to her ear and her teeth on her top lip. 'Voicemail again.' She shook her head. 'I just can't think what's happened . . . '

'OK, well, on we all get.' Tracey ushered them up the steps and nodded to the driver. The door of the coach closed with a sigh.

Maria came rushing up to the front. 'I just got a call from the hospital. They've admitted Jazzy's nan. Apparently her mum did a runner this afternoon, she didn't get her medication and when Jazzy got home from work the old dear was unconscious.'

'Oh no. The poor darling. But what about her solo?' Annie wailed. 'Her whole life has been leading up to this. She's worked so hard. I should go to the hospital and—'

'No. Annie, sit down. We're a choir,' said Tracey over her shoulder, moving down the bus and counting heads. 'A very brilliant choir,' she said more loudly, so that everyone could hear. 'POSSIBLY THE BEST CHOIR IN THE COUNTY,' she shouted to raucous acclaim.

'And not a collection of soloists.' She had moved up to the front now; this was said for Annie alone.

'Are we ready?' she called from the front.

They were.

'Are we steady?'

Some were steadier than others – in the sopranos there was a serious case of the jitters – but they all said they were anyway.

'One small change: Jazzy's not with us tonight, so Annie Miller will be taking the solo in "Lean on Me" and she will, as we all know, do it brilliantly. Enjoy the journey. Let's GO.'

♩

'... And now, put your hands together for our first contestants tonight, THE BRIDGEFORD COMMUNITY CHOIR.'

'Listen to that,' she whispered to them in the wings, flicking her thumb towards the auditorium. 'That's for you. Let's show 'em.' She grabbed Annie by the shoulders, looked her in the eye, said to her, 'You are wonderful,' and then proudly led her men out on to the battlefield.

The set could not have gone better: they gave the performance of their dreams. 'Lean on Me' was stirring, powerful and memorable, Annie's solo so deep and emotional that some claimed to see tears in the judges' eyes. The harmonies of 'Homeward Bound' were subtle and lovely, the sound surprisingly and rather wonderfully at odds with the appearance of Squat, Curly and Frank in the front there. The stalls of the Theatre Royal were full of other choirs; friends and families were up in the circle; and it was heart-warmingly, beautifully, inspiringly clear that Bridgefordians were out in force. Annie stepped forward and made her announcement: 'Ladies and gentlemen, we perform here with joy in our voices, but some sadness in our hearts. This week, our beloved Constance, who led this choir for twenty years, lost her fight for life. It is in her name that we are singing here tonight and to the memory of her spirit that we dedicate our final song.'

And how, after that, could they possibly go wrong? Even Lewis was move-perfect in 'Happy'; the audience lapped up, with soppy smiles, the unabashed joy in the faces of the awkward adolescents. Every solo was a minor triumph and the whole theatre was up and clapping along.

Performing like that had an extraordinary effect on all of them. At first, to the outsiders in the red plush seating, they had looked like who they were: a cross-generational, socially diverse collection of amateurs with nothing in common but music and geography and the determination to have a really good time. But almost at once, the transformative power of the human voice worked its magic. Both within themselves and – miraculously – in the dampened eyes of their beholders, they became something quite other. For ten glorious minutes, they stepped out of their own lives, touched each other's souls and took off into another world. When they came to the end, the noise of the audience shocked through them to their very core.

In all of their various, varied lives, this was the one thing that none of them had ever known. All those good works that Annie did in the community; all that nursing that Lewis did for his girl; the caring – the endless caring – that Maria performed for different people in different houses the whole week long; the meals that they cooked for their children; the duty with which they raised their young; the stoicism of those young in the face of poverty and unemployment; the supernatural patience that they sometimes had to summon just to get them through the tedium of their day – and the one thing that never happened to them, however much they had earned it, however much it might have helped, was a standing ovation from a theatre full of strangers.

It was a moment, not just for one, or a respectable handful – it was an extraordinary moment for them all: a great white heat of a moment of communality that would weld them together for ever more, like the very heart of a fire in a forge. Each took their neighbour's hand, raised their eyes to the spotlights, and then they dropped together in a grateful bow.

The four judges, who had been bent over their table scribbling, all looked up and smiled. Then the chairman looked up, raised his hands to clap them and mouthed the word 'Bravo'.

'Well, beat that,' mouthed Tracey as she turned around and winked at them. 'Just beat that. Come on, you lot. Let's go and watch them try.' Trembling with emotion, she led her warriors from the stage.

♪

Tracey sat in the front of the coach, her head on Bennett's shoulder, her gaze fixed on the window and the dark late night beyond.

'FUCK!' Squat shouted for the tenth time, thumping his fist on the seat in front. 'FUCKING BASTARD JUDGING FUCKERS!' He looked over his shoulder to his acolytes. 'GET THEIR FUCKING NAMES AND THEN WE CAN GO AND BREAK THEIR FUCKING STUPID JUDGEY LEGS.'

Only Squat had the energy to express his anger; the rest of them were too emotionally exhausted. Tracey had tried to make a speech when it was all over – when they were back on the coach and alone enough to cry. But her heart wasn't in it. If there were lessons to be learned, she was in no position to teach them. As far as she was concerned, the lesson was quite simple: they were robbed.

She peered out along the bypass at the lights of the strange towns as they drove by. All those houses in all those places where the

Choir just did not matter, all those people who knew nothing of their struggles and dramas and, even worse, did not care. She remembered how, just a few weeks ago, she had driven around there and seriously considered that she might move – that she was even capable of moving – to one of those towns. Breathing on the window, she rubbed a hole, stared through it and smiled. She understood it all now – that yes, of course you can live in any number of places. But you can only truly belong to one.

'I just can't explain it.' Lewis spoke up to those who were nearest. 'I simply do not understand.'

'They just thought that other lot were better, I suppose.' Kerry was lying with her head in Judith's lap.

'I mean, honestly: the Downtown Divas. Is that even a place?'

'But look how much they loved us last week at the fête. I can't imagine any of tonight's lot has ever had a reception like that one ...' Judith had tears in her eyes as she stroked Kerry's hair.

'We were on our home turf. Tonight, we were just out of context.'

Tracey sat up, looked round, alert. 'OK, so what is that? What is our context?'

Bennett shrugged. 'Just where we come from ... Bridgeford, I suppose.'

'Yet when we do try and put on a proper concert, nobody bloody turns up.'

'No,' said Tracey, deep in thought now, talking into the black beyond them. 'They don't. So next time, let's not even give them the choice ...'

Annie, three rows back, was still shaking. That solo was the most extraordinary moment of her life. All those decades in the Choir, all those years of driving the girls around to music lessons, and only tonight did she remember what she had known quite clearly in her youth: she actually had a voice of her own. Of course the result of the contest was a terrible blow; she felt for the younger members particularly. The rest of them were quite used to life's casual dispensation of pitiless injustice, but for those kids it was all quite new. And for them to be treated unfairly when they had actually tried for once – well, it was, as James would say, a bugger. You only had to look at Squat and Frank and all the rest of them to know that they had decades of defeats and disappointments ahead of them; Annie felt so bad that the first of them had happened on her watch.

But for all that, she could not buy in to this atmosphere of gloom and self-pity. The result was disappointing but their singing really was not. They had been amazing, and that she did not want any of them to forget.

On the journey there, they had sung all the way – of course they had. They were a choir on a coach trip: singing was what they had to do. So without really thinking, Annie started it again.

Oh, Danny boy, the pipes, the pipes are calling

It was what her dad used to croon to her on their end-of-the-holiday night-time journeys. She would fall asleep along the back seat of the old Rover and wake up when the pain of transition was over – home, but still with the crunch of sand between her toes.

The summer's gone, and all the roses falling

Of course, half the coach wouldn't know this one. Like *The Secret Garden* and Russian dolls and English cooking, it was a perfect joy that belonged to another age. Well, if Annie had to sing yet another solo that night, so be it ... In fact – she took a deep breath, prepared for the crescendo, pointed her voicebox at the roof rack – stand back folks and just bring it on.

But come ye back when summer's in the meadow

But now Bennett joined in – his rich and fruity tenor soaked with disappointment – and Lewis and all the others of a certain age. And as the song was picked up and carried through to the back, Annie was astonished to hear the young ones take part, too.

And all my grave will warmer, sweeter be

And they know it, she thought, as their voices merged together.

And I shall sleep in peace until you come to me.

They already know it. She beamed as they came to the end, and sank back on her headrest. They were off now. Just as they had baffled her on the way there with alien rap songs, now they were enchanting her on the way back with stuff from the past.

You'll ne-ev-er walk a-a-lone

But Annie was too happy to join in. Who could say how what they knew came through to them – via sport or adverts or YouTube or celebs? What mattered was that it came through at all. If things were good enough and relevant – if they might mean something to someone somewhere – then they lasted. And the personal implications of that for Annie were actually huge. She listened in quiet contentment as their young voices pulled off a pretty decent 'Amazing Grace'.

And she determined that it was time for her to order a skip.

When the coach drew up outside the Coronation Hall at midnight, there was a small crowd to welcome them home. Tracey and Bennett stood at the bottom step to say goodbye, thank them all individually. One by one, they went off to their waiting families. A low steady hum of consolation was filling the night air. Then Judith stepped down and suddenly a man lunged out of the dark at her with a loud and furious roar.

'Oh Christ,' said Kerry, coming down the steps with a lot of eye-rolling, looking rather bored. 'You'd think he'd let her off, tonight of all nights.'

'Who is it?' asked Lynn, behind her. 'What on earth is going on?' The couple had moved off to the hall porch to carry on the row.

'Her stupid fiancé,' yawned Kerry. 'Well, ex-fiancé. Don't worry. I'll sort him out. Night, all.'

'Fiancé?' murmured Lynn. 'Really? Fiancé?'

Judith was standing to one side now, waiting and watching while her two lovers fought it out. And Lynn tottered over to her waiting husband, muttering about fiancés and looking tired and a little bit old.

'See you next Tuesday,' Tracey said to Squat as she took him in her arms and rocked him. She had got rather fond of him in recent weeks.

'Eh?' He pulled back. 'Here, you said just till the competition ...'

'Yes I did. But something else has just occurred to me – a new idea. We've got something even bigger to work towards now. So, sorry, lads, I'm afraid I've changed my mind.'

40

Bennett reached up to the blackboard, rubbed out LEMON DRIZZLE and chalked in CHOCOLATE FUDGE. Katie had been baking well in advance of their first day of business, but everything was selling so fast that she was stuck in the back kitchen at the moment, making more. He checked his watch as he wrote: 11.40. They didn't have long, then. He had to let her out quite soon.

'How can I help you?' He took his order pad out of the large pocket of the CK-regulation butcher's apron and prepared to serve. Every time he turned round, a new lot of customers was being seated. The publicity had been great and the turnover this morning exceeded all expectations; so many customers were here to wish them well. Bennett hoped they weren't all going straight home afterwards, though. They absolutely must be made to stick around. He rubbed at his face: his skin felt hot but his insides almost freezing. He had never felt this nervous in his life.

Only one customer had been sitting in there all morning, and she wasn't there to wish anyone well. Bennett collected her empty cup on the way back to the coffee station and asked her, pointedly, if she would like anything else.

'Don't worry about me, I'm family. What about old whatser-face' – Sue pointed with her red meaty hand – 'you know, thingy' – she looked suddenly rather lost, casting around for someone, Annie presumably, to help; of course it would never occur to her that Bennett of all people might know her name – 'by the wall there? They've been waiting YEARS.' She caught a woman's eye as she settled herself down. 'Thank you for your patience, love. We do appreciate it. Please forgive him: early days.'

'Tina,' he called clearly as he walked towards her, 'I've put porridge on the menu just for you.'

'THERE YOU ARE, ANNIE.' Bennett could only presume that Sue, in her position as ex of the patron, had assumed several other *ex-officio* roles. She was the – very loud – master of ceremonies: 'AND THE WHOLE MILLER FAMILY.' The – extremely vocal – spokesperson for the CK Complaints Commission: 'HOPE YOU'VE GOT ALL MORNING. THE SERVICE IS HILARIOUSLY SLOW.' And, although they had only opened at 8.30, he was pretty sure she was already the hot contender for Most Embarrassing Customer: 'I THINK WE'LL SIT HERE. IT'S NO MENOPAUSE CORNER, BUT IT'LL JUST HAVE TO DO.'

'Mum, shit,' Lucy hissed at her. 'What did she just say?'

'Just ignore her, grab that table,' Annie replied out of the corner of her mouth before speaking up to Sue. 'Got the rabble with me this morning, we'll stick ourselves over here.'

'This,' said Lucy, grudgingly, 'is not actually uncool.'

Annie looked about, at the bleached wooden floors, the walls painted the colour of honey, the enormous blackboard and the simple tables and chairs. She had not been convinced when Bennett hired Squat and the gang to work on it for him, but she should have had more faith: it looked fantastic. The leather sofas and armchairs over against the wall were a charming new touch. She could just see herself with – who? – Tracey, probably, or Kerry perhaps, grabbing a quick bite over there whenever they could.

'I tell you what, Min's dad looks different these days, too.' Rosie was always her most observant child. 'Sort of, de-tragicked some-how ...'

Jess studied him and nodded: 'imlame.'

And Annie would have to come regularly, to bring her car to Curly's Valet Service, which he was now running on Bennett's land out the back there – must support those boys, when they were trying so hard.

'What can I get you?'

'Hey, Jazzy, that uniform's an improvement. You look gorgeous.' Annie put her hand on the girl's arm. 'We do miss you, you know, at choir.'

'I know, but I couldn't carry on with it, Mrs M.' She fumbled around for her pen in the unfamiliar pocket. 'I can't waste myself on this stuff any more, I've got to get out there and get on.' She took their order and walked away from them.

'DID YOUR MOTHER EVER TURN UP AGAIN, JASMINE?' bellowed Sue as she passed her. 'I HEAR SHE DID A RUNNER AT THE WORST POSSIBLE TIME. AND YOUR GRANDMOTHER ENDED UP BACK IN HOSPITAL. WHAT A *SHAME*.'

'She hasn't changed,' grumbled Lucy. 'Fucking witch.'

'How can you stick her?' said Jess behind a menu.

'The truth is,' Annie said through a smile, 'I can't.'

'You've changed though, Mum. Like, a bit. I mean, you know, nothing special ...'

'Oh really?' said Annie, clutching at her tummy to contain the butterflies. 'Give me a few more minutes, love. Because you ain't seen nothing yet.'

Tracey stood at the top of the slope of Bridgeford High Street, trying to look nonchalant, even though she was neatly positioned on the white lines in the middle of the road. Lewis, whose power she had noticed was less that of the average council member and more that of an over-mighty baron, had shoved up some orange notices in the dead of night, scattered traffic cones around with happy and mighty abandon and had the street pedestrianised – completely illegally, just the once and for them.

The sun was not shining unconditionally upon the CK's first day of business – it had occasionally to duck around the odd white and fluffy cloud – but it was an indisputably fine summer's Saturday morning. The bunting borrowed from the St Ambrose Fête Committee was up to its customary fluttering, and from here it looked as though the punters might just be pouring in.

Everything was going according to plan. A large box had just been abandoned in the street, as if nobody gave a damn about their own environment any more. People whom Tracey had known and worked and sung with for weeks walked past with their families and snubbed her – just did not say a word. Lewis and his gang were in what looked like an ugly political argument on the bench outside the council offices. The war memorial was covered not only with minors and their cans and their crisp packets and their fags, but even more mature individuals like Curly and Squat were there, acting like hooligans, too. Katie was looking lost and alone, unattended in her wheelchair near the traffic island, directly between Carol's newsagent and the CK. Not a soul offered to help her. Tracey, her legs crossed at the ankles, her shoulders in a mooching position, her eyes fixed down upon her phone, felt a surge of an unaccustomed emotion that she could only presume to be optimism.

As the clock on the Corn Exchange said five minutes to twelve, she saw Min emerge from the CK, position her keyboard against the outside wall and plug it into a sound system, but nobody else seemed to notice. Billy, back for a week now, still brown of skin and white of hair, came bumbling along and leaned against a lamppost. He didn't know what he was doing here, but he had got out of bed, put on some clothes and done what he was told – and that, in Tracey's view, was progress. Primary-age children started to appear, in ballet skirts and football kits or with hair wet from swimming, eager to do whatever their new choir teacher might ask them, trailing mystified parents in their wake. From the old people's home round the corner, organised by Annie and led by Maria and Lynn, came an army of Evergreens in wheelchairs and on Zimmer frames who were then positioned around the street.

The clock struck the hour. Katie picked up something in her lap and Tracey looked up and caught her eye and Katie played a short phrase on the recorder, and perhaps because she was in a wheelchair nobody seemed to give a damn. But then Min joined in on her keyboard and suddenly Annie swung through the café door, grabbed a microphone, ran into the middle of the High Street and jumped up on to the abandoned box.

SING, SING A SONG

she belted out with her newly discovered, quite extraordinary talent.

SING OUT LOUD

SING OUT STRONG

'FUUUUUCK,' shouted one of her daughters, who had all run out after her. 'SHIT. MUM'S GONE MENTAL.'

Tracey was down in her allotted place, conducting now. She pointed her baton at the newly Farrow & Ball-painted CK front door and Ben emerged, holding her old guitar.

SING OF GOOD THINGS, NOT BAD

he sang to all of Bridgeford as he walked, strumming, into position next to Annie.

SING OF HAPPY NOT SAD

'DAD,' called another of Annie's children, in a voice of pain. 'DO something.' But James was staring at her, immobile and utterly lovestruck.

Then Tracey pointed at Lewis and the council lot and they jumped up from their bench and like a boy band – yes, a slightly eccentric, niche-market sort of boy band but, hey, a boy band none the less – marched down to the singers in perfect time.

DON'T WORRY THAT IT'S NOT

GOOD ENOUGH ...

And the door of the newsagent's flung open and Judith, Kerry and Lynn and all the sopranos danced over too.

... FOR ANYONE ELSE TO HEAR

There must have been about thirty singers out there now, but the number of delighted onlookers was well into the hundreds. People were filming it and sharing on Twitter. The senior citizens were clearly enjoying the highlight of their later lives. You wait, thought Tracey, smiling as she watched them. You just wait.

SING A SONG

She pointed her baton at the war memorial and twenty hooded youths leapt to their feet, formed an orderly crocodile and swung towards them.

La la la-la-la

Le la la le-la-la

Le la la lalalala

The whole town cheered them on as they clicked their fingers and sang and danced into the centre of the whole show. The louder the cheering, the louder their singing. 'It's SQUAT!' squealed a little girl, and suddenly dozens of them swarmed towards him. 'SQUAT. SQUAT. SQUAT ... ' He raised his thumb at them, winked and carried on his song.

'That's the sound of their choir doing a flashmob in the High Street for the Saturday-morning shoppers,' said Drivetime Dave, who was standing right next to Tracey, recording a piece on community spirit. The girls were all dancing round Squat and toddlers were twirling about the pavements and the adults were clapping and the shopkeepers had all come out to enjoy. And, Ah, thought Tracey, as the whole town joined in the chorus, as she conducted hundreds of people on the left side, the right side, behind her, above her and the middle of the street, haven't I always said so? Soft pop and local radio: very heaven.

Min, laughing her pretty laugh over at the wall there, moved up another key and the chorus started up yet again.

La la le la-la

Tracey smiled at her and carried on flicking her wrists at them all in time. There was a very real chance that this might never end. The song was getting louder and louder, the sound fuller and fuller, the performance better and better the more people joined in.

There were only three faces in the whole locality that Tracey could see that were not happy ones: Ben's ex, Sue, was standing out in the street with her arms crossed, torn in half between being proud of her daughter, hating everything else and loathing, most particularly, of course, Ben out in the middle of it all being a star. Old Pat, standing beside her, rolled her eyes in elaborate despair.

JUST SING . . .

And there was Jazzy, scowling out of the CK's window, her perfectly nice voice silenced: too big for Bridgeford; only interested in the world.

. . . SING A SONG

She'll learn, thought Tracey, singing and dancing and swaying and conducting in a state somewhere near ecstasy. Eventually, like Tracey, she would have to learn: that our lives are swaddled under many layers; that that is a good thing; that even when your family lets you down, there is another microcosm, all around, just waiting and wanting to catch you. Making yourself known to the whole world out there might work for a few people, but it isn't the only answer. Because the world out there isn't for everybody. The likelihood was that it would turn its back on Jazzy, as it had on Tracey, as it had on so many. But, with a bit of luck, someone, some day, somehow would make her realise that the trapped and scrunched and narrow little lives are often, from the inside, just the best.

La, la, la, la-la

And then she too would understand just how much bigger all our lives can seem when they are lived in a smaller space.

La, la, la, la-la

She looked at Annie, in the arms of her husband, surrounded by her girls, the cynosure of her family unit. She looked at the Choir, jubilant in the middle of the High Street, still dancing; the audience, all over the pavements, hanging out of windows, still clapping. She saw Billy, over by the war memorial, dancing with the little girls from her St Ambrose Choir, and Ben, blowing her a kiss before ducking into the CK to deal with the overwhelming rush. She looked out over the houses, which all seemed today to be facing towards her.

She raised her arms to bring this one song to its end, called out a euphoric, 'THANK YOU, BRIDGEFORD.'

And then she took her bow.

Acknowledgments

I am so grateful to the team at Little, Brown – Antonia Hodgson, Reagan Arthur, Clare Smith, Tamsin Kitson and Rhiannon Smith – for their intelligence and enthusiasm, and to my agent, Caroline Wood, for her wise advice and staunch support.

Joanna Kaye, Sabine Durrant, Josephine Love, Yvonne de Jager, Judi Henson, Jonny Newell, Kle Savage and Holly, Charlie, Matilda and Sam have all helped me at some point along the way. Robert Harris has been, as ever, wonderful.

Although the choir and all the characters in this book are purely fictional, the great joy and the sense of community that singing brings are taken from life. I could not have written this book without my Monday nights with Newbury Rock Choir. They didn't know it at the time, but Caroline Redman Lusher, Kat Penn and the members were my inspiration, I thank them all.

And lastly, my mother, Margaret Hornby, who is still singing in a choir every week as she has done, continuously, for over seventy years: this book is dedicated to her.